Herons Poynte

a novel of the Chesapeake

g.m.o. callaghan

Cashel & Kells Publishing Company
Annapolis, Maryland

For Carolyn, Michael, and Patrick

Herons Poynte

Prologue

What flattery it was, History did not record. But suffice it to say, Lord Baltimore was so moved by his cavalier's kind words that he decided to reward the fawning spaniel with a noble title and a parcel of land in the New World—as much acreage, in fact, as the fellow could cover on a chart of Maria-Land with the print of his left palm.

But alas, when the time came for the gentleman to step forward and claim his prize, he had already celebrated his good fortune with an excess of ale. Despite careful aim, his ink-stained hand missed its mark completely and fell mostly in the middle of the Chesapeake Bay. By luck, the nail of his little finger just barely touched the western shore of Maria-Land while the heel of his thumb landed on a small peninsula on the opposite side of the Bay. All the rest was water.

Lord Baltimore reared back and let out a merry roar. His cartographer followed suit and soon all the worthies in the Great Hall were rollicking with laughter. Even the drunken cavalier joined in, greatly relieved to have secured even a small manor-hold in the New World.

Two Tongues

In the village it was the closest thing to outright war. Howling like a pack of wild dogs, the boys in the schoolyard were whacking each other over the head and shoulders with long crooked sticks. Elbows jabbed into ribs, knees into thighs, and fists into faces—all in an effort to gain possession of a flying rock the size of a baseball.

In the thick of the fray, the wing man arose in midair, snagged the stone in a net of woven rawhide, and brought it back to earth in the crook of his hickory stick. As his bare feet hit the ground, he glanced at his catch and for a split-second it became the head of an Englishman.

The wing man cranked and fired. The rock shot out of his net, passed through a wave of outstretched sticks, and hurtled toward the open door of a pea-green, government surplus Port-A-Potty. The goalie, a bare-chested Chickasaw half-breed, tried to block it with a garbage can lid that he wielded like a shield. Too late. Grazing his ear, the rock ricocheted around the Potty walls for a moment, then dropped straight down through the horseshoe-shaped hole.

"Shiiiiiiit!" A splatter of stinking brown goo fell on his shoulder blades and trickled down the small of his back.

"Four zip!" someone on the other side shouted.

3

The wing man held up his palm and his teammates danced around him, slapping him with high fives. Of all the boys in Dead River, he was the best. Even at sixteen, he had the broad shoulders and upper body strength of a mature man. In cutoff jeans his thighs were thick and his feet, toughened by calluses, were quick as coyotes. With either hand he could catch or throw and his eyes had the wide peripheral vision of a hawk. His sense of anticipation was serene and that alone would have set him apart from the others. He seemed to know seconds ahead of anyone else just how the action would unfold, as if he were watching from another time and place.

His name was David Waterfield, although to be correct, that was merely a convenient pseudonym assigned to him by a government agent who was not allowed to know the seven sacred syllables of his secret tribal name. The name whose meaning could never be revealed to a white man. The name that was a prophecy of things to come.

"Ain't getting that rock outta that shit hole," the goalie complained. "You go find another one."

While the other boys fanned out in search of a suitable replacement, David knelt down and adjusted the leather laces in his webbing. He was proud of his athletic prowess, but humble, too. When he was younger, Grandfather had taught him the history and meaning of the game. Baggataway, the old man said, was a sacred rite devised by the Great Spirit, himself, and played by his people for thousands of years. It was a celebration of the unpredictable nature of the world he had created, a place where life was defined by the eternal conflict between the forces of order and chaos. Tribal elders encouraged their young men to learn the game so that their bodies and minds would be trained for battle. Sometimes entire villages would compete against each other for weeks at a time. In the process, bones were broken, skin was ripped, and blood was spilled. Some players died and others were crippled for life. But those who survived the ordeal were made stronger by the experience. In times of war, Grandfather said, young men played with the heads of their enemies. It was a gruesome image that David could never forget.

"Found another one," someone shouted. Quickly, the teams lined up against each other for another face-off.

"Hurry up," they yelled to David.

But the wing man didn't move. He raised his finger to his lips and the boys on the field fell silent. Sensing a trembling in the earth beneath his feet, David cupped his ear to the ground. In the distance, he heard the roar of a hundred freight trains bearing down on them at full throttle. Overhead, the sky darkened and the clouds rushed towards the horizon like whitewater going over a falls.

"Forget it! Gotta get back!" With the other boys falling in behind him, David raced towards the one-room schoolhouse at the edge of the field. Recess was over.

Inside the small cinder block box, the younger girls were huddled around the teacher's desk, spinning a globe of the world and dreaming of far-off places. In the back of the room, the teenagers were painting their fingernails and gossiping about the boys. Their teacher, a diminutive silver-haired spinster in wire-rimmed spectacles, was standing on a step stool writing the afternoon's assignments on the black board. Grades one through four would practice spelling; five through seven would have a geography quiz; eight through ten would begin a new chapter in the History of Oklahoma; and grades eleven and twelve would correct their Algebra homework.

Pleased with herself, the teacher had just stepped down off the stool when David burst through the door.

"Miss Appelbaum! Miss Applebaum! Come quickly!"

"Why, Mr. Waterfield? What is it?"

The girls gathered around. They all thought David was cool with his sleek athletic body, so quick and graceful in its movements. They liked the way he tied his hair back in a ponytail when he was playing baggataway and his sensitive face with its high cheekbones and bright brown eyes. They were fascinated, too, by the mysterious dotted scars that lined his lids when his eyes were closed. But now he worried them. They had never seen him so agitated before.

"What is it?" they echoed. "What's the matter?"

David grabbed his teacher's hand and pulled her towards the door. "Hurry!" he insisted.

Outside, the old lady's heart stopped beating and her blood ran backwards. A monster was crawling up over the edge of the prairie like a predator in search of a warm-blooded meal. Pitchforks of lightning shot out of its body and an unearthly howl spun out of its open maw.

"Twister!" she gasped. "Big sucker!"

A Pawnee girl in black lipstick said "shit!"

Miss Applebaum whirled around and glared at her through the magnified lenses of her reading glasses.

"You know my rule against swearing, missy. Twister doesn't give you the right to disobey. You owe me two hours after this thing blows over."

"Yes, ma'am."

"Now get going, all of you. Hightail it home and warn your families."

For once, her students were listening. Most had experienced funnel clouds before. Years ago a mighty whirlwind had come roaring down the panhandle and sucked David's father into its mouth. Stone Hammer's body had never been recovered, ripped to shreds and spread over the plains for vultures to feed on. None of the children had to be reminded again. Everyone scattered to spread the alarm.

With strong deep strides, David dashed away from the schoolhouse and wound his way through the clutter of Quonset huts, tin shanties, and rusted trailers that made up the better part of the settlement. Many of the elders had seen the twister coming and were frantically boarding up their homes and reinforcing their windows with masking tape.

Veering off the path, David took a shortcut across the railroad tracks and through a field of low red mounds, taking care to leap over the bodies of those who slept underneath the soil. In the process, he squashed several centipedes underfoot and sent a pair of tarantulas scurrying into their holes.

On the far side of the burial ground, a dozen red men climbed up over the edge of the earth, their bodies pockmarked with blisters and boils.

"Run!" they warned. "Run!"

Behind their backs, the twister spun ever closer, sucking up lumber and livestock and the earth itself. Power lines had already started to fall, their severed ends thrashing on the ground like black snakes with burning tails.

Undaunted, David bolted past the frightened workmen. Ignoring a "No Trespassing!" sign, he plowed down a steep bank into the Dead River gully below. It was like descending into the underworld, itself. At the bottom, an unholy stench assaulted his nose and stung tears out of his eyes. Scattered around him were a jumble of fifty-five gallon metal drums, some with noxious fumes leaking from their lids. Stenciled on the outside were red skeleton faces that seemed to be grinning wickedly at the intruder, as if they alone were pleased by the gathering storm and the prospect of being sucked up into heaven.

David quickened his pace and raced through the toxic dump to the other side of the gorge. Scampering up the bank to a dirt road at the top, he disappeared into an exhaust cloud left by a departing eighteen-wheeler with Jersey plates.

Just ahead, through the high grass, was his mother's sod hut. Half buried in the earth, it had an exhaust pipe elbow sticking out the side and a plywood roof that was held in place by the weight of a dozen truck tires. It didn't look like much, but its thick earthen walls provided shelter from temperatures that soared to 120 degrees Fahrenheit in the summer and plummeted to seventeen below zero in the winter.

In front of the hut, David found his family in utter turmoil. The two little girls, aged six and seven, were frantically chasing chickens while his mother tugged on the horns of a pop-eyed nanny goat, hooves dug in and udders heavy with milk.

Only Grandfather Two Tongues seemed unconcerned, sitting cross-legged on the ground, oblivious to the fragments of earth and sky swirling around him. His vision was clouded by cataracts and hair sprouted out of his skull like white loco weeds, but ancient medicine still lived in his mind. Before him on the barren ground was a picture he was making with colored sands he kept in soda bottles.

With David's help, the chickens and goat were herded down through a narrow doorway into the relative safety of the hut. But the wizened, old man refused to budge.

"Please father, you've got to come in now," David's mother begged. Once she was a brave, unbroken woman who had gone by the name of Full Moon Spirit. But since the wind had snatched Stone Hammer from the earth, her demeanor had changed and so, too, had her name, as was her people's custom. Now she was Shadow Woman and would sadly remain so for the rest of her life.

"Not yet, Shadow Woman, not yet," Grandfather insisted. He had been at it all morning and wasn't about to leave his sand painting until it was finished.

"Hurry up, Grandfather," Winking Star urged.

"Yeah, hurry up," Jumping Bug repeated.

"Some things are too important to be hurried, little ones. Just a few more things to do."

"Please, Grandfather," David begged. "Can't you see a tornado is coming?"

"This is what I say to the wind," Grandfather replied. Without taking his eyes off his work, he lifted his left haunch and fired a powerful fart into the eye of the storm. "Take that," he said.

The beast in the sky roared with fury and David and his family backed away to safety. Unperturbed, the old man continued his task.

"Good," he said at last. "Now it is finished. Now we will all go inside."

He raised himself on his crooked wooden cane and followed his family into the one room hut. A moment later he was asleep on his cot with his eyes open. Shadow Woman went to her loom and tried to pretend that everything was going to be fine. Rummaging through the trash, David found an empty tin can for the nervous nanny goat to chew on. To calm the chickens, the two little girls sang a soothing lullaby.

Not long afterwards, the body of the storm hit with great force. Howling winds swirled all around them sucking the sun out of the sky and leaving nothing but a black void in its place. Inside the darkened hut, the nanny goat began to wail and the chickens fluttered around the room in utter panic. Winking Star and Jumping Bug began to cry. Surely the end of the world was at hand.

Shadow Woman left her loom and emptied a bag of dried cow dung in the fire pit and lit it with a match. Soon the air was thick with the pungent odor of burning manure and the room was warmed with a dusty, orange glow. Dark licks flickered around the earthen walls and the plywood ceiling rumbled like a kettledrum. Bending down over the old man's cot, she shook her father-in-law awake, bringing him back from his peaceful sojourn in the spirit world.

"Maybe you should tell the story now, Tequetamo," Shadow Woman said, calling out the old man's name in his native language.

"Yes, yes, it is a good time to tell the story," Grandfather Two Tongues agreed. Perhaps it would divert the children's attention from the storm. But he hadn't told the story for many, many years. Now his mind was losing its muscle and he wasn't sure he could remember all of it. Nevertheless, he had a sacred duty to repeat it to his grandchildren just as his father had told it to him and his father before him.

The frail old man struggled to his feet, pausing for a few moments to regain his balance. Then he wandered around the room looking for the hole in the wall where he kept his sacred things. At last, he remembered that he had covered the opening with a ceremonial drum and a pair of spirit rattles. Moving them aside, he reached into the hole and carefully removed a large mud brick, which he solemnly carried back to his cot. David and his sisters sat down at the old man's feet and watched with wonder as he raised the brick to his lips and blew on it with all his might. A thick crimson cloud arose from the surface and when the dust settled down, the children could see that the brick had been transformed into an oblong wooden box. Carved on it were wild creatures they had never seen before: horned animals and long-legged birds, flying fish and monsters with claws.

The old man's gnarled fingers pried open the lid and picked out an ornamental peace pipe. Its shaft was painted with lightning bolts and hung with the feathers of an eagle. From a woolen bag he took a pinch of a dried powder and tamped it into the bowl. Kindling it with a candle flame, he took a few deep drags of the sacred cactus, then held the smoke in his lungs until his chest began to burn. Two lids of dotted arcs closed over his eyes and his body began to sway and moan. A draft from under the door stirred the smoke around the room, creating wispy shapes that to the children seemed like ghosts from the past. The feathers on the stem fluttered as if they would soon take flight, taking the smoker soaring into a mysterious world of the tribal imagination.

"Choptank," Grandfather Two Tongues said at last. "We are Choptank. We do not belong to this land. We are not Cherokee or Pawnee or Tonkawa or Kaw or any of the others. We are Choptank. The earth here is not the ashes of our ancestors. It is not the ashes of anyone. No one belongs to this land. We are Choptank."

Again, he filled his lungs with the smoke of the sacred cactus and his eyes began to roll. "The earth we belong to is surrounded by water. We were born from its body. Nourished by its spirit. Our holy men called it Checepiake and spoke its name with awe. And it was revered as our Mother. It fed the earth around us and made it green and fertile. Great trees sprang from its soil and wild game abounded in its forests and its sky was thick with wings. From its rivers finned creatures of all kinds leapt into our baskets. It fed us like a Mother. The bay was called the Checepiake and our tribe was called the Choptanks."

Suddenly a painful vision wounded his eyes and a scarlet trickle oozed from his nostrils. "Then the evil spirits came. In a canoe as big as an island. With hairy faces white as death. Their silver skins were hard as stone. And they had sticks that hurled lightning into our sons. They slew our mighty werowance, our Great Standing Bear! They took trophies from our men and raped our daughters as they lay dying on the ground. They made us leave our land forever. They made us leave our Checepiake. Our Mother. Our home. We are Choptank. One day we will return and reclaim what is ours."

He took another drag of sacred smoke and sealed his eyes from the world around him. From deep down inside arose the images of his ancestors like ancient cave paintings come to life. The face of his father was followed by the face of his grandfather and the face of his father before him. In an unbroken chain that stretched back for centuries, one generation followed another, all of them chanting together the dying words of an ancient tongue. Like a song sung by spirits, they flowed through the old man's withered lips. Strange sounding words composed of colliding consonants and lilting cadences. Some were soft and gentle, others harsh and violent, like the sounds of Nature reproduced in human speech. Within them were the lapping of waves on sandy shores, the crisp rustle of leaves in an autumn breeze, mimicked songs of birds, the chirps of insects, and the yowls and yelps of wild beasts. So, too, were mighty claps of thunder, the sizzle of lightning, and the beating of war drums on hollow logs. Sacred words that had survived the decimation of the tribe and more than three-and-a-half centuries of exile. Sacred words the exhausted old man now passed on to his grandchildren for safekeeping.

"Learn these words, O my grandchildren. They are the Song of the Black Robe. Learn them well, for it is your sacred duty to preserve them in your heart and pass them on in your blood. You must never forget them."

"Yes, Grandfather," they promised.

The old man reached again into the wooden box and brought forth a great ceremonial belt, holding it up reverently for the children to see. Woven into it was an image made of black and white shell beads that had been collected long ago on ocean beaches a thousand miles away. It was a silhouette of a great tree with a row of tiny stick men underneath. All of them had their arms down at their sides except the figure in the center. His arms were raised and his hands were drawn as large squares. Turning the belt towards him, Grandfather Two Tongues leaned forward and kissed the crown of the great tree.

"This is the Center of the World," he said solemnly. "This is our home, our sacred land. One day we will return to claim it. We are Choptank."

Outside, the howl of the wind swelled into the battle cries of a thousand angry warriors. The earth shook and the walls of the hut fissured and cracked. Overhead, the plywood roof catapulted its load of truck tires into the void and went tumbling after them. The chickens were sucked up into the vacuum and the nanny goat fainted. But the old man remained calm. Drawing his family closer to him, his gaze sharpened and pierced through the clouds in his eyes like forks of lightning. He placed his palsied hand on David's head and spoke his Choptank name three times. The secret name that he alone had bestowed upon the child at birth. The secret name that could never be revealed to a white man. The secret name that was a prophecy of things to come.

Soon the storm began to dissipate and the old man's strength weakened and began to wane. It had taken all his energy to summon the sacred song from the depths of his subconscious memory. Lying back on his cot, he felt the warmth rush out of his brain like blood from an open wound. He hoped he had not left out anything important and that he had gotten what he said right. But already he was so weary he couldn't remember what he had said.

Shadow Woman put his sacred things back in the oblong wooden box and returned it to its secret hiding place in the wall. Drained of emotion, the family went to their cots in the blackness of the night, in the howling of the wind, with the ghosts of their ancestors dancing in their dreams.

The next morning, David was awakened by sounds of weeping.

"Something terrible has happened," Shadow Woman cried. "Tequetamo is dead."

He had left them without ever getting up from his cot. He had left them without even saying goodbye. He had left them forever. His spirit had been taken into the sky and with it the Song of the Black Robe. David had not only lost his mentor but his connection to his ancient past and his responsibility to the unborn future. The sacred words of his ancestors would be sung no more. David was inconsolable.

They wrapped Grandfather's frail body in a blanket from Shadow Woman's loom and carried him out of the hut using his cot as a litter. Overhead the morning sky opened like a black eye, bruised and beaten into dark purple welts. Even in the dim light of dawn, the tornado's devastation was visible all around them. Sod huts had been smashed into dust and the tall prairie grass looked like a herd of stampeding buffalo had trampled over it. With great solemnity, they bore their beloved Tequetamo across the Dead River gully and through the place where the red skeleton faces had been before the tornado had sucked them into the sky. Climbing up the steep banks of the gorge, they brought his body onto the field of mounds on the other side. With their own hands they dug a shallow grave and buried Grandfather Two Tongues in the hostile, red earth of Oklahoma. Earth that was not the ashes of his ancestors. Earth that was nobody's ashes.

Returning home, they came to the place where the old man had been sitting before the storm. David was amazed. There on the barren ground, untouched by the wind, was the painting Grandfather had made the day before. Like the image on the belt of beads, it depicted a great tree with a row of stickmen standing underneath. What ancient magic kept it safe from the storm? David wasn't sure. But of one thing he was certain. He would be the one to return to the ancient homeland, to the shores along the Checepiake. He would be the one to redeem the lost dominion. He was Choptank.

Center of the World

For centuries it had withstood the assaults of hostile elements, battling wind and tide and jagged forks of fire. Although time and circumstance had caused a precarious tilt to its carriage, its presence was still overpowering. Anchored into the earth by a deep entanglement of serpentine roots, a massive trunk the girth of thirty men rose a hundred feet into the sky. Maintaining its tenuous equilibrium were dozens of sinuous limbs that had been woven by the wind into a wild tangle of twisting boughs, diverging forks, and sudden bends. The crown that they formed was covered by a thick mantle of seven-lobed leaves hung with small clusters of acorns. Glowing green and golden in the morning sun, it cast a magical aura that could be seen from the opposite shore two miles away.

As it had since the beginning, the majestic white oak stood vigil over a place where the earth and sky came together with the water. It was a special place blessed with great natural beauty and abundance, a place where deer and wild turkeys still roamed the woods, where geese and great blue herons graced the skies, and the waters were bountiful with blue crabs, oysters, and fish of all kinds.

It was here at this sacred place, more than three-and-a-half centuries ago, that the great oak bore witness to the arrival of a three-masted pinnace from the other side of the world. Coming ashore in a small skiff, a cavalier of the king thrust his standard into the earth and claimed the fertile peninsula as his own. Soon afterwards, the Founder, as he became known to later generations, built a small clapboard house on the rise. The original dwelling, a box thirty feet square, was no longer visible, having been encompassed in a much larger structure made of red brick. Over the years, the Founder's heirs added wings that telescoped out from the sides and raised two upper stories that were now covered with English ivy and crowned with a slate roof and six double chimneys. A columned portico was extended out over the entrance to give shelter to the door and prominence to the family arms displayed on the apex above: an azure shield emblazoned with a black hand and crested with the silver helmet of a knight.

To the east of the manor house was a broad expanse of river. On this clear Saturday in May, it was roiled into a silver-gold shimmer by a stiff breeze from the south. Skimming across the surface was a fleet of sailing seesaws, each one propelled by clouds of billowing canvas counterbalanced by human weights on the ends of hiking boards.

Leading the pack of log canoes was a vessel with the image of a black bird on its main and a sedge-colored retriever sitting motionless in the bow like a carved figurehead. At the helm was the current lord of the manor, the seventh incarnation of the Founder's name. Shaded under a broad-brimmed hat, he looked for all the world like a modern-day buccaneer in search of plunder, an effect enhanced by a thin, black mustache that fell around the corners of his mouth into a perpetual scowl. Like his forebear, his eyes were embers of coal set deep in a narrow face that was disconcertingly unsymmetrical, divided as it was by a long, crooked nose. In temperament, too, he matched the Founder, with a restless mind, competitive, impatient, and quick to explode.

"Get your butts up further!" he bellowed at his crew. "Pull that goddamned jib in tighter."

A serious challenge was coming from his starboard side. *Flying Fish* was angling in towards the weather buoy.

"Tilghman's closing fast, Dad," his son warned from his perch amidship. In physical appearance, the twenty-two year-old Tavian resembled his aristocratic mother. Like her, he was pale and blonde with hooded green eyes and lobeless ears. Bisecting his upper lip was a subtle scar, a constant reminder of the hereditary flaws she had passed on to him at birth.

"Looks like a dead heat," Tavian said in an annoying lisp that sounded like the hiss of a snake.

The helmsman considered the situation for a moment. Tucking the tiller under his knee, he took a soft, leather tobacco pouch out of his pocket and scooped a bowlful of Windsor Blend into his long-stemmed, Churchwarden's pipe. Cupping it with one hand, he lit it with the other, took a few deep drags, and exhaled slowly.

"Maybe," he said. "Maybe not."

He took note of the subtle tremble that had appeared in the edge of his jib as well as the tiny ripples that ran over the surface of the swells. Factoring in the swaying treetops on shore, he calculated a subtle shift in the direction of the wind. His right hand nudged the intricately carved wooden tiller ever so slightly, catching the sun's rays in the golden shield emblazoned on his signet ring. Steering into a gust, the *Raven* glided ahead of its rival and regained the right of way.

"We're gonna have to tack." He glanced at the nine human weights perched precariously on his three hiking boards. "You fellas ready?"

From the end of the first plank, a portly, middle-aged man in a long billed baseball cap gave a hearty thumbs up.

"Okay here, Cap'n," Winston said. It was his bulging beer belly that gave the boat most of the ballast it needed to stay upright.

"Go for it," the lanky teenager on the middle board seconded. His name was Tucker and he had an IPOD headset plugged into his ears and a shock of sun-bleached hair sticking out the top of his visor.

"Ready here, skipper," an outrider atop the third plank said. A small fair-skinned fellow in a floppy hat, Emmett had zinc oxide smeared on his nose and lips to protect him from ultraviolet radiation.

"Me, too, Dad," Tavian added, his hands poised to release the starboard sheets and pull in the port.

Even the retriever seemed ready to adjust his body in anticipation of the maneuver. Everyone knew that a misstep in the ensuing ballet would cause the shallow-bottomed boat to lose her balance and topple into a cold and unfriendly river.

"Coming about," the captain shouted, swinging the tiller around as he passed the orange weather buoy.

Compensating quickly, the outriders slid down their boards and ducked under the luffing sails as Tavian released the sheets. Canvas and crew crossed to the opposite sides of the boat as *Raven* swung its beak around. *Flying Fish* abruptly steered away to avoid a certain collision and fatal penalty.

"Boards up!" the helmsman ordered as the slackened sails began to swell.

The outriders quickly reset their planks and scooted up to the ends. Their collective weight took hold and *Raven* regained its balance and increased its lead under the helmsman's steady hand.

"Got 'em!" Tavian yelled as he looked back.

Too slow to adjust, *Flying Fish* floundered for a moment and then capsized in a heap, tripping up the next two canoes in a jumble of wet canvas, tangled sheets, and wooden planks. Captains and crews were sent flailing into the river. It was as if they had fallen into an underwater hornet's nest. When they burst back to the surface, they were slimed in white jelly, their bodies ablaze with the sharp stings of toxin-laced tentacles coiled around their arms and necks.

A chase boat came roaring up to the rescue.

"Give us a hand," the captain of *Flying Fish* cried.

Raven's master looked back over his shoulder and led his crew in a round of modest applause. "Well done, gentlemen," he yelled. "Enjoy your swim."

A chorus of curses came back in response.

Tavian shot them the finger. To add insult to injury, the retriever in the bow found it necessary to raise his hind leg and piss overboard. The men on *Raven* didn't finish laughing until a blast from the committee boat signaled they had tacked across the finish line.

Drawing the strings of his tobacco pouch tight, the helmsman squeezed it lightly and slipped it back into his pocket. Once it had belonged to the Founder, himself, and was regarded in the family as something of a good luck charm. As it had passed down from generation to generation, the wealth and power of the bearers had increased exponentially. The helmsman, himself, never went anywhere without it. Today, it had proved its potency once again.

"Nicely done, Septimus" Winston said, tapping the brim of his baseball cap in salute.

The rest of the crew seconded the sentiment.

A self-satisfied smile crossed the helmsman's lips. Being called by his nickname was a form of flattery he found particularly gratifying. The allusion to the Roman numeral VII after his surname enlarged him with an inflated sense of the importance of his own pedigree.

"Couldn't have done it without you boys," he said as he altered his course towards the manor house on the point. "Time to celebrate our victory with some blue crabs and beer."

The men cheered and the dog joined in with a howl.

Alone and serene, the log canoe thrust its sails out wing-on-wing, moving forward with the grace and style of a beautiful, cream-colored butterfly. Approaching his pier, Septimus turned the boat into the face of the wind. Sails went slack and Tavian released the halyards, dropping the canvas clouds back to earth. At the same time, the nine outriders retreated from their perches and began to stack their planks neatly in the middle of the boat. Fending off with his boat hook, Septimus brought *Raven* safely to its nest.

In the bow, the retriever jumped to his feet and pointed towards the shore where a flock of mute swans had dropped in to pillage for food.

"Go get 'em, Russell," Tavian hissed. "Get 'em good."

Bounding off the boat like a rust-colored blur, the dog scampered across the dock and dove into the wetlands where the arrogant, feathered freeloaders had staked their claim. Their rubbery necks swiveled at the rude intrusion. Suddenly, the flock fragmented into the sky, hissing in alarm as they evacuated both the land and their bowels at the same time. Feathers flew before they finally reorganized their chaos into the form of a flying wedge and began to beat their wings in retreat. Russell gave chase, running the trespassers off his territory. Then suddenly, he stopped in his tracks. His nostrils dilated. Another scent had wafted across his path. The pungent smell of decay. He turned his amber eyes into the wind, then followed the invisible trail across the grounds of the estate towards the Chesapeake side of the peninsula.

After *Raven's* crew had pulled up the daggerboard and taken down her two raked masts, Septimus stepped onto the pier.

"This way, fellas," he said. "Hope you're as hungry as I am."

They were. Leaving *Raven* behind, the crew followed their captain down weathered wooden planks towards the manor house on the hill, treading carefully through a minefield of birdshit bombs left by the inconsiderate swans. Bobbing along the pier was an assortment of water toys that never failed to impress them. Next to the *Raven* was *Midnight,* a sleek, 65-foot Hylas ketch that was as black as a stealth bomber from its fiberglass hull to its high-tech graphite fiber sails. Down the pier was *Tiger Shark,* Tavian's brash orange and black cigarette boat. Powered by a pair of turbo-charged, five hundred horsepower engines, it could smoke through the water at seventy-eight miles per hour. The most impressive craft of all was the *Aria,* a floating condo that was sheltered from view inside a two-story, brown-shingled boathouse with only a glimpse of its bowsprit hinting at its magnificence. At the end of the pier, they came to a manicured lawn genetically engineered to eliminate weeds and repel insects, worms, birds, and small mammals. Uphill from there was an octagonal gazebo, screened in to protect its occupants from the summer onslaught of horse flies and other man-eating insects. Well-situated on the rise, it enjoyed spectacular water views on both sides of the peninsula. In the evening, it framed the sun as it slowly sizzled into the Bay beyond the great oak, transforming it into a sea of liquid gold. At dawn, it overlooked the orb's reemergence from the silver-blue waters of the Choptank, rising like a swimmer coming up for air after a cool, refreshing dip in the river.

Inside the gazebo, the hungry sailors sat down around a redwood picnic table covered in brown butcher's paper weighed down with wooden mallets and short-handled knives. An ageless, black man tottered down the hill from the kitchen clutching a bushel basket with steam streaming out the cracks. White splotches on his face and forearms made him appear to be a burn victim. But, in fact, his condition was the result of a chronic case of vitiligo. In a fit of whimsy, the helmsman's father, the sixth lord of the manor, had named him Nero after the mad Roman emperor who fiddled on his palace rooftop while the eternal city burned below.

"You watch your hands, gent'men," Nero warned. "They still pipin' hot."

A clatter of Number 1 Jimmies spilled out across the table, their red backs crusted over with Old Bay seasoning. They were followed by a tray of sweet white corn and a cooler of ice-cold beer brought by a pink-eyed, albino woman and her six-fingered son.

"Thank you, Cissy," Septimus said, averting his eyes from her and ignoring her son altogether.

In truth, he hardly thought of his servants as people at all. They were more like domestic animals or pieces of furniture that had been handed down from the past, worn and shabby to be sure, but sturdy and serviceable at the same time.

"You holler, Mr. B, you want more," Nero said, shooing the other two away before they caused the guests to lose their appetites.

"Don't let the crabs get cold, boys," Septimus warned.

One by one, the crew joined in on the time-honored ritual of cracking open the backs of hard-shelled crustaceans and scraping off their lungs and innards with short-handled knives. Drawing and quartering the disemboweled bodies, they picked out white nuggets of succulent backfin. Dipped in vinegar and dabbed in red pepper spice, the taste was heaven itself.

So preoccupied were they, that none of them noticed Russell returning from bayside with a new discovery clamped firmly in his mouth. He stopped at the screen door and scratched for their attention.

"Sorry Russ, no crabs for you," Tavian said without taking his eyes off the business at hand.

Not to be ignored, Russell opened his jaws and let fall his newly found prize. The distinctive thud of dead meat got everyone's attention. So did the malodorous stench of decay that sifted through the screen walls of the gazebo.

"Jesus! What the hell!"

In size and shape it resembled a deflated football. Its skin was damp and had the color of tobacco and texture of tanned leather. Just barely visible on the surface was a tattooed nest of concentric rings radiating out from the bridge of a badly broken nose. Four holes dominated the horrible visage: two hollowed-out eyes, a toothless mouth agape in a silent scream, and a bullet crater centered in the forehead.

Leaving their feast unfinished, the startled men followed Russell through the thorny underbrush of the tick-infested woods to a site just north of the Great Oak. Here, in a primeval, moss-covered clearing, solid ground turned soft and spongy. A putrid slime oozed up over the men's Top-Siders, staining their ankles red. The retriever led them on to the very edge of a peat bog that had been trapped inland from the bay centuries ago. The stench of decomposing flesh drew their attention to the grotesque spectacle in the middle of the marsh. Thrust through the surface was a mummified hand, its five fingers drawn back like claws.

The sheriff and the county coroner were summoned on cell phones. They, in turn, called in the fire department. Water pumps were brought in to drain the pond along with a refrigerated van to preserve the remains. The operation went slowly, dragging on through the late afternoon and evening and into a night lit by the harsh glare of floodlights.

As the water level gradually receded, the claw-like hand led to a solitary arm, then to a headless torso laced with scars and primitive tattoos. Beneath it was a pyramid of carcasses piled one on top of the other. Riddled with bullet holes, the bodies were mutilated beyond belief. Flesh was ripped, bones broken, and throats slit from ear to ear. Some of the men had weapons still clutched in their hands. Along with stone-headed tomahawks, there were massive war clubs embedded with the molars of carnivores and bows with flint-tipped arrows fletched with hawk feathers. There were even a few rust-covered seventeenth-century muskets. Many of the women were clutching babies and young children. It was a scene so horrifying that no expletive could do it justice.

"My guess is they're bog mummies," Winston said at last. "Courtney and I saw some in Denmark last summer at the Silkeborg Museum. Chemical stew in the peat bog preserves them. Tannic acid, I think."

"Must have worked pretty well," Emmett uttered through his zinc-lined lips. "Shit, these guys look better than Lenin."

"Hey look at that dude!" Tucker said in amazement. "Guy's humongous!"

They all gawked as the body of a big-boned warrior was carried out of the pit on a gurney. His grim face was frozen in fury, crisscrossed with battle scars and streaks of faded black war paint. In the center was a hawk-like nose and a pair of sunken eyelids arced with dotted scars. On the right side of his skull, which was shaved bare, was a prominent bullet hole. On the left, long ropes of braided hair hung down to a bearskin tunic matted with the gore of battle. His massive chest, elaborately tattooed with emblems of the hunt, had been punctured by multiple exit wounds that had exposed the tissue of his heart and lungs.

"Jesus, he stinks!" Tavian pinched his nose and turned away.

"Best we get 'em on ice as fast as possible," the coroner advised. Circulating among the men, he handed out Styrofoam face masks and barf bags.

"Seems you gents have uncovered a time capsule," the sheriff added. "I think we should contact the Department of Natural Resources."

But Septimus was too shocked to respond, his mind seized by the recognition that he had seen the dead warrior once before. When he was just a boy, he had come across the fearsome savage standing in the hallway of his home. And since then, he had often felt his unseen presence stalking him through the dead of night like an apparition hell-bent on revenge.

Now, at the edge of the bog, the seventh lord of the manor stood utterly transfixed, assailed by the imagined wails of unseen spirits rising from the dead and ascending through the tree tops into a moonless sky. After more than three-and-a-half centuries, a terrible secret had emerged from the marsh to confront him. A secret that was the family's eternal shame, and at the same time, the very cornerstone of its wealth and privilege. A secret that could destroy them forever.

Exodus

Those who survived the ambush in the woods played dead until dark, then crawled out from under the bodies of their kinsmen and crept to safety in the high rushes of the marsh. A few followed the hunter, Red-Eyed Owl, as he vanished into the horns of the moon. The others went with Burning Bow, the eldest son of Great Standing Bear.

In dugout canoes, he led them through a thundersquall of wailing winds and swirling waterspouts. Many were swallowed up in the Great Sea of Ancestors before the survivors reached the chalky cliffs of the western shore. Here the wily Patuxents welcomed their battle-weary brothers with great ceremony, filling their bellies with a feast of venison and quail. But in the blackness of the night, they slit the throat of the young werowance as he slept and set his canoes ablaze where they lay on the beach.

Those who survived their treachery, escaped into a hostile wilderness thick with thorns. Here it was that Hawk-in-the-Heart sacrificed himself to save the others, battling a wolf pack with his bare hands while the rest of his tribe swam to safety across a mighty river.

On the other side, the wisoe Counting Clouds comforted his people around a campfire, singing for them the Song of the Black Robe and telling them of a time when he would lead them back to their homeland at the Center of the World. But it was not to be. Seven times the winter snows fell and seven times they were taken back into the sun. Counting Clouds grew old and died in his dreams leaving his people to wander aimlessly in circles.

It was then that the great hunter, Talking Elk, became werowance. Following a fire that streaked across the night, he led his people farther south to a place where the river swelled with anger and roared its wrath through a granite gorge. Here he risked his life to rescue a runaway slave from the jaws of the rapids. But, alas, the black man brought with him the Englishman's pox and bewitched Talking Elk into Spotted Elk, consuming him with fever and killing a third of his people.

Medicine Dancer succeeded her father and became the only she-male werowance in the history of the tribe. With herbs and berries from the woods, she nursed her people back to health. And when locust swarms brought famine to the tribe, she led it into the setting sun in search of game. With two dead sons inside her womb, she walked until she could walk no more and the red tide came and washed her spirit away. On the devastated earth, her people lay down with her and waited for the vultures to come and take them into the sky.

It was then that the one who became the mighty Horses Head rescued the tribe with a herd of wild pintos, riding them to safety a hundred skies to the south. His nephew, High Cloud Walking, took the people up into the mountains of smoke, to the very edge of the earth, itself, where he shared the pipe of peace with the Cherokee.

The two peoples lived along side each other for a hundred years until the white man came looking for gold. The great warrior Wide Eyes was werowance then and led his Choptank braves into battle alongside their Cherokee brothers. Many warriors died that day from the fire of the long rifles. Wide Eyes and his chief men refused to retreat and were taken captive by the bluecoats. As punishment, they had their hands hacked off and were forced to live the rest of their lives as beggars among their own people.

After that, the leadership of the tribe fell to Three-legged Coyote. Under the guns of the horse soldiers, the crippled old man marched his people west into exile with the Cherokee. Through deep winter snows, they followed a trail marked by frozen limbs that stuck out of the crust like signposts. For a thousand skies, they walked, until at last they crossed the mighty river of mud and pitched their lodges on a government reservation encircled by barbed wire fences. Many of those who survived the Trail of Tears died, like their chief, of an exhausted spirit and a hole in the heart.

Fifty times the winter came and went before the white man broke his word again and hordes of settlers on horseback forced them to flee once more. Black Moon Rising was werowance then and sang the Song of the Black Robe to comfort his people as he led them into the hostile prairie beyond the falling sun. Eventually they came to a piece of land so desolate and forlorn that even the white squatters failed to follow. A place that they called "No Man's Land."

Here it was that Two Tongues came weeping into the world, he who was the first to wear the office of werowance and wisoe both, for by this time the tribe had been reduced to

31

twenty-five survivors. And after him came the last of his lineage. The one whose name could never be revealed to a white man. The one whose name was a prophecy of things to come.

Human Sacrifice

The schoolhouse was an empty shell. No roof, no door, no desks, chairs, or textbooks. All that remained inside the cinder block walls was a globe of the world which had been crushed flat under the weight of a heavy, metal drum with a grinning, red skeleton face stenciled on its yellow skin. Three others like it lay nearby flattened into compressed accordions. During the night, they had fallen through the tin roof like cluster bombs, cratering the concrete floor and exploding their toxic contents on the walls. Left behind was an unholy splatter of black liquid ooze and corrosive chemicals with noxious fumes. In addition, thousands of used syringes and broken vials of medical waste were scattered across the floor. Mixed in among them were small pellets of radioactive uranium that looked like grains of dried corn.

Lydia Applebaum slumped down on the front stoop, her anguish hidden in a cradle of arthritic hands. Speechless. Utterly devastated. Defeated. It was the only time David had ever seen his teacher that way. Without a word, he pulled the neck of his T-shirt up over his nose to filter out the fumes. Then he retrieved the flattened globe from under the metal accordion in the center of the room and set it down on the stoop next to his teacher. The miniature Atlas who had once supported the world on his shoulders had been squashed to the size and thickness of a fifty-cent piece. Somehow the brass plate on the base survived, although it was now permanently embedded in the South Pole.

"Now you can hang it on your wall like a shield," David said, trying to cheer up the old woman.

His teacher nodded sadly. The globe had been presented to her by the Guymon Board of Education in recognition of her thirty-five years of service to the Dead River School. Even flattened, it still meant a great deal to her, a professional validation of the teaching that had been and would always be her life.

"How very kind of you, Mr. Waterfield," she said softly. "Thank you."

After that, David got down to work. With his bare feet, he pushed the crumpled, skeleton-faced drums through a hole in the wall where the back door used to be. Then he scooped the syringes, vials, and uranium pellets into the pocket of his baggataway stick and took them outside to the Port-A-Potty that now lay on its back near the bell post.

Like a coffin, David thought.

Next, he fashioned a makeshift broom from buffalo grass and swept the chemicals off the walls and floor, rinsing them away with water he brought in from the well in leaking, wooden buckets.

By the end of the day, the classroom was as clean as it had ever been. It was the first indication Miss Applebaum had that anybody really cared. None of her other students had bothered to come to school at all, although she really couldn't blame them under the circumstances.

When he had finished his task, David sat down next to his teacher on the front stoop. The old woman put her hand on his arm and squeezed it.

"I was so sorry to hear about your Grandfather, Mr. Waterfield," she said. "If there's anything I can do..."

There was.

"Grandfather told us that we were Choptanks and that our tribe lived on the Checepiake Bay. Do you know where that is, Miss Applebaum?"

"The Checepiake Bay?" David's pronunciation confused her for a moment. Then she realized what he meant. "Your grandfather was probably talking about the Chesapeake Bay. That's the way we say it today."

"But where is it, Miss Applebaum?"

"Well, it's very, very far from here, I can tell you that." She picked up the flattened tin globe to show him. "We are right here in the panhandle of Oklahoma," she said, pointing to a spot near the edge. "And here, on the flip side, half-way across the country is the Chesapeake Bay, located in the states of Maryland and Virginia."

David liked the way it looked. Rich, blue water surrounded by lush, green land. It was much more appealing than the faded, brown color of Oklahoma.

"How many miles away is it, Miss Applebaum?"

"I'd guess about a thousand or more as the crow flies. A lot further by foot. Your people must have zigzagged all over the place to get here. Probably took them hundreds of years to make the trek."

The old woman got off the stoop and stepped carefully through the debris towards her beloved Rocinante, an old VW beetle she had named after Don Quixote's downtrodden nag. Red and rusted as the Oklahoma earth, it had come through the storm largely unscathed. Only a few new dents and dings had been added to the collection of battle scars it had accumulated over twenty years of faithful service. Cracking open the front door, Lydia Applebaum bent down and rummaged around under the front seat. A few moments later, she emerged holding a large book with a broken back. It was a collection of Rand McNally maps and inside was a more detailed view of the Chesapeake Bay.

"It's shaped like a tree made of water," David said. His finger traced the wide trunk that sprang up from the Atlantic and branched off into many rivers and inlets on its way north. Many of them still bore their tribal names: Potomac, Rappahannock, Wicomico, Patuxent, and Nanticoke.

"Looky here!" Miss Applebaum said. "This one's named Choptank! Must be where your people came from."

David's blood raced. The river slithered through Maryland's Eastern Shore like a winding, water snake. It had a thick, muscular body and gaping jaws with great fangs of earth on either side. Choptank! The river that ran through the veins of his ancestors. The river that circled endlessly inside in his own heart. Choptank! The very name struck deep into David's subconscious. Within its syllables he heard the sound of water lapping on a distant shore, endlessly rising and falling and calling the river by its natural name. *Choptank,* it said. *Choptank!*

"I'm going back someday," David said.

Miss Applebaum was impressed by David's resolution. None of her other students even dared to think of leaving the village.

She knew it would be almost impossible for David and tried not to encourage him.

"It's so far," she said. "How would you get there? What would you do to support yourself? You don't know anyone there. How would you survive?"

David shrugged his shoulders. "All I know is that I must return to the Chesapeake. Grandfather said so. Will you help me, Miss Applebaum?"

His determination touched her deeply. "Of course, Mr. Waterfield," she said softly, "I'll try to help you. But on one condition."

"Anything."

"That you help yourself, too."

For the first time since Grandfather's death, David's spirit lifted and the light came back into his eyes. He looked up at her with such gratitude that she almost wept.

"Thank you," he said softly.

Only yesterday, Lydia Applebaum had felt her life had been destroyed forever, flattened like her globe of the world. But now she felt herself strengthened by a strong sense of purpose and resolve. Yes, she would help him, with all her heart and mind.

One of her maxims was that education could help you accomplish anything you want. She said it many times to the class, but deep down inside she wasn't completely sure it was a rule that applied to Native Americans. Here was a test that would confirm her convictions.

"Perhaps we can find a college there that you can go to," she suggested. "One with a scholarship that will pay your tuition, room and board."

But even as she spoke, she knew how difficult that would be. None of her students had ever graduated from high school much less gone on to college. After some considerable thought, the old woman began to devise a plan. David had one thing that all schools wanted—great athletic ability. In her opinion, he had the potential to be another Jim Thorpe. Winner of the decathlon in the 1912 Olympics, Thorpe was regarded as the best Native American athlete ever, and one of the best overall athletes of all time. He was from Oklahoma, too.

But athletic prowess wouldn't be enough by itself. Good grades were even more important. David was naturally bright, but his grades were below average. He would need a great deal of tutoring if he were going to make it. Lydia Applebaum was ready and willing to do whatever it took. She decided to plan a course of action designed to get him admitted. He would be living proof of what was possible, the first of her students to go on to college, an inspiration to all the others. What Anne Sullivan was to the blind Helen Keller, she would be to David Waterfield. It was an ambitious goal to be sure, but after all, she had two years to transform her protégé into a scholarship winner.

For his part, David was determined to succeed. At last he had been given a goal to aim for. It was all the motivation he needed. He began to listen carefully in class and do his homework faithfully. Every day, Miss Applebaum tutored him after school and during the summer, she worked with him on a reading list. It wasn't long before his grades began to improve dramatically.

In October of his senior year, David rode the Greyhound to Guymon and took the SAT's with a roomful of rich, Caucasian kids. Two months of anxiety followed before he finally got the results. David had scored in the top five percent.

"My word!" Miss Applebaum pressed her hand over her heart. "This is even better than I hoped for!"

She sank back down in her chair to catch her breath. A profound sense of achievement passed over her. She had done it. David Waterfield was going to be the first of her students to go to college. She had proved her point. Education could do anything.

The next hurdle was to decide which college he should go to. With a little research, Miss Applebaum came up with the ideal candidate. The United States Naval Academy! She couldn't wait to show David the catalogue.

"Looky here. It's located right on the Chesapeake Bay. Best of all, it's completely free! You even get a small salary to attend!"

"What's the catch?" David asked skeptically.

"All you have to do is serve in the Navy a few years after graduation. It would give you a chance to see the world."

David was thrilled with the idea. The Naval Academy! The Chesapeake! The World! All for free!

Miss Applebaum quickly paged to the back of the catalogue and her big bug eyes rapidly scanned the section on admission procedures.

"Hmmmm. Says here that to get admitted you're required to have a nomination from either your Congressman, Senator, or the President or Vice-President of the United States."

"Hey, no big deal," David said. "Got to know all those dudes pretty well down in the Dead River Dump. I'm sure they wouldn't mind giving me a nomination."

"Really, Mr. Waterfield, you don't have to know them personally. The Academy is administered by Congress. The admission requirements are just a way to insure that all the states and congressional districts get their proper representation. They don't expect you to know anyone personally. Each elected official has a number of slots to fill. All you have to do is write them a letter stating your qualifications and test scores. Everything is judged on the up and up."

David believed her. He wrote to everyone and hoped for the best. Surely, one of them would see the merits of his case. Several weeks later, form letters followed from his Congressman, two Senators, the President, and the Vice-President of the United States. All of them said the same thing. Someone else had been selected.

"Oh, damn!" Miss Applebaum said. It was the first time David had ever heard her break her own rule against swearing in the classroom. She just stared at the letters in total disbelief. "Damn, damn, damn," she said. He had never heard her repeat herself either.

David was stoic in accepting rejection. He was deeply disappointed that his dream had ended so quickly. But he wasn't surprised. Native peoples never really expected help from the government. After all, none of the peace treaties they made with the white man had ever been honored for very long. Once again, the government had failed to make amends. Instead of going back to the Chesapeake, he would have to spend his life working in the toxic waste dump at the edge of town.

After stewing a few weeks, Miss Applebaum renewed her determination and vowed not to take "no" for an answer.

"There must be some mistake," she declared to David. "Maybe they didn't receive your transcripts or SAT's or something. We must leave nothing to chance."

She decided to forget about the President, Vice-President, and Senators and concentrate all her efforts on Congressman Jesse P. Snyder from the 3rd District, which included the panhandle. His support seemed the most attainable and his office was the most accessible, even though it was almost halfway across the state in Stillwater. After eighteen telephone calls, a meeting was finally arranged.

David washed and polished Rocinante just for the occasion and her dints and dings never looked better. Neither did Miss Applebaum. She had dressed up for the occasion in her finest church-going clothes. Despite the hundred-degree heat, she wore a winter-weight, navy-blue frock decorated with tiny white polka dots. Resting on top of her head was a cream-colored pillbox hat with a narrow black veil across the brim. She carried a pair of spotless white gloves in her purse to avoid getting them sweaty.

At Shadow Woman's insistence, David wore the clothes his father had left behind when the wind took him away. Stone Hammer's long-sleeved, red flannel shirt was a size too small and his sun-bleached blue jeans were an inch too short. With great difficulty, David worked his feet into his father's cowboy boots, each of which had a hole in the sole.

"A perfect fit," he had told his mother. And Shadow Woman smiled proudly.

Miss Applebaum had offered to give her star pupil a haircut, but David was superstitious and feared, like Sampson in the white man's Bible, that he would lose his strength. Instead, he tied his hair back into a ponytail the way he did when he was playing stickball.

At dawn on the appointed morning, the two of them set out on their journey. Stillwater was six hours away in a car that had a top speed of forty-five miles an hour, wasn't air-conditioned, and already had 275,000 miles on its odometer. The radio was broken but music of a sort was provided by the rhythm of a rattling muffler and a whistle from a hole in the tailpipe.

"Miss Applebaum, Rocinante is like a musical instrument," David said. "When I close my eyes, I see Grandfather shaking his spirit rattle and my mother playing her wooden flute. My sisters are dancing around the fire and the chickens are clucking and clapping their wings. It's really cool."

"Never thought of it that way, Mr. Waterfield. But now that you mention it, I think I hear it, too. It's lovely. Really lovely."

She glanced over at her young passenger. His eyes were still closed and there was a happy smile on his face. She couldn't help but notice the mysterious dotted scars that lined his eyelids. There were many things she didn't know about her protégé, but she had to admit that he had a wonderful imagination.

Mid-way to their destination, a red light flashed on the dashboard and Miss Applebaum steered over onto the gravel shoulder.

"Rosie's overheating again," she said. "Inconsiderate little thing."

"I need to stretch my legs anyway," David said.

Without the breeze coming in the window, the hundred-degree heat was stifling, lifting off the blacktop like fumes from a frying pan. All around them the land was flat and grassy, punctuated by a single vertical pole with a historical marker on top. While they waited for the engine to cool, they walked down for a closer look.

Boundary Line it read. *1889 and 1893.*

"This is where the great land runs began," Miss Applebaum said. "First one was to the south by proclamation of President Harrison. The second one was to the north by proclamation of President Cleveland."

David closed his eyes and a gunshot exploded next to his ear. Screaming hordes rushed across the line. Frantic horsemen whipped their mounts and dug their spurs into bloody underbellies. Following them were hundreds of buckboards, stagecoaches, and prairie schooners heavy with homesteaders.

On the plains ahead of them, an Indian family abandoned their tepee and ran frantically to get out of the way. The father carried a small boy in his arms and his wife had a papoose on her back. But it was too late. The hooves of destiny and the wheels of progress ran them down, trampling their brown bodies into the earth. Oblivious to the tragedy underfoot, a hundred thousand land-hungry boomers surged over the plains, stabbing wooden stakes into the land. When it was over, the Cherokee were left with less than one-third of one percent of the seven million acres that the Treaty of New Echota had conveyed to them in 1838 as payment for uprooting the tribe from their ancient homeland in the east.

"They stole it from them," David said. "They had no right."

"I'm sorry, Mr. Waterfield," his teacher said sadly. "It was a great tragedy for the Cherokee and for your people, too."

When the engine had cooled, Miss Applebaum gave Rocinante a drink of water from a plastic jug she kept on the floor of the backseat. Back in the bug, they headed down the highway in a deep and profound silence. They hadn't gone far when a rust hole the size of a basketball fell through the floor boards on the passenger side.

"Hey!" David yelled.

"Sorry, Mr. Waterfield. I've been meaning to get that fixed."

David propped his fee up on the dashboard. "It's okay, Miss Applebaum. In this heat an extra window comes in handy."

His teacher managed a worried smile. "Only hope Rosie doesn't fall apart all at once like the 'One Hoss Shay' did."

"Oliver Wendell Holmes wrote that. It was on my SAT."

"Very good. Very good, indeed, Mr. Waterfield." She was so proud of him that she all but forgot the gaping hole in her floorboard.

David settled back and watched endless miles of macadam race by through his legs. The effect was almost hypnotic, interrupted by occasional potholes and road kills.

"Hey, we just ran over a skunk!" He held his breath and pinched his nose.

"Lot of 'em around these parts," Miss Applebaum replied. "Down here they call 'em politicians."

And they both laughed out loud.

After stopping a few more times to let the engine cool, they finally reached the outskirts of Stillwater. Under the curious gaze of longhorn cattle, Rocinante sputtered ever onwards, passing fields of oil pump jacks that dotted the landscape like Don Quixote's windmills. A series of billboards floated by informing them that Stillwater was the home of the Oklahoma

State University Cowboys. Another urged them to visit the National Wrestling Museum. A third promoted the Largest Button Collection in the World.

The town itself was small and flat with a population of forty-two thousand. They easily found the Honorable Jesse P. Snyder's office in the heart of the historic district, catty-cornered from a white-columned, Georgian-style Court House. It was located in a contemporary structure that at four stories high was the tallest building in town. As they approached it on foot, the silvered-glass facade reflected back their distorted images like an overgrown, fun house mirror. It was one of those places that you could see out of, but nobody else could see in. A perfect hiding place for a five-term, pork barrel politician.

The visitors were kept waiting for over an hour, sunk into a soft, calfskin sofa. Facing them was an oversized portrait of the congressman hung in a western-style frame made of woven lariats. As captured on canvas, His Honor was a weasel of a man with a snout-like nose, black eye slits, and sharp, pointed teeth. Arrayed around him on the other walls were dozens of autographed pictures of adoring friends, high-powered constituents, movie stars, sports heroes, and prominent politicians. They were a not so subtle reminder to those who ventured here that Jesse P. Snyder was a man of widespread influence and power.

Eventually, a busty young blonde with penciled-in eyebrows and bright red collagen-inflated lips appeared. She introduced herself as Jocelyn Barbanell, Congressman's Snyder's administrative aide.

"Jesse P was so looking forward to meeting you all," she lied "but he was called back to Washington late last night. But don't worry, I can handle things for him."

Somehow they both thought she was pretty good at that.

"We can meet back in my cubby," she added cheerfully. "Care for something to drink?"

"Nope," Miss Applebaum said curtly.

They followed the nubile young woman as she flounced through a labyrinth of small cubicles to an office adjoining the Congressman's. It was empty except for a small desk on one side and a folded sofa bed on the other. Miss Barbenell discreetly nudged a pair of black panties under her desk and wriggled down into her chair.

Dispensing with small talk, Lydia Applebaum voiced her complaint in the strongest language possible. She introduced David and described his accomplishments, one after another.

"Mr. Waterfield has earned a B+ average and has served as his class president for the past two years. His SAT scores are in the top five percent. Not only that, he's a terrific athlete to boot."

"What sport do you play, Mr. Waterfield?"

"Baggataway."

"He means lacrosse," his teacher corrected. "It was invented by American Indians, you know."

"I play wing attack," David said. "Either side."

"How nice," Miss Barbanell said, forcing a tight little smile. "Unfortunately, Jesse P gets so many outstanding applications that we submit them to the Academy and let them recommend the best one."

She followed up with a file folder from her desk drawer. It belonged to the winning candidate. Inside was a newspaper clipping with a headline that announced *Local Boy Navy Bound*. It included a photo of Congressman Snyder congratulating the chosen one—a good-looking, athletic Anglo-Saxon named John Leland. The boy's father, a weathered man in a cowboy hat and fringed buckskin jacket, stood by his side beaming proudly.

One by one, the vacuous blonde enumerated the reasons for the Leland boy's selection. According to the file, he had earned straight A's and his SAT's were superior. He was captain of the football team, president of the debate club, commander of the drill team, and stroke on the varsity crew. The boy lived and breathed Navy.

"I'll bet he even looks good in blue," Lydia Applebaum added sarcastically.

"Perhaps next year Mr. Waterfield can resubmit his application," Miss Barbanell suggested. "Of course, I can't promise anything, but maybe the competition won't be so keen."

There was nothing they could say. They were defeated fair and square. Or so it seemed.

The young lady ushered the visitors out of her office and back through the maze of partitions. As they went out into the lobby, Miss Applebaum's eyes zeroed in on one of the pictures on the power wall. A familiar man in a cowboy hat and fringed buckskin jacket was caught in the act of handing over a campaign check to the Honorable Congressman Snyder whose mouth was broken into a saw-toothed grin.

"Mr. Leland, you know, the boy's father," she said to the aide. "He's the Mr. Leland of Leland Oil, isn't he, missy?"

Miss Barbanell didn't care for the question. "Yes," she admitted reluctantly. "I believe...uh...he is the...uh... same Mr. Leland."

Lydia Applebaum understood it all very well now. The congressman's girl friend had thrown up a smoke screen about how candidates were chosen. It might be true most of the time, but not in this case. Her instincts told her a political favor was being repaid from one multi-millionaire to another.

That evening, on the long journey home, Miss Applebaum tried to be positive. "It's not over yet," she declared. "I'm not through by a long shot."

"But what can we do?" David asked. "They've already chosen."

"I've taught you just about everything I know, Mr. Waterfield. English, History, Math, Geography. Just about everything. But there's one thing I haven't taught you and that's practical politics. It's the way things get done in this country. Sometimes you gotta fight fire with fire."

David didn't quite understand what she meant, but he saw that his teacher didn't want to talk about it anymore. Her mind shifted into automatic pilot and she spent the rest of the trip mulling over her options, driving slowly down highways littered with flattened snakes and decaying deer carcasses. Occasionally, she would stop altogether to give Rocinante a drink. When darkness fell, she turned on her one good headlight and went even slower, wheezing and sputtering down bumpy dirt roads. To David the music of the rattles and pipes now seemed like a funeral dirge.

The next day Miss Applebaum knew just what to do. According to the newspaper clipping, John Leland had graduated from Stillwater High. It so happened that an old college friend worked in the guidance office there. A telephone call brought surreptitious Xeroxes of the boy's attendance records, report cards, teacher's notes, and SAT scores.

"Ahah!" Miss Applebaum said.

It was just as she suspected. John Leland was really only an average student with mediocre SAT's. He wasn't captain of the football team, just a second string tailback. And he was constantly in trouble with the principal. The congressman's girl friend had just been covering her boss's tracks with a lot of hype.

Fortified by a shot of whiskey, Lydia Applebaum plotted her strategy. She wrote the Honorable Jesse P. Snyder and pointed out that revelation of the political favor would surely make unfavorable reading during the upcoming elections, particularly when she knew such a highly qualified young applicant was still available. And he was an underprivileged minority to boot. She enclosed copies of John Leland's report cards and SAT scores along with a copy of the letter she intended to send to the newspapers. And sealing the envelope, she knew she was sealing her fate as well.

Two letters came by special delivery return mail. The first was from the Congressman's office to David. In a friendly manner, it informed him that an opening had just occurred at the United States Naval Academy due to the decision of the previous candidate to attend another institution. The slot was now being offered to him. David was ecstatic. He couldn't believe his eyes. Miss Applebaum's magic was powerful indeed.

The second letter was from the School Board and she didn't open it for several days, allowing David time to celebrate his success. When she did, it was what she feared would happen. Her contract was not being renewed. No reason was given, but none was needed. She knew she was being punished for having brought pressure to bear on a United States Congressman. The retaliation had been swift and sure. They were taking away the one thing that she loved. But it didn't matter. She had made her point. She had made a difference. She felt as if her sacrifice had begun to undo, in some small way, the centuries of injustice that had been committed against native peoples by the white man. She had reversed the tide of history. She had turned back the forces of nature. She had given David Waterfield his ticket home.

Black Steeple

In the morning light, it looked like a fresh wound. Carved into the top of a cliff just a hundred yards north of the great oak was a crescent of red clay, three feet deep. Spaced at one-foot intervals around its perimeter were a series of discolored ovals, the rotted remains of wooden poles that had once formed the outer ring of a palisadoed village. In the centuries since the site had been abandoned, half of its circumference had crumbled into the bay, the victim of water erosion. The other half had already yielded up a treasure trove of native artifacts including awls, axe heads, and numerous pottery shards.

Despite the early hour, a bushy-haired man with caterpillar eyebrows was already hard at work. Whistling through the gaps in his front teeth, he shoveled loose debris into a six-gallon plastic bucket. His assistant, a woman seven months pregnant, was working nearby at the sifter, rocking the rickety wooden stand back and forth as if it was a baby's cradle.

"When you think about it, Dolores," Carter Seymour said, "this must have been a great place to live. The Bay provided protection from surprise attacks from the west and was also a perpetual source of seafood."

Dolores agreed. "Must have been a pretty pricey piece of property in its time. You know what the real estate guys say— location, location, location."

A steady stream of loose dirt filtered through her screen and settled into a small pyramid on the ground underneath. So far, all she had found in her sifter were some small pottery fragments, nothing of importance. Until now.

"Hey, Carter! Look at this!"

Resting on top of the wire mesh was a large, jagged arrowhead. Brushing away the debris around it, Dolores held it up to the light. Both faces had been flaked and the edges were completely translucent.

"Looks like white agate to me," she said. "And it's shaped like a laurel leaf!"

Seymour snatched it from her and examined it in his own hands. "By Jove, Delores, you've found a Solutrean point!"

Both of them immediately understood the significance of their find. Solutrean points were calling cards left by Paleoindian hunters of the Ice Age as they stalked wooly mammoths and giant bison across the continent. They were so called because identical points had been discovered at Solutrea on the northern coast of Spain. Finding one here buttressed the latest theory that some of the continent's first inhabitants had sailed across the Atlantic in boats made from animal skins.

"You know what this means, Dolores?"

"Yes, Carter. This site is at least fifteen thousand years old."

They had just found the earliest human habitation on the Chesapeake.

The joy of their discovery was shattered by the harsh chop of rotor blades and a powerful downdraft that kicked up a cloud of dust. The seventh incarnation of the Founder's name arose from behind the great oak in a black, four-bladed, twin-turbine Sikorsky helicopter.

At the controls was a big-boned, hairy-handed man in mirrored sunglasses. "Wonder what the geeks are looking for today, boss?" he asked into his mic-boom.

"History, Chuck," Septimus said through the speaker in the back seat. "History in the form of beads and pottery shards. Maybe even a few skeletons."

The village site had been discovered a few months after the recovery of the bog mummies from the marsh and was being excavated by archaeologists from the American Anthropological Society, the Smithsonian Institute, and the University of Maryland. Like the mummies, it was expected to be a treasure trove of information about the early inhabitants of the Chesapeake. When the bodies had first been discovered, Septimus's first inclination was to have them all incinerated. But with the sheriff and so many witnesses present, that would have seemed suspicious. The next best thing was to get the carcasses off his property and into a museum where he could control the questions surrounding their demise. As it turned out, this course of action reaped unexpected rewards. The Choptank remains turned out to be extremely valuable. As the first bog mummies ever found outside Northern Europe or the state of Florida, they netted Septimus thirty-two million in tax deductions. More was expected from artifacts uncovered at the newly discovered village site.

Banking around to the northwest, Chuck put his nose down and headed out across the Chesapeake. To mask out the noisy rotors, he piped some music back to the boss's headset. Attired in imperial-purple pajamas and a royal-blue robe, Septimus adjusted a black sleep mask over his eyes and settled back into the soothing strains of the Pachelbel Canon.

Below them, the Chesapeake was practically deserted, its broad surface broken only by the wake of a solitary crabber on his morning rounds. Once the great estuary had been a virtual protein factory. But no more. Deep beneath the surface, a zone of death was spreading down the main stem and into the rivers on either side. Chemical runoff from factories, farms, and excessive real estate development was robbing the water of its oxygen. Suffocating aquatic life, it was gradually threatening the collapse of the delicate ecology of the entire Bay.

"It's so beautiful. So delicate and uplifting. The balance, the harmony. Don't you think Chuck?" As usual, Septimus was so tuned into his music that he was oblivious to the damage his industries were causing deep beneath the surface of the Bay.

"If you say so, boss," the pilot said. "I'm into Techno-Gothic myself."

"Barbarian."

"Just kidding, boss. I like whatever you like."

Up ahead on the western shore, the colonial city of Annapolis became visible, its narrow lanes radiating out from the wooden dome of its historic state house like spokes from an eighteenth-century wagon wheel. As it passed nearby, the Sikorsky cast an ominous shadow over the manicured grounds of the United States Naval Academy, standing sentinel at the water's edge. Already the middies were out in the athletic fields doing their morning exercises.

Just over the horizon, two great steel spans arose to meet them. Vaulting more than four miles across the Bay, they connected the Eastern Shore to the rest of Maryland. The gulf that divided them was more than just a geographical barrier. It separated two distinct ways of life. On the one side was the relatively unspoiled Eastern Shore where great landowners like Septimus lived on private fiefdoms that were visible only from the air and water. On the other was the heavily populated western shore and an endless urban sprawl of subdivisions linked to each other by congested highways and a sense of quiet desperation.

Beyond the twin spans, an ugly brown river ran down from the city of Baltimore. As it swept past the dilapidated factories and mills that lined its banks, it gathered up their liquified waste and flushed it into the Bay like a gigantic sewer.

Wallowing through the murky water was a rusted freighter that was making its way towards the docks of a decaying steel mill on the point. The size of an inner city slum, it was an unholy conglomeration of smoking towers, massive blast furnaces, mountains of iron ore, chemical lagoons, and open hearth sheds the size of airplane hangers. Along the shoreline, a series of huge pumps discharged a torrent of crimson-colored waste into the water. From the air, it looked like the mill was lying in a pool of its own blood.

This was Herons Point, the place where the tip of the Founder's fifth finger had so fortuitously fallen centuries ago. It was here, at the dawn of the industrial age, that his great, great grandson, the fifth incarnation of his name, had the foresight to build the integrated iron-and-steel mill that had so enlarged the family fortune. The graceful, long-legged birds that gave the place its name had abandoned their rookeries long ago, leaving Herons Point a geographical misnomer. No living thing could ever survive in the alternative environment that had been created here.

As the copter churned through columns of dense black smoke, the skyline of Baltimore loomed ahead. Jutted with concrete and steel monoliths, it resembled a bar graph in an economics textbook. The shorter ones were older buildings from the thirties distinguished by art-deco motifs that mimicked the classic structures of Manhattan. The taller ones were modern designs of gleaming glass and stainless steel. One, in particular, stood out above the rest—a sleek ebony structure with smoky one-way windows that not only housed the family's corporate headquarters, but also served as an architectural metaphor for the family's immense prestige and power. In the city it was known as Black Steeple.

Slowly, the chopper screwed its way down through the sky and onto the giant B that had been painted on the roof. Septimus disembarked, feeling a bit like a god leaving his winged chariot after an exhilarating ride down from Mount Olympus. Underneath his feet were all his earthly riches—fifty-two stories of vertically integrated corporations. Starting with the steelworks at the top, they descended in the order of importance down to the grubby sidewalks of Charles Street. Among them were companies in shipbuilding, real estate, chicken farming, trucking, investment banking, a law firm, accountant, cattle ranch, and advertising agency—all of them wholly-owned subsidiaries of the steel mill.

From out of the shadows, Laurence Roche stepped forward to greet his boss. He was an unctuous, little gnome clad in a cheap seersucker suit and plaid, clip-on bow tie. At five-foot two, the diminutive attorney seemed only half a man, but his enormous brainpower more than made up for his physical deficiency. Roche had a mind that computed data at speeds faster than the latest, high tech microprocessor. His eyes, bleary and bloodshot from reading volumes of small print, always appeared to be squinting, like he was looking into the sun.

"Your eight o'clock is here already, Mr. Chairman," Roche announced. "A half hour early."

"A half hour!" Septimus smirked. "Let them wait."

The Chairman proceeded into the building and up one flight of stairs to his penthouse apartment. Created by Sebastian Lumma of London, it was an ultra contemporary space defined by a pyramidal skylight and plate glass walls. In contrast to the ebony facade of Black Steeple, the interior was rendered in subtle shades of white. There were glossy, lacquered tables topped by porcelain vases, rugs of arctic fox fur, frosted crystal luminaries, and a semicircular sofa of bleached suede created by Vertucci of Barcelona. The interior walls were covered in creamy limestone, textured with seashells, and hung with a collection of abstract expressionist paintings by Robert Rauschenberg. All white on white. There was even a built-in scent-control system that emitted the soothing fragrance of pure vanilla into the room.

The magnificent space was imbued with all the essential luxuries of the day: a large, flat-screen, high-definition TV that vanished into the wall; an invisible Bose sound system; and radiant heating under the floor. The master boudoir was furnished with a sumptuous round bed covered in silk and fleece and encircled by tastefully mirrored walls and ceiling. Adjoining it was a white marble bathroom as large and decadent as a Roman bathhouse. Along with a glass-enclosed shower, Jacuzzi, sauna, and bidet, it featured a high-tech Japanese toilet. At the punch of a button, you could activate a heated seat, noisemakers, a deodorizing fan, and a bottom-washer and blower that made toilet paper completely obsolete.

Best of all, the penthouse came equipped with a state-of-the-art, Tokyo trained, geiko geisha with a black belt in the Karma Sutra and breast cones the size of Mount Fujiyama.

"Good morning, master-san," she said with a supplicating bow. "I hope you sleep velly well last night and that your day will be a most pleasant one."

Her name was Mikada and her services had been given to Septimus by a Nagasaki industrialist as a token of his appreciation for the successful consummation of a business venture. Her new master had freed her from her traditional kimono and time consuming makeup, preferring to see her in skin-tight, black leotards that showed off her curves and crevices to best effect. She was grateful to be westernized and did her best to please him. Part of her daily ritual was to administer the Chairman's morning ablutions, starting with the massage table where she was a master of exotic, tantric techniques and amazing, muscular manipulations. With strong, Japanese milkmaid hands, she stroked away nocturnal stress, thus ensuring a harmonious mind-body balance beneficial to the business decisions of the day. After that, she soaped his limp body with her bare hands, rinsed him off with buckets of warm water, and evaporated the remaining moisture with a blow drier. Next, she dressed him in a dark blue pinstriped suit from

Savile Row and a cream-colored dress shirt that was woven from Egyptian long staple cotton and was as smooth as silk. Around his neck she placed a custom-made tie that bore an endless repetition of the family crest. A pair of silk, ankle length hose eased his way into shoes fashioned from the finest grade of black leather from the House of Gucci, brightened with a champagne shine.

A full hour behind schedule, the Chairman entered the reception area outside the boardroom, the silver streaks in his hair masked by a deep obsidian dye. Waiting patiently for him were three men in dark suits with American flags pinned to their lapels. Power ties in various shades of red hung down from their necks like streaks of blood.

"Wonderful to see you again, Septimus," Senator Randolph Brookes said. Jumping to his feet he offered him a well-manicured hand. A smooth-looking politician with slicked back hair, he had a toothy smile that could blind a constituent at twenty paces.

"Sorry for the delay, gentlemen," Septimus apologized.

"No problem," Karl Darren responded loudly. "No problem at all." As a small man, the Secretary of Defense found it necessary to compensate for his lack of stature with a big booming voice and an overly strong grip. Knowing this, the Chairman preempted his handshake with a hearty slap on the back.

The third man, Christopher Harmon, simply nodded. The Director of the CIA was a man of few words. As always, he was wearing an opaque pair of wrap-around dark glasses that would have given the average person a severe case of eyestrain.

As they followed the Chairman into his inner sanctum, their eyes were drawn, as always, to a wall of windows that afforded a striking panorama of downtown Baltimore. Modern sculptures fashioned from stainless steel frolicked in the corner while a striking assortment of surrealist canvases practically wallpapered the rest of the room.

Septimus directed his visitors to a long glass conference table that was so transparent that the china and silver settings placed on it seemed to float on air. The wall-to-wall carpeting that ran underneath was so white that visitors were almost afraid to step on it for fear of soiling it and leaving tracks.

When everyone was seated, a pair of towering, black chefs crowned in white toques strode in like Zulu kings bearing a dazzling array of carved cantaloupes and honeydews, fancy cheese omelets, breakfast steaks, freshly squeezed orange juice, and gourmet coffee.

In between sips and swallows, the men made the standard small talk, exchanging sailing news, hot IPO's, and salacious gossip about the antics of various and sundry mistresses.

When they finished scarfing down their food and their last burps were muffled inside thick, Irish linen napkins, the Zulus bounced in to clear the dishes and the meeting finally hunkered down to business.

The Chairman scooped a bowl of Windsor Blend out of the Founder's pouch, musing as he always did on the legend that surrounded it. Lighting up his pipe, he took a few puffs, then turned to the subject at hand.

"On the phone, you said you had something pressing, Mr. Secretary." How he loved to address his guests by their official titles when business was being discussed. It elevated the tone of the conversation and made everyone feel so important.

"Project Minerva," Karl Darren said, lowering his loud voice a few decibels. "The President gave the go-ahead yesterday."

"Refresh my memory."

"It's the new boomers, Septimus," Randy Brookes said. "Upgrades on the Ohio class. These go faster and dive deeper than what we have now. Six hundred feet long with a displacement of twenty thousand tons."

"And its got some new bells and whistles that the agency is interested in," Chris Harmon added. "Next generation stealth technology."

"Ah, yes. The project from the black budget."

The visitors showed their teeth. The black budget was the Defense Department's secret stash. Unaccountable to Congress, it was estimated at thirty-six billion a year, or around a hundred million a day.

"And just how much is this Project Minerva going to cost?"

"Not cheap. Each one is two billion," Darren said. "Give or take a few million."

"And we need seven," Senator Brookes added.

"One for each sea, I suppose," Septimus joked.

There were three good reasons to have a project in the black budget. First, it was necessary for funding top-secret projects; second, it was ideal for hiding embarrassing boondoggles; and third and most importantly, it was an ideal vehicle for skimming off profits with no one the wiser. In this case, the last reason was the controlling factor.

These kinds of black budget projects were the Blackburn corporation's bread and butter. In the past, the steel business had been a source of dynastic wealth, but in today's world, most steel manufacturing had been forced overseas where labor costs were far less. Unable to compete, all but a few domestic mills were forced into receivership and bankruptcy. A decade ago, the Chairman had foreseen these shifts to third-world factories and had steered his business into the lucrative world of unbid black budget defense projects. To maximize his profits, he had acquired a shipbuilding subsidiary in Newport News that made his steelworks one-stop shopping for projects like this one.

"So how much steel are we talking about?" the Chairman asked.

Secretary Darren took a file from his briefcase and shoved it across the table. "Seven thousand tons each, forty-nine in all. And we need it quick. President Cannon has given us a tight ass deadline. We need the first sub in the water by the end of this fiscal year. The rest in six month increments."

Septimus shook his head and projected an aura of mock concern. Frank Cannon was a fly-fishing friend and had entrusted him with these details weeks ago.

"Building the ships on his timetable shouldn't be a problem, Mr. Secretary, but the steel could be a holdup. We're back-ordered on a couple of major commitments. I'm not sure we can handle it." A little drama to make the meeting more interesting.

The faces at the table looked like they had just tasted cat pee. If Septimus couldn't handle the order, they would have to go legit with another domestic supplier and miss out on the Chairman's standard under-the-table kickbacks. In other words, goodbye Swiss bank accounts, hello credit card debt.

The Chairman arose and drifted over to the window that looked out over Charles Street. Picking up the hotline to Herons Point, he speed-dialed his foreman's cell phone.

A barge full of coal was being unloaded by crane when the call came in.

"Shit!" Bull Wolinski said when he saw the caller ID on his phone. "What the fuck does he want now?"

A pair of gigantic steel jaws took another bite out of the black mountain and swung out over the pier dribbling a shower of soot behind it. A few lumps of coal fell at the foreman's feet and one bounced off his hard hat. Turning his back on the scene, Bull yanked down his Styrofoam face mask and stuck a finger in his ear.

"Morning, sir," he said in a polite tone that was completely out of character. A thick-necked pig of a man, Bull rarely spoke without swearing.

"Shipbuilding needs forty-nine thousand tons by next June," the Chairman said abruptly. "That possible?"

The jaws of the crane opened and an avalanche of coal fell into the empty steel bed of railroad car.

"No way, boss. We already got a couple of big ass, suspension bridges and a fifty-five floor skyscraper in the works now. We're three months behind as it is."

The Chairman's stony silence spoke louder than words.

"Guess we could double production," Bull continued. "Trouble is, there'll be more complaints about emissions from the folks in Dundalk. That will end up pissing off the EPA. They could fine us four or five million, maybe more."

Septimus dismissed the fine right away. Compared to the profits on a fourteen billion dollar contract, the penalties were in the minuscule to picayune range.

"Go on, Mr. Polanski."

"It's Wolinski, sir."

"If you insist. Go on."

"Worse than that we'd be forced to take shortcuts," Bull continued. "Lots of shortcuts."

"Like?"

"We'd have to lighten up on our carbon and alloys to have enough to go around. Hardenability would suffer a bit and we'd have to cut down on the tempering and quenching processes, too."

"What does that mean in English?"

Bull's face flushed, bringing a spider web of broken blood vessels to the surface. "Bottom line is our steel would be no better than the shit they make in India. You ask me it's too big a risk for a sub."

Septimus cradled the receiver without saying goodbye. If there were an accident to any of the subs because of defective steel, he knew very well that he would face an enormous lawsuit from the federal government. He remembered the case of the *USS Thresher* back in '63. During deep-diving tests some 220 miles east of Boston, it had broken apart in 1,400 fathoms of water. Sixteen officers, ninety-six enlisted men, and seventeen civilians perished. Later, the bathyscaphe, *Trieste*, went down to investigate and found that the sub had broken up into six sections. No evidence was ever found of the release of radioactivity from the reactor fuel elements and no reason had ever been given for the accident. The moral of the story:

accidents to subs usually happen in the depths of the ocean where stress is the greatest. If anything happened to the subs of Project Minerva, it would be almost impossible to pinpoint the cause.

The Chairman turned back to the three men perched on the edge of their seats. They looked as apprehensive as outriders on the end of hiking boards, not knowing whether the Captain's next move would keep them on course or catapult them into a school of jelly fish. Septimus let them stew for a few moments before speaking.

"Anchors aweigh, my boys," he said at last, "you've got yourselves a deal."

G.M.O. CALLAGHAN

City of the Sea

From the crest of the hill, the view was spectacular. Lying before David was a river of quicksilver filled with a flotilla of white sails and colorful spinnakers. On the far shore, at the edge of Colonial Annapolis, the United States Naval Academy glistened in the morning dew, a modern day Atlantis risen from the sea on a landfill of oyster shells. In the center, soaring up from the high ground, was the Cathedral of the Navy with its stately copper dome, greened by the elements and crowned by a golden cupola. Arrayed around it were magnificent columned edifices built in the Beaux Arts style and topped with great mansard roofs. Complementing them were clean-lined contemporaries with large picture windows that drank in the magnificent water views.

Coming over the high arch of the Severn River Bridge, David was filled with excitement. To the southeast, the Chesapeake, itself, was in view. Somewhere across the Bay, his ancient homeland awaited his return. How he would find it remained a mystery. His only clues were Tequetamo's story and the pictograph of the great tree in the belt of beads. It wasn't much to go on.

On the other side of the river, the airport taxi passed an athletic field, a large satellite dish, and several low-rise apartment buildings before pulling over and letting David out at Gate 8. A Marine with bulging eyeballs stepped smartly out of the guardhouse and reviewed David's papers.

"Welcome aboard, Mr. Waterfield. Check-in point is straight ahead." He thumbed back over his shoulder towards an enormous gray building a quarter of a mile down the road.

In his size-too-small, cow-pie-encrusted boots, the trek was painful. And hot, too. It was ninety-four degrees in the shade and the humidity was that of a tropical rainforest. To compound the problem, David had worn his father's clothes in honor of the special occasion. His long-sleeved, red flannel shirt and beat-up blue jeans were already soaked in sweat. All told, he felt a bit like a hobo, an image reinforced by the wooden lacrosse stick he carried over his shoulder and the small duffel bag that hung on the end. Inside were his toothbrush, a change of underwear, and a gift his mother had given him earlier that morning.

"Grandfather Two Tongues would have wanted you to have this," she had said, her voice trembling with emotion, double felt for her dead father-in-law and newly departing son. The gift was wrapped in red cloth and tied with a piece of blue yarn, both woven on her own loom.

From its oblong shape, David guessed what it was. "I still miss him," he said. "I will always miss him."

"Tequetamo would have been so proud of you. We are all proud of you. You are our last hope now." Tears streamed down his mother's wrinkled face. Tears that were the only rivers the village had ever known.

And now he had found himself in a place surrounded by water. Crossing over Dorsey Creek, he hobbled past the parade grounds and a row of stately, red brick homes with classy blue-and-white-stripped awnings. Up ahead, on the far side of Decatur Road, was his destination. On closer inspection he could see the massive gray building had dozens of doors and several white information tents in front. Already hundreds of young men and women were converging there from every direction.

During the academic year, Alumni Hall was used primarily for basketball games, concerts, and theatrical productions. But today the hardwood floor was partitioned into dozens of processing stations. After waiting in line for an hour, David was issued a name tag and assigned to a twelve-man squad, one of the few all male outfits in the platoon.

They were a rag tag bunch characterized by decidedly unmilitary hairdos. Among them were a short, white kid with dreadlocks; a black beanpole with bangs; a freckled-faced redhead with spikes; and another dude with white sidewalls topped with curly blonde hair that resembled a mushroom cloud. With his coarse brown ponytail, David fit right in.

Their squad leader was a saucy black upperclassman with a flat chest and a mouth like a bullhorn. "My name is Sasser," she roared. "I am woman. You boys got any problem with that?"

"Ma'am, no, ma'am!" they shouted.

"Good, 'cause I got a black belt in kickboxing, run the hundred in twelve-three, and can throw the javelin one hundred and thirty-five feet. Got the message?"

"Ma'am, yes, ma'am!"

"For the next seven weeks, you will rise at zero dark thirty. You will run until your legs turn to rubber. You will learn how to handle a rifle until it becomes your third arm. Your brains will be transformed from mush into muscle. You'll be lucky if you have enough time to breathe or go to the head. It's my job to make men of you boys and frankly, from the looks of you, it ain't gonna be easy."

She looked up at David standing a foot taller than she was. "Nice ponytail, Mr. Waterfield. Had one like that myself when I was in junior high. Bet you look good in pigtails, too."

The other men started to snicker.

"Hey people! I didn't give permission to laugh. Down and give me twenty."

The squad dropped to the hardwood and dutifully pumped out their punishment. When they got back to their feet, Sasser wasted no time in bringing some much-needed discipline to her bunch of misfits. She taught them the basics. How to stand at attention, snap to parade rest, and give a proper salute. After that, she marched them through the stations on the field house floor. They changed into blue-rimmed T-shirts and Dixie cup caps, filled out medical forms, got vaccinated with inoculator guns, and had their hair shaved to the consistency of sandpaper.

Sasser seemed especially pleased when David lost his ponytail. "Hair today, gone tomorrow, Mr. Waterfield. You'll get over it. The short look is all the fashion this year."

Next, they got measured for dress uniforms and collected the rest of their clothing, shoes, and toiletries in large, white laundry bags. For the first time in his life, David knew what Christmas was like.

Loaded with bags and boxes, Sasser led them out of Alumni Hall and marched them like a big game safari across the grounds towards their new quarters in Bancroft Hall. David was impressed. The "Yard", as it was called, was neatly landscaped with stately trees, ornamental shrubs, lush flower beds, and even a Victorian bandstand. And everywhere in-between stood great monuments in remembrance of past glories—statues of heroes, historic weapons of war, and trophies of hard-won victories and uncommon valor.

"That there is the Herndon Monument," Sasser said, pointing out a tall, granite obelisk across from the chapel. "Some people think it's a phallic symbol. I think it looks like a knitting needle. What do you men think?"

"Ma'am, knitting needle, ma'am."

"Excellent choice. Anyone know what happens here during Commissioning Week?"

A hand shot up. "Ma'am, they put a Dixie cup cap at the top. We gotta climb up and replace it with a hard hat. After that we officially become Third Classmen, ma'am."

"Right you are, Mr. Quinn," Sasser said. "Legend has it that whoever gets to the top first becomes the first Admiral in *her* class."

"Ma'am, what if the *her* is a *he*, ma'am?" David dared to ask.

"We have ways of taking care of that, Mr. Waterfield. Remember what happened to your ponytail. Snip snip."

Presumably she was joking but the men knew better than to laugh.

Next stop was a large bronze bust of an Indian warrior. His face was lean and fierce and his skull was shaved bare and crowned with feathered plumes. A great quiver of arrows hung from his broad shoulders and a battle-axe was tucked under his belt.

"I understand you're a Native American, Mr. Waterfield, I bet you know all about the fellow up there."

"Ma'am, yes, ma'am. His name is Tecumseh, which means 'Crouching Panther' in your language. He was the great Shawnee chief who fought the last great battle against the bluecoats. He was defeated at Tippecanoe and later killed in the Battle of Thames."

"You know your history, Mr. Waterfield, I'll say that for you." Sasser turned away and addressed the group at large. "This bust of Tecumseh is a replica of a figurehead off the U.S.S. Delaware. At the Academy, he's known as the God of 2.0. It's customary to flip a penny in the chief's quiver on your way to exams and he's supposed to help you eek out a passing grade."

David closed his eyes and underneath his dotted lids the great Tecumseh lay amid the bodies of his slain enemies, mortally wounded. His buckskin was soaked in blood and his tomahawk was still gripped in his hand, covered with the grime of battle. A group of "long rifles" in coonskin caps dragged him into the woods. They tied a rope around his ankles and strung his body up over a limb. Then they took out their hunting knives.

"They skinned him," David said.

"What was that, Mr. Waterfield?" At first Sasser was shocked that he failed to address her properly. Then she realized what he had said.

"Three men from Kentucky. They skinned Tecumseh like a deer and sold the strips for razor strops, ma'am."

Sasser was stunned. "I'm sorry, Mr. Waterfield. I'm really sorry. I never heard that before."

David nodded. There were many versions of the death of Tecumseh but this one had come down from his ancestor, Fire-in-the-Sky. He had fought alongside the great chief and was with him at the end.

The lynching and mutilation of Tecumseh made Sasser sick. As a black woman she knew a great deal about genocide and racism and she felt sorry for the pain she had caused David. Vowing not to harass him anymore, she turned away and led her squad on in silence. The big game safari had become a funeral cortege. None of them would be throwing any pennies at Tecumseh any time soon.

Along with the rest of the platoon, David's squad was housed in a third floor wing of Bancroft Hall. The sprawling building was said to be the largest dormitory in the world. It had almost two thousand rooms that were spread over five floors and linked by five miles of corridors. Most of the quarters were just big enough for a pair of modular wall units constructed of blonde-veneered, particleboard. One half was a desk-and-bookcase combination and the other, a closet with a sliding door and set of drawers. Overhead, just a few feet from the ceiling tiles, was a narrow bunk. Each room had its own sink and shower and a community head just a short trot down the hall. They were intended to be spare and Spartan. But to David, they were the best he had ever seen. It was the first place he ever lived that didn't have a dirt floor.

His assigned roommate was the freckled-faced redhead who had shown up earlier that morning with his hair in spikes.

"Unger, Archibald," the guy said in a squeaky voice. "My friends call me Archie."

David shook his hand and introduced himself. And as he did so, he heard Grandfather Two Tongues sing out his secret Choptank name.

"Sorry about what happened to the chief out there," Archie said. "No excuse for that sort of thing."

David nodded. "Thanks man, but that was a long time ago. Time to forgive and forget." But deep down inside, the atrocities committed against his people still bled like an open wound.

"Where you from, Dave?"

The Center of the World, Grandfather said inside. "Oklahoma," David answered out loud. "How 'bout you?"

"I'm a townie. Lived here all my life." He glanced down at David's wooden stick.

"See you're into stickball, too. I'm a goalie. What do you play, Dave?"

"Wing attack. Either side."

"Ambidextrous, huh. That's cool. A double threat."

They exchanged sticks. Archie's pole was made of titanium and had an enlarged head with downsloping sidewalls, the latest in high tech weaponry. He was amazed by David's wooden antique.

"Far out, man. Never saw a stick like this before. Totally awesome."

"My grandfather made it for me," David said proudly.

It had taken Two Tongues three months to make because of the arthritis that had crippled his hands and the cataracts that blurred his vision. For a shaft, he had selected a hickory walking stick that had been cut from a hardwood forest in Georgia. It had a history to it, having crossed the country in the hands of Three-Legged Coyote when the crippled old man walked with the Cherokee on the Trail of Tears. For several weeks, Grandfather had steamed the end of the stick over a pot of boiling water, gradually bending it into a shepherd's crook. When it had hardened into shape, he strung its jaws with tendons taken from the kicking leg of a mule. Around the shaft he carved the body of an eastern diamondback. Its skin was painted gray and decorated with a pattern of yellow hexagons, twelve brown rattles, and a gaping red mouth with a pair of extended fangs.

"Looks dangerous," Archie said. "Like it's got some bite. What do you call it? Weapons like this gotta have a name."

"Grandfather called it 'ZaStakaZappa.' It means 'stick that strikes like a rattle snake.' "

"Awesome."

"Plays pretty good," David said. It was a modest understatement, for he knew well that the power was not in the stick but in the arms that wielded it, the legs that gave it speed, and the eyes that guided the ball from the pouch and directed its flight through the air.

Archie tossed it back to David. "I brought along an attackman stick, too. You know, in case I don't make goalie. It's also made of titanium. You can use it if you want, you know, so you don't risk breaking your wooden stick."

"Thanks," David said. "But I'm kinda used to ZaStakaZappa." He thought of it in a sentimental way, like it was a mystical extension of his grandfather's arm and of the arms of his ancestors all the way back to the beginning of the game. When he scored a goal, it was triumph for all of them.

"Going out for fall ball?"

"Yep. You?"

"Wouldn't miss it. Just gotta keep up my grades."

They spent the rest of the afternoon getting their quarters squared away. Only a few personal items, like athletic equipment and photographs, were allowed to stay. Street clothes were packed away in duffel bags destined for storage lockers in the basement. Before he zipped his bag, Archie pulled out a picture of his girlfriend and showed it to David. She was a toothy, brown-eyed blonde with a snub nose and clunky gold braces.

"This here's Helene," he said proudly as he set the frame down on his desk. "She's gonna live here, too. Our third roommate. I call her Babe. You can call her Helene."

David laughed. "You got lucky. She's good looking." He was too polite to crack any jokes about whether Archie was up on his tetanus shots.

"Thanks. I miss the hell out of her already. Babe was planning on coming to the Academy with me, too, but had to drop out of school last semester. Too bad. She could have had a KIA nomination."

"What's a KIA nomination?"

"Means 'Killed in Action.' If you had a parent that was KIA, you get admitted to the Academy almost automatically. Helene's mom was one of the first women to graduate back in '80. Got blown away in Iraq a year ago. Fucking car bomb."

"Sorry."

"Babe has never gotten over it. Her old man turned into an alcoholic and got his ass fired. Now Babe has to work two jobs to put food on the table and pay for her braces. She's also taking a few courses in night school this year so she'll finally get to graduate. I'm sending her my pay and the plan is for her to get admitted here next year."

"Hope it works out for you, Archie."

"Me, too. What about you, Dave? Got a girl?"

"Three of them. My mom and two sisters. No real girlfriend."

"Don't worry about it, man. After Plebe Summer, we'll get out of these clown suits and into a real midshipman outfit with a snappy hard hat and spit-shined shoes. The girls will be all over you."

The clown suits that Archie referred to were white jumpers with floppy square bibs in back and white duck pants with slightly flared cuffs. Sasser had ordered the squad to change into them for the formal swearing-in ceremony. Capped off with demeaning, blue-rimmed Dixie cup covers, David and Archie were ready for the Big Top.

Along with the rest of the squad, they formed up in the hallway outside their room. Under Sasser's command, the new plebes marched through a maze of identical passageways until they finally left the building and found themselves in Tecumseh Courtyard. Fourteen hundred white folding chairs had been set up for the ceremony with a row of family-filled bleachers in back. As they filed in, Archie gestured to one of a multitude of camcorders that was sticking up out of the crowd.

"That's my dad. I recognize his watch. My folks have photographed my every move since birth. They even have my ultrasounds."

"Know what you mean," David said. But he didn't really. Shadow Woman was too poor to have even a simple disposable camera. The only picture of him had been a sand painting Grandfather Two Tongues had created to celebrate his seventh birthday, the day the old wisoe told him the meaning of his secret Choptank name. The name that could never be revealed to a white man. The name that was a prophecy of things to come.

Taking their seats, they found themselves facing a podium that had been set up on a landing in front of the formal entrance to the building. Its massive columns, arches, pediments, and portals reminded David of a cross between a neoclassic temple and a fancy wedding cake richly ornamented with images of Neptune's trident, Roman torches, and gargoyles of sea serpents. At either end of the balustrade that crossed the top of the building were the bows of two great ironclad ships of state, laden with flags. Each had a figurehead of a winged eagle and a turret ringed with guns.

Suddenly, four F-18 Hornets swept across the sky dropping their sonic booms like bombs. Everyone, plebes and parents alike, jumped out of their skins, hearts pounding at the awesome display of raw Naval air power. Immediately thereafter, the Superintendent of the Naval Academy came striding up to the podium, resplendent in dress whites with gold shoulder boards and a chestful of ribbons.

Oliver Shaw loved dramatic entrances. It amused him to think there probably wasn't a dry set of skivvies on any of the trembling plebes assembled at his feet. Or on their parents either. But that didn't matter. At least he had everyone's attention.

"Five years ago," he began, speaking in a voice as deep and resonate as the sea, "the boys in those birds were sitting in your seats. Now they're landing on aircraft carriers in the dead of night. Their friends and classmates are commanding destroyers and nuclear subs that can slip silently under the Arctic ice cap. A few are even up there orbiting around us in the international space station. Some of them may end up on the moon or the planet Mars. The moral is—you men and women can be anything you want to be. We'll give you the tools. We'll give you the chance. All you have to do is reach out and seize it."

The audience applauded. But David wasn't thinking about a career. Somewhere across the Bay were the tribal lands of his ancestors. All he wanted to do was find them. As of yet, he had no idea how to go about it.

For the next hour, Admiral Shaw rambled on about his hopes for the future. When he finished, he asked the class to stand and raise their right hands. For David Waterfield, there was no turning back. In a voice firm and full, he committed himself to spending the next eight years of his life in the United States Navy.

When it was over, the new plebes were allowed a few private moments with their families. With no place to go, David wandered out into tearful farewells that were taking place in the shade of the tall, stately trees that lined Stribling Walk just past the statue of Tecumseh. In the distance he saw Archie hug his mom, shake his father's hand, and plant a kiss on the mouth of a petite blonde in a yellow sun-suit that just had to be Helene.

David thought about his own loved ones, remembering them as he had last seen them. The Greyhound bus had come too soon and there was hardly any time to say a proper goodbye. The driver, a moley-faced Caucasoid, was impatient and slowed down just enough for David to jump on board, then blasted off like a rocket ship. Miss Applebaum was furious, stamping her foot down and smacking her hands together like she did in class when somebody was misbehaving. Hurriedly, she loaded his mother and sisters into her beetle and chased after the bus. Pulling alongside, they waved at David through the windows until Rocinante lost her tailpipe and the Greyhound raced out of sight. He had been gone only a day, but already David missed them terribly.

That night, after Archie had fallen asleep in the arms of an imaginary Helene, David reached under his pillow and retrieved the gift his mother had given him at the bus stop. Officially, the oblong, wooden box was now contraband. But it was an heirloom David couldn't live without and he was willing to risk the consequences. Taking a penlight from under his mattress, he unwrapped the cloth and cracked open the lid.

For the second time in his life, he beheld the sacred artifacts of his ancestors. The peace pipe with the lightning bolts on its stem and the belt of beads woven with the image of the great tree were as he remembered them. But there was more! Something Grandfather Two Tongues had not shown him the night of his death. Lining the bottom of the box was a deerskin parchment the same color as the wood. Its edges were crumbling and it appeared to be very old.

David lifted it out of the box and carefully unfolded it. Written on its face was a strange language that he had never seen before. The letters looked English but the words they formed were not. Composed of long difficult syllables, they were strung together without any punctuation. Some of the letters were printed while others were linked together in a cursive script. Over many of the vowels were a variety of accents, double dots, bars, and half moons of the kind that are used to aid pronunciation. Some of the words were long strings of consonants without any vowels whatsoever.

Slowly sounding them out to himself, David realized that he had heard them once before. They were the mysterious Choptank words that Grandfather Two Tongues had chanted the night of his death. The Song of the Black Robe! It had not died with Tequetamo after all. Someone had carefully written down what it sounded like. But who and why? Two Tongues, himself, must not have known what it was, for the old man had never learned to read or write.

At the bottom of the page was a crudely drawn X, the color of clotted blood. Underneath it was a florid signature composed of overlapping loops and flourishes. *Caecilius Blackburn*, it said. *Court-Baron of Lord Baltimore.*

The name of David's ancient enemy was a secret no more.

Inferno

A resounding boom shook the steel-girdered cavern on its foundations. Inside the Blast Furnace a hundred-and-fifty tons of molten pig iron spewed out of the wickey hole like lava from an erupting volcano. On the platform above, workmen in flame retardant coats and red hard hats heaved bags of manganese and river coal into the boiling liquid causing angry flames to leap up at them like solar flares from the surface of the sun.

Through darkly tinted welder's goggles, a light-skinned black man gauged the color of the fire. As the impurities burned out, the flames turned violet and then orange, causing hissing clouds of noxious steam to rise off the sickly yellow and red witches' brew. When the heart of the fire turned white, the man in tinted goggles turned and signaled his boss on the floor below. A small, diamond stud flashed in his left earlobe.

Watching from his post by the fuel throttle was a big-boned black man in grimy, sweat-soaked overalls. His face was crusted over in a layer of soot and the hair that stuck out from under his rusted hard hat was singed white. Over the deafening roar of gigantic machines, he turned and bellowed to the crane operator. Buttons were pushed, levers were pulled, and a pair of huge hooks hoisted the ladle off its trunnions. Groaning under the massive weight, the crane hauled its load across the floor to the teeming pit, where it emptied a torrent of liquid steel into ingot molds on the back of flatbed railroad cars. Sparks flew like tracer bullets in a nocturnal firefight, sending a three-legged mutt howling and hobbling to the far side of the cavern where he stopped and lifted his phantom limb to take a pee.

No one seemed to mind. The stench of urine and feces already permeated the premises, emanating from a network of underground pipes that connected all the workstations of the mill. Because of the expense of fresh water and the corrosive effects of brackish bay water, heavy machinery was cooled by effluents purchased at bargain rates from the Baltimore City Sewer System. To the management of Blackburn Steelworks, the pungent aroma of wastewater was the sweet smell of money saved.

When the ladle had been emptied, the boss man lumbered over to three executive hardhats huddled in the corner, as far away as they could get from the infernal heat and noxious stench of the blast furnace. His eyes went first to the attractive young brunette in snug-fitting blue jeans. She was holding a handkerchief over her nose with one hand and cradling a clipboard in the other.

"Afternoon, Miss Mancini," he hollered over the din. "Welcome to Hell."

She smiled back with her indigo-colored eyes and nodded. "Hey, Lee. It's kind of hot in here. How about turning on your air conditioner."

"Wish I could, Miss Mancini," he deadpanned, "but our window unit melted down yesterday. Sorry about the stink, too. We all out of Airwicks."

Then he turned his attention to Bull Wolinski and the other man. "Wassup, Bull?" LeGrande shouted. "How come you folks from the front office come down t'here?"

"Show and tell time, Lee." The foreman hollered back. "This here's the boss's boy, Tavian Blackburn. He's our new GM."

From the looks of him, LeGrande was pretty sure the guy had never worked a day in his life. The dude was wearing a pink cotton shirt, navy blue blazer, cream-colored duck pants, and Top-siders without socks. It was like he had just stepped off a yacht. He was pinching his nose between his thumb and forefinger and didn't look happy to be there.

"Tavian's gonna help gear our asses up for the DOD job," Bull explained.

"Gonna need all the help we can get, Gravian," LeGrande shouted.

"Tavian," Bull yelled in his ear. "His name is Tavian."

Liz bit her tongue so she wouldn't smile. As the eighth incarnation of the Founder's name, the boy had been nick-named Octavian, which had later been shortened to Tavian. The Latin name was an allusion to the adopted son of Julius Caesar. Descended from the clan of the "eighth child," he was destined to become Emperor of Rome and the living god, Augustus.

"Sorry," the big steelman apologized. "Don't hear so good no more."

"LeGrande here is the head man," Bull hollered to Tavian. "The Keeper of the Blast Furnace."

LeGrande peeled off his thick leather glove to shake but Tavian only nodded recognition, hiding his hands in his pockets to avoid any chance of contact. Confronted with the harsh reality of the mill itself, he could hardly mask his horror at the rank smelling, grime-encrusted environment around him. He made a mental note to spend as little time here as possible. He much preferred working from his swanky office suite in the Steeple or, better yet, from the hot tub on the polished teak deck of the *Aria* with a topless secretary snuggled up at his side.

"Tavian's an efficiency expert. Got a degree from Princeton and just did two years at Horton," Bull bellowed through cupped hands, making it sound like the boy had just been released from prison.

"Wharton," Tavian yelled in his ear. "Not Horton." But the distinction was lost on Bull Wolinski. He just looked puzzled and nodded.

The Keeper managed a smile. *The guy is such an efficiency expert he hasn't worked a day in his life,* he thought.

"Don't let us disturb you. Just gonna look around, okay?"

"Be my guest, Bull," LeGrande shouted back. "Just don't make a mess, understand?" His attempt at humor fell on deaf ears.

Tavian rudely turned his back on the Keeper and followed his foreman down the rust-covered railroad tracks that connected the Blast Furnace to the other workstations of the mill.

"Good-bye, Miss Mancini," LeGrande hollered, ignoring Bull and the boy boss completely.

She waved her clipboard at him and hurried after the others, stopping briefly to feed a biscuit to the pitiful three-legged mutt who hobbled after her. He was a frightful-looking beast with mangy skin and yellow-red eyes, but was as friendly as a puppy. The poor creature had followed one of the men to work one day and they had all taken a liking to him. He was a downtrodden mongrel like them, beaten up and bloodied but still kicking, even if it was on three legs. No one could come up with a name for him and it was a month before Liz suggested "Cerberus" as a possibility. It was a name she had remembered from a literature class she had taken in college. According to Greek Mythology, Cerberus was the three-headed hound that guarded the Gates of Hades. The Blast Furnace Boys loved it. It made them feel like well-educated *literati* even though they hadn't cracked a book since flunking out of the company grade school.

Liz had a knack for always making the people around her feel good. Everyone liked her. She had a warm, radiant smile and a personal magnetism that seem to work in reverse polarity, repelling the dust and ashes that settled on everyone else, but left her untouched. No one could ever figure her out. Why would a girl like Liz be working at a hellhole like Herons Point?

As the contingent from the front office made their way out of the Blast Furnace, a half dozen steelmen gathered around LeGrande Collins. They were men with names to match their might: Kenyatta, Tsonka, Mandala, J'Rod, and Qwazi. Well-muscled blacks of different hues, it was as if their skins had been tanned lighter or darker by their proximity to the fire. In reality, they were all mulattos whose blood had mixed in varying degrees with that of African slaves, aboriginal natives, and the poor whites of the region. Their jobs were handed down from one generation to another. It wasn't nepotism, of course, for no sane man would work at Herons Point if he had any other option. Or live there either. For like their enslaved ancestors who were confined to rundown log cabins on white plantations, the steelmen were forced by economic necessity to live behind the mill in run-down shanties built on a landfill of factory waste. They were the lowest of the low, the only men desperate enough to withstand the heat and oppression of the Blast Furnace.

"Who be the boy?" the small man with the tinted goggles and diamond ear-stud yelled at the Keeper.

"Our new boss," LeGrande shouted.

Qwazi Lightfoot slipped his welding goggles up on his forehead. "Miss Mancini," he said, "she best watch her ass with him. All I gotta say."

"Yeah," Mandala agreed. "Us too, by the look of him." At six foot-eight, three-hundred-and-fifty pounds, the gentle giant seemed completely oblivious of the fact that no one would ever want to mess with him.

Liz followed her two bosses down the railroad tracks past the open mouth of the Rolling Shed. Inside she could see steel being shaped into gun barrels of all sizes, a reminder that the manufacture of weapons of war had always been the principal mainstay of Blackburn Steelworks.

"Dad has authorized time-and-a-half for the first four hours of OT, double after that and on weekends," Tavian told Bull in his annoying hiss. "Give the Blast Furnace first crack. After that, draw from the Open Hearth, Rolling Shed, Coke Oven, and Melt Shop in that order. Miss Mancini, I want you to get a memo out to all our employees as soon as possible."

"Sure thing."

"Finding the fuckin' labor ain't gonna be a problem," Bull said. "These fuckin' guys are animals. They always need money, the shit they buy."

After two years at the mill, Liz was immune to the constant stream of expletives that served as the primary mode of communication.

"Then what's the problem?" Tavian asked.

Bull turned around and looked out at the river sweeping by them like an open sewer after a heavy storm, laden with clumps of chemical waste, sulfur suds, oil slicks, and bloated fish carcasses. He gestured to the run-down tenements across the river, squinting and frowning as if the sight of them actually hurt his eyeballs.

"It's those pain-in-the-butts over there in Dundalk we gotta worry about. They got the EPA's number written on their walls in magic markers. Call 'em up even if we take a piss in the river."

The efficiency expert with the C-minus grade-point average came up with a brilliant solution. "What they can't see won't hurt them. Schedule the second shift to start after it gets dark. That way we can double the output and no one will see the smoke in the sky or the discharge in the river."

"That should work," Bull shrugged.

"Miss Mancini," Tavian continued, "we need to remind the people in Dundalk that there are a lot of good things we do for their community. The library we built. The community center. The new wing on the high school. Things like that they should be thankful for. A couple of well-timed press releases to the *Sun* wouldn't hurt."

"I'll get on it right away," Liz said.

She made a note on her clipboard before following the men towards a point of land where the river emptied into the Chesapeake Bay. Once the area had been a fertile wetland surrounded by tall trees crowned with rookeries of Great Blue Heron. Now, more than a hundred and fifty years later, it had been transformed into a desolate blacktop with a brick building in the center. Only two stories tall, the Administration Office boasted a pretentious castellated roof reminiscent of the battlements and turrets found atop medieval fortresses where boiling oil was dumped on invading armies.

Tavian stopped by the entrance and waited impatiently while Bull removed the black Satin Stretch cover from his sports car. Underneath was a hot orange Ferrari Enzo. The design was breathtaking in the extreme. A sculpted Formula One body with two large air intakes in front and a spoiler in back. Stuck inside the rear window was a Princeton sticker that showed a leaping tiger with an angry snarl on its face.

"Nice," Liz said, trying hard not to be too impressed.

"One of 399 ever made," Tavian said proudly. "Six-hundred-sixty horses and a V-12 engine. Top speed is 217 mph. Goes from zero to sixty in 3.5 seconds."

Bull carefully shook out the layer of ash that had accumulated on the cover in the hour and a half that the car had been parked there.

"I'd like to meet with you further on these releases," Tavian told Liz. "This evening's good for me. I'll pick you up at five and we can work over dinner."

"Evenings are out for me," Liz said firmly.

"Oh?"

"Night school. Five times a week."

"Liz is gonna be an attorney," Bull added, carefully folding the car cover into a triangle like it was an American flag. "Works harder than anyone I know."

"Impressive," Tavian hissed. He was deeply disappointed that she didn't jump at the chance to ride in his car and get to know him better. "The company is always on the look-out for bright young attorneys." A hook in the water.

"Good to know," Liz said. *Not my kind of attorney,* she thought.

"You're coming to the shore next Saturday, aren't you?"

"Yes, of course." She had planned the affair and had to attend to make sure everything was in order.

"Maybe we can put our heads together then."

Liz tried to look agreeable. "Works for me." It wasn't smart to reject him completely.

Bull's piggish face burned red, ticked off that the boss hadn't seen fit to invite him to the party.

Oblivious to the slight, Tavian punched the remote button on his key chain and his gull wing doors flew upwards. The Enzo looked like an airplane ready to take flight.

"Last chance," he told Liz as he slid into his ergonomically designed seat, richly upholstered in plush black leather. "I'll write a note for your teacher."

"Sorry. I'd be too far behind."

Not used to getting turned down, especially when he was ensconced in his magnificent flaming orange throne, Tavian's expression soured visibly.

"You're the one who'll be sorry," he said.

The gull wings dropped down and he took his hurt out on the accelerator. Peeling out, he leaned on his tiger growl horn and roared down the two-mile long gravel access road and out the front gate.

"You could do a lot worse, girlie." Bull chided.

Liz didn't answer. She was already walking a thin line. Tavian's budding interest in her was going to make things much more difficult.

Without any further conversation they made their way up two flights of rickety stairs to the office on the second floor. It was a dreary place with two-toned, puke-green walls, government surplus metal desks, cardboard file cabinets, and a wire mesh window with a spectacular view of the ugly brick towers of the coke ovens. Overhead, a flickering bank of cold-white fluorescent tubes made migraines a common affliction for everyone who worked there. Bull took refuge behind the door of his rat's nest and Liz sank down behind her desk.

The three other women in the office were buried in files and ledgers. All of them were ashen-haired widows whose husbands had made the ultimate sacrifice for the company. Petra's had been run over by a flatbed truck, Gudren's had been crushed by a falling crane, and Olga's had been incinerated by an explosion at the Blast Furnace. All that was left of him was a pile of ashes that at least saved his family the cost of cremation. Without life insurance, none of the widows had any way to make a living other than at the mill.

Liz found the old crones to be an endless source of gossip about the Chairman and his family. Especially his love life. Since his divorce twenty-two years ago, Septimus had been photographed in the society pages of *The Baltimore Sun* with a seemingly endless string of beautiful women. The crones delighted in showing Liz a manila folder that contained clippings they had collected over the years. Among them were pictures of the Chairman with a blue-blooded Manhattan socialite, a prima ballerina from the Bolshoi Ballet, an Oscar-winning leading lady, a double-jointed Olympic gymnast, a twosome of tacky twin centerfolds, and a platinum-blonde pop diva.

"This one my favorite," Petra said. She showed Liz a picture yellowed with age. "Twenty three years ago I clip it from the Sunday paper. The color was so beautiful before it faded."

It was the official wedding portrait of the Chairman and his first and only wife, Felicia. She was a pale blonde aristocrat with an immaculate complexion and hooded green eyes that seemed unnecessarily downcast for such a happy occasion.

According to Gudren, the bride had been born into an Austrian branch of the fabled House of Habsburg. Unfortunately, her father, the 12th Viscount, had squandered his inheritance on the baccarat tables of Monte Carlo and in the brothels of Paris, leaving the family ripe for a corporate takeover. Septimus jumped at the chance to enrich his own bloodline by acquiring a titled consort at bargain basement prices. After his plastic surgeon had repaired the hereditary harelip that had kept Felicia single until she was forty, their merger was consummated in a lavish, three-day celebration that was held in Venice during *Carnivale*. Nine months later, his investment paid off handsomely when his bride's precious bloodline was siphoned into the veins of a newborn son. A few months later, the couple divorced under mysterious circumstances.

"A pity," Olga lamented. "Such a beauty." Then the three crones would look at Liz as if they fully expected her to be next in line, if not for the Chairman, then for his only son and heir. They hadn't failed to notice Tavian's interest in her.

The very thought of a private meeting with Tavian made Liz extremely uneasy. She couldn't afford to alienate him completely, yet she didn't want to encourage his interest in her. After some further consideration, she decided to be courteous to him, but not overly friendly. She would, at all times, maintain a professional distance. Her job, and indeed, her future, depended on it.

She began to type up the memo he had asked her to write. In her naturally upbeat style, she praised the mill's workers for all their hard work during the year. Because of their dedication, she said, demand for the company's steel was increasing. As a result, management had decided to add a second shift to the Blast Furnace. This opportunity for employees to earn overtime would extend through the Christmas Holidays and into the foreseeable future.

When she had finished, she slipped a draft in Bull's in-box and went back to her desk to ponder the press releases that Tavian had suggested. She decided not to spin her wheels on them until she got further instructions from him the next Saturday. How she wished she could find a way out of that encounter. But it was impossible. The Chairman was throwing a celebration at Kings Oak for those involved in the finalization of the Project Minerva deal. Even though it was to be a mid-day luncheon, he wanted it to be a swanky black tie affair. As the Director of Public Relations, it was her responsibility to oversee the event and she was understandably up tight about it. The affair was to be a sit-down dinner for fifty. Even the formal ballroom in the manor was not large enough to accommodate the guests, so Liz had arranged for a large three-peaked party tent to be set up on the Choptank side of the estate. At the time, dining outside had seemed the ideal plan, but the current weather report filled her with trepidation. Rain was a distinct possibility with temperatures in the mid-fifties. It was too late to change plans now.

She looked over the guest list one more time. It was a compendium of the most influential people on the east coast. Included were high-ranking government officials, business executives, and independently wealthy non-working socialites. The seating chart had been Liz's biggest headache. The Chairman had insisted on an order of proximity to his person based on rank, as if he were the President of the United States hosting a state dinner. She solved it to his satisfaction by placing guests in descending order from the head of the table on the basis of the annual budget, personal or official, that they controlled. Money, as always, had its privileges.

A shrill siren shattered her concentration. It was quitting time. All over Herons Point, the weary worked-out remains of once robust men turned down their furnaces, put away their tools, and shuffled through the clock houses to stamp their time cards. Most headed home on foot to their humble shacks in the landfill behind the mill.

Liz looked through her wire mesh window at exhausted men rushing to make their escape. It reminded her of a prison break. Unfortunately, they would all have to come back the next day. In the office, the three widows said goodbye to Liz and made their way down the stairs as somberly as if they were descending into their graves.

An hour remained before it would be time for her to leave for class. Liz put away the seating chart and pulled a two-pound textbook out of her backpack. Opening it up to the assigned chapter, she began to underline the important passages with a yellow magic marker. A moment later, she retrieved a peanut butter-and-jelly sandwich from her lunch bag and fed it automatically into her mouth.

Bull came out of his cubbyhole across the room and locked the door behind him. As he approached Liz, she could smell the odor of cheap bourbon on his breath.

"You've got some dedication, girlie. All I can say."

Liz managed a smile. Dedication had nothing to do with it.

"A rich husband would be a lot easier," Bull said as he clunked down the stairs in his heavy steel-toed boots.

A moment later, she heard the din of the mill come roaring in the front door, then cut off with a slam. In five minutes Bull would be safely out of the way, his wide ass perched on a barstool somewhere in Dundalk, irrigating his ulcers with even more alcohol.

When she was sure it was safe, Liz put down her book and crept across the room to Bull's office. Taking a credit card out of her wallet, she wedged it in between the frame and the lock, then pushed open the door. As usual, it was a parakeet's cage inside. A week's worth of newsprint was strewn haphazardly on the floor. Crushed beer cans overflowed from the trash can next to the desk and several dog-eared porno magazines lay on top of the file cabinet. Next to Bull's chair was a white porcelain spittoon full of floating butts that made it look like an unflushed toilet.

"Pig," Liz said.

Then walking inside, she quietly closed the door behind her.

Pharos

In September the upperclassmen returned to the Yard fresh from their summer training cruises abroad. Bronzed young gods in starched summer whites and black-brimmed hats, they were ready and willing to heap scorn on the pitiful new plebeians.

Even though they had exchanged their demeaning Dixie cup caps and crackerjack jumpers for the Uniform of the Day, the newcomers stood out like targets on a firing range. An upperclassman could spot a plebe a hundred yards away by the fear on their face. At every encounter, they quizzed them mercilessly. Plebes were expected to recite on command all pertinent Academy rules, names of the officers of the watch, uniforms of the day, the menu in the mess hall, and even newspaper headlines and sports scores—all for the convenience of the upper-class deities. Failure to comply resulted in a punishment of countless pushups, star jumps, or a trip into the shower fully clothed.

Taking refuge in his studies, David avoided the upperclassmen as best he could, numbing his mind on calculus, chemistry, leadership, and literature. All the while, he kept his mind focused on the sacred task ahead of him. His ancient homeland lay somewhere across the Chesapeake on the banks of the Choptank River. But where?

Amazingly enough, he soon found the trailhead to the past right in the middle of his own room. In fact, right in the center of his computer screen. The signature of Caecilius Blackburn had been the critical clue. Googling the Internet, David discovered that Blackburn had provided his patron with an account of his settlement in the New World. The original document was in the rare book room of the British Museum in London. Miraculously, there was a facsimile edition on the shelves of the Library of Congress in Washington. A research librarian in Nimitz had helped David submit an Interlibrary Loan Request. For two weeks, he had been checking his e-mail for notification of the book's arrival, but no luck.

Then one night as he worked at his computer a soft chime alerted him to the arrival of a new message. It was the one he was hoping for.

"It's here!" David yelled. Jumping up, he grabbed his cover and bolted for the door.

"Hey, man! Where the fuck's the fire?" Archie asked in his squeaky voice. He was sitting on his bunk lacing his goalie stick.

"Nimitz. Be right back."

"Watch where you're going, Dave," Archie warned. "It's dangerous out there. Might want to take ZaStakaZappa with you and your helmet and pads, too."

"I'll be okay, mother."

The passageway outside his room was deserted at this hour. Most midshipmen were chained to their desks or hunkered down in the library. Nevertheless, David double-timed down the halls, squaring his corners with a smart click of his heels in case anyone was looking.

Taking the stairs two at a time, he pivoted onto the first floor. Suddenly, he was face-to-face with a pair of ornery-looking upperclassmen, each with a third class chip on his shoulder.

"Hey! You call that a ninety-degree turn, squid?" The guy had a prizefighter's nose and squinty eyes.

"Sir, yes, sir!"

"Looked like a hundred to me."

"Very sloppy," the other one said. A scrawny-looking junkyard dog.

"What da ya think? Twenty pushups?"

"Forty, at a minimum. This is a major infraction."

"I'll handle this, gentlemen." A first-class lady mid materialized in back of them.

"Yes, ma'am," the guy with the bulbous nose said.

"On your way, men."

"Yes, ma'am."

The lady mid gave David the once-over, stopping to check out his nameplate.

"So you're Mr. Waterfield!" she barked. "I've heard about you! Down and give me fifty!"

She was so close to him that David could smell her Binaca Breath Spray. It was spearmint. Dropping to the floor, he began pumping out pushups. Satisfied that the offending plebe was being properly punished, the third-classmen disappeared around the corner. David had completed five pushups when the lady mid interrupted him in a much softer tone of voice.

"Very good, Mr. Waterfield. That will be all."

"Ma'am, yes, ma'am." A bit confused at the reprieve, David bounced back to his feet.

"Where are you headed, Mr. Waterfield?"

"To the library, ma'am."

The lady mid broke into a broad smile. "Very good, Mr. Waterfield. Stay out as long as you like. No need to rush back."

They exchanged salutes and she pivoted away smartly, then looked back and winked at him.

David couldn't believe it! A wink! For a moment he convinced himself that he imagined it. But no, she had definitely winked at him. It suggested a certain degree of familiarity. She seemed to know him but just where he had run into her before was a mystery.

His thoughts returned to the book that was waiting for him at Nimitz and he hurried on his way before he ran into another upperclassman.

Luckily, the library was just a brisk walk from Bancroft Hall. It was an imposing contemporary structure with immense plate-glass windows that afforded a spectacular view of the Severn River during the day. After dark their radiant glow transformed the building into a great lighthouse. Like the legendary Pharos of Alexandria, one of the seven wonders of the ancient world, it guided wanderers through the shoals of uncertainty into a safe harbor deep with knowledge. No less than 650,000 volumes sat on its shelves, including rare books and special collections. With access to books housed in other major libraries and with its computers connected to the World Wide Web, there was nothing that couldn't be learned here. Or so it seemed.

Inside, David found that the premises were crawling with upperclassmen. Fortunately, they were too occupied with their own assignments to harass a lowly plebe. After storing his cover on the top shelf of a coat rack, he hurried to the checkout desk. The duty librarian behind the counter was a tall willowy lady with a pageboy haircut and very long fingers.

"Lord Blackburn you say," she whispered. "I'll take a look-see."

She slipped on her reading glasses and turned back to the reserved bookshelf. Slowly she ran her long index finger down the spines, carefully checking each title. A few minutes later, she came back empty-handed.

"No, I don't see it. I'm afraid it's not here."

"Not here? But it must be here!"

"Sssh. Please lower your voice so as not to disturb others."

David did. "Sorry. But I got an e-mail that said it came in from the Library of Congress on interlibrary loan."

"I'll look again, son, but I'm sure I didn't miss it."

David was dismayed. So close and yet so far.

Once again she ran her long fingers down the backs of the reserved books. "Oops. Maybe this is it," she said.

Wedged in between two thick history tomes was a tiny sliver of a book the size of a postcard. It was barely big enough for its title: *A Generall Historie of Caecilius Blackburn His Colonye in Maria-Land.*

With great excitement, David checked it out and hurried across the reading room to the nearest unoccupied seat. Opening the cover, he suddenly came face-to-face with his ancient foe in the form of a tinted portrait. In it, the Court-Baron had been idealized by the artist as a gentlemen cavalier of noble bearing, resplendent in gold-plated chest armor, white ruffed-collar, and green velvet cloak. These accessories of civility belied the crude features of his face, divided as it was into asymmetrical halves by a long, crooked nose. In an attempt to render his countenance in a more pleasing manner, his thick lips and sunken cheeks had been liberally rouged in the fashion of the day and his long black hair had been curled into ringlets to suggest the mane of a lion. Carefully cultivated above his upper lip was a narrow mustache that formed the crossbar of a crucifix-shaped goatee designed to lend his face the appearance of devoutness. The gentleman was posed with his right hand resting on the basket hilt of his ceremonial saber while his left palm was firmly implanted on a chart of the Chesapeake Bay.

On the next page, the air came back into his dead lungs and Caecilius Blackburn began to speak.

A Generall Historie

On the tenth daye of Aprile in the yeare of our Lord sixteen hundred and thirty five, we sailed from Cowes in the Mary Deere under the command of Captain Jeremiah Coxe. Our faire ship was bound for our landes in the New World that I had claimed by the print of my left hand on Lord Baltimore his chart. Besides our brave Captain and his valient crew I had on bord a priest, ten gentlemen, five and twenty yeoman, fifteen soldiers, six servants, one chirugeon, nine women, a cabin boy, a dozen chickens, four jersey cows, two dogs, and a flock of ten sheep. Sturdy stock they be for the planting of a new colonye in Maria Land dedicated to the greater glory of God and King. To guarantee our good fortune, we replaced the buxom mermaid on the bowsprit with a wooden statue of the Holy Virgin. A golden halo sat upon her head and her right hand was raised in benediction. It was our fervent hope that the Queen of Heaven would bless our brave undertaking and keep us safe from harme.

For fifteen dayes and nights our Captain sayled on a sea as genteel as a childe his rocking horse. On the sixteenth daye, the devil himself blew up a mightie storme to try the rightnesse of our faith. The heavens responded with grate shaftes of lightning that smoked the sky and sizzled in the sea. Not a man on board was not taken sicke by the perpetuall heaving of the shipe and falling of the skie. Grate waves as tall as our mainmast broke over us. Our priest, chirugeon, three saylors, all our livestock, and ten barrels of provisions were lost to the deep. For three dayes and three nights the battle waged. Then on the morning of the fourth day we heard a grate hissing from above and saw blue flames burning at the top of the mainmast. The smell of sulfur offended our noses. It was St. Elmo his fire which we understood, like mariners of olde, to be a sign that our Holy Virgin had interceded for our souls. Our knees did bend unto the deck and a hundred Hail Marys each one said in her honor.

Thereafter the wind did abate and the sea was eerie calm. We repaired our sailes with the shirtes off our backs and the britches off our bums. With no milk to be had and lyttle meate, we wasted into living skeletons and the rotten stench of mutinie hung heavy in the aire.

To save ourselves we ate the cabin boy, a young lad of thirteen yeares. Many had savored him before but none enjoyed him more than when our cook did fry his parts upon the galley stove covering his gamey taste with spices and hot sauce. Tender he was and plump and meaty as a pig. His uneaten parts we saved and salted for another daye. God save our soules!

For a fortnighte we prayed that our Holy Lady would send us manna from Heaven to protect us and our most worthie enterprize. But it was not to be. A cloud of gulls flew o'er our heads and mocked our plight with fearsome squawking and much ado. They shat upon our faire ship with such velocity that we took refuge in the captain his cabin. But our Lady worketh in wondrous ways. Within the waste of these intruders we divined the half-eaten remains of blue berries and leaves. I took these to be a sign, like the olive twig the dove brought to Noah his ark, that our Lady was leading us to our salvation in the New Worlde.

And so it was. After forty days on the uncertain sea, we found our way into the safe arms of the Checepiacke Baye. This is the most delightfull water I ever saw, with a channell 8 fathoms deep and 10 leagues broad. Of fish there were the most abundant that I have ever observed. Great schools swarmed over the surface, some leaping from place to place as if they were a birdes in flight. But alas, our nets and lines had been lost overboard and we could feast on them only with our eyes.

Onwards we sailed towards the point of land where my fifth finger had fallen on Lord Baltimore his chart. At evensong we saw great fires leap up along the bankes and heard the drums of war heralding our arrival. In daye we saw heathen salvages running hither and yon brandishing spears and sending forth a rain of arrowes to warn us from setting our boots upon their sacred soyle.

That night under a moonless sky, we sett our ankor at the mouth of that mightie river which Captain Smith his map called Patowmacke. At second watch I was awakened by loud alarums from the crow his nest. In the blacke of night we spied the head of a ghoste floating in the aire and chanting an unearthlie high-pitched wail. The goule raised a lantern to his face and we saw his eyes were dreadful hollow and he wore a crown of hair around his bare pate. Behold our spirit was nothing but a monk dressed in black robes and standing on a raft of logs.

On board our shippe he tole us he had spied the statue of the Virgin on our bowsprit and took us for kindred soules for he himself was an ordained priest of the Society of Jesus. Though he was of Spanish blood, he spake well our English tongue and told us his name was Francisco de Genoa. As a young man, he come to the New Worlde on the shippe of Captain Francisco Fernandez de Ecija to spye on the colonye of Jamestowne. One daye when he had gone ashore to study the native plants, an Englishe warship appeared out of the fog and chased his shippe away. But he did not despair, knowing in his hart that it was the will of God that he staye in the New Worlde and propagate the Catholic faith among the salvages in word and deed.

For twentie and sixe years, he roamed the Checepiacke learning the natives their tongues so he could translate the word of God to heathen ears. Many lost soules he had saved from the eternal fire before he himself fell victim to the temptation of the flesh. Overcome by the beauty of the Indian maidens in all their shameless nakedness, his vow of celibacy had been forgot and he had planted his seed in many a fertile mound. A multitude of half-breed babes he did sire before the twin cullions of his lust were flattened between a pair of Indian stones. Now in his old age and as penance for his misdeeds, sikened with the palsy and overwhelmed with guilt, he wished to return to the Holy See and make confession of his sins to the Holy Father. Thinking his knowledge of the native tongue useful, and in need of priestly guidance having lost our first at sea, we granted the good father passage to London when the Mary Deere should be sent back for supplies

The next daye we sailed north passing six more rivers to the west until we reached the mouth of the seventh which the salvages call Patapsco. Here at the poynte of a peninsula we found the very spot where the tip of mine own fifth finger had fallen on Lord Baltimore his chart. Praise God and the Queen of Heaven, it was a fortuitous choice. The land was thicke with trees and sweete with the scent of sassafras. Fishing along the shore were hundreds of noble birds with long legs and great wings. Father Francisco tells us that the land is a sacred place known in the Englishe tongue as the Poynte of the Herons.

Our shallop did we take ashore and on the beach did plant our flagge and arms and claimed this lande for ourselves in the name of our noble patron and our mightie King. The forest is alive with game of all sorts. We spyed great antlered elk, beaver, and smaller beastes too numerous to name. We saw no trace of humankynd upon the lande for it is as unspoyled as the daye it was created.

Amid such wondrous plentie our stomaches ached from wanton emptiness. Too weake to hunte the game, we devised a plan to bring the beastes to us. On the southern banke of a small brooke that flewed across the poynte, we mayde a line of fyre to run all game into the river from whence we sat in wait upon our faire shippe in the manner of the King his own stag hunts. Alas the winde grew fickle and gave way to a whirling gale. The fyre leapt across the stream and headed north as well as south and east and west.

All acrost the land, a grate wall of flame rose into the skye and swept all living creatures into the river where we sat in safety on the deck of our faire shipe. They swam to us like animals to Noah his Ark, predators next to prey. Bears swam with deer, antlered stags with mountain lions and fork-tonged snakes. Those we could, we slaughtered with our cross-bowes and muskets and fetched aboard for food. At the river its edge, the flames did quench themselves, leaving a land of ashen black where once the heron ruled in verdant green.

A grate feast we did have and bellies fill with all manners of birdes and beastes. We made most merry and Father Francisco lead us in a prayer of thanksgiving for the reap of our grate harvest. On the thirde daye of June by our reckoning, we set our sailes on a southeast course towards that land we had claimed with the base of our own thumb. Two dayes later we entered a river wondrous wide. Father Francisco told us it was called the Choptanke after the heathen that inhabit its shores.

We found the heel of our left thumb implanted on a lush peninsula marked by a giant oak the girth of twenty men. From its bodie a hundred wooden arms reached out and touched the roof of the skye itself. We dubbed it the King His Oak after our most gracious sovereign Majestie whose royal roots and branches unite the heavens and the earth. In the shade beneath, we beheld a group of native maidens casting their nets upon the waters. In our small shallop we did venture forth holding up our empty hands in signs of peace. Transfixed they were by the sight of our coming like gods from another world, all white of skin and silver in our armour. And we, too, were in awe of them. Naked they were, and all buxom in the prime of their ripe young womanhood.

We chose the comeliest of the maidens to send as presents to Lord Baltimore along with a small boy, the taste of His Lordship being universal. Suddenly our enterprize was rudely interrupted. From the thicknesse of the woods beyond appeared a great paynted giante. His fearsome visage and huge trunke were smeared in blood and his massive neck was encircled with talons and claws. Upon his head sat a ridge of hair like unto the comb of a gamecock. One side of his skull was shaved bare as a pigge his bottom. From the other hung long strands of hair like braided rope. The skin of a bear covered his privy parts and the bodie of a snake was wrapped round about his grate girth and knotted at the neck. In his hand was clutched a mightie war club stinking of freshlie smashed braines. Lurking behind him were a dozen devils besplattered in mud and armed with bowes and arrowes, bludgeons and spears. Three were wounded with a multitude of feathered shaftes sticking out their armes and legs. Another dragged a prisoner bound in vines. His horrid face was paynted hideous blew.

Father Francisco had been among this giante and his companye before and hallowed him in his own tongue. Wondrous to beholde, the two of them held forth like olde friends. To our sweet Englishe eare, this salvage speeche is passing strange. Within it are darke gutterals that soundeth like the growls of wilde beastes and also soundes of grate softenesse like unto the falling of pine needles on the forest floor. The pitch of the voice doth vary up and down like notes played by a piper on his flute. Oft times it doth seem to mimick the trill of song birdes, the hoot of owls, and the hiss and rattle of a serpent. Despite their fierce visage, the salvages seem to be a friendly people much given to laughter which soundeth like the cackling of a campfire.

The Emperor of the Choptankes is called in our English tongue Grate Standing Bear although our learned priest says that be not his given name but a title won through a brave adventure. His real name is held secret in his heart and is not for us to know.

The giante was well pleased to have Father Francisco back in his companye for two year previous our priest had bathed his dying son in holy water and made him whole againe. Beholding our shippe that rode at ankor in the river, the Emperor was sore amazed. He queried our jesuit whence grew the mighty tree of which so great a canow should be hewen for he supposed it to be mayde all of one peece as were his canows.

Father Francisco replied that it had come from across the grate water from a powerful lande where forests grew up into the clouds and trees hath a hundred times the girth of the grate oak. He tole him that our kingdom was ruled by a grate and mightie Majesty who hath in his infinite grace and wisdom dispatched us to the Emperor of the Choptankes bearing grate greetings and high salutations. As a token of his esteeme, he hath sent giftes of precious jewels and gold to seal our friendship with Grate Standing Bear. We shewed him a chest full of wondrous trinkets which were colored glass and nuggets of fool his gold. Silvered mirrors we gave to his five and fifty wives with which they were much taken, vanity being a universal qualitie of the female flesh. To his

*fearsome warriors we gave divers hoes and rakes that caused
them to marvel at our Englishe ingenuitie.*

*The Emperor himself was much taken with our muskets
which he deemed to be a weapon of torture thinking that the
metal hammer which we had cocked for our defense was
meant for the crushing of a thumb. We fired into the skye and
brought down a multitude of ducks and geese. The King and
his companye were much startled and fled into the woods
until Father Francisco beeseched them to return with open
armes. In their tongue they called our musket a thunderstick
and were much amazed by the rain of waterfowl that
followed the firey discharge from its throat. Our jesuit tole the
Choptanke Emperor our Grate Majestie commanded ten
thousand thundersticks. Grate Standing Bear was sore
amazed at such grate power and beseeched us most ardently
for our friendshipe for they live in constant fear of attacke
from the fearsome Susquahannocks in the north.*

*In gratitude for our gifts and show of peace, the Emperor
took us to his seat which was a palisadoed village on a cliff
which o'erlooked the Checepiake Baye. His people came from
hiding in their simple huts to cheer us. In number they are
some three hundred soules, filthie in appearance with red
mud smeared about their body and hair. We are told they use
it to keep away the stinging mosquitoes which are plentiful in
their kingdom. Their chief instructed them to prepare a great
banquet for us. A wild stag was skinned and skewered and
roasted over a fyre whilst nine naked maidens danced to
beating of hollow logs and the rattling of gourds. This passeth
for musick in their heathen eares. We dined on meate and
oysters and divers fish and crabes and our stomaches were*

filled wondrous goode. From the hold of the Mary Deere we brought forth two casks of port to celebrate our good fortune.

Whilst we ate and drank the Emperor ordered an entertainment for us which in their language is called baggataway. Fiftie young warriors armed with long sticks smote each other for the blew and bloodied head of their captive which they carried in a woven basket like a mother her new born babe. There was much shouting and merriment in the enterprise and the sporte lasted until the last limbs lay down upon the earth exhausted.

That night we sat with Grate Standing Bear in the Emperor his lodge. Before we spake, a wild man with an owl on his head entered our companye. One eye was sewn shut and a string of dried tongues hung down around his neck. He shook his spirit rattle at us three times and threw a yellow powder into the fyre which made it leap exceedingly high. In a voice that reeked of raw meat, he sang a chant to ward away evil and falsehoode from our person. Father Francis says he is the wisoe, One-eyed Fox. The tongues around his neck he plucked from enemies who spake his secret name against him in a magic spell that took his eye.

When the wild man fell exhausted on the floor, Father Francisco shewed the salvage werowance Lord Baltimore his charte of Maria-Land and my letter patent stamped with Lord Baltimore his grate waxen seal. He tole him in his heathen tongue that by these instruments our leige lord hath granted me the land so covered on the charte by the print of my left hand. In return I pledged to my lord an annual fealty in the amount of one-forthe the crops raised thereupon and one-thirde the minerals taken from the ground. The salvage

Emperor was ignorant of such legal nicities and was much vexed that another lord, however omnipotent, who dwelt across a grate ocean should dare to take away the very ground under his feet. His blood stained face darkened into menace and he arose from the campfire and shouted for his guards.

To avoid all occasion of dislike and colour of wrong, we tole the salvage King that we wished to compensate him most generously for his loss. A second grate treasure chest we offered him but to no avail for he clamped his hands o'er his eares and turned his backe upon us, breaking winde and speaking not a solitary word. Father Francisco explained to us that this place is sacred to his tribe for they believe it is the center of the earthe where the grate oak tree stands so mightily.

We formed a circle to protect our backs and feared that we would have to force our royal claim by use of armes. At length the Choptanke King on consultation with his wisoe and chief men turned away from his silence and spake his mind. Besides the giftes we had already granted, he did demand ten crosse-bows and twenty muskets to defend his tribe against the fearsome Nanticokes and Susquihanocks who are his sworn and constant enemies. To cement the bargain between us we agreed to trade five crosse-bows and ten muskets along with ramrods, wads, flints, two barrels of black powder, match, and divers other blandishments to ease their withdrawal from our land. As if he had won a grate victorie, he seemed much enlarged and powerful and strutted from his lodge to the hurrahs of his men and cheers of women and children. Too ignorant was he in the mechanics of our muskets to ask for leaden shot in trade. We offered none fearing that his friendshipe with such weapons in his hands might prove to be of temporary character.

Our learned Jesuit scribed our bargain down in the Choptanke tung which he sang to them in their own speeche like a choirboy. They in turn sang the song back to us like it was a grate opera for their memories are prodigious and filled with the historie of their people. We placed our seal and signature upon it and the salvage King pricked his finger with his knife and made his own marke in his bloode. The bargain sealed, the morning next they abandoned their camp and left in their cannows with the bounty we had given them. Thus did we gain in peace the possession of the land which our gracious sovereign hath vouchsafed us in the New World.

Moses

The University of Maryland Law School was temporarily housed in historic Davidge Hall in downtown Baltimore while a renovation to the original was taking place a few blocks away. The Environmental Law class was quartered inside a small, seven-tiered amphitheater that had been originally built during the Civil War so that medical students could study the corpses of confederate dead that were wheeled into the well for autopsies. Tonight, the only dissections on display here were performed on the bloodless body of the law for the benefit of two-dozen working stiffs and would-be attorneys.

All eyes were fixed on the big-boned, fifty-five year-old black gentleman behind the podium in the well. As was his habit, Dr. Moses was eclectically attired in denim overalls, tweed sport jacket, starched white dress shirt, plaid bow tie, and penny loafers. Pulled down over his forehead at a jaunty angle was a green plaid Ivy League cap that had become his trademark. He never appeared anywhere without it and some joked that it was glued permanently to his bare pate. All-in-all, Raymond Moses was a walking fashion statement that said Harvard Law School by way of the cotton plantation. Besides his unconventional uniform, Moses exuded a certain charisma that made him the focus of attention wherever he went. Legend had it that he had won a full scholarship to Johns Hopkins at age fifteen, graduating *summa cum laude* a year ahead of his class. The same rapid success was repeated at Harvard Law where he became legendary for a razor-sharp mind softened by a good sense of humor and a proclivity for sophomoric pranks. During a wild commencement weekend, he mocked his people's slavery by having a barcode tattooed on his ass. The existence of the latter was verified by police reports from prominent members of the white establishment who had witnessed the barcode on a pressed ham in the window of a passing car.

The Living Legend had risen to become one of the country's leading experts on Environmental Law and the University of Maryland was fortunate to have him even if he was a bit long-winded. This semester he was expounding on Toxic Torts. Speaking without the benefit of notes, he held forth in great detail on the procedure for class action lawsuits for plaintiffs who have suffered damages as a result of environmental pollution.

In the horseshoe above, his students raced to write down his every word. Some keyed them in at warp speed on their laptops. Others wrote crisply in shorthand. A few scribbled feverishly in illegible longhand while recording the lecture on tape as a backup. From her seat in the top row, Liz just listened without lifting a pencil to take a single note, a practice that could not fail to capture the professor's attention when the rest of the class was in such a flurry of activity. Her eyes and ears were completely focused on the lecture, assessing and evaluating each piece of information. She made it a habit of never writing anything down. If she didn't understand, she asked questions. If she couldn't remember the answer, then it wasn't worth knowing.

"In conclusion, ladies and gentlemen," Dr. Moses said at long last, a good thirty minutes after class was supposed to have ended, "remember your class projects will be due in four weeks. I'll be in for the next hour if you need to speak to me. Good evening or good morning or whatever it is."

When he reached his office down the hall, he was surprised to find his star pupil waiting for him.

"You must know some sort of short cut, Miss Mancini," he said.

"A secret passage, Doc. Can't tell you about it."

"You didn't slide down the coal chute, did you? That's how they got the cadavers down here during the Civil War. Put 'em in a barrel of whiskey to preserve 'em."

Liz laughed. "No. Nothing like that. Actually, I just came down the stairs and passed you when you were talking to someone else."

"Alas, my powers of observation are not what they once were as Louisa constantly reminds me. And speaking of my wife, she really enjoyed chatting with you again at the faculty party. Wants us to have you over for dinner sometime soon."

"That sounds like fun. Hopefully I'll have some free time after I finish my project."

"Good. But I gotta warn you up front—Lou's home cooking ain't that great."

Liz smiled. "That's one of the benefits of having a doctor for a wife."

"Tell me about it," the professor said. "The woman uses a stomach pump as the centerpiece on our dining room table."

He laughed at his own joke, then sat down at a small desk with a large flat-screen computer monitor on top. Slipping off his loafers, he put his feet on a vibrator under his desk and switched on the power with his big toe. Leaning back in his chair, he turned his full attention to his favorite student.

"This is the best part of the day," he sighed. "My dawgs are so tired."

"I really hate to bother you, Doc..."

"That's what I'm here for, young lady. Guess you've finally decided on a subject for your project and are dying to tell me about it."

"I have."

"And..."

"It's Blackburn Steelworks."

"Blackburn Steel!" The professor's pleasant smile flipped into a frown. He detested the Blackburns and everything they stood for. On one occasion, he had even crossed swords with them in court, suing them for unjust enrichment on behalf of the descendants of slaves the family once owned. Twenty-five million dollars worth of unjust enrichment to be exact, including interest accrued since the time of captivity. Though he was not listed on the suit as one of the plaintiffs, he had been motivated by the knowledge that one of his own forebears had been among those sold into slavery at Kings Oak.

"Blackburn Steel," he repeated. "Take a seat. Tell me what the villains have done now."

"More of the same, I'd say. They're in a constant state of non-compliance with the Clean Air Act, the Clean Water Act, and the Resource Conservation and Recovery Act."

"And how do you know these things."

"A whistle blower."

"Someone who works at the mill?"

"Yes."

"You?"

"Who else?"

"I see. Just what evidence do you propose to put forth in your paper?"

"I'm not writing a paper, Doc. I'm filing a suit. In Baltimore County Circuit Court."

The professor sat bolt upright. He knew Liz was a serious student but not this serious.

Digging down in her backpack, Liz retrieved the papers she had pilfered from Bull's file cabinet and handed them over to the professor.

"This is a copy of the latest Emission Report that the mill filed with the EPA."

Raymond put on his reading glasses and scanned the numbers in front of him. "From what I can see, they seem to be compliant with federal emission standards. Well within what is allowed, if these figures are to be believed."

"They're a pack of lies," Liz said. "As you know, the EPA inspectors are so overworked that the mills are allowed to do their own emission inspections."

"The Honor System," Raymond said sarcastically.

"A misnomer if there ever was one." Liz handed him another sheaf of papers from her backpack. Written in pencil, they were covered with dirty black fingerprints.

"These are the foreman's worksheets for the period covered by the EPA Report. They tell a far different story."

"Why am I not surprised?" Raymond asked.

"To summarize, Blackburn Steel has 210 coke ovens which produce a by-product of 380 tons of carcinogens and solid particle waste a year. Twice what they reported."

"That a fact?"

"Yes it is. And you might find it interesting to note that the annual cancer rate for Dundalk across the river is forty-two percent higher than the area norm. Draw your own conclusions."

"They'll deny any wrongdoing, of course. Claim their works sheets were stolen or fabricated. You'll get fired and maybe even do some time for stealing documents."

Raymond Moses was well aware of how ruthless the Blackburn's legal team could be. Their chief barracuda, Laurence Roche, had no scruples at all. It was he who successfully defended his employer against the slave reparation lawsuit, basing his argument on the fact that slavery was completely legal at the time. Raymond was forced to pay court costs in the amount of fourteen thousand dollars. And it still hurt.

Liz shrugged off the warning. "To make matters worse, they're doubling production by adding a night shift in a couple of weeks."

"So no one in Dundalk will actually see the new emissions."

"You got it, Doc. More pollution. More cancer. More pulmonary disease. More birth defects. And they get away scot-free."

"The EPA will slap them on the wrist with a token fine. Twenty, thirty grand at most. Not even as painful as a mosquito bite."

"Not talking EPA here, Doc. I'm talking class action suit. Damages for lives ruined in flagrant disregard for the law. I'm talking hundreds of millions of dollars. That ought to make them think twice about doing this stuff again."

The professor slipped off his reading glasses and studied the earnest face of the indigo-eyed, ivory-skinned crusader in front of him.

"So to summarize, let me get this straight. You, Miss Elizabeth Mancini, a second year law student, want to take down Blackburn Steelworks, a member in long-standing of the Fortune Five Hundred?"

Liz nodded.

"For your class project?"

"Uh huh."

"They've got all the pols on their payroll and the best-fed law firms on fat-ass retainers. And you want to take them down."

"Us. I want us to take them down. I'll do the research and build the arguments. Your friend Max has volunteered to help, too. But I need you to file the papers and present the case in court."

Raymond Moses leaned back in his chair and marveled at the outrageous audacity of his favorite student. Raising his right foot off the floor, he punched his vibrator's high-power button with his big toe, sending it up to the next level.

"Know what?" he grinned. "Sounds like a mismatch to me. Those dumb crackers aren't gonna know what hit 'em."

Fall Ball

There she was again! The winking lady from Bancroft Hall! For a split second, David took his eye off the ball. Enough time for it to bean him on the side of his helmet and send him tumbling to the turf.

"Hey, Dave! You okay?" Archie asked.

David sat up slowly. For a moment, his brain was scrambled. Looking down field, he thought he saw grown men running around in purple gowns and pointed white hats, all of them waving golden shepherd's crooks in their arms. But no, the figures came back into focus. It was the varsity warming up at the far end of the field. The purple men in funny hats belonged to a story Grandfather Two Tongues had told him long ago.

"They were Jesuits," the old man had told him, "Foolish Frenchmen who thought they were saving our souls. When they first saw our beloved baggataway, our little brother of war, they disapproved of it and renamed it to please their own god. Our sticks reminded them of their holy men. They wore purple gowns like women and silly pointed hats. And they carried shepherd's crooks with crosses on the top. 'Crosiers' they called them. And so they renamed our game 'la crosse.' The great spirit was not amused."

It had been, however, an amusing image for a young boy. Now, whenever David thought of the name "lacrosse," he always imagined the men in purple gowns batting the ball around the field with their golden shepherd's crooks.

Back up on his feet, David wobbled about uneasily.

"How many fingers am I holding up, Dave?"

"I'm okay, Archie. It's this damn helmet. Never played in one before. Interferes with my peripheral vision. Never played in shoes either. Cleats really mess me up. Can't get the hang of cutting. Gloves, too. Makes ZaStakaZappa hard to handle."

"Gotta wear 'em for your own good, Dave. Otherwise you might get injured. You'll get used to 'em. Just takes a little time."

"I'll be okay," David assured him. Adjusting his helmet, he looked around for the winking girl. But she was nowhere to be seen.

Someone else was watching him now.

"Who's the clutz?" Coach Sleazak sneered. He was a temperamental little man with a jack-in-the-box personality made up of nervous pent-up energy that could explode without warning.

"Water-something," his assistant said. "Indian Kid."

"Shit! You mean that's the guy from Oklahoma? Thought he was supposed to be blue chip!"

"Guess not, coach. Runs like he's got cement in his shoes."

"That a wooden stick he's playing with?" Sleazak couldn't believe his eyes.

"Either that or a crab net. Ain't seen one of them for forty years."

"Jesus! Ship him back to the reservation, or casino, or wherever the hell he came from."

Down at the far end of the field, David and Archie continued warming-up with the other plebe wannabes. Archie gestured down field.

"Hey, Dave, you see that hotshot showing off over there?"

"The big guy? Number 1 on his jersey?"

"That's him. Name's Armbruister. The varsity's star attackman. That's the guy you gotta beat out to start."

"Yeah?"

"Armbruister is totally awesome. He played for the Annapolis High Panthers when I was a freshman. A real fanatic. In the off-season, during the winter, he'd round us up to practice with him after school. It was dark by then and the field didn't have any lights. Somehow he got the crazy notion of painting the ball black."

"Hard to see."

"That was his point. You really had to focus and pay attention. Helped the concentration."

"Did it work?"

"Did for him. His eyes are like night-vision scopes. The rest of us—all it got us was a lot of bruises, black eyes, and lost balls."

The whistle blew. Warm-up was over and Coach Sleazak waved the players to the bench. He broke them up into two teams—varsity returnees versus the lowly plebes wannabes. Archie was picked to start at goalie. As the eleventh man on a ten-man team, David was consigned to the bench.

As the scrimmage began, David's mind turned inward and he started to think about what he had read in the *Generall Historie*. He had found the tone of the account highly offensive. It was as if the English lord was making fun of the simple quaintness of the Choptank people. But more than that, David was outraged that he had tricked them into trading their land for a few muskets and cross bows, some glass trinkets, mirrors, rakes, and hoes. But no ammunition. The guy was a seventeenth-century shyster. The agreement was written down in the Choptank tongue by the Jesuit priest. But the natives couldn't read and so the words had been memorized by the elders and passed down through the centuries. The Song of the Black Robe they had called it. He was not surprised that there was no mention of the massacre that Two Tongues had described so vividly. It was not something one would want to record for history. How had it happened? Had Great Standing Bear returned when he discovered the muskets had no ammunition? David was determined to find out. As for the location of his ancient homeland, it had been generally described as a peninsula between the Chesapeake and Choptank. Navigation charts would help narrow that down. What David had no way of knowing was whether the great tree of his ancestors was still standing or not. To his people it was the Center of the World, but to the Englishmen it was something else. They called it "Kings Oak" and regarded it as a living monument to the eternal glory of their sovereign. But that didn't guarantee that the tree wouldn't vanish under condos or shopping malls if the price were right or succumb to the natural processes of erosion or disease.

There was a big thud on the field in front of him. A fellow plebe was lying on his back unconscious. Armbruister was standing over him in a victory stance, cradling a stolen ball in his net.

"Hope he ain't dead," Sleazak said. "Probably just a concussion," the trainer replied as he ran out with some smelling salts. A couple of whiffs and the guy came to.

A couple of teammates dragged him off the field.

"I'm okay coach, I can still play," the dazed plebe said before he bent over and vomited.

Sleazak turned away and looked at the solitary figure on his bench. "Hey Chief, go in for Dutton."

The moment of truth was at hand. David Waterfield arose, tossed aside his gloves, took off his helmet, stepped out of his cleats, peeled off his sweat socks, picked up ZaStakaZappa and walked onto the field.

"That ain't safe!" the trainer complained.

"Fuck it," Sleazak said. "Give the Chief a chance. See what he can do."

It was only then that they got a good look at David's feet. Blister craters and chemical burns ran from his soles to his ankles.

"Jesus! What the fuck is that?" the trainer asked.

Sleazak shrugged his shoulders. "I've heard of athlete's foot, but this is ridiculous."

David ignored them. No one could imagine the pain he had suffered from exposure to the toxic waste in Miss Applebaum's schoolroom. Unfortunately his blisters had never completely healed and had a way of flaring up at the most inconvenient times. Sometimes when he walked, it was like he was stepping on a prickly pear cactus and when he ran it was like he was running on red-hot coals. But he wasn't about to let anyone know it bothered him.

The ref blew his whistle and play resumed.

Armbruister charged inbounds and headed towards the plebe's goal, the stolen ball cradled in his net. David stuck out his wooden stick and closed in on the varsity's star attackman.

"Try to stop me, sister, and I'm gonna break your fuckin' toy in two," Armbruister screamed.

Up close, he looked fearsome with black greasepaint smeared under his eyes and a Breathe Right Strip across his snorting nostrils. Taunting David with stutter steps and side fakes, he tried his best to stamp his cleats on his defender's blistered feet. But David would not be intimidated. He would not be fooled. Like an image in a mirror, he matched Armbruister's every move, holding him at bay until at last the energy of his attack began to wane.

Then, like lightning on a clear day, ZaStakaZappa struck. With blinding speed, David smacked the ball from his opponent's stick and snagged it in his own pocket. He feinted twice then pivoted away into the clear. Legs twisted, Armbruister tumbled to the ground and watched in dismay as David blazed down field. Zigzagging through onrushing defenders, he heard the wind singing in his ear, chanting out the seven sacred syllables of his secret Choptank name. Racing beside him, he saw fierce warriors with painted faces and bleeding wounds. Urged onwards by their strident cries, his long legs ate up the turf in front of him. And before his eyes, the ball that was cradled in his net became the disembodied head of an Englishman.

A pack of varsity long sticks converged on him, but David was not to be denied. Roll dodging around them, he raced straight for the goal. The defenders took his fakes and found themselves guarding nothing but the wind that followed in his wake. Launching their bodies at him, they missed their target completely and collided into each other instead. In mid-flight David spun around and whipped the hard rubber ball over the goalie's left shoulder and into the net.

"Not bad," Jesse Sleazak mused. "Not bad at all."

But the best was yet to come. All afternoon long, David raced up and down the field wrecking havoc on the varsity midfielders and long sticks. His skills were the catalyst that made his teammates play up above their potential. He stole passes, led the fast break, and made unbelievable behind the back assists. He ignited his teammates pride and made them believe in themselves. At the net, Archie's shaky stick work suddenly became strong and self-assured.

The last goal said it all. With the score tied, David galloped down the center of the field with the ball in the mouth of ZaStakaZappa. The varsity defenders backed down around their goal. David feinted to the crease, then outflanked them and ran around to the back of the goal. The long sticks followed as best they could, but David's natural speed put him a step ahead. And that was all he needed. The goalie wheeled around and saw David coming from behind the net, powerless to stop him. At the last moment, David leapt high into the air and slam-dunked the ball from the back of the goal.

Although it only took a fraction of a second, it was a moment replayed for minutes at a time in the minds of those who had witnessed it. The figure of David Waterfield hanging high in the air. The slo-mo fake to the right that committed the goalie to the wrong side. The quick slam back to the opening on the left. The ball careening off the goalie's shoulder pads and ripping into the back of the net. Then and there everyone knew that David Waterfield was something very special. Only a few of the very best players in the world were capable of slam-dunking from behind the goal.

"Fuck me!" Coach Sleazak screamed. "National Championship here we come."

After that, no one ever called David Waterfield 'sister' again.

Night Burn

It seemed like the moon and stars had been extinguished all at once leaving only a cold and desolate void in their place. In reality, however, it was just an unholy illusion created by thick thunderclouds of black smoke that billowed out of the coke towers of Herons Point. At the same time, in the bowels of the mill, corroded holding tanks of heated wastewater were flushed out into the river, turning the Patapsco into an open sewer. Downwind and downriver, thousands of innocent souls were unaware of the nightly poisoning of the basic elements that sustained their lives. Everyone, that is, except for the occupants of a black minivan. With its headlights and motor turned off, the vehicle coasted slowly down a gravel incline that led through a shipping terminal and down to a vacant rat-infested dock that overlooked the mill at Herons Point.

Behind the wheel was a balding, potbellied man with a toothpick wiggling in his teeth. He wore a Ravens Super Bowl cap on his head, catcher style, and was steering with the aid of night vision goggles that he had brought home with him after the first Gulf War. Seen through them, the world around him was rendered in grainy shades of black and green. The goggles made him feel like he was on the front lines once again, only here there were no Iraqi soldiers jumping out at him with their hands in the air. Instead, long blocks of corrugated containers stood alongside the road like a barricade, one stacked on top of the other. Packed inside were trade goods from the four corners of the world—household appliances, apparel, toys, television sets, and maybe even a terrorist or two. By morning they would all be gone, loaded onto flatbed trucks and railroad cars that would take them to warehouses all across the country. Coasting past them, the driver headed down toward the massive derricks and straddle carriers that were waiting patiently for the next cargo ship to arrive.

"Don't drive off the edge, Max," his passenger warned.

"Don't worry, Miss Mancini, I can see just fine."

Suddenly there was a thud on the hood and a bird bounced off the windshield. A second one followed and another ricocheted off the roof.

"Shit!" Max said. "It's raining birds."

"It's the fumes from the mill killing them," Liz said. "They've been finding carcasses all over Dundalk. Mostly sparrows with black soot on them. People there think it's some kind of plague."

"Wouldn't be far wrong."

"No they wouldn't," Liz agreed.

Max continued on a little further before easing on the brakes and shifting into park.

"Time to boogie," he said.

Max was one of the most experienced videographers in Baltimore, having learned his craft while on active duty with the Army. After retirement, he was forced to supplement his income with occasional freelancing assignments. Eventually, Max found his niche taping crime scenes and other evidence used to bolster legal arguments in court. It was steady work in a city where crime was becoming a growth industry.

His night vision goggles scanned the premises. "Looks like the coast is clear. Only ones here are you and me and about a hundred dead birds."

Liz checked her watch. "The security guard is on his rounds now. We've got ten minutes before he comes back."

Max slipped off his goggles, popped opened the back of his van, and jumped out to collect his gear. Tonight he was shooting with a Pyron-Electric Videcon camera that converted heat into Infrared Thermography. Snapping it on the head of a tripod, he held a tiny penlight between his teeth and fiddled with his camera controls. Satisfied with his settings, he peered out into the pitch-black night.

"Where the hell is it?" he said. "Can't see shit."

"That's because they turn off all their mercury vapor security lights so no one will see what they're doing," Liz explained. She took a compass out of her pocket, checked out the lighted dial, and then pointed it into the blackness. "Fifteen degrees south east will get it."

A few minutes later Max was rolling, panning slowly across the black horizon until an image suddenly flared up in his eyepiece monitor. He jumped back as if his eyeballs had gotten singed.

"Son of a bitch!"

A monster made of fire had suddenly materialized from the void. Its blazing temperatures were rendered in vibrant tones of orange, red, purple, and violet. To Liz's eye, it was a raging forest fire in the shape of Blackburn Steelworks, a forest fire that was secretly destroying the world around it. Max zoomed in for some close-ups. In one, a complex of towers vomited mustard-colored fumes. In another, molten lava burst out of discharge pipes, turning the river red. Before his lens, the Patapsco was transformed into the river of liquid hellfire.

"This ought to wow them in the courtroom," Max said.

The date and time were recorded digitally at the bottom of the tape. It was compelling evidence that Blackburn Steelworks was grossly exceeding its emissions quotas without regard for the health and well being of their neighbors, not to mention the employees who worked at the mill itself.

"We'd better hurry," Liz whispered. "It's about time for the guard to come back."

"If we can't see him, he can't see us," Max replied.

"Yeah, but his Rottweiler can," Liz said.

"He's got a Rottweiler?" Max gasped.

The sound of vicious barking came as if on cue. Their eyes were suddenly blinded by the glare of a powerful flashlight.

"Stop or I'll be letting the bitch go!" came a warning out of the dark.

Liz shielded her eyes with her hand. "We can explain, sir," she said as pleasantly as she could under the circumstances. "Please call off your dog." The Rottweiler was growling and throwing back gravel as he strained on his leash.

"Explain what? You people be trespassing your asses on private property." The light beam panned over to the Voyager and stopped on the camera and tripod. "Fuck you doing? Spying or some shit, looks like."

"Calm down, sir," Max said. "We can explain..."

"Don't you move your white asses, got a gun here."

Suddenly, the air went out of his voice as a pair of massive arms wrapped around his waist and levitated his body a foot off the ground.

"Hey T-Bone, watch who you be messing with. Miss Mancini, she be a friend of mine."

"Hey, put me down muthafucker! You crackin' my ribs."

From the thud, Liz realized the guard had been dropped in the gravel. An invisible black hand picked up the light. A moment later it shined it up on a familiar face.

"Hey! Miss Mancini, it's me, Manny Mandala from the house."

"Manny! I didn't expect to see you here."

Of all the boys at the Blast Furnace he was the biggest: three-hundred-and-fifty pounds on a six-foot-eight frame. He was wearing his hard hat and was carrying a lunch pail in his hand.

"You neither. On my way to the late, late shift. My girl live over t'here and I taking a short cut." He flashed the beam on the watchman crumpled up on the ground, a skinny runt in a rent-a-cop uniform. "T-Bone here don't mean you no harm. He's my cousin. Ain't got no gun and his dawg's blind in one eye and ain't got no teeth. Not gonna hurt you, none."

"Got my job to do, is all," T-Bone said apologetically. "Gotta put food on the table."

"It's okay, T-Bone," Liz said. "No harm done."

Mandala panned the flashlight over to the camera on the tripod. "Whatcha all doing, making a movie or something?"

"Something like that. This is my friend, Max. He's a videographer."

Mandala turned the beam back on Max. "How you gonna shoot dat? Aint' got no light out t'here."

Max held his hand over his eyes. "Heat," he explained. "We're doing it with heat. Look here."

Mandala crunched over the gravel and peered into the monitor eyepiece. Violet and orange flames leapt up and down.

"Shit! That be the mill, ain't it?"

"Yes," Liz said.

"Looks like hell in there. Feels like hell, too."

"Only hotter," Max added.

"Bad enough we gotta work dere in da day," Mandala said. "No way we should work at night." He looked Liz in the eyes. "You trying to get us out, ain't you Miss Mancini. Dat's what you be doing here, ain't it?"

Liz nodded. "I'm trying, Manny. I'm trying. Don't tell anyone you saw us here, okay."

"Hey, me and T-Bone don't see nuthing. Did we, T-Bone?"

"Hell no. Ain't seen nuthin. It so black out here I thought I gone go blind."

Across the river, the invisible monster roared like a fire breathing dragon with a hundred burning tongues.

Sea of Ancestors

The fierce visage of the great Tecumseh was smeared with streaks of crimson, black, and gold. His chest and shoulders were painted navy blue to resemble a midshipman's uniform.

David shook his head in dismay. During football season, it was a long-standing tradition to decorate the bronze bust with Bon Ami war paint in the hope that the spirit of the great chief would lead the team to victory. Last Saturday, Tecumseh was apparently displeased with his makeup and the Middies lost to Notre Dame by a landslide.

The chief didn't look too optimistic about today's game against the Air Force Academy either. Despite a sunny forecast, the morning sky was dark and ominous. From the looks of it, Tecumseh's bust would soon be washed clean of its desecration. But the prospect of inclement weather didn't dampen David's enthusiasm. It was the Columbus Day Weekend and the brigade had been granted ten hours of town liberty. Most midshipmen would march uptown to the Navy-Marine Corps Stadium and fill the stands in support of their team. But David had other plans. What better time to go exploring than on the holiday that celebrated the discovery of the New World? But this time the roles of the principals would be reversed. This time the native would go in search of the white man. Like Tecumseh, David was embarked on a mission to regain his people's stolen lands, even if it cost him his life. Swearing a silent oath to his ancestors, he took leave of the great Shawnee chief and continued down the red brick path towards the crossroads of his destiny.

David made his way across the Yard and through the Maryland Avenue Gate. He found himself on an elegant brick-cobblestone street lined with grand eighteenth-century homes. David fell in behind a walking tour led by an exuberant woman in colonial garb. Waddling down the lane, she took delight in pointing out historically significant sites to the visitors.

"To your left is Hammond-Harwood House, one of the jewels of Annapolis. It is reputed to possess the most beautifully ornamented door in colonial America. Try finding one of those at Home Depot today. And right across the street, surrounded by that elegant white picket fence, is the wonderful Chase-Lloyd mansion. It was once the home of a signer of the Declaration of Independence. And behind us you can see a genuine Naval Academy midshipman. One of our country's finest."

The tourists turned around to stare at the interloper in dress blues and a black raincoat. Then someone started to applaud. David blushed as much as a red man could blush.

"We'd be pleased to have you join us, son," the guide said.

David nodded his appreciation. He was going that way anyway.

Three blocks later, the merry guide led the group onto State Circle, the highest elevation in the city. Dominating the center was Maryland's historic capitol, a columned brick building with a white wooden dome.

"It was here during a session of the Continental Congress in 1783," the guide explained, "that George Washington resigned his commission in the Continental Army."

The tourists were duly impressed. As they followed the guide into the capitol, David broke off from the group. Crossing the street, he squeezed through an alley that separated an art gallery from a bed-and-breakfast. Exiting near the top of Main Street, he was impressed with the view of the city below. For the most part the historic buildings had maintained their colonial facades despite the demands of contemporary commerce. Time had transformed them into a variety of small stores, ranging from restaurants with sidewalk cafes to real-estate companies, banks, and fancy boutiques. Even on a drab day it was a colorful scene. Flowers hung from the arms of street lamps and overflowed from terra cotta planters at their feet. Visitors in yellow slickers were bravely bustling down the brick sidewalks toward City Dock determined not to let the threatening weather ruin their holiday.

David went inside the first clothing store he saw. When he came out, he was incognito in a new pair of old-looking stone-washed jeans, black T-shirt, hiking boots, waterproof wind breaker, and a backpack which now contained his hat, uniform, and raincoat. His taste in fashion was pretty limited, confined to the kind of second-hand castoffs he had always worn but which were now locked away in the basement of Bancroft Hall. He felt extravagant having forked over almost a month's pay. But it was a necessary expense. It wouldn't be wise to wear his uniform where he was going. If he got caught outside the twenty-two mile liberty radius, he would be put on report or "fried" in the parlance of the Yard.

David continued on down Main Street toward City Dock. This weekend it had assumed the appearance of a medieval fair with a collection of large white tents and hundreds of masts festooned with flying banners and pennants. The Annual United States Sailboat Show was in town and, despite the grumbling of storm clouds, the faithful were flocking in to see the latest in high-tech racers, cruisers, and multi-hulls packed cheek-by-jowl around floating piers.

As David passed the Market House and crossed the street to City Dock, he became aware that he was following in the footsteps of another man. Sitting on a wall at the corner of the channel, cordoned off from the festival by a chain link fence, was a life-like bronze storyteller who was reading to three small bronze children at his feet. Like David, Alex Haley had come to the shores of the Chesapeake in search of his lost heritage. He, too, had visited this place of infamy many years before, this place where shiploads of African slaves had once been sold at auction to the highest bidder. Their lives, so desperate and sad, had been immortalized in Haley's best-selling novel, *Roots*.

For a moment David saw the past as the present. Frightened captives huddled together on the dock, chained in iron, swaddled in rags, and stinking from three months in steerage. A fast-talking auctioneer was hawking them like they were bales of tobacco. Standing downwind was a crowd of curious onlookers. Perfumed gentlemen in powdered wigs, fancy breeches, and long silk stockings fortified themselves with snuff while their finely gowned ladies held their noses with one hand and twirled their fancy parasols in the other. Standing discreetly behind them were thick-necked overseers carrying ropes and chains. At the auctioneer's command, a Mandingo warrior was separated from his wife and children and stripped naked for inspection. Prospective buyers prodded him with walking sticks. Some examined his hair for lice; others checked his teeth for rot. One of them even measured his genitals to make sure he was big enough to stud.

Filled with disgust, David turned away from the scene and made his way down Compromise Street past crowded ticket booths, thriving barbeque stands, and a swanky waterfront hotel. Traffic came to a standstill at the Spa Creek Bridge. While the center spans were being lowered, David studied the sleek glass and wood decks of the Annapolis Yacht Club. An eerie sense of *déjà vu* came over him. It was as if he had been there before, not in the past, but in the future.

The drawbridge arm lifted and traffic began moving again. Once over the bridge, David found himself in a quirky Bohemian community the locals called the Maritime Republic of Eastport. Years ago it had declared its independence from the rest of the world and now boasted its own mock-government complete with a premier, national anthem, flag, passports, currency and even a makeshift navy.

David headed for a small run-down marina that was flying the Eastport ensign, a yellow banner with the motto "We Like It This Way" emblazoned across the top. Docked between a skipjack and a yawl was a bay-built boat with a large handwritten sign hanging from her starboard rail. "For sale! Boat Show Special!" it read. And it was no wonder. The craft had seen better days. White paint was peeling off her plywood and barnacles were visible at the waterline. To make matters worse, the rickety wheelhouse on her bow looked like it was about to collapse under the weight of dozens of crab pots. Her captain, a tanned-to-the-bone white man in orange overalls, was crawling around on the deck chipping paint.

"Excuse me, sir," David said, breathing through his mouth to bypass the smell of rancid eel bait.

The owner looked up. "She's a good boat and I'll give you a fair deal," he replied.

"Not in the market," David said.

The man's toothless mouth compressed into a pucker as he spat a wad of tobacco juice over the rail.

David began again. "Look Mr..."

"Not a Mr. You can call me Cap'n. 'Til I sells *Emma Anne* anyways. Cap'n Roark they call me. Josuah Roark to be exact."

David identified himself by his American name and the old geezer gave him a nod.

"Look Cap'n Roark, I have to get across the Bay. It's important."

Cap'n Roark shook his head. "Small Craft Advisory out thar today. Twenty-five knots, maybe more. Gonna rain like cold piss." He glanced up at the anvil-shaped clouds overhead. "No day for a boy like you to be out on the water."

"It's really important. I could pay you."

"You could try."

"How much would you charge?"

"Much you got?"

"Fifty okay?"

"Fifty'll just about pay for my gas. Nuttin' for my time."

"Hundred's all I have."

"Hundred will get you over there. How you gonna get back? Swim?"

"Yes, sir," David said. "With my thumb."

Roark considered the proposition for a moment, gumming off another chaw of tobacco. "Don't have nothing better to do but I hope you ain't in no hurry."

"Just gotta make sure I'm back in seven hours," David said.

"With a little luck, maybe. No guarantee."

Climbing aboard, David paid Cap'n Roark his hundred bucks and the deal was struck in a hard-callused handshake. David zipped up his windbreaker and unfolded the collar to form a hood over his head while the old codger went in the cabin and fired up the diesel. Pushing away from the dock, he swung a U-turn and headed out toward the open water.

"Whereabouts exactly you be going to?" he asked.

That was a good question. Even after studying the *Generall Historie,* David hadn't been sure he could actually locate his ancient homeland. His first thought had been to emulate Caecilius Blackburn and plant his own palm on a modern navigation chart. He had no trouble finding Herons Point at the tip of the Patapsco River. Unfortunately, when he put the little finger of his left hand on it, the heel of his thumb fell on the south shore of the Chester River. Either Caecilius Blackburn had a strangely shaped hand or he had gotten the names of the rivers mixed up. Another possibility was that the Choptank chieftaincy extended up to the Chester River. It was only later, when David came across a book of antique maps that the answer became obvious. The earliest chart of the Chesapeake had been drawn by Captain John Smith during his exploration of the Bay in 1608. One look and David could see that it was drawn well out of proportion. Blowing it up on a copy machine, he found that when he put his little finger of his left hand at the end of the Patapsco, the heel of his thumb fell squarely on a tip of land on the north shore of the Choptank.

"Near Tilghman Island," David answered at last. "You know it?"

"Yep. Take us about an hour-and-a-half to git there. If the weather holds."

Already the sky had dimmed so much David could just barely make out the boat show on the other side of Spa Creek. Expensive yachts were bobbing wildly in the water, banging into each other. One of the large vendor tents collapsed in a gust, trapping screaming visitors underneath. Undaunted, Cap'n Roark followed the Academy seawall out of the harbor, creeping past Trident Point and the resurrected foremast of the sunken Battleship Maine, a memorial to those lost in the Spanish American War.

As they entered the Bay, the water roiled into white caps and the *Emma Anne* lurched up and down in the turbulent surf. Overhead, the sudden booming of thunder sounded like the guns of a naval bombardment. Flashes of sheet lightning exploded on the horizons. And it began to pour. David took refuge in the cabin. Visibility was next to zero. Navigation seemed impossible. But Cap'n Roark just squinted his eyes and kept on going.

"Got a GPS, huh?" David asked.

"Too expensive," the Cap'n said.

"Where's your compass?"

"Don't need no fuckin' compass."

"How do you know where you're going? We can't see the markers."

"Got the markers up here," Cap'n Roark said, tapping his temple. "Born on the Bay, you get a set of markers in your mind. Know 'em like I know the moles on my Mrs." He spat a wad of tobacco juice across the cabin and into a tin can for emphasis. Everything was in complete control.

Far from reassured, David felt dizzy and disoriented. His breakfast and bowels hinted at mutiny, intent on evacuation from opposite ends of his vessel. Still the *Emma Anne* rolled on, braving twenty-eight knots of wind, three-foot waves, and rain that intensified from a downpour into a deluge.

"Be not afraid of the storm," Grandfather Two Tongues had told him when he was a child, calmly holding him to his breast and whispering the soothing sound of his secret Choptank name. *"Be not afraid, for it is your ancestors returning to earth in a different guise."*

As time went by, David had come to understand the truth of that statement. Science had confirmed that every human being was made mostly of water with a little earth thrown in to hold the shape. What then was the storm but the water spirits of the ancient ones traveling down from the clouds in rivers of rain? What then were the oceans and bays but great seas that held the sacred essence of his ancestors? All around him he imagined the great ones of the past falling to earth as the thunder applauded their return. Here was Great Standing Bear attended by his five and fifty wives. And after him came the wisoes, One-eyed Fox and Counting Clouds, shaking their spirit rattles and pounding their drums. Brave Burning Bow and Hawk-in-the-Heart followed along with many other fearless warriors, their bodies interlaced with tattoos and battle scars. Medicine Dancer was there, too, hung with garlands of herbs and berries, the only she-male werowance in the history of the tribe. And after her were the hunters, Spotted Elk and Horses Head, they who could understand the unspoken speech of wild animals. And here, too, was the water spirit of Grandfather Two Tongues, himself. David was in good company.

A half-hour later, the waterfall ended abruptly and the ancient ones rested from their long journey in the great sea of themselves. David imagined them mingling together and getting re-acquainted with each other. Some of them were smoking peace pipes, others swapping stories of hunts gone by. Great-grandfathers greeted great-grandsons and ancestors introduced themselves to descendants they never knew. Each of them passed their time patiently, waiting to be taken back into the sky by the sun, waiting to be reborn in the earth in a different guise.

Relieved of its liquid burden, the dark sky lightened. Visibility returned to normal in the nick of time. Dead ahead, a black mountain was speeding toward them on a collision course. Cap'n Roark spun the wheel hard. David was thrown to the deck and the crab pots on the cabin top slid overboard. *Emma Anne* passed so close that the Cap'n reached out and snatched a rock out of the base of the mountain and tossed it into David's hands.

"Hey!"

"What's the matter, boy? Ain't you never seen a piece of coal before? Get your hands dirty, did ya?" He chortled as he shifted into neutral.

David got back to his feet and threw the black rock at the departing barge, causing a small avalanche of coal to cascade into the water. Unaware of the near miss, the barge continued blithely on its way. Pulled by a tiny tug at the head of a thousand-foot cable, it swung back and forth like the pendulum of a grandfather clock.

"They could have killed us!"

"Could have," the Cap'n said. "But didn't. Today must be our lucky day." He shifted into reverse and began backing up to retrieve his pots.

"Always amazes me, that little tug pulling that big ass barge. Must have been two-hundred fifty tons of coal."

"Where did they come from?"

"Norfolk, I 'spect."

"And where are they headed?"

"Where they always go. Up to Herons Point for to make steel."

The name struck a cord with David. "Herons Point? You mean there's a foundry there?"

"You bet. Big ass fucker. That's it over thar," the Cap'n picked it out on the horizon with a crooked forefinger.

Beyond the bridge, on the northwest side of the Bay, a plume of thick, black smoke hung motionless in the air.

"Looks like a tornado," David said. "Only standing still."

"Just as dangerous, you ask me. Place makes poison, not steel. Used to set my lines and traps up there but the catch ain't fit to eat. Fact is, it makes you wanna puke." To emphasize the point, he arched a stream of tobacco juice overboard.

"Shit, son, this here Bay's a'dyin'. Besides the steel crap, we got a dead zone running right down the center where nothing can live. Too many chemicals and shit taking all the oxygen away. Only a matter of time for she goes."

"Can't the government do something?"

"Doesn't seem to have the will. Too many payoffs from the fat cats."

"Maybe the people will rise up."

"When the Bay turns to tar. But then, it'll be too late. Here, help me get my traps up."

David leaned over the gunwale and helped the old fisherman retrieve his pots. And as he did so, he cleansed his blackened hands in the sacred waters of the Bay. The Bay that was the mother of his people. The Bay that was the resting place of his ancestors. The Bay that refueled their rebirth in a thousand different guises—all the plants and trees and fish and birds and animals and insects and people that composed the sacred cycle of life on the Chesapeake. Now it, too, was sick and dying. He held his hands up to the sun and closed his dotted lids. Within him, arose the swelling voices of his ancestors singing forth the seven sacred syllables of his secret Choptank name. The name that could never be told to a white man. The name that was a prophecy of things to come. It was all up to him now. He was the one.

A half-hour later, two dozen wire cubes were stacked back atop *Emma Anne's* cabin. Cap'n Roark revved up his engine and got back on course. Completing its miraculous transformation, the once-grey sky morphed into a deep cobalt blue, streaked by long wispy contrails. Wind-roughened water became as smooth and silvery as liquid mercury. Reflecting both sky and boat on its sun-rich surface, it created a double image that converged on a distant point of land as invisible as infinity, a point of land where the past, present, and future intersected at the Center of the World.

Overhead, flocks of Canada Geese were winging their way to their wintering grounds on the Chesapeake, their journey imprinted in their genes. Underneath the surface, another mysterious pilgrimage was taking place as hundreds of thousands of eels slithered through the dead zone toward their spawning grounds in the Sargasso Sea, half-way across the Atlantic Ocean. Elsewhere, blue crabs migrated to the mouth of the Bay to lay their eggs in saltier water and finned creatures of every kind were compelled by Nature to return to their natal rivers to begin their life cycles anew. So, too, was David Waterfield urged ever onwards by the call of the ancestors that lived in his blood.

Suddenly, a monarch butterfly landed on his shoulder, followed by several more. The air around him became sweet with the smell of wildflowers.

"Hey! I'm being attacked."

"Don't worry none," Cap'n Roark laughed. "It's their migratory route. They come down from Canada this time of year on their way to Mehico. Heard it said that they go to the same branch on the same tree every year."

"Amazing."

"Long trip you ask me. Guess they just need a place to sit their asses down and rest a spell."

More monarchs alighted, drawn by some unseen instinct to fan their golden wings on David's arms and shoulders, to pay him some kind of special homage. And then, just as suddenly, they were gone, en route to their ultimate destination a thousand miles away. A mystical feeling descended over David Waterfield. It was as if he had been anointed by Nature in a coronation carried out by kings.

Kings Oak

A pair of steel wings cut across the shimmering surface of the Chesapeake and stole the sun away. In the sky above, a restored twin-engine Grumman Goose amphibian was making its way towards the Eastern Shore and the Manor at Kings Oak.

Inside the cabin, Randy Brookes, Karl Darren, and Chris Harmon were in high spirits. The consummation of the lucrative Project Minerva deal had made serious-minded men giddy with glee. Ahead of them was a lavish weekend celebration at the Manor, made all the more enjoyable by the knowledge that Septimus had kicked back a percentage of his windfall profits into their numbered Swiss and Cayman accounts.

Leaving the sumptuous comfort of their plush leather seats, the men couldn't wait to get out of their blue jeans, safari shirts, and fishing vests and into black tuxedos, red cummerbunds, and white bow ties.

"And to think our wives think we're going fly fishing," Secretary Darren said loudly.

The only fishing they would be doing would be for the high-priced call girls that their host routinely mixed in with his Eastern Shore cronies and Ivy League blue bloods.

"My worm is wiggling already," Senator Brookes declared.

The man in the dark glasses seconded the thought.

Lowering its wing flaps, the Grumman Goose gracefully descended over the wide waters of the Choptank, a thing of beauty from a previous gilded age. Diffused in the window ports like an exquisite watercolor by J. M. W. Turner was the mighty oak, itself, crowned in rich fall foliage. Across the peninsula was a view of the historic red brick manor house perched atop a green velvet hill that gently sloped down to the Choptank. So blue was the river that it appeared the sky had fallen down on it. A large white party tent with three peaks had been set up on the lawn and a full-piece orchestra was tuning up next to a portable dance floor that had been laid down over the swimming pool. Work crews and caterers were scurrying to get off stage before the curtain rose.

Gently the Goose set down, her prow kissing the surface of the river and sending a spray of silver out on either side. When she had come to rest, the amphibian turned around and taxied toward the pier.

Without warning an orange-and-black rocket roared up alongside and gunned across the Goose's nose. It was *Tiger Shark* with Tavian Blackburn at the wheel and a boatload of Baltimore babes cavorting in the cockpit, their shrieking laughter drowned out by the thunder of a thousand rampaging horses.

"It's junior," Randy Brookes yelled. "And he's got our gals."

His cronies sent up a rousing cheer.

The Goose unloaded its precious cargo of VIP's at the end of the pier. Tavian was waiting for them there with his boatload of windswept ladies. The babes looked almost ludicrous, with their bosoms falling out of their formal gowns and their fancy hairdos in total disarray, a contrast to Tavian and his buddy, Cyrus Van Aiken, who had dressed down for the trip in ratty T-shirts and jeans. After a round of matchmaking and horse-trading, the group headed down the pier towards the bar that had been set up in the gazebo.

With their cargo safely delivered, Cyrus retrieved his garment bag from the cabin of *Tiger Shark*. Walking with a slight limp, he followed Tavian up towards the manor house to change into formal attire. Cy was Tavian's closest friend, an old prep school chum who now headed up Internal Security at the Naval Academy. The two of them had first met at Boy's Latin Boarding School in Baltimore. When Tavian was on the verge of flunking out, it was Cy who slipped him the answers to his math exam. Tavian returned the favor by giving him a few puffs on his bong and sharing occasional lines of coke. After his family's bank collapsed, Cy was forced to use their connections to get a free education at the Naval Academy while Tavian headed on to pricey Princeton and another set of student retainers. Graduating from the Academy as a Marine, Cy went on to fight in Afghanistan. A misstep in a minefield caused him to lose his left leg just under the knee. The pain had subsided with time, but the shock of his wound would remain frozen on his face forever in his squinty eyes and the clenched teeth he hid behind a tight smile. Eventually, he had become resigned to his fate. The plastic limb he strapped on each morning made walking a bit awkward but came in handy in other ways.

"Hey! Those babes are primed for action," Cy told his buddy. "Mine's greased up and ready to go. Can't wait to get it on."

"You'll like Glynda," Tavian said. "She's a lot of fun. Got a shaved bush that looks like Charlie Chaplin's mustache."

"I get it. That's why you call her the Little Tramp."

"Right on target as usual, Captain. Anyway, you can use the V-berth in the *Shark* if you want. Just don't poke a hole in it."

Cy laughed. "So how come you didn't take one of the babes for yourself?"

"Already hooked up. That's my lady over there." His hooded green eyes honed in on the party tent where a brunette in the snug-fitting blue jeans was working.

"She's really hot for me," Tavian said.

Liz felt the intensity of Tavian's gaze and her face flushed. Turning away, she buried herself back in her work.

"Great ass," Cy said.

"Tell me."

Out of the corner of her eyes Liz saw the two men laugh, then continue up towards the manor house. She continued to check her seating arrangement against the place cards on the dining table. It was a stunning sight. Draped in Irish linen, it was dressed with twenty-four place settings of Wedgwood China, Waterford Crystal, and silver flatware in the Baroque style. The centerpiece was an elaborate ice sculpture of a pair of sea serpents with coiled tails that stretched up and down the table. The menu was equally spectacular. The appetizer was to be Chesapeake oysters on the half-shell, each implanted with souvenir pearl earrings for the ladies and cufflinks for the men. That was to be followed by Terrapin soup prepared from diced Diamondback tenderloin set in buttery cream laced with sherry. The main course was roast goose a l'orange, served on a nest of wild rice. To insure freshness, Septimus insisted that the waterfowl be shot out of the sky the very morning of the event from blinds hidden in the marshlands of Kings Oak. Dessert was to be Grand Marnier Soufflé followed by a wide variety of after dinner cordials.

Liz was beginning to panic. She was behind schedule and there didn't seem to be anyway she could finish her chores on time.

"Let me help you, Miss Elizabeth," Nero said, coming into the tent. "I can fold those napkins for you. Know how to do it so they look like butterflies."

"Thanks, Nero. That would be a big help."

Like the other servants, he wore a cream-colored dinner jacket and black bowtie. Liz couldn't help but notice that there was something different about him this morning. Then she got it. The white splotches on his face and hands. They had all vanished.

"Oh shoot," he said. He had left a black smudge on the corner of one of his linen butterflies.

"Nero."

"I sorry, Miss Elizabeth, I sorry. Gotta be more careful."

"Nero, tell me what happened? What did he do to you?'

His eyes watered and he was so upset he could hardly speak. "Master made me put black shoe polish on my spots. My cheeks and my hands! So I wouldn't frighten the guests he said."

"You couldn't frighten anyone, Nero. You don't need to wear that stuff."

"I need the job, Miss Elizabeth. Cissy and I got nowhere to go."

"He be right about that," Cissy said as she came into the tent.

Liz turned and saw that her appearance had changed, too. Cissy's eyes squinted and were ringed in red. She hadn't gotten used to the brown contact lenses that now masked her unearthly pink eyes. With them and her albino skin, she could pass for white, which is exactly what her master wanted her to do.

Now Liz hated him more than ever.

Upstairs in his bedroom, Tavian kicked off his clothes and took a quick shower while Cy started to undress. When Tavian came back out, he found his buddy sitting on the edge of the bed in his skivvies with his plastic leg crossed over his knee. It was a sight Tavian had never quite gotten used to. With both hands on his ankle, Cy pulled off his prosthesis as casually as if he were taking off a riding boot. Underneath was a stump of flesh that looked like the puckered end of a giant salami. Tavian almost puked. Turning his limb upside down, Cy shook out the contents of a hollow compartment. A virtual pharmacopoeia of painkillers and trendy street drugs fell onto the pillow: Batmans and Banana Splits, E-bombs, Peepers, Coke, Party packs, Goop, Toonies, Tweety Birds, and the ever popular Sextasy.

"Party favors," he said. "Take your pick."

Tavian selected a small bag of coke for himself and an assortment of other goodies, which he intended to distribute to selected guests. The high government muckety mucks were not on his list since their drug of choice was alcohol. Instead, he planned on giving them as party favors to some young society bucks he wanted to ingratiate himself with. Ever the prankster, he planned on secreting some Sextasy into the drinks of an elderly grand dame and her teenage nephew as an experiment to see if the drug had power to surmount cultural taboos. All in good fun, of course, and in the name of science. In payment, he handed Cy an envelope, fat with cash, which he, in turn, deposited in his hollow leg along with the remaining drugs. A few minutes later, Cy was suited up in his dress uniform. It consisted of sky blue trousers with a red stripe down the side and a dark blue coat with a blue belt at the waist and high collar at the neck. Four gold buttons ran down the middle of his chest next to a Purple Heart and three rows of ribbons. A black-brimmed, white barracks cover with a Marine Corps Insignia and a pair of white gloves completed the transformation. No one would ever suspect Captain Cyrus T. Van Aiken III was a drug mule for Tavian Blackburn.

Outside, at the top of the peninsula, a cortege of stately limousines crept through gilded gates and down the tree-lined cobblestoned drive as if they were going to a funeral. The cadavers inside were blue-blooded society people with translucent skin that showed spider webs of imperial purple lurking beneath the surface. Decades of selected inbreeding had rendered them so sedate that their hearts were barely pumping. One by one, they stopped under the covered portico and were eased out of their seats by doormen in black livery bordered in gold and adorned with the heraldic arms of the Founder and first Lord of the Manor. The corpses kissed each other lightly on the lips as if they were practicing mouth-to-mouth resuscitation. Then they turned and walked slowly down a petal strewn path to the field below where an orchestra was performing the first suite of Handel's *Water Music*. Royal music for a royal occasion.

After his distinguished guests had arrived from land, sea, and air, the present Lord of the Manor made his grand entrance down the riverfront stairway. On his arm was a stunning redhead. Her sleek body was shrink-wrapped in a knee length, green satin sheath that featured major cleavage down the front and a long slit up the side. She wore a large, halo-like hat and high-heeled shoes that she held on with leashes as if she were merely taking her poodles out for a stroll. It was the latest fashion statement from the runways of Milan. The effect was as intended. With such a prize on his arm, Septimus was the envy of every man there. And a few women, too.

Inside the tent, Liz was sure the guests would converge on her before she could change into her party clothes.

"You best get going to look after yourself, Miss Elizabeth," Cissy said. "Me and Nero can finish up here."

"Thanks for your help, guys," Liz said. "I'll be back in a few minutes."

Quickly, she left her post and hurried across the lawn towards the two-storied, brown-shingled boathouse next to the pier—the lair of the legendary yacht, *Aria*. She had heard a lot of gossip about the craft but had never actually laid eyes on it. The ninety-two foot Italian mega-cruiser boasted an aerodynamic body sculpted in the boatyards of Viareggio. There was a Jacuzzi on the top deck behind the glass-enclosed bridge; a gourmet kitchen and entertainment center on the second level; and a master bedroom below equipped with a king-size waterbed, gas-burning fireplace, and a bidet in the adjoining bath. It had a five man live-aboard crew ready to fire up the engines at a moment's notice, a galley manned by three

Filipino stewards, and a standard guest list that included some of the most outstanding topless swimsuit models in the country.

In hopes of a glimpse, Liz peeked through the boathouse window. Like a thoroughbred eager for the starting bell, the *Aria* strained impatiently on its lines. Its swept-back shape was a paradox, both contemporary and classic at the same time. It reminded her of one of Leonardo da Vinci's futuristic designs transformed into a fiberglass sculpture. The light sound of laughter drew her attention to the top deck. The Honorable Randolph Brookes, Chairman of the Senate Armed Services Committee, was frolicking in a hot tub with one of Tavian's Baltimore bimbos, a topless redhead with boobs as big and bouncy as a boxer's gloves. A Filipino steward, his head lowered and gaze discreetly averted, brought in a magnum of Champagne and two long-stemmed glasses.

Isn't that cozy, Liz thought. Septimus did everything he could to get his hooks in his contacts, even providing them with sex. She wondered if he had outfitted the staterooms with two-way mirrors and hidden cameras in case a little blackmail was needed someday.

Leaving the window, she scampered up the rickety stairs on the side of the boathouse and entered the loft. It was a cluttered, unfinished space used mostly for the storage of sails, oars, and other boating equipment. Quickly, she stepped out of her jeans, pulled off her blouse, and tossed them on top of a stack of cockpit cushions. Retrieving her plain black evening dress from a peg on the wall, she slipped it on over her head, careful not to mess up her hairdo. When she emerged through the neck she was startled to see a man in a black tux standing in front of her. Tavian!

"Alone at last," he hissed.

"Oh shit! I mean—you scared me. I didn't see you," she said lamely.

"But I saw you."

Slowly, he backed her into the wall, a lascivious grin spreading over his face like an oil slick. His nostrils were running and a trace of white powder was visible over his harelip.

"Excuse me, but I'm running late." Liz darted around him.

Tavian grabbed her from behind, his hands cupping her breasts.

"You're not going anywhere," he hissed.

Turning her around, he pulled her to him and thrust his tongue between her lips.

Liz twisted away. "No, no, please."

Tavian tightened his grip, too turned-on to stop now. "You know you want it, you little prick teaser. Now you're gonna get it."

If she refused, it was the end of her employment at Blackburn Steel. No more inside information. No more reports for Dr. Moses. No possibility of a judicial proceeding. She had to stall for time.

"What I mean is—I'm having my period."

Tavian's face turned to disgust. His grip went flaccid and he released her.

"Sorry. It seems to always come at the wrong time."

But Tavian was not so easily put off. "You're not bleeding in your mouth, are you?" He unzipped his fly and stuck his hand inside.

Suddenly, the door flew open and banged against the wall, jangling the windowpanes. Standing at the threshold was the Director of the CIA, his arm around a striking blonde with short mannish hair and sharp pointed tits.

"Oh fuck!" he said succinctly.

While Tavian stood there speechless with his hand in his fly, Liz broke away and shot through the door. Shoeless, she didn't stop running until she was safe inside the circle of celebration.

Sacred Ground

David Waterfield was wonder struck. Leaning out over the water, ablaze in bright autumnal foliage, was the mighty oak of his ancestors. Fanned by the wind, a thousand red and yellow leaves flickered and flashed like the flames of a signal fire, welcoming him back to his ancient homeland after more than three-and-a-half centuries of exile.

Slipping his backpack over his shoulders, he leapt off *Emma Anne* and waded ashore onto a sandy beach, then scampered up to an open meadow where rushes rippled in the wind like waves rolling across the ocean. In the center was the great oak itself, its large roots radiating out from the base of its trunk, weaving through the earth like serpents through an uncharted sea.

It was at this very spot, Grandfather said, that the Great Spirit began his creation by planting a sacred acorn in the void. As it flourished, the earth formed around its roots and the sky arose from its limbs like a sweet-scented perfume. So happy was he with his handiwork, that the Great Spirit flooded the earth with tears of joy. Welling up on the land, they formed a great bay that mirrored his creation back to his home in the sky. It was then, Grandfather said, that the water spirits of their ancestors crawled up on the shore and dressed themselves in earthen clothes and lived peacefully at the Center of the World. Later, when the water spirits passed into the sky, the ashes of their earthen shells were sown into the soft loamy soil around its trunk. Drawn up by its roots into its mighty shaft, they lived again in the great annular rings that encircled its heart, the great rings that chronicled the history of the world.

The smell of the sacred oak permeated David's soul and intoxicated him as if it were an exotic perfume. He felt himself drawn like a magnet towards its massive trunk. Running his hands over its rough bark, he sensed the essence of his ancestors dwelling within. Looking up into its crimson crown, he felt the sky spinning around him, as if the great oak were the very axis of the earth, itself.

He turned and waved Cap'n Roark away, then set out to explore the bank along the Bay side of the peninsula. As he made his way through the tall grass, the land gently lifted him upwards. Soon he found himself walking on the edge of a cliff. Below him was a beach cluttered with seaweed and the empty husks of horseshoe crabs. Fragments of seashells lay scattered on the sand like pieces of a broken jigsaw puzzle.

The meadow grass ended abruptly. Cut into it was a field of naked earth, three feet deep, scraped flat, and strung with a grid of yellow string. Inside, a semi-circle of rotting post-molds outlined the remains of an ancient palisadoed village, half of which had been eroded into the Bay. Nearby, a wooden sifter rocked gently in the breeze. Stacked underneath were a nest of empty buckets and several cardboard boxes. In one of them was a collection of flint points and fishing hooks; in another, hide scrapers and axe heads.

David knelt down and ran his open palms over the brushed earth. In this space, in a time long past, his ancestors lived and died. Their spirits perhaps lingered still, speaking to him in the sounds of nature that they had mimicked in their speech. He listened again to the rustling leaves of the great tree, the cry of geese overhead, the chirp of cicadas, and the gentle lapping of waves on the beach below.

"Checepiake" the water seemed to say as it rushed forwards onto the sandy shore, then slowly receded back into itself. *"Checepiake. Checepiake."*

Its soothing rhythm evoked the peaceful tranquility of lives connected to nature and its seasons. David could well imagine how his people's world had been forever shattered by the advent of a floating island manned by white devils with thunder sticks.

Suddenly, the subtle snap of a twig cried out a warning. The hair on the back of his neck rose and he had the feeling that he was being watched. David's eyes turned eastward and beheld the image of a sedge-colored retriever standing at the edge of the woods. Although trained to guard his territory, Russell made no move and uttered not a sound, as if he sensed the return of the rightful owner. Eyes locked together, Russell backed slowly away as if he were trying to pull the visitor after him.

David arose and followed the dog through thick woods burning with the fire of autumn. Poplars, maples, hickories, and elms blazed all around him. Leaves scorched with scarlet, orange, and yellow fell on him like cinders from a forest fire.

Leaping over a small stream, David's boots sank into the soft, spongy soil at the edge of a marsh. Russell ran ahead then turned and waited for him beside a drained bog stinking of tannic acid. As David approached he could feel a sense of doom pervading the place. Something terrible had happened here long ago—a painful tragedy which nature chose to preserve in the plaintive cry of the loon and the eternal tears of amber which bled from the bullet-riddled trunks of ancient trees.

The retriever continued on apace. Wild, untamed growth gradually gave way to more stately trees with Latin names screwed into their bark on black plastic labels like specimens in an arboretum. At last, the curtain of fire parted, revealing a magnificent topiary garden. Here the hedges, shrubs, and trees had been trained and sculptured to form grand, geometric shapes. Spheres and circles, spirals and cones—all were displayed like works of art on an emerald green lawn. Centered in the middle was a classical, multi-tiered fountain fashioned of Italian marble. On four sides the garden was encompassed by a series of arches fashioned of English ivy. Some led to ancillary alcoves, others served to frame classical statuary. Through one of them, David could see a distant stable with a cupola on top. Prancing about in the paddock next to it were several finely tuned thoroughbreds with ornately braided manes. Sensing the presence of a stranger, they raised their heads and snorted, then turned around and swatted their tails at him like he was a fly.

Beyond the topiary was a stately Georgian manor set on a rise that overlooked the river beyond. It reminded David of the great estates that he had seen in books on England. Like them, it was a red-brick palace dominating the countryside, a habitation fit for a King. Adorning the apex over the entrance was a baronial coat-of-arms: an azure shield emblazoned with a black palm and crested with the silver helmet of a knight. From a distance, the place seemed deserted. But even from afar, he could see the double doors under the columned portico were flung open, as if in anticipation of important visitors.

Slowly, and with a deep sense of trepidation, he made his way out of the garden and up the rise for a closer look. A cobblestone drive looped under the covered portico and ran back toward a distant gatehouse on a road lined with stately elms. Parked under them were a string of empty black limousines. Outside the gatehouse, chauffeurs had assembled in a circle to share flasks of scotch whiskey, forbidden cigarettes, and the latest, malicious gossip about their employers.

Two stone lions, rampant and ready to pounce, guarded the steps that led up to the double doors. Worn down by the footfalls of countless supplicants who had for centuries come to pay their respect to the Lord of the Manor, the steps now gave rise to a visitor who had come on a different mission. At the top of the landing, David paused between two fluted Corinthian columns and gazed through the open doorway into the opulence within.

On either side of the grand foyer were twin staircases that swept down to a polished marble floor composed of alternating black and white tiles. Hanging from the ceiling in the center of the room was a magnificent, three-tiered chandelier, its crystal prisms gently clinking into one another. Dancing off their facets, the afternoon sun cast refracted rainbows on priceless tapestries that decorated rich mahogany walls.

"Hello. Anyone home?"

Nothing.

Boldly, David stepped inside onto the chessboard of black and white tiles. The irony of the situation did not escape him. He was a pawn stalking a king, a trespasser in his own land, a pauper in his own principality.

The sound of orchestral music drew him towards a central hallway that led to a second set of open doors on the river side of the manor. Its walls were finished in red silk damask and hung with family portraits. Remembered there were thirteen generations that had claimed this place as their home. Some were confined to simple ovals or small squares, while others were displayed in gilded wooden rectangles embellished with elaborate carvings. Among them was a big-chested farmer, the size of three men. It was he who first cleared virgin forest into fertile fields—with a little help, of course, from African slaves who were depicted in a distant field uprooting a ten-legged stump. Looking on in approval from the opposite wall was a colonial planter, puffing proudly on a clay pipe. It was filled, no doubt, with tobacco harvested from verdant fields that ran in profusion to the horizon behind him, an endless supply of the broad green-leaves that were as close to growing money as one could get at the time. Next to him, with a prominent nose held high in the air, was the gallant figure of a revolutionary war general. Regally posed in powdered wig and ceremonial uniform, he was shown accepting the sword of a Hessian officer. He had been the first of his family to break with the English Crown, giving up his hereditary title and serving without pay in the Maryland Battalion commanded by General Willliam Smallwood. At the end of the war, the new government of Maryland allowed him to keep possession of his land at Kings Oak. In addition, he was awarded title to the confiscated property of his royalist neighbors, thus increasing the family's holdings five-fold.

Scattered in among these illustrious gentlemen were elegant ladies in period gowns and fragile children who had never lived to adulthood. In addition to the oils, there were sepia-toned daguerreotypes of estranged brothers who fought on different sides in the Civil War, now separated forever on opposites walls of the picture gallery, glaring each other into eternity. There were photographs of prosperous, pink-cheeked merchants and prudent bankers with double chins who insured that the family fortune would grow and compound itself over the centuries.

The grandest portrait of all belonged to the family's most successful entrepreneur, the fifth incarnation of the Founder's name. An obese man with mutton chop sideburns, he was decked out in a silk top hat and Prince Albert frock coat. Behind him at the water's edge were three smoking towers made of brick. At the dawn of the Industrial Revolution, it was he who had the foresight to build a great steel mill on the family fingertip across the Bay. From its foundries came the steel that would one day build the city of Baltimore, the Bay Bridge, and a thousand ships at sea. It was an investment that multiplied the family's fortune a hundred-fold.

Following in his hard-to-fill footsteps were smaller pictures of black-robed judges and shrewd politicians who had protected and enlarged upon their vast inheritance, insuring that future generations would continue to be the richest and most powerful family in Maryland.

The last and largest canvas took David's breath away. Under the shade of a mighty oak, a group of splendidly attired English cavaliers stood facing a small band of idealized natives. The composition was similar to that of the primitive images on Grandfather's sand painting and wampum belt. Only here the great tree had been rendered in amazing detail and the stick figures underneath fleshed out, costumed, and individually personalized by the skilled hand of a seventeenth century master.

With his curly black mane, burning eyes, crooked nose, and crucifix-shaped goatee, Caecilius Blackburn was unmistakable. Like his portrait in the journal, he was depicted in a fancy plumed hat and ceremonial breastplate. This time the artist had posed his subject with one hand on his hip and the other resting on the sword sheathed at his side. An ostentatious gold signet ring was displayed on his little finger.

Facing him was the towering figure of Great Standing Bear. Inspired by the description in *A Generall Historie,* the artist had painted the werowance as a tattooed giant with half of his head shaved bare and strings of talons and fangs hanging down around his neck. Wrapped around his loins was the skin of a black bear with its snarling head covering his private parts. One hand grasped a spiked war club; the other, a baggataway stick with a ghastly blue head resting in the basket.

Standing between the two wary adversaries was an austere black-robed Jesuit with sallow skin and sunken eyes. A large silver cross hung from his neck like an anchor, bending his body into a perpetual state of genuflection. His arms reached out to the adversaries on either side of him, just like the central stick figure in the belt of beads. Only instead of squares, his hands were holding two sheets of parchment.

Why two? David wondered. Then it became clear. The parchment that was being handed to Great Standing Bear was the one he had retrieved from Grandfather's oblong box, the one his people called the Song of the Black Robe. The parchment being given to Lord Blackburn must surely have been written in English. The Jesuit priest would have composed it first so that he could transcribe the terms of the treaty into the Choptank tongue. Perhaps the mysterious words of his ancestors could be deciphered after all!

The title of the painting was engraved on a gold plate set into the bottom of a wooden frame decorated with carved oak leaves. *The Founding,* it said simply. Underneath was the name *Bartholomew Boynton* and date, *1658.*

Like the account in *A Generall Historie,* the painting depicted a peaceful accommodation between the white man and Indian. But David knew better. It was nothing more than a clever piece of propaganda designed to rewrite history, to counter to the bloody clash of cultures that Grandfather Two Tongues had so vividly described the night before he died.

> *Then the evil spirits came. In a canoe as big as an island. With hairy faces white as death. Their silver skins were hard as stone. And they had sticks that hurled lightning into our sons. They slew our mighty werowance, our Great Standing Bear! They took trophies from our men and raped our daughters as they lay dying on the ground. They made us leave our land forever. They made us leave our Checepiake. Our Mother. Our home. We are Choptank. One day we will return and reclaim what is ours.*

A peace treaty had been signed, that much was true. But it was at gunpoint and under extreme duress.

Outside, a smattering of polite applause signaled the end of the third suite of Handel's *Water Music*. David looked past the painting to the open door at the end of the hallway. Approaching cautiously, his back against the wall, he slowly inched his way to the open door and peered out into the daylight. His eyes were filled with the silver sheen of the river, the silhouetted peaks of the party tent, and clusters of elegantly attired guests. For a moment the clapping gave way to sounds of polite chatter that, in turn, died away with the commencement of another movement by the orchestra. Suddenly a deep gravelly voice shattered the calm civility of the scene.

"Hey you! Get the hell out of there!"

The words came from a man in his mid-fifties. His appearance was all too familiar. It was as if the cavalier in the painting had come to life. Instead of a crucifix goatee, he had a black mustache that was curved down around the corners of the mouth into a scowl. Instead of armor, he was wearing a black tuxedo with a cream-colored bow tie and a crimson cummerbund. On his finger, a gold signet ring caught a beam of light and hurled it like a javelin at the intruder.

Startled guests turned to stare at the stranger in the doorway. What they saw was a clay-colored skinhead with a suspicious-looking backpack on his shoulder. He was definitely not one of them. David found himself the unwanted center of attention.

Septimus reached out and grabbed a passing waiter by the arm. "Hey fella, I told you not to let your people in the house," he said angrily.

The waiter took a quick glance at David. "He's not one of my men, Mr. Blackburn. I swear I've never seen the guy before."

David's eyes sharpened, his pulse quickened.

"I'll take care of it, Dad," Tavian said.

"Make sure he hasn't stolen anything," Septimus ordered.

As his son hurried toward the dark-skinned interloper, the lord of the manor calmly took out his pipe and filled the bowl with tobacco from the Founder's pouch.

David stepped out of the doorway onto the porch as Tavian scampered up the stairs two steps at a time.

"I can explain," he said.

But Tavian wasn't interested in explanations. "Okay, man, up against the wall."

He grabbed David's wrist, spun him around, and thrust him forward so hard that he skinned his forehead against the rough brick wall before he could brace himself with his free hand.

Suddenly, David felt like a common criminal. Tavian ripped the backpack off his shoulder and tossed it down in front of Liz's bare feet.

"Check out his knapsack," he yelled to her. Then he thrust his hands into the pockets of David's windbreaker.

"I didn't take anything, man."

"Yeah, well maybe I don't believe you."

Tavian knelt down on one knee and let his hands run up and down David's legs. The indignity was too much. From deep within his chest the drums of war began to beat. Enough was enough. It was time to set things straight, not only for himself, but for all his people. He was the end of the line, the tip of a tree that had its roots in the beginning of time. In his blood were the living genes of all who had come before. The immortal

Choptank was he. And within his breast stirred the indignation and rage of a thousand werowances and warriors. It was time.

In a sudden burst, David turned and grabbed Tavian's wrist, twisting it behind his back so hard he heard a bone crack.

"Shit!"

David brought his foot up to the small of his back and kicked his antagonist back down the steps. The crowd backed away as the son went sprawling face down at his father's feet.

"What the hell!" the elder Blackburn erupted.

Tavian rolled over, gasping for air. His face and the front of his tux were smeared with grass stains.

"I think my arm's broken," he whined.

Several guests rushed to his aid. One appeared to be a doctor.

David Waterfield slowly descended to the lawn below. Guests scattered before him like frightened game spooked by the approach of a hunter. Boldly, he walked closer to his adversary, invading the perimeter of his private space. Septimus took a step forward before his shrink-wrapped companion put her hand on his shoulder and pulled him back.

"Don't, darling. He might have a knife."

David held his palms out. "My only weapon is the Truth."

"Who the hell are you?"

"My American name is David Waterfield. My Choptank name is not for you to know."

"An Indian, huh? Well what the hell are you doing here? We don't have any Indians around here."

"Not anymore, Mr. Blackburn, but my people lived and died here along the banks of this river for ten thousand years."

"That doesn't give you the right to trespass on my property."

"Your property, Mr. Blackburn? The very soil that you're standing on is composed of the ashes of my ancestors. The ashes of Choptanks. Not the ashes of Englishmen. The very air you breathe are the spirits of my people. The water you drink was once their blood. It is not I who am trespassing here today, Mr. Blackburn. It is you."

An icy chill spread over the gathering. Never before had anyone spoken that way to Caecilius Blackburn, VII. Never.

Standing face-to-face, David stared into the burning embers of his enemy's eyes and through them into the eyes of the forefathers who nested within him like a series of Chinese boxes—all the way back to the Founder himself, living eye to living eye.

"In the name of my people," he said to them all, "I have returned to reclaim the stolen legacy of my ancestors."

A collective gasp came from the guests.

David snatched his backpack out of Liz's hands and walked away, the lost honor of his ancestors welling up within him, all of them singing out the seven sacred syllables of his secret Choptank name.

The seventh incarnation of the Founder's name spoke not a word. His exterior was as calm and cool as freshly quenched steel. But deep down inside, a burst of adrenalin turned his blood into fire. Deep down inside, he knew that an ancient enemy had returned in the guise of a new generation to do battle with the Blackburns over their lost dominion of the Chesapeake.

Kindred Souls

North of Kings Oak Manor, a rutted dirt road led David through vast fields of decaying corn stubble. Around a bend, he came upon a clutter of one-room shanties. Their rotting sides were propped up by wooden braces and they looked exhausted, like patients on crutches that would rather just lie down and die. None had windows and most were missing their doors. Inside one of them, he caught sight of a dirt floor and the scattered remains of a straw mattress.

Slave cabins, he thought.

The rapping of a wooden door on one of the other cabins caught his attention. At first he thought someone had gone inside, but no, it was only the wind swinging it open and slamming it shut. A glimpse of mahogany caught David's eye. Opening the door, he was surprised to discover the aging skeleton of an antique four-poster.

A bit fancy for a slave, David thought.

Carved roses decorated its side boards and it had overhead rails that once held a privacy curtain. The center of the headboard was badly battered and the tapered ends of all four legs had been driven into the dirt floor as if by a hammer. A set of broken slats were lying under the frame.

Disturbed by the image, David backed out of the cabin and continued on his way. Nearby was an overgrown cemetery with wooden markers just visible over the weeds. He could just barely make out a few of the names carved into them: Bessy, Father John, Cissy, Toby, Little Tom, Delia, and Abraham. Blackburn slaves from time long past. One marker surprised him. It was much larger than the rest and was made out of granite. The name Silena was chiseled on it. Arrayed around it were six small wooden crosses with no names on them at all.

David suddenly remembered the time. He had two hours to get back to the Academy or face the consequences. He guessed it was about fifty or sixty miles back to Annapolis. His best bet was to get to a major highway and start hitchhiking west toward the setting sun. But fifteen minutes down the road, the blisters that peppered his feet were beginning to throb in his unbroken boots. The pain was so intense, he was sure he could go no further. Then he recalled the example of Three-Legged Coyote whose memory lived in his blood. During the Trail of Tears, the crippled old man had walked a thousand skies from the dense woodlands of Georgia to the desolate Indian Territory of Oklahoma. Suddenly, a fifty or sixty mile walk to the Academy didn't seem that far after all.

Behind him, David heard the sound of an approaching car. Turning around, he walked backwards and stuck out his thumb. Only it wasn't a car. It was a green Toyota Tundra truck. Behind the wheel was an attractive brunette in a black dress—the same woman who had handed him his backpack at the party.

Pulling up next to him, she eased on the brakes. "Need a ride?" Liz asked, shielding the sun from her eyes with her left hand.

Up close, David couldn't help but admire her long wavy hair, bright indigo eyes, and smooth, lightly tanned complexion. And her fingers were ringless to boot. But he couldn't forget that she was the woman he had seen with his attacker.

"Not from you," David said. He turned away and continued on down the road.

The truck crawled alongside.

"I overheard them report you to the sheriff. Said you were stealing things from inside the house."

"I'm not a thief."

"I know. It's the rest of the bunch that belongs in jail."

David studied the driver further. "You're not one of them? I saw you helping the son."

"Tavian? He's a slime ball. Unfortunately, I work for him."

Her words were punctuated by the distant wail of an approaching police car.

"Look, Mr. Waterfield, you'd better hop in now. The sheriff is on his way."

"I didn't do anything wrong."

"You'll like Sheriff Turner once you get to know him. Very civic-minded. He's President of the Kiwanis and a Kleagle in the local chapter of the Ku Klux Klan."

The siren was getting louder.

David stopped. "On second thought, maybe I could use a lift."

"Better make it quick." Liz pushed open the passenger door as David slipped out of his backpack and jumped inside.

Shifting back into gear, Liz stepped on the gas pedal, leaving the dead fields of Kings Oak Manor behind her. Up ahead, a car with a flashing light bar came into view. David bent down and zipped open his backpack like he was an ostrich trying to find a hole to hide in.

As he approached, the sheriff put his hand out the window and waved the truck over to the side of the road. His blue-gray, Crown Victoria nosed in parallel to it. Sheriff Turner rolled down the window. He was a short, stocky man with a loose-fitting leather face that made him look like a bulldog. He wore a light-brown shirt with sweat stains under the armpits and a tan trooper hat with a back strap that fit nicely between the fat folds in his sunburned neck.

"Afternoon, Miss Mancini," he said politely.

"Afternoon, sheriff."

His dog eyes shifted to the man in the passenger seat. Cocked down over his head at a jaunty angle was a black-brimmed white hat with a gold band and anchor insignia in front.

"Afternoon, sir," the sheriff said, touching the edge of his hat to show his respect for the military. He, himself, had lucked out in the draft lottery way back when and the truth was he always felt a little guilty about not serving his country.

David nodded back, relieved that Turner's line of sight precluded him from seeing the rest of his "uniform"—his decidedly unmilitary black T-shirt, stone-washed jeans, and hiking boots.

"Mind my asking, you folks pass any drifters on the road?"

"If you mean that boy that caused the commotion at the Manor, sheriff, yes we did," Liz said. "Saw him running into the cornfield about half a mile back. Disgraceful what he did."

"Won't be doing it again, Miss Mancini, I get my hands on him."

"Good luck," Liz said.

"You folks have a good afternoon," Sheriff Turner said. Nodding to David, he peeled out in a cloud of dust, light bars blazing, siren screaming.

"I knew you were a middie," Liz said. "Saw your uniform in your backpack. Might not have picked you up otherwise. Everyone at the party thought you were a skinhead. Anyway, you're in luck. I'm headed back to Fells Point. I can do a short detour through Annapolis and drop you at the Academy."

"That'd be great. Thanks."

"No problem."

The corn fields of Kings Oak Manor gave way to a timberland of loblolly pines bowed over in obedience to the constant and sometimes quite stormy wind that came off the Chesapeake. Through the trees on the other side of the peninsula, David could make out silvery patches of the Choptank and the steeple of an old stone church.

"That really true what you said back there at the manor?" Liz asked. "You know, about your tribal lands?"

David repeated Grandfather's story: the belt of beads, the tree of colored sand, the phonetic parchment in the bottom of the oblong box, and the archaeological dig he had just stumbled across. He told her, too, about the account of the founding in *A Generall Historie.*

"This parchment," Liz said, "your ancestors must have saved it for a reason."

"They felt cheated, I'm sure. The muskets they traded for didn't come with lead shot."

"The traditional Blackburn deal. You really think there was an English version of your parchment?"

"That's my guess. Why else would the priest in the painting be handing out two copies?"

"Wonder if the Blackburn's still have theirs?"

David shrugged his shoulders. "After today, I don't think they'd let me see it if they did."

"Guess you're right about that."

The dirt road grew into a two-lane blacktop. Several miles later, it stopped abruptly at a raised drawbridge. A skipjack was coming in from the Chesapeake under power. In the middle of the deck was a windlass and a long chain connected to a metal dredge with iron teeth. Workmen in rubber boots and foul weather gear were busily sorting through a small pile of oysters, throwing the empty shells overboard.

"Doesn't look like they caught much," David said.

Liz signed. "The beds are pretty depleted nowadays. Used to be the Bay had mountains of oysters. Nowadays over-harvesting, disease, and pollution have taken a heavy toll."

"Too bad."

"A tragedy really. Oysters filter out impurities and help keep the water clean."

As the skipjack steered into the dock of an oyster shucking plant, a clanging bell brought the drawbridge back down. Liz's Tundra rumbled over the metal grate and continued on it way.

"I was just thinking," she said "if your parchment was a deed or peace treaty, a copy might have been filed in the Maryland State Archives."

"Maybe so."

"My friend Phyllis works at the Archives. She knows about things like that. If you want, I'll ask her to look for it."

David studied his benefactor for a few moments.

"If you don't mind my asking, Liz, why are you helping me?"

"That's easy. Anyone who's against the Blackburns is a friend of mine."

David looked perplexed. "Then why are you working for them?"

"That's a long story. A really long story."

She fell silent as they entered the outskirts of St. Michaels. A quaint waterfront village, it was famous for its charming shops, cozy inns, seafood restaurants, and the Chesapeake Bay Maritime Museum. The main street was decorated with hanging plants, flower boxes, whirligigs, windsocks, and blue-and-red Union Jacks.

"What's with all the British flags," David asked.

Happy to change the subject, Liz filled him in on a little local history. "St. Michaels is known as the 'Town that Fooled the British.' It was a major Eastern Shore port during colonial times. One night, during the War of 1812, some British gun ships paid a visit. The townsfolk hung lanterns in treetops and the English canons fired over their heads. Guess they were gone before daylight and the townspeople had the last laugh. Now all is forgiven and they fly British flags in commemoration of the event."

"Thanks for the info," David said with a smile. "It might come in handy in my Naval Warfare class."

"You never know."

On the other side of town, Liz slowly resumed her speed and returned to the subject of her grievance against her employer.

"My father worked for Blackburn Steelworks for forty years. I'm so proud of him. Emigrated from Italy when he was only fifteen. Couldn't speak a word of English but somehow landed a job at the mill shoveling coal. Thirty years later he had worked his way up to be foreman of the Coke Ovens. He got sick and died when I was twelve."

"Sorry," David said.

Liz nodded. "There were no benefits then. No life insurance or pension. My mother had to work in the mill office to support me. It took everything she had to send me through Essex Community College. A year after I graduated, she passed away. She was just exhausted by it all. I took over her job after that. You could say working for Blackburns was part of my heritage. I was born into it. Like being born into slavery."

"What is it you do for them exactly?" David asked.

Liz glanced over at him and smiled. "At first I was just a clerk-typist, but last year I got a promotion. Don't laugh. I'm the Director of Public Relations now. I try to make the mill look good."

"Must be a tough job."

"You have no idea." She paused and then added. "One of the things I was supposed to do was make sure the dinner today went well. There were a lot of important people there."

"Guess I ruined that."

"Doesn't matter. It was great. I've never seen Septimus so flustered in front of his friends. It was a real treat, believe me."

"Why don't you quit if you dislike them so much? Must be a lot of jobs out there you can get."

"Plan to when I finish grad school. I've got just two years to go and then I'm outta there."

"Grad school?"

"Yeah. University of Maryland in Baltimore. Three nights a week. It's pretty tough."

"Public Relations?"

"No way. I'm going to be a lawyer."

"A lawyer! I'm impressed. What kind of law?"

"Environmental. I want to shut down industries that are harming the Chesapeake."

"Like Blackburn Steelworks for example?"

"You got it. They have a long history of completely ignoring EPA's guidelines on emissions. Right now they've expanded their operations with a secret night shift."

"So no one can see what they're doing."

"Exactly. They're doubling the amount of pollution they discharge in the water and the carcinogens they release into the atmosphere. The Bay's dying and the surrounding area has the largest lung cancer rate in the state. Something has got to be done to stop them."

"Wow," David said. "You and I have a lot in common."

"Yes, we do," Liz said. "Yes, we do."

Ahead of them, the twin spans of the Bay Bridge arose majestically, curving gracefully over the water like a pair of playful dolphins leaping in tandem. On either side, white canvas wings sailed over the surface of the Bay en route to their nests in the branches of the great Chesapeake water tree.

"I hate to tell you this, but a lot of Blackburn steel went into making this bridge," Liz said. "Back in the early fifties."

The bridge seemed to shake and the drainage grates rattled. David imagined a rain of rusted bolts and nuts falling into the water below.

"Hope it wasn't low bid," he said.

"Probably was on paper. State project and all that. They say that a year before the project was made public, Septimus, acting under a pseudonym, bought up a lot of acreage on either side of the proposed site. When the bridge was announced, property values shot through the stratosphere. He made a fortune out from the deal."

"Actually, I was more concerned that the bridge might fall apart than worried that the man might not make enough money to pay his mortgage."

"You've got a point," Liz said.

Once over the bridge, Liz drove past the tollbooths and pulled into the first gas station she could find. David disappeared into the restroom and returned in his dress blues.

"Hey, you look pretty snazzy. Why didn't you wear that to the party? You would have made even more of a splash."

"We're not supposed to go any further than twenty-two miles from the Academy," David said. "I was afraid someone might spot me."

"You have a point. I saw some military brass there. The Blackburns have a lot of connections."

"Yeah," David said. But so did he. Only trouble was they were all dead and living in his blood.

Several miles later, Liz took the 450 Exit towards Annapolis. She pulled up near the Maryland Avenue Gate just as a group of middies were returning from valiant, but ultimately vain, attempts to pick up some townie babes at a local bar.

"Thanks for the lift," David said as he climbed out the door. "I hope you'll let me return the favor by buying you dinner."

"That's a deal."

"Great. The only time we lowly plebes get liberty is on holidays. I'm afraid you'll have to wait until Thanksgiving."

Liz laughed. "I should have a pretty big appetite by then. Just give me a jingle." She took her business card out of her wallet and handed it to him. "My cell phone number is at the bottom. Call me anytime."

"Thanks. Would you mind if I leave my backpack here? Got my civvies inside. Can't take 'em back to my room."

"No problem. I'll hold them for you until you can get them. Rent's cheap."

"Great. I'll talk to you soon."

Liz waved goodbye, then drove away leaving David alone on the sidewalk.

"Hey Waterfield! How'd someone so ugly get so lucky?"

David turned and saw Archie standing next to a lady mid with First Class stripes on her shoulders. He couldn't believe his eyes. She was none other than the winking woman of Bancroft Hall!

"Want you to meet Helene Friedman," his roommate said proudly.

"He means Zankowski," she corrected awkwardly, the scent of spearmint heavy on her breath. "I go by my mother's maiden name." She tapped her nameplate and smiled broadly at David, revealing a set of bright, gold-plated braces.

David's head spun. Helene's brown eyes, snub nose, and clunky braces were right out of the picture on Archie's desk. But David distinctly remembered him saying that his girl didn't go to the Academy. And yet here she was in the uniform of a firstie. Not wanting to take chances, David snapped a quick salute.

"Good afternoon, ma'am."

Helene returned it smartly. "Good to see you again, Mr. Waterfield. Heard a lot about you from Archibald." Then she leaned over and whispered. "Hope you don't mind, but he showed me your wooden stick. It's so neat. Zataka something."

"ZaStakaZappa."

"Yeah. ZaStakaZappa. It's so cool."

"Thanks."

A taxi pulled up to the curb and Helene got into the back seat. "I've got to run now. Look after Archibald for me, Mr. Waterfield."

"Yes, ma'am."

And with that she was gone.

"We'd better hurry to muster," Archie said.

They made tracks toward the Maryland Avenue gate. David was totally confused. Liberty was over in five minutes. And yet Helene was driving away. Was she a middie or wasn't she?

"Can you keep a secret, Dave?"

"Sure, Archie."

"You probably figured it out anyway. Babe isn't actually a real middie yet."

"Go on."

"Like I told you, her mom was an Academy grad. Got killed in action in Iraq. Babe was planning on going to the Academy with me but had to drop out of school last semester to support her old man. Guy's a basket case. But she's gonna apply again next year. Anyway, I guess she went a little bit crazy. Took her mom's uniforms out of her closet and ripped off the Navy insignias and sewed back the old Academy ones. After she made a few alterations, the uniforms fit perfectly. Now she feels like she can come over to the Yard anytime she wants to. Fact is, she was on her way to see me when she rescued you in the hall the other day."

"I'll have to thank her for that. But, I mean, isn't that slightly against the rules? She's guilty of impersonating the military."

"I guess."

"Not to mention that plebes are forbidden from dating other middies, real or imagined, or bringing any outsider onto the Yard or into Bancroft Hall."

"Yeah, yeah, yeah."

Archie had violated the Honor Concept in spades. Theoretically, David was supposed to turn him in.

"You're not gonna rat on me, are you, Dave? Babe's just having a hard time. When she puts on her mom's uniform it's like she's seeing things through her eyes, reliving the life she had at the Academy."

David sighed. He was trapped in a moral dilemma. He had promised to keep Archie's secret and a Choptank warrior never went back on his word, no matter what. But if anyone ever found out, they could both be kicked out of the Academy.

"It's okay, man," he said. "I'll never tell."

"Thanks, Dave."

As they approached the guardhouse, a marine in woodland camouflage demanded to see their IDs. They flashed their cards at him and he waved them through.

"Don't the guards ever check her ID?" David asked.

"All the time. Babe uses her mom's. Made a few changes to it and no one's ever questioned it."

"You mean she falsified an ID!"

"Sssssh. Not so loud. I know it's risky. But it's worth it. Babe will be able to come up to my room whenever she wants. Hope you understand."

"It's okay, Archie. Just let me know when she's coming again and I'll disappear."

"I'd do the same for you, Dave."

"I know, man. Thanks."

Picking up their pace, they followed the brick walkway around the Administration Building and toward the chapel, anxious not to be late for evening muster in Bancroft Hall.

"Aren't you guys afraid you're going to get caught?" David asked. "You could get booted out and Helene could go to jail."

"Yeah. But it's a chance we have to take. We love each other so much, we can't bear to be apart. After we get our commissions, we're gonna get married in there."

They stopped for a moment to take in the chapel. It was a magnificent building that some referred to as the Cathedral of the Navy. Outside the entrance were a pair of massive, three-ton iron anchors, symbols of the steadfastness of faith in the life of the Academy. The chapel, itself, rose out of the high ground in pristine white limestone crowned with a majestic, green and gold dome. Adorning the sides were five large stained-glass windows including one of Christ walking on the water. In a chamber underneath the altar was the crypt of John Paul Jones, father of the United States Navy. Hallowed ground.

"Great place to get married," David said.

"Yeah. Babe's mom and dad got hitched here. Saw their wedding album. After the ceremony, when you come out the door, there's an honor guard waiting with drawn swords. They make an arch for you to go under."

"Pretty neat."

Archie stared at the front steps for a moment trying to envision the future that lay ahead of him. But the scene was off his radar screen. The Honor Guard didn't materialize and the front doors remained closed.

"Anyway, you gotta book the place a year in advance," he said. "After graduation everyone wants to get married here. There's one ceremony every fifteen minutes."

"Like the Elvis Chapel in Vegas," David quipped.

Archie ignored him. "Who knows, maybe you'll be right behind me. Your chick looked pretty cool."

David smiled and his thoughts returned to the indigo-eyed brunette in the green truck who had rescued him on the road. It had been a truly remarkable day; a day of great discoveries, both of long lost tribal lands, and of a kindred soul. Maybe there was an arch of swords in their future, too.

Fried

Admiral Oliver Shaw leaned back behind a mahogany desk the size of an aircraft carrier and sized up his visitor. On the far side of his flag-filled office, the rigid form of David Waterfield stood on a thick blue carpet, frozen at attention. Two minutes elapsed in icy silence. David was barely breathing. It was the first time in memory that a plebe had ever been summoned to the Superintendent's office. He wondered if he were going to get booted out of the Academy for keeping Archie's secret.

"Normally, I don't get involved in these matters, Mr. Waterfield," Admiral Shaw said at last. "Like to leave discipline up to the Commandant. But under the circumstances, I thought I'd better see you myself."

Seen up close, the Superintendent was larger than life—the bravery of John Paul Jones and vision of Chester Nimitz rolled into one, with a dash of Jimmy Carter's honesty and Roger Staubach's leadership thrown in for good measure. At fifty years old, he appeared a decade younger, with steel-grey eyes, straw-colored hair, and chiseled features that could have come off Mount Rushmore.

"Haircut gave you away," the Admiral said.

"Excuse me, sir?"

"The buzz. Not too popular these days with civilians, is it?"

"No, sir."

"The new civvies were another sign. You still had a price tag stapled to your back pocket."

"Yes, sir." Rotten luck. Shaw had been at the Blackburn party, too.

"Guess you figured you'd be outside the twenty-two mile radius. You'll have to report to your platoon leader for discipline on that."

"Yes, sir." A vision of interminable marching came to mind. His feet were already swollen from all the walking he had done at Kings Oak.

"And you weren't supposed to ride in a car."

"I went over in a boat, sir."

The Superintendent just stared at him.

The Honor Concept kicked in. "But I came back in a truck, sir," David admitted.

"See your platoon leader about that, too."

Admiral Shaw rose to his feet. His six-foot-four frame ambled around to the front of his desk. Sitting down on the corner, he folded his arms and studied David further.

"And, finally, I'd be lying if I said I didn't recognize your name. You're the lacrosse whiz Coach Sleazak's been telling me about. The Native American kid who plays barefoot with a wooden stick. Am I right?"

"I have a wooden stick, yes sir."

"Coach says he's never seen a player like you in all his life. Says you've got the speed and the savvy. Every move in the book and the mettle to go with them. Predicts you'll be an All-American in your first year. That is, if you learn how to run in cleats and don't get booted out of the Academy before then."

"I didn't steal anything, sir. I never stole anything in my life."

The Admiral moved away from his desk and over to a wall-sized bookcase stocked with picture frames and athletic trophies.

"Look, son, I'll be square with you. Lacrosse is my game, too." He selected a picture off the shelf and held it up for David to see. "I was a midfielder, team of '75. Third from the left, second row. Just a plebe back then. Did pretty well though. Got to the finals of the National Championship. Lost to the Terps, 20-13. Thirty-one years ago and that old wound still hurts like it happened yesterday."

He paused for a moment of introspection. The picture of his old teammates led him to think about their years later as Navy Seals. In 1981, President Reagan dispatched their outfit into El Salvador to neutralize the death squads of the Farabundo Martí National Liberation Front. He and four of his buddies were patrolling a river the color and texture of liquefied ox shit when they were hit with a grenade. His four buddies were instantly blown apart, but his life was miraculously spared. Thrown overboard by the blast, he was taken prisoner by two machine-gun-toting guerillas. Their ragged uniforms couldn't disguise the fact that they were mere boys, not more than twelve years old. Before they could decide who would execute him, he kicked their guns out of their hands and cut their throats with a hunting knife he had hidden in his boot. That was El Salvador. Two boys, four buddies, and his innocence lost forever.

Filled with a sense of melancholy, Oliver Shaw refocused his attention on the situation at hand. "I always wanted us to have a second chance," he said, his words weighted with double meaning. "But life doesn't give you that. I always thought someone else would carry on and set things right but we've had a long drought since then. You may be our ticket back, Mr. Waterfield. Maybe we'll win the conference. Maybe even the National Championship. Believe me, son, I don't want to have to kick you out of here."

"Thank you, sir."

"But if I find out you've lied to me, that's a violation of the Brigade's Honor Concept. I'd have no choice."

"I've told you the truth, sir," David said. "I didn't take anything from them."

Oliver Shaw studied him further. "I believe you, son. Like to think I'm a pretty good judge of character."

The Admiral set the picture back on the shelf, put away his painful memories, and went back to his seat.

"At ease, Mr. Waterfield."

David forked his legs and folded his hands in the small of his back.

"Off the record, Septimus Blackburn is not what I'd really call a friend. He's more of a friend of a friend. That's why Mitzi and I were at the dinner in the first place. Our mutual friend being, Karl Darren. I'm sure you've heard of him. Karl's the Secretary of Defense. My boss's boss. Darren and Blackburn are pretty tight, so you might say officially I'm friends with him, too."

"Yes, sir."

"Bottom line is I think Blackburn was out of line with you. You may have crashed the party, but that's not a capital offense. And you may have broken junior's arm, but he got what was coming to him, you ask me."

"Yes, sir, he did."

"I don't pretend to understand the forces that drove you to Kings Oak in the first place, son, but I advise you to stay clear of those people and don't provoke them anymore. Blackburn is a very powerful man and well connected, too. Only last month, he took President Cannon fly fishing. Last winter they went duck hunting together. He does a ton of business with the Defense Department and that's why Secretary Darren likes him. If you cross him again and he finds out you're a midshipman, I may not be able to help. So do me a favor and keep away from him."

David held his tongue and fixed his eyes in a blank stare. It was a promise he couldn't make.

The Admiral waited impatiently for a reply and then realized the futility of his request.

"Very well, son. You may go now, but don't say I didn't warn you."

David Waterfield clicked his heels to attention, pivoted around, and disappeared out the door.

Styx

Everything was gray. Through the front of the bus, David could just barely make out the massive girders on the steel arch over the Francis Scott Key Bridge. Thirty-six stories high, the span was built on the spot where its namesake had watched the night bombardment of Fort McHenry during the War of 1812. Today the historic Fort was almost invisible, its star-like shape shrouded in a dense fog that had rolled in from the Chesapeake. A little further over the bridge, David realized it wasn't fog, it was smoke and it was coming from the north bank of the Patapsco where a sprawling steel mill sat shimmering in its own fumes like a desert mirage.

Once over the bridge, David got off at the first bus stop and immediately felt out of place. Dress blues and spit-shined shoes seemed inappropriate in the midst of an industrial wasteland that resembled a war zone. A pregnant woman, like a refugee with no where to flee, passed in front of him dragging a child with Downs syndrome behind her, casualties of the ignorance and inbreeding that permeated the place.

Following the railroad tracks, David made his way through acres of high weeds and stony rubble towards the smoke enshrouded mill at Herons Point. The closer he got, the more he could feel the temperature of the air rise on his face.

Like getting a suntan without the sun, he thought.

In a gully where the weeds were trampled flat, he came upon an abandoned campfire, several cardboard mats, and a scattering of tin cans—a sure sign that the homeless of the area knew where they could come to keep warm in the winter. As he continued through the murky gloom, David's senses were gradually assailed by the increasing rancor of heavy machinery, the foul odor of rotten eggs mixed with human waste, and the presence of air borne chemicals that made his eyes burn so much he felt like they were bleeding. Suddenly, a chain link fence materialized in front of him, the kind that had several rows of barbed wire strung across the top.

Beyond it, the full extent of Blackburn Steelworks emerged from the haze. Its size was overwhelming, stretching for miles along the waterfront in an unsightly conglomeration of smoking towers, blackened brick buildings, chemical vats, and large sheds that flashed flames through their open mouths. A trio of gigantic cranes swung through the sky, their jagged jaws eating away at mountains of coal, limestone, and iron ore. Their contents were dumped into large hoppers and carted up a conveyor belt to the top of a gargantuan blast furnace. From within its thick steel walls came a massive explosion that shook the twelve-story building like it was an Atlas rocket about to take off for the moon.

Undaunted, David followed the chain link fence over a rise and down across the edge of a crowded parking lot. Perpendicular to it was a gravel access road that paralleled the river and led to a security gate with a lowered barricade. David couldn't help but notice a row of remotely controlled metal spikes embedded underneath.

Sitting in the guardhouse next to the gate was an armed man in a face mask and goggles. As David approached, he slid back the window. His voice was muffled by his mask, but David understood the question.

"Just waiting for a friend," he explained.

Without a word, the window slapped shut and the barricade remained down. David made his way over to the river bank and peered down into the opaque waters of the Patapsco, coated over with the iridescent hues of an oil slick. Down the length of the waterline, he saw great pumps disgorging themselves into the river. Discolored by chemicals, it stank like a chemical stew. Dead fish floated by on their bellies, half-eaten eyes wide with wonder.

Like the river Styx, David thought. The river that ran through the circles of Hell. He recalled the description of Herons Point that the Founder had written in his journal. Back then, it had been described as a natural paradise, thick with fish and fowl and four-footed game. But now there were no fish to catch, no trees for the birds to perch in, and the four-footed game had been reduced to a single three-legged mutt that David had seen hobbling around near the garbage cans at the front gate. Paradise had turned into a wasteland. Herons Point had become a place of sorrow.

David noticed a half-dozen barges and a rundown container ship tied up at several long wharves that jutted out into the river. In stark contrast to them was a sleek white luxury yacht that was docked in a private slip next to a boxy brick building with a turreted roof. Parked next to the gangplank were an orange Ferrari and a black Cadillac stretch limousine.

Inside the yacht's dining salon, the three principals of Project Minerva and their dowdy wives had just finished a lavish Thanksgiving feast hosted by Septimus and his son. As they sat sipping coffee under a magnificent crystal chandelier, Filipino stewards in immaculate white jackets removed messy plates streaked with the remains of herb roasted turkey, cranberry-orange relish, Waldorf salad, candied yams, steamed broccoli, and pumpkin cheesecake. When the table was cleared, Septimus presented his guests with gift-wrapped souvenirs of their visit. The men received Zeiss Victory binoculars in leather cases emblazoned with their initials and the ship's logo. Their wives were given gold brooches in the shape of the Roman goddess, Minerva.

"She was the deity of Wisdom," Septimus informed the delighted ladies as he took his pipe and tobacco pouch out of his vest pocket.

"Most of us are," the wife of the Director of the CIA responded. "Isn't that right, dear?"

"Yes, Mildred," Christopher Harmon replied meekly, rolling his eyes under his darkly tinted glasses.

"Minerva was a very, very unusual woman," Septimus said, his voice taking on a dramatic tone. He let his guests hang for a few moments while he lit up his pipe and took a few puffs. "Legend has it that she wasn't born in the normal way. Seems Jupiter had a migraine and Vulcan cracked his head open with a hammer."

"Vulcan always had a delicate touch," Karl Darren joked.

"Out popped a full-grown Minerva," the host continued. "She was wearing a plumed helmet and body armor. Had a javelin in one hand and a shield in the other."

"Wonder if that's the cause of my headache," the Senator's wife asked as she massaged the deep creases in her brow.

"I'm pretty sure it's the three glasses of wine, Blanche," Randy Brookes teased. "No cause to worry. Just take a couple of aspirins tonight and get a Botox touchup tomorrow. You'll be back to normal."

Shortly afterwards, the dutiful husbands escorted their tipsy wives down the gangplank and helped them into the back seat of the black limousine. As the women were whisked away towards their suburban homes in nearby Virginia, the men returned to the boat for some unfinished business on Project Minerva. The General Accounting Office required them to conduct on-sight inspections both of the steel foundry and the Blackburn shipbuilding facility in Newport News, which was on the schedule for the next day.

Their host led them up the ladder towards the bridge. "This way, gentlemen," he said. "Don't forget to bring your binoculars."

Not wanting his three VIP's to soil the soles of their five-hundred dollar Italian shoes by actually setting foot inside the grimy workstations of the mill, or to offend their nostrils with the dreadful smell of the place, Septimus had cleverly devised a way to inspect the facility from the incomparable luxury of *Aria's* glass enclosed, climate-controlled bridge. Directing their binoculars to the open sheds that faced the water, he conducted a sanitized telephoto tour of his sweatshops, devoid of hard hats, earplugs, and Styrofoam face masks. His narrative was modulated by classical music and the entire presentation softened by an environment of plush furniture, priceless works of art, and an endless supply of alcohol.

"Hey!" Tavian yelled. With his right arm still idled in a sling, he held up the binoculars in his left hand and trained them on an approaching red SUV. "Looks like the entertainment has arrived."

Stopping in front of the gangplank, Captain Cy Van Aiken hopped out of the driver's seat and slid open the side cargo door. One by one, six pairs of long, lean, freshly-waxed legs emerged from under scandalously short mini-skirts. Tavian's contingent of high-priced party girls had arrived.

"I've got to hand it to you, Septimus," Karl Darren said, "in all my years in the Pentagon, this is the best on-site inspection I've ever been involved in."

The other men wholeheartedly agreed.

"Doesn't hurt to mix a little pleasure with business, gentlemen," Septimus said.

On the grounds of the mill, the shriek of a steam whistle signaled the end of another long day. Soon afterwards, workers in the day shift began to leave their work sheds and punch their time cards in the clock houses. Most walked with their eyes to the ground as if they were ashamed of the way Fate had forced them to make a living. There would be no holiday leave for them. Almost all of them would be back at work the next morning.

"There's your gal from the party," Randy Brookes told Tavian. It wasn't hard to pick out someone as attractive as Liz in the midst of the herd of dirty steelmen.

"That stupid bitch? I dumped her ass," Tavian said in his annoying lisp. Lying came as naturally to him as it did to his father.

Liz was wearing a raincoat and holding a handkerchief over her face. There was still a note of grace about her even at the end of a hard day's work. Coming through the gate, her eyes smiled at the sight of David pinching his nose.

"Got a clothes pin?" he asked in a nasal twang.

"Wish I did," she said through her handkerchief. She was just as beautiful as David remembered her—the long, dark brown hair; the indigo eyes; the same radiant glow to her skin.

"Place smells like an open sewer," David said.

"You're not far wrong." Liz went on to tell him about how the mill was cooled with cheap wastewater from the city of Baltimore.

"Isn't that kinda harmful?"

"Not according to the Department of Public Health. They gave Blackburn Steelworks a certificate of compliance—right after Septimus made a donation to one of the local politicians."

"That stinks even more."

"The smell isn't the worst part," Liz continued. "The sewage acts like fertilizer and causes algae to bloom on the surface of the water. When it dies and decomposes, oxygen is taken out of the Bay and aquatic life suffers. It's one of the main reasons for the dead zone in the middle of the Bay."

"I had no idea," David said.

"To be fair, there is plenty of blame to go around. Runoff from sewage treatment plants and heavy industry is a big problem, too. So is fertilizer from farms and irresponsible real estate development. Something needs to be done."

"Beginning with Blackburn Steel?" David asked.

"We gotta start somewhere," she said.

On the bridge of the *Aria*, the newly arrived party girls paired up with the VIPs they had first met at Kings Oak. The pint-sized

Karl Darren tried to impress his statuesque beauty by allowing her to look through his expensive Zeiss binoculars. While she was doing so, he took the opportunity to check out the amazing boobs that overflowed from her low-cut blouse.

"Hey look at that!" she said. "There's that guy who crashed the party at Kings Oak!"

"What are you talking about?" Darren snatched the binoculars away from her and focused them on the navy blue blood next to Liz.

"Jesus! It is him!"

The other binoculars panned around to take a look.

"It's that Indian kid!" Randy Brookes said. "And he's in a Navy uniform!"

Septimus was incredulous. "What the hell!"

Tavian's face flushed with anger and shame. Not only had David Waterfield broken his arm, but now the punk was with the one girl he hadn't conquered.

"Looks like she dumped you," Christopher Harmon chided.

"Get him the hell off my property!" Septimus screamed into the ship's intercom. His wrath was multiplied ten-fold by the stereo speakers on each deck. The crew of the *Aria* flew around in utter confusion.

Unaware of the turmoil he had caused, David followed Liz into the parking lot.

"Remember, I promised you Thanksgiving dinner," he said. "There a good restaurant around here?

"Know just the place."

"Five star?"

"Actually, it's unrated. But don't worry, you'll get a square meal. I promise."

David smiled. Her comment reminded him of the "square" meals he was forced to eat during Plebe Summer. He could visualize Sasser sitting at the head of the table barking out four-count cadences to the squad. On "one," the fork speared the food; on "two," it lifted it straight up; on "three," it thrust it into the mouth; and on "four," it dropped down to the plate again to complete the outline of a perfect square. It was good for discipline perhaps, but decidedly bad for the digestion.

At the far end of the lot, they came to her Toyota Tundra. David remembered it as being forest green, but a layer of soot had turned it into charcoal gray and rendered the windshield opaque.

Liz unlocked the door, started the engine, squirted some cleaning fluid on the windshield, and waited patiently for the wiper blades to do their work.

"You do a lot of off-road driving?" David asked.

"Yeah. I like to get off the beaten path and do some exploring. Never got enough Nature when I was growing up, I guess."

"You can never get enough of that," David said.

Liz nodded. "Truck's great, but it's kinda expensive to run."

"Yeah. Gas is sky high now."

"No. Wiper fluid. I go through a couple of gallons a week. Otherwise, I'd have it paid off by now."

David found her sense of humor attractive. Liz liked to laugh and didn't take herself too seriously.

On the way out of the parking lot, she fell in behind six lumbering black giants, their feet encased in heavy steel-toed boondockers.

"Those guys are friends of mine," Liz told David. "Work in the Blast Furnace. Always hang out together."

She slowed down as she drove up next to them, rolling down the window. Their eyes were red, their skin peeling and blistered, and their clothes drenched in sweat.

"Hey, LeGrande!" she said. "You guys headed where I think you're headed?"

"Half of us is, and half of us ain't, Sister Mancini." The Keeper's long, white-singed hair looked like a cross between a skunk and a porcupine.

"Some of us gotta work the graveyard shift," the three-hundred-and-fifty pound Mandala said. "Gotta get our beauty sleep."

"While the rest of us gone get loaded," the slightly built Qwazi added.

"Well, this is my midshipman friend, David Waterfield, and we're gonna get a bite to eat. Hop in back and I'll drop half of you at home and the other half can come with us. I assume you know who's who."

"By the time you get there," LeGrande said, "we'll have it all figured out."

With that, a ton-and-a half of blackened beef jumped in back, dropping the Tundra's suspension down to the top of its treads. Even with the added weight, the truck still moved, although just barely. Creeping slowly over the railroad tracks, Liz made a hard right down a narrow asphalt slab that led into the old mill town behind the Blast Furnace. The road was named Maple Avenue but there wasn't a stick of wood growing anywhere in sight. Shabby clapboard row houses lined the street. Each had its own dirt patch in front that was supposed to be a yard. A layer of black soot covered everything—even the laundry on the clotheslines.

"Mine's the brick mansion in the middle of the next block," Kenyatta yelled out. "The one with the helipad out front." Humor was his way of coping with an ugly reality. He was the Don Quixote of the steel mill.

Liz eased to a stop and Kenyatta, Mandala, and J'Rod hopped out. After thanking her for the lift, they hurried off in different directions. A four-year-old in an Orioles baseball cap toddled out of the imaginary mansion with the helipad to greet Kenyatta. His father picked him up and swung him around, eliciting a squeal of happiness from the boy. Turning to Liz, he grabbed his child's left hand and helped him wave. The other arm was deformed.

Liz returned the wave and continued down the road. "The way Kenny talked about his son, you would have thought the boy was ready for the major leagues."

"Must be the mill," David said. "I saw a child with Downs syndrome on the way in."

"Birth defects are a by-product here," Liz said. "That and lung cancer."

When she came to a corner row house at the end of Maple, Liz slowed down. A warm, amber glow bled through the cheap, lace curtains.

"My family used to live there. When I was five, I saw a strange man coming up the walk. Caked in grime from head to toe. I ran inside and cried to my mother about the strange man following me. It was my father, of course, and I hadn't recognized him. Then one day he didn't come home at all. Black lung disease had taken his last breath. I knew then that it wasn't steel the mill was making. It was death. That's when

I decided I wanted to be a lawyer and put people like the Blackburns out of business."

David covered her hand with his. Comforted, she drove on in silence, burying her memories as best she could. Crossing back over the railroad tracks, she drove out onto the open highway, taking the first exit into the seedy side of Dundalk. She found a parking place in front of a second-hand sports store with a pyramid of used bowling balls stacked in the window. LeGrande, Qwazi, and Tsonka piled out and jaywalked across the street towards the neighborhood bar. A narrow building with a fake-brick facade, it was squeezed in between a pool hall and pawn shop. It was aptly named "The Pig Iron Pub."

"Pretty fancy place," David joked.

"The inside is pretty classy, too," Liz said.

As they opened the door, they were enveloped in a cloud of second-hand cigarette smoke. A flickering neon light above the bar illuminated a linoleum floor sticky with dried beer and littered with a carpet of peanut shells. The place was already beginning to fill up with weary steelmen and stevedores intent on turning a hard week into a dim and distant memory. Bull Wolinski had already beaten them to the bar. Sitting hunched over a drink, his fat cheeks spread out over the stool like a toxic mushroom. Oblivious to their presence, he farted as they passed behind him.

"Most sensible thing I heard him say all day," Liz said.

"He's making sense all right," Tsonka joked. "What my nose says."

The others laughed and hurried to safety.

They all sat together in a family-sized wooden booth in the no-smoking area in back. The waitress, a sixty-five year-old woman in a curly, brown wig came over to wipe the grease off the Formica-topped table.

"Hey Gladys," Liz said. "How's Jacob doing?"

"The hospice said he could come home next week," she said in a sweet, innocent voice that sounded like it belonged to a ten-year-old girl. "Not much more they can do for him, I guess. Just keep him out of pain."

"Sorry to hear that."

"Talked to him about what you told me. Said he wanted to help you out with that ...uh...disposition."

"Deposition," Liz corrected. Jacob had contracted lung cancer as a result of living too near the mill. His testimony would help her class-action case against the Blackburns.

"Whatever. Next Saturday morning would be a good time. Around ten if that's alright with you."

"That's fine, Gladys. You won't be sorry. We'll make them pay. I promise."

"Yeah, well..." Her voice trailed off for a moment and when it came back she was her regular upbeat self. "You folks ready to order yet?"

Everyone looked down at the menus.

"What do you recommend," David asked Liz.

"Not the chicken, that's for sure," she said. "Chances are pretty good it comes from the Blackburn Poultry Farms on the Pocomoke River. Been a lot of fish kills there recently. Pfiesteria."

"Fisss...what?" David asked.

"Pfiesteria. It's caused by chicken waste that runs off into the river. Fish are infected with lesions and die. They're not sure about the effect on humans who eat the fish, but I'm playing it safe. Besides, I've heard the chickens are treated inhumanely. Small cages, forced moulting, debeaking—that sort of thing. They kill them by throwing them against a wall. No choice but to boycott them."

"If the fish ain't from the Pocomoke, is it okay to eat?" Qwazi asked.

"Probably. As long as it doesn't come from the Potomac."

"What's the matter there?"

"Smallmouth bass for starters. Males have been found recently with eggs growing inside their sex organs. Scientists think it's caused by some kind of chemical pollution in the river that interferes with their natural hormones."

"I'm gonna scratch that one from my list," LeGrande said. "Don't want no eggs messing around with my bubba."

"Mine neither" Qwazi added.

"What about the beef?" Tsonka asked.

"I boycott that too. Septimus owns thousands of head of cattle up on the Susquehanna. Every one of them poops about a hundred pounds of manure a day and he doesn't do a thing to help prevent it from running off into the river and Bay."

"Disgraceful," LeGrande said. "Them cows ought to be diapered."

"That would be a start. Their waste causes excessive algae blooms and is largely responsible for the dead zone in the middle of the bay."

"That's it. I'm never gonna have any more of that beef shit," Qwazi said.

"Is there anything on the menu you will eat?" David asked Liz.

"Soft-shell crab sandwich looks good. I don't know if they've got mercury or lead in them or not, but they taste so good I'm willing to take a chance."

Following Liz's lead, David signed up for a soft-shell crab sandwich and ice tea. Playing it safe, the three steelmen each ordered a pitcher of beer and a couple of sides of potato skins, nachos, and cheese fries. Gladys hurried off into the kitchen like a stockbroker anxious to place an important order. While they were waiting, Liz filled LeGrande and his friends in on David's run-in with the Blackburns.

"That explains it," Qwazi said. "I saw the boy zoom up in his fancy orange rocket car this afternoon. Saw his right arm in a sling. Sorta limped up the gangplank to that big white boat. Guess he got what was coming to him all right."

"Way to go, bro." LeGrande slapped David on the back. "I've been thinking one of these days I'm gonna tow that car of his into the Melt Shop and put it back in his parking place as a block of metal."

"He's so stupid, he'd probably call Triple A," Liz said.

When the laughter died down, the conversation turned serious. Liz told them about David's background and his search for the stolen land of his ancestors.

"Most of us got Indian blood, too," LeGrande told David. "Mixed in with our black blood."

"Like cherry juice mixed in oil." Tsonka added. His black skin had a distinct reddish tone to it. "What it does, makes our blood come to a boil slower, how come we can work so close to the fire and keep our cool."

"What you mean cool, man? You sweat like a open sewer," Qwazi said.

"What tribe do you guys belong to?" David asked.

"Hell, our people have intermarried so many times, we done forgot our roots," LeGrande said.

"Speak for yourself, man," Qwazi said. "I got me a little English cream mixed in with my cherry juice and oil. Thinking about having my gynecology traced back. Feel sure I must be related to the Queen."

"You mean genealogy," Liz said, barely able to suppress a smile.

"Yeah. Genealogy. What I mean."

"Could be true you related," Tsonka said. "Queen like to wear diamonds, too." They were always teasing him about the ear stud he wore. Like he was a rock star or a basketball legend.

Gladys brought out their order, carefully balanced on a big, round tray and plopped their plates down in front of them. David was a little taken aback by the appearance of his sandwich: a pair of mushy claws and back fins sticking out the corners of a Kaiser roll. Inside was the fried carcass of a recently molted blue crab, internal organs intact, resting peacefully on a bed of lettuce and a slice of tomato. But the look of the thing didn't stop him from chomping into it.

"What do you think?" Liz asked.

"Tastes great," David said. "Kinda sweet and crunchy."

"Doesn't freak you out?"

"Naw. I've eaten stranger things at home. My mother liked to serve deep-fried scorpion steaks and tarantula kebabs on special occasions."

"Nothing like home cooking," Qwazi said with a straight face.

During dinner, the conversation turned to David's life at the Naval Academy. None of the Blast Furnace boys had even finished elementary school and were greatly impressed by David's drive to excel. They were especially curious about his participation in the sport of lacrosse, which they had heard about but not actually seen.

"How could you beat someone on the head with a stick and not get arrested?" Tsonka asked. "What I want to know."

David laughed. "I'll have to show you. This spring I'll get you some free passes. You can come down and see for yourselves."

They looked at him like he had just asked them to travel to the moon. None of them had ever been ten miles from Milltown before.

"It's all right guys," Liz said. "I'll drive you down and make sure you get home safely."

"You say so, Miss Mancini," LeGrande said. "All right with us."

The others agreed. It would do them good to see what the rest of the world was like.

Liz's wristwatch alarm went off. "Hate to eat and run, guys, but I've got a ton of reading to catch up on."

"You keep working hard on those law books, Miss Mancini," LeGrande said. "Someday you gonna help us get a better shake at the mill."

"I'm gonna try my best, Lee."

"Just don't go shutting her down all the way," Tsonka added.

"We need the work, Miss Mancini," Qwazi said. "Alls we know how to do."

"I know, guys. Don't worry. I just want Blackburn Steelworks to care as much about the community and its employees as it does about its own bottom line. That's all."

David got up and let her slide out of the booth. He was sorry the evening had come to an end so soon. But he admired Liz's industry and independence.

"Okay, if I go with you? I can catch a bus from downtown."

"Glad to have the company. We'd better hurry."

David snatched the bill from Gladys and paid for everyone.

"Thanks, man," LeGrande said on behalf of his crew. "We owe you."

David waved them off and followed Liz out of the place.

Outside it was as dark as a World War II blackout. Vandals had broken the streetlights and most of the stores had closed early for lack of costumers. The only traffic now was from occasional rats that darted to and from overturned garbage cans and gutter openings. David followed Liz across the street to her truck. As she was unlocking it, three Filipino thugs in black jumpsuits rushed out of a dark alley swinging baseball bats. The first blow struck David on the back, breaking a rib. As he turned to defend himself, a second one fractured his kneecap. David's mouth dropped open, too shocked to utter a sound.

Liz screamed. A bat just missed her head and shattered her side window. Another blow put a big dent in her hood.

Inside the bar, the Keeper and his crew were roused by the ruckus.

"That Miss Mancini's voice," Legrande said.

"She need help!" Qwazi shouted.

The steelmen arose in a body and stormed through the bar.

Everyone fell in behind, with the exception of Bull Wolinski who was passed out in a puddle. But help didn't come soon enough for David Waterfield. He fended off several blows with his forearms before one glanced off the side of his head, knocking him unconscious. The attackers were poised to finish him off when the steelmen burst out onto the street.

One took a swipe at LeGrande causing him to fall back through the plate glass window of the sporting goods store. A second smacked Tsonka on the shoulder, cracking his collarbone.

"Base hit!" the goon yelled.

Liz rushed at the batter. Before she could get to him, Qwazi grabbed her around the waist, threw her inside the truck, and slammed the door shut.

"Stay put, Miss Mancini," he yelled. "We take care of things now."

Cut and bleeding, LeGrande climbed back out the broken window with a sixteen-pound Global Assault bowling ball in his hand.

"Hit this muthafucka!" he roared, shot-putting the ball at his attacker. The thug in the black jumpsuit caught it in his chest and fell over backwards.

Qwazi picked up his bat and turned it on the other two with a fury, swinging it at them like it was a laser-edged light sabre. LeGrande reloaded with a bowling ball in each hand. The thugs got the message and fled down the alley, a Fat Man and Shock Zone Pro thundering down after them.

Liz hurried to David's side. His body was broken and his blood streamed into the gutter. His open eyes stared blankly into the black sky. She was sure that he was dead.

Last Rites

Kneeling in the front pew of the hospital chapel, Liz lowered her head and began to sob uncontrollably. For most of her adult life she had been a lapsed Catholic who rarely set foot inside a church. But now she prayed like never before. She hardly knew David Waterfield. They had met on only two occasions. And yet she had been drawn to his person and the rightness of his cause. Deep down inside, she realized that her admiration for him had begun to turn to love, both for the purity of his soul and the integrity of his quest. And now this terrible tragedy had happened. She felt responsible for having drawn him into danger.

The door opened and a shaft of light crossed the figure of the crucified god above the altar. "They did all they could for him, girl," a husky voice announced. Standing in the doorway was a stocky black nurse with an elaborate cornrow that resembled an alien crop circle. Tinted maroon, it matched the tattoos on her forearms, a by-product of her previous life as a street-ball star on the asphalt courts and chain-link hoops of the inner city.

"I Shakela," she announced proudly. "Dr. Zegusa will see you now."

With great trepidation, Liz followed her to the Trauma Resuscitation Unit on the second floor of the University of Maryland Hospital. The double doors opened and David was wheeled in on a gurney. Still unconscious, his face was bruised black and purple and his eyes were swollen shut. A bandage was wrapped around his brow and both his right arm and left leg were in plaster casts. He was hooked up to a ventilator to help him breathe.

Dr. Zegusa came in a few moments later. He was a mid-sixties gentleman with a face that had been pulled tight with plastic surgery in a vain attempt to regain his youth. His farsightedness had been corrected by laser surgery, and his graying hair had been dyed a lustrous shade of brown. Far from comic, his macabre appearance was almost Faustian.

"Your friend is in critical condition, I'm sorry to say," he told Liz. "Suffered a serious concussion, three cracked ribs, shattered left knee, broken left leg, and multiple bruises, abrasions, and contusions. He had internal bleeding as well."

Liz was almost afraid to ask. "Do you think he'll make it?"

"Depends on his will to live. The next 24 hours are crucial."

"Would it be all right if I stayed with him? He doesn't have any relatives in the area."

The old man with the young face nodded. His patient would need all the help he could get to pull through. In David's case, even a deal with Mephistopheles might not be sufficient.

Two inner-city orderlies decked out in doo rags, baggy green scrubs, and Nike sneakers carefully transferred the patient to a hospital bed. Shakela attached electrodes wired to a life support system and hooked David up to a rack of plastic bags and tubes. Then she ripped the wrapper off a syringe, wadded it up, and tossed it in the wastebasket on the other side of the bed.

"That be a three if I ever saw one," she said, disinfecting a spot on David's arm with a cotton ball.

"Your feet on the line," one of the orderlies countered. "That only a two."

Shakela filled up the syringe and gave David a shot in the arm, then walked away wagging her finger at the two orderlies. "It a three and you bad boys know it."

As she left the T.R.U., a striking, light-skinned, black lady strode in like a high-fashion model on a runway. Her face was elegantly sculptured and cover girl beautiful without benefit of an ounce of makeup. Only a smattering of grey in her short, woolly hair gave a hint that she was, perhaps, a bit older than she looked. She wore a pair of red high-heels that clicked smartly across the tile floor accompanied by the tinkling of long, dangling earrings that looked like miniature wind chimes. Only her white lab coat and the stethoscope around her neck revealed her true calling. A name tag on her lapel identified her as Dr. Louisa Lumamba, the maiden name she was too proud to relinquish when she married Raymond Moses thirty years earlier.

"I came in tonight to deliver some C-sections and saw your truck parked outside the ER," she said as she hugged Liz. "I was afraid you'd been in a wreck. Told me downstairs it was your friend that got beat up bad."

"It was awful, Lou. I can't even talk about it."

"You gotta believe he's gonna be okay. You brought him to the right place and Zegusa is the best in Baltimore. Andre will have him up and kicking in no time."

Liz nodded and managed a weak smile.

"Is there anything I can do to help you, hon?'

"Tell Doc what happened. I'm staying here with David until he gets better."

"Your young man is more than just a friend, isn't he?" Louisa asked.

"Maybe."

"Well you just stay out of class as long as you need to, hon. I know Ray will cut you a lot of slack. I'm sure you guessed by now that you're his favorite student."

"Thanks."

Louisa glanced up at the clock on the wall. "Time for me to go deliver a set of twins. I'll be praying for you both. Remember—you need anything, anything at all, just call." And with that she hurried off to welcome her new arrivals into the world.

Alone with David at last, Liz pulled a chair over and sat by his side. She held his hand gently and watched over him for hours, hoping for some subtle sign of recovery. But he remained as still as a corpse, animated only by the rhythm of his automated breathing machine. It was during this time that she noticed the mysterious lines of dotted scars across the top of his lids. *A tribal thing,* she thought. There was so much she didn't know about him, so much she wanted to learn.

By midnight, she had fallen into an exhausted slumber when David Waterfield suddenly arose and pulled off his ventilator mask. One by one, he removed his bandages, stripped the electrodes from his chest, cut off his cast, and pulled out the plastic tubes that were his lifeline. Battered and bloody, he left his bed and walked naked into the woods toward the funeral pyre by the river's edge. His mother waited with a flaming torch that would return his ashes to the earth and send his water spirit high into the sky where it would fall back into the Great Sea of Ancestors. He lay down upon the kindling wood, crossed his bruised and broken arms over his chest, and closed his swollen eyes for the final time.

From a chasm deep inside the earth, the trembling voice of Grandfather Two Tongues arose and began to chant his grandson's secret name. And one by one, the ancestors emerged from the sea to join his song. Great Standing Bear was the first to arise, his mighty war club resting on his shoulder. In his giant footsteps followed brave Burning Bow and Spotted Elk. Then came the hero, Horses Head, ascending from the water on the back of a wild pinto with Medicine Dancer sitting on the rump behind him. And after them, High Cloud Walking and Eagle Nose led their people down from the sky in a stream of canoes. And from frozen lakes and ponds and underground rivers burst forth the other ancient ones— Three Legged Coyote, Black Moon Rising, and Fire-in-the Sky. In a swelling chorus, they encircled the funeral pyre and filled the heart and soul of the dying man with the seven sacred syllables of his secret Choptank name. Now was not the time for him to join them in the earth and sky and sea. The sacred mission of his secret name remained unfulfilled. And so Shadow Woman turned away from her only son, turned away from the funeral pyre and threw the flaming torch like a tomahawk into the mouth of the river. The moon went out and the world turned black.

Slowly the sight seeped back into David's swollen eyes and the radiant face of Liz Mancini melted into focus above him.

He had no way of knowing that he'd been in a coma for three days. Her soft and caring fingers touched his cheek and he managed to send back a subtle smile. Their eyes welled up in tears and at that moment, they both knew how much they meant to each other.

When Dr. Zegusa came in to examine his patient again, he was very positive about his prognosis. "Got a strong will, this guy," he told Liz. "Gonna be just fine."

Liz didn't know how or why, but she was sure she had just witnessed a miracle.

G.M.O. CALLAGHAN

Dying Wishes

River View Terrace was a low-rise apartment complex located at a noisy nexus of railroad tracks and highways that converged together at the southern edge of Dundalk. Built back in the sixties, it was a garden-style structure with a blonde-brick facade and tiny balconies enclosed in chain link. Over the intervening years, regular deposits of soot from the mill across the river had discolored the brick into a sickly shade of gray. The landscaping around the entrance had been poisoned so often that the management company had decided it was cheaper to substitute impervious plastic plants instead. In an effort to brighten the place with some Christmas cheer, a string of colored light bulbs had been placed on the shrubs and were blinking on and off like a neon sign in front of a cheap motel.

At 10 a.m., Liz pulled her battered green Tundra into a vacant space in front of the building and left her motor running to stay warm. The morning had arrived with a bone-numbing chill and snow flurries were expected later that afternoon. She sat on her hands for a few moments until a shiny Harley Davidson Fatboy roared up next to her. The rider, a big man in a black leather outfit dotted with silver studs, dismounted and stomped the kickstand down. Turning towards her, he took off his helmet and quickly slapped an Ivy League cap over his bald pate.

"It's a bit cool for a cycle, don't you think, Doc," Liz said as she got out of her truck, rubbing her hands together. She was enveloped in a thick, down-filled parka and hood.

"Not so," Professor Moses said. "Hog's got a heated seat that works pretty good. Lou gave it to me for my birthday last month. Makes me feel forty years younger."

"Just don't go trying any wheelies on that thing, Doc. Don't want you to have an accident, too."

"Speaking of that, Lou told me what happened to your friend. How's he doing?"

"Dave is getting better. His spirits are strong. Thanks for asking."

"Sure hope they find those thugs."

"Yeah, me too."

A backfiring tailpipe trumpeted the arrival of a black minivan. Behind the wheel was a familiar balding, potbellied man with a toothpick wiggling in his teeth and a Ravens Super Bowl cap on his head, catcher style.

"It's your buddy, Max," Liz said. "Punctual as usual."

Bundled up in a Navy peacoat, the driver got out with bags under his eyes and a cup of coffee frozen to his right hand.

"Jeezus. Any colder and I'd be farting snow cones," he said amiably, spitting out his toothpick. He used his free hand to tip his hat to Liz, then high-fived the professor.

"Cool bike, Ray."

"From the wife. Just breaking it in."

"Figured you for more of a Segway kind of guy. You know those scooters with the big wheels you ride standing up on. Safer at your age."

"Thanks."

"How'd it go last night, Max?" Liz asked.

"Pretty much like it has since we started. Got it all down on tape."

"T-Bone bother you any?"

"Naw. Just walked by me like he was a blind man with a seeing-eye Rottweiler."

Liz smiled. Manny Mandala had come along at the right time. He had made everything so easy.

Max clinched the rim of the Styrofoam cup between his teeth, popped opened his hatch, and began to get out his video gear.

"Guess it's time to boogie again," he said.

Liz turned to Raymond. "We've been documenting the mill for a month now, Doc. Think that's good enough?"

The professor nodded. "I would think it would be more than sufficient to show the court that the mill is routinely exceeding its emissions quotas. That and the depositions we'll be getting today should build a pretty solid case against them. Who's first on the list?"

"Guy's name is Jacob Danzig. He and his wife Gladys live up on the third floor. I know her from the Pig Iron Pub. Jacob hauls concrete block, or at least used to. Anyway, he and Gladys have lived here for the last thirty-five years. Neither of them ever smoked a day in their lives and now Jacob's a ninety-eight pound skeleton wasting away from lung cancer."

"Can't say I'm surprised," Doc said. "Steel mill's upwind across the river."

Max slammed his hatch shut. Stacked in front of him was a fluid head tripod, hammered-metal camera case, lighting kit, ditty bag, battery box, and a coil of extension cords. Seventy-five pounds in all.

"Tell me there's an elevator, Miss Mancini," he said.

"Afraid not, Max. Don't think they were invented when this place was built."

"Let me help you with some of that stuff," Raymond said, bending down and hoisting the tripod over his shoulder.

"Me, too," Liz said. She picked up the battery box and a coil of extension cords.

"Okay, but watch your step," Max warned. "Looks like its been raining birds here. Got carcasses all over the place."

Liz started to nudge them aside with her boots. "Always are, Max. Gladys says they keep the groundskeeper busy. Bags them up and gives them to the Public Health folks. Guess he hasn't gotten around to them this morning."

"It's kinda eerie," Raymond said, following in their footsteps. "Like we're in an Alfred Hitchcock movie."

"Yeah, it's like we're doing a remake of *Birds,*" Liz said. "I'm playing the Tippi Hedrin character."

"And I'm Rod Taylor," Max said. "Who are you, Doc?"

"Guess I must be Hitchcock," Raymond said. "Can't remember, did I have a cameo in that movie?"

"Yeah," Max said, "you were one of the birds. There were about a million of them."

"A bird extra. Just my luck," Raymond lamented.

Stepping over a squished carcass, he followed Liz and Max up three flights of stairs to the Danzig's apartment. At the top of the landing, they put down their loads and Liz tapped politely on the dingy, dung-colored door. The peephole went dark followed by the sound of an unlatching deadbolt. Gradually, the door cracked opened until it was restrained by a security chain. Gladys' face appeared in the narrow slit. Without the wig she wore at work, her hair was short and grey. Red rings around her eyes indicated she had been crying.

"Morning, Gladys," Liz said, trying her best to be pleasant.

"Miss Mancini," Gladys answered in her little girl's voice. "I tried to call you."

"Is this not a good time?" Liz asked.

Gladys shook her head. "Jacob, he changed his mind. Says he's not gonna help you."

"What's wrong?"

Gladys dabbed her eyes with a tissue. "That gang that attacked your friend—bartender at the Pub says they were off the Blackburn boat. Seen 'em at the bar a couple of time. Once, they got so drunk he had to send them back in a cab. Jacob don't want to go up against the Blackburns. Afraid they'll get me after he's gone."

Raymond broke in. "With the settlement you'll win, Mrs. Danzig, you could move away from here. No way they could hurt you."

"You the lawyer?"

"Yes, ma'am."

"Get him the hell outta here," a frail voice screamed from the back bedroom. "Asshole just wants his cut."

"This is *pro bono*, Mrs. Danzig. I'm not getting a fee."

Sounds of coughing and hacking came from the back room.

"I'm sorry," Gladys said. "Maybe you can get someone else."

The door clicked closed and the deadbolt slid shut.

Dejected, they picked up their loads and headed back down to the parking lot.

They got a similar story from two other victims who lived in the same neighborhood. No one was willing to testify against the mill after what happened to David Waterfield.

"Three strikes and we're out," Liz lamented. "So much for my class action suit."

"You tried your best," Raymond said, trying to hide his deep disappointment from his favorite pupil. I'm giving you an A-plus on your project anyway. Best you can do now is to alert the EPA. Send them the video tapes and let them handle it from here on."

"A token fine?"

"Better than nothing."

Liz sighed. "I'm not through with them yet, Doc. There's got to be another way."

And there would be. Raymond Moses would see to that.

Lady in the Leaves

Dr. Zegusa cracked as wide a smile as his tight-skinned face would permit. "You're healing well, Mr. Waterfield. If all goes according to plan, you could be released by Christmas. With a cast and crutches, of course."

"Wonderful," Liz said. "We can't thank you enough."

"What about lacrosse?" David asked. "Will I be able to play this spring?'

Zegusa shook his head. "Sorry, son. Even I can't perform a miracle. I'm afraid you'll have to wait until next year."

In the silence that ensued, the doctor filled out his chart and left without another word. David could hardly mask his disappointment.

Liz sat down in the chair next to him. "Got to look on the bright side, Dave. The attack could have been a lot worse."

"I know. I'm lucky to be alive."

"Cheer up. Got some good news for you."

"Just seeing you cheers me up."

Liz felt herself blush. "On my way over here, Phyllis called me on my cell phone."

"Who's Phyllis?"

"You remember. I told you about her when I gave you a ride back from the shore."

"Your librarian friend who works in the Maryland State Archives?"

"So you were listening."

"To you. Always."

"Anyway, I asked Phyllis to research the Blackburn documents that might be on file there. She searched the Rare Manuscripts Room and found the original charter from Lord Baltimore and a map of the Chesapeake with Lord Blackburn's handprint in the center. But she hasn't been able to find evidence of any treaties he made with the Choptanks."

"Guess I'm not surprised."

"In fact there's very little information in the Archives on the Choptanks at all," Liz continued. "Phyllis found a census from 1727 that showed there were approximately 37 left in the state by then. She says that those who survived took refuge with other tribes, black slaves, and poor white sharecroppers. Almost all of them eventually took English names. Today, those who claim to have a little Choptank blood in them have no knowledge of their lost heritage or their ancient language. She doesn't think they would be any help to you."

"This news is supposed to cheer me up?"

"Be patient. I'm not finished. Phyllis had a great idea on how you might get your parchment translated. Said there's a guy at the American Anthropological Society in Washington who specializes in American Indian Cultures. He's supposed to be an expert in native languages. If you want, I'll call him and set up an appointment for us sometime between Christmas and New Years. You'll be out of here and on leave by then."

"Excellent idea. I'd appreciate that. Thanks."

"Think nothing of it. Like I told you before, any enemy of the Blackburns is a friend of mine. Especially now that my class project has blown up."

"Sorry about that," David said.

"It's okay. I'm never going to give up trying. I'm never going to let them beat me."

"Good," David said. He shut his eyes for a moment and once more Liz saw the mysterious dotted scars lining his lids.

"Do you mind if I ask you something personal?"

"Shoot."

"It's about your eyelids. The dots. You don't have to tell me if you don't want to."

"It's okay. It was a custom passed down by my ancestors. They were warriors who always slept with their eyes wide open. You know, ready to react to any sudden movements or threatening sounds. When I was just a boy, my grandfather trained me in the practice by piercing my eyelids with a needle and thread and tying them open before I went to sleep."

"What a horrible thing to do."

"Didn't hurt much at all. About what a woman would feel when her ears are pierced."

"Or her nose or tongue," Liz said.

"Whatever. Anyway, I grew up with great night vision. Only thing is, sometimes I can't tell if I'm really seeing something or if I'm just dreaming."

"That's really interesting, Dave. Thanks for sharing that with me."

David paused for a moment. "There's something else you should know."

"What's that?" She was hoping that he would say he really liked her, or better yet, that he was falling in love with her.

"David is not my real name."

"Not your real name?"

"Neither is Waterfield."

"What are you telling me? Are you a spy or something?"

"Nothing like that. My people believe that names are sacred. They embody your real identity. If someone knows your name, then they have power over you. So our names are kept secret in our families."

"Doesn't that make communication with the outside world rather difficult?"

"We are given a second name for that. One that we earn by our actions. My grandfather was known as Two Tongues because he could speak Choptank as well as a little bit of English. My mother is Shadow Woman because she is still in mourning for my dead father and my sisters are Jumping Bug and Winking Star..."

"Don't tell me. I can just picture them," Liz said. "All energy and excitement."

"Yes."

"How did you come to be named David Waterfield then? It doesn't sound like the others."

"After I was born, my mother said a man from the Bureau of Indian Affairs came to our hut to make a record of my birth. Grandfather chased him out of our house with a stick, cursing at him in Choptank. The agent figured that was my name and wrote down what it sounded like in English."

"David Waterfield. Good choice."

"Guess it kind of stuck with me."

Shakela rushed into the room to take David's temperature and blood pressure. As she was bending over him, Liz got a good look at the intricate pattern in her maroon colored cornrows. She was amazed. It looked as if it had taken a week to weave it.

"I really like your hairdo, Shakela," Liz said.

The big black nurse looked at her and beamed. "Same one Netambo got. Plays for the City Rats in the Summer Neighborhood League. First time he wore it, dude scored 42 points."

"Very impressive," David said.

"You want to see impressive, check out this needle." She held it up in front of his face. "Don't worry none. Won't hurt more than just a little."

David looked away as she stuck him in his arm.

"Check on you later," Shakela said as she was leaving. "See if you still alive."

When she was gone, Liz turned to David and laughed. "Girl really loves her basketball."

"Just realized that's probably how she got her name," David said. "Shakela is the female version of Shaq. You know, the big star used to play with the Lakers. Now he's with the Miami Heat."

"Maybe so," Liz allowed. "Speaking of names, are you ever going to tell me your real one?"

David shook his head. "I can't. It would violate my oath. Besides it's seven syllables long and very hard to pronounce. Like a tongue twister. Even my little sisters have trouble with it."

"Can you give me a hint about what it means?"

"Well, I'm not named after anything that I did or anything that happened to me."

"What does that leave?"

"The Future. Grandfather told me my name is a prophecy of things to come."

"A prophecy! My goodness! Why did he think that?"

"He was a wisoe. What you would call a wise man or medicine man. He told me my name is like a wish that you hold deep in your heart. If you say it out loud it won't come true."

"I see." She looked away from him.

"What's the matter? Have I disappointed you?"

Liz shook her head. "No, no. I'm happy that you've confided in me. It's just...there will always be part of you that I will never know."

"Don't worry, you'll know my name sooner or later. You'll know it because of my actions. That will explain who I am. Or rather who my Grandfather wanted me to be."

Suddenly, there was a rap on the door. They looked up to see a hulk in a heavy, blue overcoat standing in the hallway.

"Admiral Shaw!"

The Superintendent strode into the room with his hat under his arm and a dutiful aide trotting behind him.

"Came over as soon as I heard you could have visitors, Mr. Waterfield. Brought you a get-well present."

The aide set a heavy cardboard box down on the tray table next to the bed. On top was a thick Calculus textbook. Turning smartly, the young Ensign quickly retreated out the door.

"Thought you might enjoy a little light reading during your convalescence," Admiral Shaw said.

"Thank you, sir."

After an awkward pause, David nodded at Liz. "This is my friend, Liz Mancini, sir."

She offered her hand and the Superintendent squeezed it gently.

"A pleasure, ma'am," the Admiral said gallantly.

"Liz works at the mill, sir. She was with me when I was attacked. Helped saved my life, in fact."

Oliver Shaw shook his head. "We're all in your debt, then, Miss Mancini."

Liz nodded. "Won't you have a seat, sir?"

"No thanks, ma'am. I can't stay very long." He looked down at David. "About those thugs who attacked you—-the suspicion is that they may have come from the Blackburn yacht. Someone from the Pig Iron Pub may have recognized them. The police are investigating."

"Good."

"The bad news is that the Blackburns now know you are a midshipman. The Secretary of Defense, Karl Darren, was on the boat and saw you with his binoculars."

"Damn."

"Darren called me directly to suggest that you be thrown out of the Academy indefinitely for your hostile actions at Kings Oak."

David tensed up.

"I reminded him that the Uniform Code of Military Justice required that we hold a hearing on the matter. Everyone at the party would be called to testify. I added that I wouldn't be surprised if those on board the *Aria* at Thanksgiving would be called as well. Including the three Filipino stewards."

"What happened then, sir?"

"He said he had to take a call from the White House and hung up. Haven't heard from his since."

"Thank you, sir."

Oliver Shaw nodded. "Hope to see you back at the Academy soon, Mr. Waterfield. Try not to worry about your missed classes too much. We'll make sure you have plenty of opportunity to make up your work."

"Yes, sir. I should have plenty of time to catch up. Dr. Zegusa told me I won't be able to play lacrosse this year."

The Superintendent sighed. "Such a pity. Coach Sleazak has been suicidal since he heard about your injuries. But we can wait another year to win the championship. Better late than never as they say."

As they were speaking, Archie and Helene walked in. Both were wearing service dress blues with their overcoats folded neatly over their forearms. At the first sight of Admiral Shaw, they snapped to attention.

"At ease, people."

"Admiral Shaw," David said "this is...uh...my math tutor, Ms. Zankowski, and my roommate, Mr. Unger."

"Nice to meet you both."

"Nice to see you, sir," they responded, almost in unison.

"Your name's familiar," the Superintendent said to Archie. "Our new goalie as I recall."

"Yes, sir."

"We'll be depending on some stiff defense from you this year without Mr. Waterfield."

"I'll do my best, sir."

"I'm sure you will, son."

Archie and Helene had not met Liz yet and David made the introductions. While he was doing so, the Admiral studied Helene. There was something about her that intrigued him.

"Zankowski is not a common name," he said. "When I was at the Academy, it was in the late seventies, I knew a classmate with that same name. Any relation?"

Tears bubbled out of Helene's eyes. "That was my mother, sir. I took her maiden name after she died."

"I'm truly sorry," Admiral Shaw said. He put his arm around her and gave her a hug.

"She was killed by a car bomb in Baghdad, sir." Archie explained. "Babe...I mean Helene, still hasn't gotten over it."

Helene sniffed back her tears and regained her self-control. "I'm sorry, sir."

"Nothing to be sorry about. You should be proud. Zank was a fine woman. We were in the Masqueraders together."

"I'm in drama, too." Helene said. At the moment she was performing her greatest role.

Admiral Shaw looked off into the distance. "I remember now. We had supporting parts in the musical, *Grease*. I couldn't sing and she couldn't dance. It was a helluva lot of fun."

David and Archie exchanged glances. Somehow it didn't compute—the future Superintendent swiveling his hips and singing rock and roll. But then again Oliver Shaw was something special. He had a sensitive side, too. The man was definitely not your ordinary knife-wielding, throat-cutting, Navy seal.

"Zank was wonderful in the show. Really wonderful."

"I'm going to be an actress, too," Helene said. "After I complete my active duty," she added hastily.

The Superintendent was familiar with a wide variety of post-active duty careers but this was the first time he had heard of a midshipman wanting to be an actress.

"Let me know if you're in any productions this year, Miss Zankowski. Mitzi and I would love to come see you perform."

"I will, sir." She was doing a pretty good job of it already.

"Fine." He checked his big, stainless steel diver's watch. "I'll let you young people alone. Mitzi is expecting me to take her to the movies this afternoon." He zeroed in on David. "You get better soon, son, and that's a direct order."

"I'll do my best, sir," David promised.

Admiral Shaw shook Liz's hand, exchanged salutes with Archie and Helene, and marched out the door.

There was a moment of silence and then everyone breathed a great sigh of relief.

"I think we just witnessed an Academy Award winning performance," David said.

"Am I missing something?" Liz asked

"Helene isn't really a midshipman," Archie explained. "She just likes to wear her mother's uniforms so she can come over to the Yard and see me."

Helene smiled, revealing her clunky, gold braces.

"Wow," Liz said. "Isn't that kinda risky?"

"Not really. I'm a method actress."

Shakela came back in the room, her thick tattooed arms pushing a medicine cart. "Times up! You people move your butts out of here or you're gonna help me change the bedpan."

"Hate to run," Archie said.

"But we're outta here," Helene added.

They wished David well, said goodbye to Liz, and hustled out the door before they found out if their services really would be required.

"It's almost noon," Liz told David. "I promised Lou that I'd do lunch with her. I'll come back later and check on you."

"Coward," Shakela said as Liz retreated out the door.

The Department of Obstetrics was on the other side of the medical complex about a block away. Decorated with tinsel garlands and glass ornaments, the nursery was all ready for Christmas. The presents had come a week early. On display behind the plate glass windows were dozens of newborns of every size and color: white, yellow, brown, black, and every shade and nuance in between. Watching over them were proud poppas already worried about how to support the new dependents. Next to them were haggard moms in hospital robes, worn out from the ordeal of childbirth and the demands of small siblings who were already beginning to get jealous. And yet Liz envied them all. Her family was gone now and she missed them terribly. She could only hope that she would be lucky enough to have a child of her own someday.

Louisa came out to join her and they took the elevator down to the sub-basement.

"So how many deliveries have you had today?" Liz asked.

"Two newborns," Louisa said "and one sixty-year old."

"The sixty-year old being Doc."

"Correct. Had to drop him off at the university this morning. His Humvee's in the shop and someone stole his Fatboy."

"That's awful. Any idea who took it?"

"Yep. Me. I snatched it back when he wasn't looking. Way he drives he was gonna break his fool neck on that thing. I'm gonna give him a motorized wheel chair instead."

Liz laughed. Doc and Lou were always playing jokes on one another. But then again, maybe this wasn't a joke.

Exiting the elevator, they walked down the new wing to the cafeteria. The decor of the place came as a complete surprise. Large, artificial skylights in the ceiling tricked the mind into believing you were at street level rather than deep underground. The space was filled with elegant sculptured shrubs, potted trees, and trellises woven with English ivy—all decorated for the holidays. Glass topped tables with Santa Barbara umbrellas completed the illusion that one was in a garden pavilion of some kind, a suggestion underlined by the brick floor that was laid out in a circular pattern reminiscent of an upscale patio.

For a public cafeteria, the food was surprisingly good. It featured a garden-fresh salad bar and a variety of organic foods mixed in with the standard fare. Despite Liz's protests, Louisa was insistent about picking up the tab.

"My treat," she said. "Consider this a business lunch. I need all the tax write-offs I can get."

"Okay, you win this time. But I'll get you back."

They took their food to a vacant table with a vase of sweet-smelling gardenias in the center. At the far side of the room, outside an open enclosure, Liz noticed a woman staring at her. She was a sophisticated lady in a broad-brimmed straw hat and white linen dress. Something about her was familiar but Liz couldn't quite place her. Behind the lady was a receding array of topiary arches and ornamental shapes of exquisitely sculpted shrubbery. It was a moment before Liz realized she was actually looking at a painting. A fine example of the *trompe l'oeil* technique, it tricked the eye into perceiving the lady and her garden in three dimensions. Now Liz understood the decor of the cafeteria. It was intended to be an extension of the scene depicted in the painting, a clever illusion that drew together the past and the present and made the woman in the picture part of both. She looked to be in her late thirties or early forties with soft blonde hair, hooded green eyes, and a complexion that was flawless except for the hint of a vertical scar on her upper lip. Liz suddenly realized she had seen her before in Petra's newspaper clipping.

"That woman in the garden over there—is she who I think she is?"

Lou nodded. "The same. Your boss's ex-wife, the Countess Felicia Von Habsburg. It was she who endowed this new wing. A really lovely lady. I helped tend to her when she came in for a caesarian. I was in the first year of my residency."

"Tavian?"

"Yes." Louisa paused to ponder whether she should go on. She looked around to make sure she wasn't overheard, then leaned forward and spoke in a whisper. "She almost died giving birth to him, you know. And...I shouldn't tell you this...only the people in the operating room know and they were sworn to secrecy... but the baby was born...defective."

"I know about Tavian's harelip," Liz said. "Had one just like his mother's. Septimus fixed them both up."

"More than that, hon. His body had hair all over it"
"Yuck."

"Not only that—he had a four-inch tail."
"A tail!"

"It's a rare genetic defect caused by a mutation during the development of the fetus. There were no bones or nerve cords inside, so it was surgically removed before his father saw him. The hair fell out after a few hours."

Liz lost her appetite.

"Felicia was horrified, of course. Absolutely hysterical. She was a very religious person and thought he was a child of the devil, himself. She was certain that Satan had impregnated her through her husband."

"My God!"

"Septimus on the other hand, blamed the defects entirely on her. Too many inbred genes in the Habsburg line. Hemophilia, cleft palates, poor eyesight, overgrown jaws, things like that. Anyway, that was the end of the marriage. Felicia filed for divorce citing adultery as the prime reason for the dissolution of their marriage, but it was really the baby. Septimus didn't contest it. He had plenty of other women in waiting. He married Felicia for her blood line and didn't have much use for her after that."

"Was there a big settlement?"

"For most people it would have been huge. Thirty-five million in 1980 dollars. For Septimus, it was pocket change."

"Such a creep."

"Exactly. Like I said, Felicia was very religious. She credited the hospital for saving her life and she gave us her entire settlement to build the new wing."

"All of it?"

Louisa nodded. "The woman didn't need the money. She had renounced her worldly life and was preparing to enter a nunnery on the Eastern Shore. Convent of the Blessed Virgin, I think it was called."

"I know where it is," Liz said. "I've seen a historic marker on the road to Kings Oak."

"Yes," Louisa said. "But it's worlds away from all that."

"I know," Liz nodded. "As far away as Heaven is from Hell."

Crucible

Herons Point shook like the epicenter of a major earthquake. Tongues of fire leapt out of coke towers and plumes of sulfur dioxide billowed into the night sky, turning the full moon black. It was Christmas Eve at Blackburn Steelworks and still the ovens and furnaces ran at full throttle. Inside the open sheds, sweat-drenched human machines went about the grim business of muscling steel from tons of raw iron ore amid deafening noise, infernal heat, and the unholy stench of shitwater wafting up from the grates in the floor.

Despite the deplorable conditions and the physical strain of a double shift, LeGrande and his crew were uplifted by the holiday spirit. During their break, they gathered together for some Christmas cheer—a glass of green Gatorade and some sugar cookies LeGrande's wife had made. J-Rod switched his boom box on full blast and tuned to a station that played hip-hop holiday rap.

> *Covered in ashes, covered in coal,*
> *Saint Nick come out of his chimney hole.*
> *Rocks in our stockings, sticks under the tree*
> *Nuthin' in presents for you and me.*
> *Bad little girl, bad little boy,*
> *Be good next year if you want some toys.*

"Makes me wish we had some dancing shoes," J-Rod yelled over the lyrics. "Can't move real good in these things."

He was referring to the steel-toed work boots the crew was required to wear. Cut-up truck tires had been nailed to their soles to protect them from the hot-brick floor. They made walking clumsy and dancing impossible.

"Don't need no special shoes," Mandala said loudly. "Put your fat butt down on the floor and do some break dancing. It thick enough."

"Maybe do some head spins, too," Tsonka added. "Won't cause no harm."

Qwazi came over and turned down the volume. In his hand was a small aluminum Christmas tree.

"Looky here what Miss Mancini sent us," he said. "Had a dog bone underneath it and a tag says it be for Cerberus."

He held the biscuit up and the yapping, yellow-eyed mongrel hopped up and down on its one hind leg like a pogo stick before finally snatching it in his mouth.

"Too bad we didn't get anything for the lady," LeGrande said.

"Maybe we can make her something nice outta steel," Mandala suggested.

"A suit of armor would be good," Kenyatta said. "Protect her butt from the boss man. Like the ones I gots in my castle over there in Ireland."

The others ignored him as usual. Turning up the volume on the boom box, they went about decorating the tree with steel rivets, bolts, and nuts. Their weight made the limbs a bit droopy but no one seemed to care. After it was finished, they moved it as close to the Blast Furnace as they dared.

"Not too close!" Tsonka yelled out over the din. "Santa don't leave presents under melted Christmas trees."

"Old Saint Nick gonna get a rude surprise, he come down this chimney," J'Rod hollered. He pointed to the massive, metal furnace that soared through the roof of the shed.

"Look like the Jolly Old Elf already been here," Mandala said, gesturing to a railroad car loaded with coal. "Must be he think we all been bad boys."

"Not bad, just lazy," LeGrande said. "Time to get your butts back to work. We got steel to make tonight."

"Scrooge," Kenyatta called him.

Reluctantly, the crew ended their break and went grudgingly back to work: J'Rod and Mandala to load iron oar, coke, and limestone into the top of the furnace; Kenyatta to operate the blowers; and Tsonka, the crane. Qwazi slipped his welding goggles over his eyes and climbed up a ladder to the grated-platform that overlooked the empty cauldron below, his diamond ear-stud twinkling in the hellish firelight.

When the temperature gauge told him the contents of the Blast Furnace had been heated to 1,400 degrees Fahrenheit, LeGrande yanked down a bright red lever. With a thunderous roar, a fiery Niagara of molten pig iron shot out the wickey hole and into the crucible below, sending up clouds of sparks and geysers of fire.

Through darkly tinted goggles, Qwazi judged the blaze in the cauldron to be more intense than it should be. He and his crew began to frantically throw in large bags of scrap metal to bring down the temperature. Maybe it was the steam, or maybe his cataract-afflicted eyes just didn't see well anymore, or maybe he was just worn out from the double shift, but whatever the reason, he suddenly tripped and lost his balance.

LeGrande saw the railing give way. Saw Qwazi go down with it. Falling fast. Arms flailing helplessly. Trying to catch the thin air. Trying to reverse the laws of gravity. All the way down into the swirling maelstrom of molten pig iron.

The other men saw it, too. Screams filled the open shed like shrieking brakes on a runaway train. Cerberus wailed and ran in circles. Qwazi surfaced once, his face melting off his skull like hot fudge off a vanilla sundae. And then he went under and resurfaced no more.

LeGrande grabbed a shovel and probed around for his friend like a lifeguard trying to rescue a drowning man. As if somehow Qwazi would be able to grab hold and extricate himself from the molten metal. But it was not to be. The end of the shovel melted and the frustrated Keeper just threw it in and watched it dissolve, horrified by the realization of what had just happened. In desperation, he signaled Tsonka to lift the cauldron with his crane and empty its white-hot steel into the molds on a flatbed railroad car. Nothing. No body. No bones. No remains at all. His friend had dissolved like an ice cube in boiling water. Qwazi Lightfoot was no more.

Gravesend

There was no grave to dig, no body to bury. There was only the memory of Qwazi Lightfoot to inter in the minds of those who knew him best: LeGrande, Mandala, Tsonka, J'Rod, Kenyatta and a few others from Qwazi's years in the Melt Shop. They stood together in the graveyard at the edge of Milltown with their arms around each other, covered in snow that had turned black from the soot in the air.

Qwazi Lightfoot had no wife or children to mourn him. Nor did he have any living relatives to grieve his passing. He was not a church-going man either, and so the Keeper took it upon himself to step forward and say a few words in remembrance of his friend.

He was about to begin when a filthy green truck drove up next to the cemetery. Liz got out, bundled up in a down parka. Quickly, she hurried around to the passenger side and opened the door. With great difficulty, David Waterfield stepped out. His left leg was encased in a plaster cast and his body was supported by a pair of crutches. Draped over his shoulders was a double-breasted, navy-blue overcoat with gold buttons down the front. He had a white scarf around his neck and a bandage around his brow that was just barely visible under his black-brimmed hat. With great solemnity, he crutched his way through the soot-covered snow toward the gathering of mourners. The steelmen nodded, appreciating the show of respect for their fallen brother. When the group had settled back down, LeGrande began to speak.

"We come here to our burying ground to honor the memory of our little brother, Qwazi," he said solemnly.

"Yes, we have," Tsonka said. "Yes, we have."

"Don't know about you," the Keeper continued, "but I'm always gonna see that big-ass smile of his. Even when he was ticked off, he was grinning ear-to-ear."

"Yes he did. He sure did."

"And that diamond stud he was always wearing. Thought he was a superstar. And he was, too. Qwazi never let down. Never. Always worked hard. Gave more than he needed to. Had a lot of pride, too. And that's what killed him. We all know he shouldn't have been working that double shift, none of us should. OSHA's gonna hear about it for sure."

Liz nodded. She would see to that. But deep down inside, she knew that OSHA would only administer a slap on the wrist. Since Qwazi had no immediate family, there would be no suit for punitive damages.

"But money ain't gonna bring Qwazi back," the Keeper went on. "The man's gone and we got no gravestone to lay down with his name chiseled on it."

"We ain't gonna forget him," J'Rod said.

"No way," LeGrande declared emphatically. "No way. I say let the steel he died in be his tombstone. The girders they're gonna use in the skeleton of some high-rise somewheres. The hull of some big ass ship or the backbone of a suspension bridge. Maybe even the skin of one of those jumbo jets."

"You right brutha. You right."

"Our Qwazi ain't gone. He just turned into steel, that's all. And we all know that steel last forever."

"Amen, brutha," Mandala said.

After a few moments of silence, it seemed there wasn't anything else to say. One by one, the mourners left the graveyard and trudged back through the black snow to grieve alone in their humble ash-covered shacks.

When they were by themselves, Liz led David to a site on the far side of the cemetery. Two warped wooden markers stuck out of the ground brightened by bouquets of plastic flowers that were just barely visible under the soot-blackened snow. A third plot lay vacant next to them.

"My mom and dad," Liz whispered as if somehow her voice could disturb their sleep. "You can see they left room for me."

Her composure gave way and she started to sob. David took her in his arms and hugged her tightly, pain searing through every bone in his battered body. But at that moment, she needed him. And he needed her, too, more than ever before.

A Veil of Alabaster

Washington was a city painted in a hundred shades of white. From Capitol Hill to the monuments on the mall, its marble facades blended seamlessly into the freshly fallen snow and cloud-enshrouded sky. For the tourists who had braved the weather, the scene was a picture-perfect postcard. But lurking underneath the pristine surface was a dark history of bloodshed and butchery.

As Liz drove past the White House, David closed his dotted lids and saw the snow begin to melt. Striding across the mush was the ghost of a white-haired general in a *chapeau de bra*. He was wearing a high-collared blue coat with a ruffled cravat at the neck and a pair of gold epaulets on his shoulders. His white breeches were spotless and a crimson sash was wrapped around his waist. In this right hand he carried a long curved saber. As the snow disappeared under his black riding boots, the bloody carnage of a battlefield began to emerge. Strewn across it like fallen trees that had been stripped of their bark were the skinned carcasses of Indian braves. Some of the General's men were curing the skins in salt and tanning them into leather. Others were making them into belts, hat bands, and harnesses--souvenirs of the battlefield to remind the troops of their great victory. The Indians called the General

Sharp Knife. The whites knew him as Old Hickory and elected him President of the United States.

David turned away from the vision in disgust. A hundred and eight-three winters had come and gone since the atrocities committed by Andrew Jackson at the Battle of Horseshoe Bend. But no amount of snowfall, however pure and unsullied, could cleanse the bloodstained hands of the Great White Father, although Nature seemed intent on trying once again.

Several blocks from the White House, Liz found a parking place near the Corcoran Gallery of Art. It was only a short walk from there to the exhibition hall of the American Anthropological Society. Like its more famous cousins on the mall, the museum had a marble facade and a pediment supported by a half dozen Doric columns, their flutes streaked from acid rain. A Conestoga Tours motorcoach from Ft. Wayne, Indiana, was parked in front and a group of senior citizens were filing inside.

David and Liz made their way up the handicapped ramp and through the rotating glass door. At the information kiosk, a woman in a brown blazer inspected the contents of Liz's shopping bag and issued her a receipt. Then she unfolded a floor map and directed them to the third floor office of the Director of Native North American Cultures.

On the way to the elevators, they passed through an exhibit of Mayan artifacts recently discovered in the ancient city of Chichén Itzá. On display were golden jaguar masks, fragments of a mural that depicted blood sacrifice, and several large stones carved with elaborate glyphs.

"If they can interpret those hieroglyphics," Liz told David, "they ought to be able to decipher your parchment."

"Yes," David joked, "but my parchment's not written in stone."

"Very funny," Liz said.

The third floor was very different from the public rooms below. Like a vast attic, it housed artifacts that had been donated to the Society but had not yet gone on display. The main corridor was lined with shelves full of primitive stone tools, arrowheads, animal skins, stuffed animals, feathered headdresses, and clay urns. There was even a collection of totem poles.

The office of the Director of Native North American Cultures was at the end of the hallway. It was as cold as a meat locker inside and filled with stacks of long slatted-wood crates. On the other side of the wall of crates, a bushy haired man in a down-filled jacket was hunched over a cluttered desk examining a fragment of pottery.

"Excuse me," Liz interrupted. "Are you Dr. Seymour? Dr. Carter Seymour?"

"Last time I looked," the man answered, not bothering to turn around.

"We're your ten o'clock appointment. I'm Liz Mancini and this is David Waterfield."

Putting aside the pottery shard, the man swiveled around and confronted them with an enormous left eye. "And you're out of focus," he said, pausing for dramatic effect before flipping up the magnifying lens on his spectacles. "That's better. By Jove! You're in bad shape, young man. Let me get you a seat."

"Actually, it's easier to stand," David said, leaning forwards on his crutches.

"How about some hot chocolate then? Nothing better on a day like today."

"Thanks," Liz said, "that would be great." Her breath was visible and she couldn't stop shivering.

"Forgive me, but I keep the temperature down in the interests of science."

"We're fine," David said through chattering teeth.

Dr. Seymour cleared a path through the stacks of crates and made his way to the kitchenette in the corner of his office. A few minutes later he brought back two mugs of steaming, hot cocoa with a sprinkling of marshmallows on top.

"This should warm you up," he said. "Pardon me for not drinking with you but I've already had three cups this morning."

"I appreciate your taking time to see us," David said after a few sips. "As Liz told you on the phone, we were wondering if you could help us understand some artifacts of mine."

"Ah, yes. Now I remember. You're the people from Oklahoma."

"Yes." Liz said. "David is anyway,"

"Excuse me while I do a little house keeping," the bushy haired man said. He leaned over and swept a pile of computer paper, post-it notes, yellow tablets, scholarly journals, several bottles of pills, and dozens of pencils off his desk and into an empty cardboard box.

"My filing system is a little primitive, but it's quick," he explained. "At least the initial phase."

He nudged the carton under his desk with his foot. All settled, he was ready to get down to business. "Now let's see what you brought me."

"My grandfather gave me these things," David said. "They were handed down from our ancestors."

He reached in the shopping bag and brought out the oblong box. Before he could open it, the man with three eyes lurched forwards and grabbed his wrist.

"White gloves, young man, white gloves. The oils from you hands can speed deterioration. Let me do it. I've already got them on."

Taking the box from David, he opened the lid carefully, as if he were about to defuse a pressure-sensitive time bomb. He removed the long-stemmed pipe first and turned it over under his lamp.

"Peace pipe. Seen a million of 'em. Average workmanship." He took a whiff of the bowl and perked up at the telltale smell of narcotics.

"Peyote," he said.

"It was last smoked by my grandfather two years ago. Took him into a trance."

"Yes, yes. I'm sure he did. This is pretty strong stuff and it's just the residue. A couple of puffs and it would be like your brain was struck by lightning."

"Hence the jagged yellow bolts on the stem," Liz said.

Dr. Seymour nodded. "Yes, of course. My guess is that the peyote probably came up from Mexico. It was a hot trade item on the reservations."

He put the pipe aside and carefully picked up the wampum belt with both hands and set it down on his desk. Flipping his jeweler's lens down over his left eye, he leaned forward and examined it closely.

"Exquisite work here, really top notch. These kinds of things were made to commemorate peace treaties and such. Notice the difference in size of the stick figures. The ones under the left side of the tree are much smaller in size than the others. They're natives. They thought of themselves as inferior to the English invaders and drew themselves that way."

"Guns have that effect on people," Liz noted.

The three-eyed man ignored the comment. "What intrigues me are the squared hands on the central stick figure. Very unusual."

"They're parchments," David explained. "Like this one at the bottom of my box."

Seymour's eyes lit up. "Goodness. I didn't see that before. Same color as the wood."

With trembling hands, he lifted the deerskin parchment out of the oblong box and carefully unfolded it. As he scanned the long, laborious words, his eyes brightened ten-fold.

"By Jove, I haven't seen one of these in quite a while. A phonetic parchment! No doubt the work of a Jesuit missionary. Black Robes, they were called. Learned native tongues so they could translate the word of God to the heathens and save their souls from damnation. This specimen is in great shape. Dry heat of Oklahoma, no doubt."

"No doubt," David said.

"The words are onomatopoeia, of course. The earliest language of man. Sounds of nature mimicked in human speech and recorded on parchment as close as the ear can discern. See here, the writer has helped us out with pronunciation marks above the vowels. The accents tell us which syllable to stress. Then you have these horizontal bars, macrons we call them, that indicate a long vowel. The smiley marks or breves tell us a vowel is short. The dots over these two adjacent vowels are a dieresis. It tells us to pronounce each vowel as a separate syllable. And, of course, some of the words have no vowels at all."

"Can you make any sense of what it says?" Liz asked.

"In onomatopoeia, sound is sense. Here's a good example over here. The word *zaka-kraakatuma*. What does it sound like to you?"

"Not a clue," David said.

"To me it suggests a crack of lightning followed by a roll of thunder. Maybe it means 'storm.' Who knows? Here's another obvious one. A funny hyphenate with no vowels. *Crrrrrrrp-crrrrrrrp.*"

"A bird call," Liz guessed.

"Or maybe the chirp of an insect or something all together different. Who can say for sure?"

"What about abstractions? How can imitating the sounds of nature convey that?"

"Good question, young man. The answer is sound symbolism. The onomatopoeia here is richly enhanced with it. Some of the finest I've ever seen. A virtual cornucopia of plosives, fricatives, glides, liquids, nasal stops and such."

David and Liz looked confused.

"I see you're not familiar with them. Let me explain. They're all ways of articulating speech to suggest, not only the sounds of nature, but actions and abstractions, too. With plosives air is expelled through parted lips, suggesting power. Like this first word here. *PotaPowHatant.* It may not actually be an attempt to reproduce a naturally occurring sound, but the 'p' sound successfully conveys an impression of strength and power. Down here is a good example of a fricative—*frshhisss*. To pronounce it, the speech tract is narrowed somewhat. As the air is let out, there's a good deal of friction and even some hissing in some cases. This could be an object whizzing by in the air..."

"An arrow," David guessed.

"Perhaps. Or the sound of a snake."

"Or symbolic of a person who acts like a snake."

"Precisely, young lady. You're catching on. Nasal stops are consonants that end abruptly and resonate in the nasal cavity. Hence, they suggest the onomatopoeia of impact. Like this one here—*dzunkk*."

"A heavy stone being dropped," David guessed.

"Or the stone itself. Or symbolically, a heavy decision or action. The words can be verbs, nouns, adverbs, and adjectives all at the same time."

"What about the cursive letters mixed in with the printed ones?"

"Haven't seen that before, son. I would guess it indicates that we should let those letters run together. Like this word here—*sssmissiana*. It suggests to me the idea of liquidity. Maybe it means 'stream' or 'river.' Symbolically, it could mean 'water' or even 'life'."

"Any idea of what it all adds up to?" Liz asked.

"I'm afraid I can't help you there. The text sounds rather like poetry or even music when you speak it. Like this line— *ShumMaTecu tanKamatu mazaKanna Beku*. It's very beautiful, but making sense out it—why it's like trying to decipher the meaning of Egyptian hieroglyphics without a Rosetta stone to go by."

His jeweler's eye went to the florid black scribble at the bottom of the page. "I see it's signed, too. Letters overlap. Rather hard to make out. One below is easier, a crude X."

"The mark of the werowance," David said.

Dr. Seymour leaned closer. "Yes. I see that. It looks browner than the other writing. You ask me, I think it was made in blood." He turned his attention back to the knotted signature above.

"Caecilius Blackburn," David said. "If you stretch it out."

"Blackburn?" Seymour's face went slack. He looked back up at David and raised his third eye. "I thought you said you were from Oklahoma."

"I was born there but my ancestors were from the Chesapeake. The Choptank River to be exact."

"Your people are Choptanks? By Jove! What an amazing coincidence! The museum is conducting a dig at the Blackburn estate on the Eastern Shore. The current owner has generously underwritten the entire project."

David was unsettled. The three-eyed man was on his enemy's payroll. Suddenly, he didn't trust him anymore.

"You should visit there, Mr. Waterfield. It's most interesting. I can arrange it for you."

"Thanks. But I've already been to Kings Oak."

"Oh, I see. Enterprising young fellow, aren't you?"

"You have no idea," Liz said.

"Your stick figure was holding out two squares," Seymour said. "I assume there is a second parchment."

David nodded. "At Kings Oak, I saw a painting of the scene depicted on the belt of beads. In it, a Jesuit priest was handing another parchment to Lord Blackburn. My theory is that it must have been the original one and written in English."

Liz agreed. "How else could he have understood it? I don't think they were teaching Choptank at Oxford back then."

"Exactly," David said. "And the priest would have needed an English version to translate into Choptank."

"A logical conclusion, young man," the professor said. "I've never heard anything about that. Why don't you leave this with me and I'll give it some further study? The Society is mounting an exhibit in March and we might be interested in displaying it."

"Can't do that."

"Let us buy it from you then." The three-eyed man was starting to drool.

"It's not for sale."

"Name your price. I'll see what I can get you."

"I said no."

David took the parchment out of Dr. Seymour's gloved hands, folded it back up, and put it back in the bottom of the oblong box along with the belt of beads and the peace pipe.

The doctor reached over and grabbed his wrist again. "You've got to reconsider, Mr. Waterfield. Science demands it."

"Let go," David insisted. "Like I said, it's not for sale. No way."

Seymour snatched the oblong box with his other hand. David yanked it away from him. In the ensuing tug-of-war, David's crutches slipped out from under him and he fell back into the slatted-wood crates. Several broke open and spilled their contents on the floor.

"My God!" Liz gasped.

Before them were the grotesque figures of mummified bodies in shrink-wrapped wooden frames. Eyeless faces, scalped heads, and bullet-riddled bodies contorted in agony.

"Don't touch them!" Seymour warned.

David backed away, horrified at the remains that lay around him. "Where did you get these?" he demanded.

Dr. Seymour ignored him and rushed towards a telephone.

"It's here on the shipping label," Liz said. "Kings Oak, Maryland."

David put his hands over his ears as the wails of Grandfather Two Tongues filled his head.

"Grave robber!" Liz screamed.

"Get out or I'll call security," Seymour yelled, brandishing the telephone receiver at them.

"You'll be hearing from me again," David warned as he got back on his crutches.

Liz led him out of the room before they really got in trouble.

The Second Square

The sudden blast of a shotgun shattered the calm and knocked the ice off the trees with a clatter. In the flock overhead, a solitary canvasback froze in mid-air, then dropped lifeless into the thin crust that had formed over the shallows, leaving behind a pink mist to stain the morning sky.

Crawling out of the marsh grass at the river's edge was a hunter clad in snake-patterned camouflage. His weapon was a sixty-five-thousand-dollar, twelve-gauge, double barrel antique Remington with a golden fowl chiseled into the plate on the stock. Except for two dark eyes, his face was hidden behind a mask that replicated the scaly skin of a copperhead.

"Fetch it, Russell," he commanded. Immediately his sedge-colored retriever emerged from the reeds and carefully worked his way across the thin crust, past a half-dozen canvasback decoys.

This morning, Septimus was hunting alone. One of the things he liked best about the solitude was that it gave him time to think. The cold and dark served to clarify his thoughts, to crystallize them so he could turn them over in his mind and examine them from every angle. One of the most troubling was last month's incident with the trespasser. Hopefully the punk had gotten the message to stay clear. Baseball bats had a way of doing that. To insure that the attackers did not get traced back to the *Aria,* he had ordered his three Filipino stewards to leave the ship when it had docked in Newport News. His attorney, Laurence Roche, saw to it that they boarded a plane back to the Philippines. Afterwards, he contacted the police to report that the stewards had gone AWOL from the *Aria* and had taken some priceless antique silverware with them. It was a good cover story since there was virtually no chance of them being caught. By now, the little yellow men would have been met at the airport in Manila by a company limousine and whisked back to their squalid cardboard hovels in the slums of the city. How Septimus had hated to see them go. They were the best stewards he had ever employed, working night and day in return for room and board and all the loose change they could steal off the bureaus in the guest staterooms. Every day, the black satin sheets on the beds were replaced with a freshly dry-cleaned set. In the dining room, black linen tablecloths and napkins were ironed before every meal. Folds and creases were one of the Chairman's pet peeves. The Filipinos even ironed his socks and underwear so they were warm when he dressed in the morning. Yes, he was certainly going to miss them. But he had no doubt there were more to be found where they came from.

His hunting done for the day, Septimus broke open the breech and ejected his shell casings. A few moments later, Russell returned with the kill in his mouth. It was an especially large specimen, a drake with a thirty-inch body and a wingspan of three feet.

"Good boy, good Russell," his master said, pulling off his mask. He looked around and spoke into the woods.

"It's all yours, Zaccariah."

A black boy materialized from behind a tree and trotted through the snow with a burlap bag. Kneeling in front of the dog, he carefully removed the kill from his jaw with his six-fingered hand. Four small wounds had brought the creature to earth. One each in his rust-colored head and black chest and two in his white belly.

"Got it good, Mr. B," Zaccariah said.

As usual, Septimus was pleased with the kill, especially a canvasback this size. "Tell Cissy to send this one to the taxidermist for mounting. She can roast one of the smaller ones for dinner tonight."

The boy grunted, putting the bird in the bag with the others. Then he set about pulling the decoys off the ice with a long pole that had a crook on the end. Each was beautifully hand-carved in wood and painted as close to life as the hand of man could make it. Afterwards, Zaccariah ran back to the duck shed with a string of decoys in one hand and the blood-soaked burlap bag in the other. Hanging from hooks inside the shed were his master's world-class collection of waterfowl decoys. Among them were Red Heads, Coots, Pintails, Ring Necks, Bald Pates, Canada Geese, Swans, Doves, Great Blue Herons, and other species whose migration routes took them over the Eastern Shore, a great many for the last time. The six-fingered boy hung the canvasbacks on their hooks, then latched the door shut and hurried up towards the manor house kitchen for a morning of feather plucking with Cissy.

The lord of the manor trudged after him, following a trail of splattered blood through the foot-deep snow. He was well pleased with the seven canvasbacks he had bagged that morning. True, he was three over his limit for the day but who on earth was ever going to know? Three was nothing. How well he remembered hunting with his father and grandfather when ducks were as thick as locusts, darkening the sky when they flew overhead and blanketing the surface of the water when they landed. Back then, they hunted in the middle of the night in a small, flat-bottomed boat with a canon-like punt gun in the bow, drifting right up to a raft of unsuspecting fowl. Five ounces of black powder and two pounds of scrap iron were guaranteed to deliver close to a hundred birds in one blast. Those were the days!

He climbed up the back stairs and left his gun propped next to the door to be cleaned and oiled for the next shoot. Without bothering to scape off the soles of his rubber boots, he entered the house and tracked mud down the antique Tibetan runner than ran the length of the portrait gallery. Cleaning up after him was something he expected his servants to do. It was a task that always kept them busy.

Turning into the den, he found the great fieldstone fireplace ablaze and crackling, just as he ordered. Pulling off his gloves, he backed up next to the flames and warmed out the winter chill. And as he did so, his eyes wandered around the room. Of the thirty-two in the manor, it was his favorite place, the inner sanctum where he felt most at home. It was a masculine space with rich mahogany paneling and plush leather sofas and chairs. On the floor in front of the hearth was the skin of an immense black bear with its head, teeth, and claws still intact. It had been bagged sixty years ago by his great-grandfather, the steel baron, and was thought to be the last of its kind on the Eastern Shore. Hanging from the walls were other trophies of the hunt, taken by Septimus, himself, and preserved and enhanced by an artful hand of the taxidermist. His favorites were a pair of waterfowl in full flight, the head of a growling mountain lion, and a prize-winning white marlin, its body forever arched in midair.

Mounted above the hearth was a 17th Century musket that once belonged to the Founder, himself. It was a magnificent piece with a fire-blued damascene muzzle and carved wooden stock inlaid with ivory and fitted with a snaphaunce firing mechanism. A piece of flint was attached to a spring-loaded arm and when the trigger was pulled, the cover slid off the flash pan, and the arm snapped forward striking a metal plate. The resulting sparks ignited the black powder and sent a two-ounce lead shot exploding from the mouth. The recoil was so violent that the Founder, in his later years, often complained of a chronic dislocation of his left shoulder. It was an ailment that stayed with him to the end of his days and was principally responsible for the deterioration of his once elegant penmanship.

The far wall of the den was reserved for signed photographs of the power elite that the Chairman had cultivated over the years. One of his favorites, taken when he was only fourteen, showed him deep sea fishing with his father and Maryland Governor Spiro Agnew. It was taken seven years before his honor had become the first Vice President of the United States drummed out of office for income tax evasion. Next to it was a large, glossy photograph of the twenty year-old Septimus teeing off with Tricky Dick and Bebe Rebozo at the Breakers golf course in Palm Beach. The shot of the 37th President always left him a little cold. The family had poured a fortune into Nixon's last campaign but unfortunately the bum was booted out of the White House before they could get a return on their investment.

With his head full of memories, the seventh incarnation of the Founder's name plopped down in the antique, cock fighting chair that faced the fire. It was one of two that the Founder had brought with him from England on his maiden voyage. Each was built with caged compartments under the seat that once housed ferocious roosters trained to fight and kill. Miner Blues, Roundheads, and White Hackles were the Founder's favorites, each bred for size, strength, speed, and intelligence—traits that gave them a distinct advantage in the pit. The Founder favored the naked spur style of combat. It could go on for hours and provide endless opportunities for wagers and good fellowship. In the colonies, cock fighting was a favorite pastime of the sporting elite. Prominent among them were George Washington and Thomas Jefferson who bred and fought their own stock. The chair gave Septimus a link to the past and, it must be said, a sense of power that those connected to blood sports seemed to relish.

A small turn of the hand, like the discreet signal he used at auction houses, brought his black manservant out of the shadows. Septimus lifted up his foot and, without further instruction, Nero pulled off his master's rubber boots, one after the other.

"Boy said you had a good day shoot, Mr. B.," he said.

Septimus nodded, avoiding eye contact. He was never one to carry on a conversation with a servant if he could help it, especially one with white splotches all over his face and hands.

"Cissy, she starting to pluck the big one already."

"No, damn it! I told the boy that one was to go to the taxidermist!"

"Sorry, Mr. B. You know Zaccariah, he be a little slow. I'll go tell Cissy to stop what she doing. Maybe the taxi man can stick the feathers back in."

Nero trotted off towards the kitchen with his master's boots under his arm. Septimus was of half a mind to fire the lot of them. The only thing stopping him was that they had worked for his family forever. They were loyal employees even though they were sometimes incredibly stupid. Even so, they were a notch above the other blacks that lived down in the stables like farm animals. Genetics, he thought. Inbreeding.

Calming down a bit, the lord of the manor leaned back and reached for his long-stemmed, Churchwarden's pipe and the old, leather tobacco pouch on the table next to him. He scooped up a bowlful of Windsor Blend, lit it, and took a few deep, soothing drags. Relaxing, he put his feet up on an ottoman and was soon transported into a satisfying sense of calm. A successful kill always had that affect on him. Perhaps it was a primitive response evoked after the next meal had been assured. It was time for the hunter to let down his guard in anticipation of a full belly. Fiddling with his tobacco pouch, he found himself, once again, musing on the legend surrounding it. It had been passed down in the family from father to son for many generations. Even now the leathery skin was as soft and supple as when the Founder first had it made, a remarkable example of the tanner's art.

Nero came back with a portable phone in his mottled hand. "It for you, Mr. B.," he said. "Cissy say the bird okay."

Annoyed, the Chairman put the receiver up to his ear and waited for the caller to speak.

"Mr. Blackburn?" the man on the other end asked after a few awkward moments had gone by. "It's Carter Seymour from the American Anthropological Society."

It took a few seconds for Septimus to recognize the name as one of the archaeological ants who'd been rummaging around his property for the past two summers.

"What can I do for you, Mr. Seymour?" he said at last. He knew, of course, that the caller was a Ph.D., but it pleased him to downgrade people like that. He felt that it gave him the upper hand.

"I've got some exciting news to tell you about."

"Go on." The only thing the Chairman found exciting about archaeology was the tax deductions he had been accumulating.

"Some folks came to see me this morning with an old, deer-skin parchment written in phonetics. I was astounded to see that it was signed by the Founder himself. Believe it or not, it's the Choptank parchment mentioned in the *Generall Historie*."

Waterfield! Septimus tensed up.

"The young man has deduced that it must have been written from an English original that you might have. Made me think that if we could compare them, we could begin to reconstruct an entire language that has been lost for more than three-and-a-half centuries!"

"That would be truly wonderful, Mr. Seymour," Septimus said. "Yes, there was an English version. I remember my Grandfather and father chatting about it several times. All very boring to me as a child, of course. Never was that interested in history. But I distinctly remember grandpapa saying it was written by a Jesuit priest. A peace treaty of some sort, I believe he said it was. Signed by both the Founder and the leader of the tribe."

On the other end of the line the three-eyed curator could not contain his excitement. This unexpected discovery could cap off his distinguished career. He could envision a cover story in the society's magazine and perhaps a documentary on the Discovery Channel. Maybe he could even get a book deal that would give him something extra to retire on.

"I tried to get the young man to sell his copy to the museum," Seymour continued "but he was reluctant to let it go. But I'm sure he must have his price. Every man does. If you were interested in underwriting its purchase, it would be a wonderful addition to our February exhibit."

"I doubt if the young man would part with such an heirloom for any price," Septimus said. "Besides it would be of no use. I must not have mentioned it, but the English parchment was destroyed in a dreadful fire back in the forties. The east wing of the Manor was struck by lightning and burned to the ground. Several servants died trying to save our valuables. We lost a Reynolds painting that was worth a fortune. A terrible tragedy for all of us."

The curator could hardly contain his disappointment. "So sorry I'm not able to help on this one, Mr. Seymour. But I understand you will be returning to Kings Oak this summer. Perhaps you'll find some new treasures to make up for it."

"We'll keep looking, Mr. Blackburn," Seymour said. "Thank you for your time." He was about to mention the fracas with the mummies but Septimus hung up without another word.

That Waterfield punk! The seventh lord of the manor arose immediately and strode across the room to the wall safe that was hidden behind a painting of a Great Blue Heron. From inside its stainless steel chamber, he retrieved a long safety deposit box. Inside, wrapped in a red velvet cloth, was the English original of the Choptank parchment. His eyes rapidly ran down the page. His face turned pale and the veins in his temples rose. It was just as he remembered when his father had first shown it to him thirty years ago—a revelation so damaging that it frightened him to think that somehow the Indian punk might lay his hands on it, either by outright theft, or court subpoena. The Nixon tapes came to mind. If Tricky Dick had destroyed them, he would never have been booted out of office. Without another thought, Septimus took the priceless old parchment over to the hearth and tossed it on the fire.

The taut lines in his narrow asymmetrical face relaxed as voracious red flames ate into the family secret, nibbling away its edges and gobbling up its heart until there was nothing left but a crumbling sheet of ashes. Freed of its body, the spirit of the secret escaped up the chimney flue in a curl of dense black smoke. Like an ominous shadow, it drifted slowly over the snow-covered peninsula before settling down in the anguished arms of the gnarled oak that stood alone and mourning at the Center of the World.

Chopped Liver

A Humvee painted in olive, black, and brown camouflage, and flying a purple Ravens' pennant from its antenna, roared down Martin Luther King, Jr. Boulevard, past the twin stadiums, and out of the city of Baltimore. A wind spoiler in the rear smoothed the ride and spinning silver wheel disks gave it some glitter. With its 16-inch ground clearance, four-wheel drive, and GPS system, the Humvee was designed for the rugged, off-road performance necessary in military campaigns. The driver often fantasized about veering off I-97 and taking a short cut to his destination, climbing over artificial berms and churning through marshes, backyards, and shopping malls. Had it not been for the presence of the state police, he would have been tempted. Raymond knew most of the officers by sight, if not by name, since they spent a good deal of time kibitzing at the courthouse. This morning, as an upstanding, law-abiding citizen, he confined himself to the highway and left his fantasy off-road adventure for another day. Going just a little over the speed limit, Raymond made the trip to Annapolis in less than forty minutes. Luckily, he found an empty meter on Main Street in front of Chick & Ruth's Deli and right behind Liz's truck.

The deli was something of an institution on Main Street. Lying in the shadow of the State House a block away, it was a convenient place for lobbyists to meet politicians attending the annual session of the General Assembly. Inside, it was a narrow bus-like diner with a Formica counter on one side and small two-seater booths on the other. The color scheme was a cheerful mix of yellow and pale orange. Politicians who became famous, or even infamous, were rewarded by having their favorite sandwich named after them and added to the menu that was displayed in large colorful circles on the wall behind the counter. Among them were former Governor/ convicted felon Marvin Mandel, former Camelot princess/ Lieutenant Governor Kathleen Kennedy Townsend, and an assortment of lesser known state and local officials. Conspicuously missing from the all-star menu was Spiro T. Agnew's beef and lamb gyro. After the veep's resignation in 1973, it was yanked down faster than if it had caused food poisoning.

The booth across from the cash register was cordoned off from the *hoi polloi*. As always, it was reserved for the sitting Governor of Maryland, currently a sandy-haired WASP with a mouthful of scrambled eggs. He quickly recognized the big-boned, black man in the intentionally mismatched denim overalls, tweed jacket, and the ever-present Ivy League cap. Swallowing quickly, the Governor cracked a big fake smile and rose to shake the big, black sharecropper's hand.

"Good to see you, counselor. What brings you to Crabtown?" The Governor discreetly wiped the germs off his right hand and onto the leg of his pinstriped trousers.

"Just hoping to have a sandwich named after me, Trent. Chopped liver would be nice."

"I can arrange it, Ray. But you'll owe me."

"A cheap price for immortality," Raymond said. The exchange of pleasantries complete, the Governor returned to his brunch and the professor continued on to the back of the bus.

On Saturday mornings, the joint was crowded with tourists and midshipmen on town liberty. Among them he found Liz having coffee with her wounded plebe, the nasty scrape on his forehead still visible. Turning sideways, Raymond sucked in his stomach and squeezed into the vacant booth next to them.

"I'm impressed, Doc," Liz said.

"That I could fit in?"

"That, too. Didn't know you knew Governor Thomas, either."

"From way, waaay back. Fact is we threw moons together at Harvard Law. That won't help us now though. Blackburn hands are in his pockets and he's lost his balls. Excuse the figure of speech."

David laughed and suddenly Liz realized she hadn't introduced him.

"Doc, this is my friend, David Waterfield."

Raymond turned to him and shook his hand. "Glad to meet you, Dave. Liz told me a lot about you. Don't worry. It's all hearsay. Can't be introduced into evidence."

"I've heard a lot about you, too, sir," David said in return. "Thanks for coming."

A harried waitress interrupted them and took the professor's order for a chopped liver sandwich and a glass of lemonade, then disappeared behind the counter.

When she was gone, Liz started in. "As I told you on the phone, Doc, Dave and I really need your help."

"I hear ya," he nodded. "And as you know, *pro bono* is my middle name."

Liz filled the professor in on Grandfather Two Tongue's tale, the mysterious parchment, and the grisly discovery of Choptank mummies in Dr. Seymour's office.

"We want to file a criminal suit against the Blackburns," David said. "The mummies are proof that their ancestor murdered my people and stole their land."

For a moment, Raymond paused and reflected on the misery that the Blackburns had inflicted on his own forebears.

"I know how you must hate them, son," he said. "I hate them, too. Some of my own people were owned by the scoundrels."

"Sorry, I didn't know."

"I'm sure your grandfather's story is true. But the hard fact is it would be thrown out of court as hearsay. You have no real evidence that it was Lord Blackburn and his men who killed your people. It could have been a hostile tribe or another group of white settlers. As far as the parchment goes, you say it can't be translated. Maybe the Blackburns do have an English copy, but it would be hard, if not impossible, to pry it out of their lily-white hands. Even if we could, and it showed that they cheated your ancestors out of their land, it wouldn't help. Under English law, the property belonged to Caecilius Blackburn because Lord Baltimore gave it to him. He had gotten it from the King and it was the King's by Right of Discovery. The title can't be contested."

"What your saying, Dr. Moses," David said bitterly "is that the Blackburns stole my people's land fair and square."

"I'm afraid so, son. A great many colonists with royal land grants paid the tribes some token amount for their land. Not because they needed to legally. They felt it was insurance that would prevent the tribes from warring on them later. I'm sure Lord Blackburn did the same thing. But it wasn't legally necessary."

The waitress rushed back with Raymond's order. Stuck in the sandwich was a toothpick with a small oval placard that read "Dr. Moses' Chopped Liver Sandwich." The professor roared and looked down the diner and through the crowd to the smiling Governor.

"You owe me," the Governor mouthed.

"Damn!" Raymond swore. "I'm in trouble now."

"A toothpick in the sandwich is better than a spike through the heart," Liz noted.

"You gotta point."

David allowed the professor a few bites before he returned to the subject at hand. "I'd settle for just having my people reburied on their homeland. The Society is planning on putting the mummies on display in March. Like some kind of freak show."

"They are?"

"Yes, sir."

"Really?"

David nodded grimly.

"That's distressing."

"Isn't there something we can do to stop them, Doc?" Liz asked.

The professor chewed his food slowly for a few moments. He thought about the captivity of his own people and the hardships and cruelty they had suffered at the hands of their slave-masters. He thought about the costly trial for reparations that had ended so badly and Liz's futile attempt at a class action suit. He swallowed hard and washed the liver down with lemonade.

"Well, what do you think?" Liz prodded.

"Very tasty. Like I said, chopped liver is my favorite." He blotted his mouth with his napkin and when it came down he was smiling like a panther about to pounce.

Glass Coffins

As a private non-governmental institution, the American Anthropological Society relied heavily on public support for its operating budget and was therefore more adventuresome in its programming than the other Federally funded museums in the city could be. Recently, the Society had gained fame, and a bit of notoriety, for its exhibitions of the desiccated corpses of Egyptian pharaohs and the Inca Ice Maidens of the Andes. The Choptank Bog Mummy Exhibition was expected to draw better crowds since they were the first specimens to be found outside Northern Europe or the state of Florida, where mummified brains had been identified inside the craniums of ancient skeletons.

Attendance to the premiere was by invitation only. To give a sense of scientific *gravitas* to the exhibition, Carter Seymour had encouraged the presence of a distinguished group of anthropologists and archaeologists, some from as far away as China. As patron of the affair, Septimus insisted on bringing several society friends and a few of his closest political cronies, including the Project Minerva group and several Supreme Court Justices. The liberal press was specifically excluded from the guest list for fear that they might attempt to stir up a hornet's nest in the Native American community.

271

G.M.O. CALLAGHAN

As curator of the exhibit, it was Carter Seymour's responsibility to escort the Blackburns and their party of VIPs through the exhibit. They began in the museum's outer chamber where artifacts uncovered in and around the village site at Kings Oak were displayed. The ladies in the Minerva group were attracted to the exquisite terra cotta pottery which was decorated with the images of long-legged birds, crabs with gigantic claws, and graceful flying fish. Their husbands gravitated to a collection of ceremonial masks which included a roaring black bear with a bloody maw, an angry-looking elk with blood-tipped antlers, and a hawk head with a rattlesnake in its beak.

Also on display were bracelets made of hammered copper and necklaces strung with eagle talons and bear claws. One case displayed several archaeologically significant Solutrean points along with dozens of scrapers and axe heads. Next to them was a huge war club that had the molars of wolves embedded in its head.

But the most interesting part of the exhibit was confined to the inner chamber. Before entering, visitors were invited to watch an introductory video presentation on bog mummies. According to it, over a thousand had been discovered in Northern Europe since the early fifties as a result of peat harvesting. It told how the tannic acid in the bogs stained their bodies brown and carbon dating indicated some of them were almost 2,500 years old. The video went on to describe in technical detail how their soft tissue had been preserved by the special chemistry of the peat bog—the acidic and oxygen free environment that prevented the decaying effects of bacteria and fungi. Because of this, scientists were able to thoroughly analyze the bodies and develop theories about the world in which they lived.

After the video was over, the dignitaries proceeded into the next chamber, dimly lit for dramatic effect. Of the two hundred and ten mummies recovered at Kings Oak, only fifteen were on display. Lying in glass cases pumped full of krypton gas, they appeared to be in an excellent state of preservation.

The VIP ladies left their husbands and gathered around several cases that contained the remains of beautiful young Choptank women. As always, the society ladies were eager to study the fashions of the day, including the popular hairstyles and accessories. They greatly admired the squaws' elaborate braids and fringed deerskin frocks, both of which were decorated with shell beads and feathers. Of particular interest to them was a young mother who was cradling a small baby boy in her arms.

"Oh, he's so cute," Rosalyn Darren whispered to the others, as if the baby were only sleeping and might wake up from his nap in a really bad mood.

Septimus and the other men in his party were more interested in the male mummies. Among them were fierce-looking braves in war paint, an old man with a hatchet in his hand, and a young boy clutching a bow.

"We think this specimen over here was the tribe's wisoe, or medicine man," Carter Seymour told them in the tone he used with school children. "The Founder called him 'One-Eyed Fox.' You'll notice his left eye has been sewn shut."

"Very interesting, Mr. Seymour," Septimus said, ignoring the man's doctoral degree as usual. He was pleased to see that the wisoe's body, and indeed all of the mummies, had been positioned so that the bullet holes in their backs were not visible. From the start he had insisted that the focus of the exhibit be on the scientific importance of the bog mummies rather than on the discovery of massacred bodies in a mass grave.

"The articles he's wearing support our thesis," Dr. Seymour continued. "Notice the owl headdress, the spirit rattle still in his grip, and the string of dried tongues around his neck."

"Interesting," Senator Brookes said. The others around him agreed.

Ignoring the "No Smoking" signs all around him, Septimus took out his pipe and tobacco pouch. "Mind if I smoke, Mr. Seymour?"

"Not at all," the curator replied. After all, who would dare say "no" to the man whose philanthropy had made the exhibit possible?

Lighting up, the Chairman inhaled deeply, then let out a series of big puffs as he continued on through the exhibit with his retinue trailing behind. A painted face with an exposed white skull caught Christopher Harmon's eye.

"Looks like this fellow has been scalped," he said. "From his eyebrows on up."

"And this other guy's ears have been cut off," Karl Darren noted.

"Quite so," the curator agreed. "Vanquished warriors were often mutilated by rival tribes. Trophies were taken, usually a scalp, sometimes a whole head. Other body parts as well. Some of the dead were even skinned."

"Barbaric practice," Septimus said.

"We didn't put the damaged specimens on exhibition for obvious reasons," the curator said, giving his benefactor a faint smile. They both knew that the mutilations of the bog mummies had not been committed by hostile tribes.

"Hey, Dad, look what they've done to the giant," Tavian said. "Got him all spruced up for the show."

The Chairman and his party joined him in front of an oversized glass case. Squeezed inside were the remains of the fearsome savage that the young Septimus had first encountered in the portrait gallery of Kings Oak Manor, and later when his mummified body was pulled out of the peat bog. The giant's face was frozen in an angry snarl and the bullet hole in his head had been plugged up with mortician's wax. The exit wounds in his massive chest had been sewn shut with the skill of a cosmetic surgeon. His black bearskin tunic was fluffed up and looked like it had just come back from the dry cleaners. The shaved half of his head had been polished to a sheen and the hair on the other side had been cleansed of its gore, shampooed, and braided by the hands of a skilled beautician. Even the yellow-orange fangs of the copperhead coiled around his waist had been whitened.

"We think this is the werowance or chief," Carter Seymour explained. "He's obviously much larger than the other men and he matches the description of Great Standing Bear in the *Generall Historie*."

"Fierce-looking fellow, isn't he," the Chairman noted.

Standing on his tiptoes, the diminutive Secretary of Defense peered over the curator's shoulders. "Wouldn't wanted to have tangled with him," Karl Darren said.

Not unless you had a musket in your hand, Septimus mused.

275

"Seems as if the werowance is in pretty good shape," Christopher Harmon said.

"Sure does. Still got his scalp and his skin intact," Christopher Harmon noted.

"Looks can be deceiving, gentlemen," Dr. Seymour said. He looked around to make sure he wouldn't be overheard by the ladies or any of the other guests, then lowered his voice. "Don't tell anyone, but the chief here was castrated."

"Indeed?" Septimus said. "How appalling."

Now he knew, once and for all, that the family legend was true. The Founder's tobacco pouch had been made from the balls of Great Standing Bear, taken by the Founder, himself, as a trophy of war. Preserved for posterity by the tanner's art, the bulbous leather bag had been passed down through generations from father to son, a symbol of power and good fortune.

Squeezing the pouch hard, it pleased Septimus to think about how loudly the mighty werowance would have yowled. All over the peninsula, flocks of blackbirds would have launched themselves into the air. Beasts of the forest would have fouled themselves and run for cover. A thousand warriors would have subjugated themselves on the ground. And five and fifty royal wives would have wailed and doused their hair in urine. Septimus felt enlarged. Now the great orbs of authority rested in his hands, the mighty jewels that had fathered over five hundred children and cemented the peace between countless warring tribes. Slowly releasing his grip, the Chairman slipped the balls of Great Standing Bear back into his pant's pocket. The power of the werowance was his and his alone.

A commotion at the entrance to the exhibit diverted their attention. Septimus turned and through the crowd caught sight of a lumbering, black oaf dressed in overalls, a tweed sports coat, and Ivy League cap. From the eclectic nature of his wardrobe, the Chairman's first thought was that the creature was a homeless man who had drifted in off the street. But no, that wasn't it. The oaf was making his way through the crowd followed by a pack of media hounds—TV crews with Betacams rolling and still photographers firing flashes.

"Who's in charge here?" Raymond Moses bellowed.

Rattled by the noisy intrusion, Dr. Seymour left his benefactor's side and hurried over to intercept the intruder.

"What's the meaning of this? This reception is by invitation only."

"Here's my invitation," Raymond said. He reached inside the vest pocket of his tweed jacket and pulled out a blue-backed lawsuit and a Cease and Desist Order issued by the District Court of Maryland. Then he turned to address the cameras.

"This exhibit is in violation of Federal Law—the 1990 Native American Graves Protection and Repatriation Act, or NAGPRA for short. These mummies have been stolen from their grave site and should be returned immediately to their tribe for reburial."

A chorus of shrill voices started hurling questions at him.

"Hush," Raymond said sticking out his palms. "I've brought along someone who can answer your questions about this matter better than I can."

The media horde parted and a midshipman in dress blacks walked into their midst with a noticeable limp.

Septimus reddened like he had taken a fist in the face. He wheeled around to Tavian. "Get him the hell out of here."

"But my arm, Dad..." Tavian whined.

Laurence Roche quickly intervened. "Not here, Mr. Chairman. Not now. Not in front of the press."

"This is David Waterfield," Raymond announced loudly. "He's a midshipman at the United States Naval Academy from the state of Oklahoma. David is a direct descendant of the Choptank people displayed in these cases. I'll let him tell you how he feels at seeing this...this ...atrocity."

At once David was surrounded by electronic flashes, boom mikes, and TV cameras. "It's like seeing your relatives' bodies in the crematory at Dachau or Auschwitz," he said.

And it got worse from there. He repeated Two Tongue's account of the massacre of his people by Lord Blackburn. He told how their ancient homeland at the Center of the World had been stolen from them and how the survivors had been forced to migrate halfway across the country to some of the poorest land on the continent. He spoke of the mysterious Choptank parchment and his desire to set things right.

The Chairman glared at the black oaf with the jaunty Ivy League cap on his head. He recognized him now. The bastard had sued him once before, trying to get reparations for black families whose ancestors once worked at the manor as slaves. Raymond Moses had lost that suit. He would lose this one, too. The seventh incarnation of the Founder's name would make sure of that.

Secret Admirer

Twelve long-stemmed roses awaited Liz's arrival, a dozen blood-red dots that were already starting to wither in the sulfuric stench that permeated the office.

"From a secret admirer," the note said.

David! Liz thought when she saw them on her desk. She was so proud of the way he had handled himself on TV—so smart and articulate. And his picture had made the morning paper as well. The flowers were his way of thanking her for all her help.

"Your young man's waiting for you outside," Olga said, the poison of envy dripping from her voice.

"He's so handsome," Gudren added.

Petra agreed. "And so polite, too."

"Yes, he is, isn't he?" Liz said. She put down her bookbag and hurried back down the stairs.

He must have been hiding, she thought, *or I would have seen him when I came in.*

Rushing outside, she found her secret admirer waiting for her by the door.

"Oh! It's you." Liz quickly stepped back inside.

Tavian looked a bit sheepish. He hadn't been to the office in five months, not since the episode at Kings Oak. "Hope you'll accept my peace offering," he said with a slight hiss. "My deepest apologies for the boathouse thing. I'm truly sorry. It was unforgivable."

The "boathouse thing" to him. An attempted rape to her. Once again, Liz thought it was best to downplay the incident in order to keep the information pipeline open and flowing.

"The roses were beautiful. What a surprise."

"The surprise was you didn't report me to the cops. I really appreciate it."

Liz managed a weak smile. She had her reasons and none of them had to do with him.

"If you're not still mad, will you take a walk with me? There's something I want to discuss with you."

"Well... I..."

"Relax. It's a business matter."

It was daylight and people were constantly coming in and out of the worksheds. It seemed safe. "Okay, but I can't be gone too long. I've got an appointment in a half hour."

Tavian smirked, making his harelip scar more noticeable. She was lying and he knew it. But his proposition wouldn't take very long. Overcoming her sense of trepidation, Liz ventured outside, shutting the door behind her. They started walking in awkward silence along the riverbank. Several ducks floated by, all of them dead and in various stages of decay. Fortunately, the wind was blowing the stench to the north and so it wasn't as unpleasant as it usually was.

"I remember you said you were studying law," Tavian began.

"Yes, at night school," Liz said. "Takes up all my free time. A real bummer." She was letting him know that she wouldn't be making any time for him soon.

"What a pity."

As they approached the Blast Furnace, a rush of hot air shot out of its open maw, raising the temperature outside a full fifteen degrees. The cranes and cauldrons inside generated such a clamor that the continuation of their conversation was impossible for the moment. In spite of the infernal noise, Cerberus was curled up near the door, sleeping like a baby.

"Filthy mutt," Tavian said when they'd gotten past the din. "They ought to get rid of him."

"Cerberus is a nice dog," Liz defended. "The men love him and take care of him. He's no problem to anybody."

"Whatever," Tavian said curtly, his face flushing. He was never pleased when someone disagreed with him. Turning abruptly, he led her down an alley between the Melt Shop and Blast Furnace. Parked up ahead was a familiar shape shrouded in a black Satin Stretch car cover.

"Wondered where you hid your wheels," Liz said.

"Had to," Tavian replied. "If I'd parked the beast out front, it would have ruined my little surprise."

The sibilant hiss at the end of "surprise" reminded Liz of Tavian's harelip and the other birth defects Lou had told her about in the hospital cafeteria—the hair that covered his new born body and the awful four-inch tail.

Suddenly, Tavian turned, and fixed his unsettling green eyes on her. "You may recall that I once told you the firm is always on the lookout for legal talent."

"Yes, I remember."

"Anyway, I was just thinking—how would you like it if I transferred you to our legal office? Laurence Roche is the best attorney in Baltimore. You could intern under him and get a lot of valuable experience. And it would make amends for my bad behavior."

Liz opened her mouth, but she couldn't think of anything to say.

"Of course, you'd have to work downtown in the Steeple. And we'd have to give you a raise to make it worth your while."

"That's very kind of you."

"Think of it as on-the-job training. If you want to work for the company after you graduate, you'd have a leg up on anyone else. It'd be your decision. No obligations to accept the job. No strings attached."

Talk about conflict of interest, Liz thought. She'd be working both sides of the street, privy to the defense's strategy in the bog mummy case. She'd be able to tell Doc just what arguments they were planning to use. Their invincible lawyers might still win in the end but the case would be long and drawn out and create a public relations nightmare for the Blackburns.

"Your generosity is overwhelming..."

"Take your time to make your decision. Let me know next week."

"Actually," Liz said. "I can let you know now."

Tavian wasn't surprised. The offer was too good for anyone to refuse.

"I'm going to have to say no."

"No?" Her answer both surprised him and confirmed his deepest suspicions.

"Mind if I ask why?"

"I just think...."

"Conflict of interest, isn't it?"

"I don't know what you mean?"

"You're working with them, aren't you?"

"Who?"

"That Indian punk and the black bastard."

"I don't know what..."

"You fucking traitor!" His hands clamped onto her shoulders.

"Stop it! You're hurting me!"

He put his hand over her mouth and dragged her towards a portable john at the side of the workshed.

"You're gonna get it now!" he screamed, kicking open the door.

Suddenly, a fierce pain shot up his leg.

"Fuck!"

It was Cerberus! His sharp yellow fangs were embedded in his ankle!

"You bitch! You fucking bitch!"

Liz broke out of his grasp and ran away as fast as she could. Tavian ripped off his mangy attacker and hurled him into the open john. Cerberus rebounded, eyes glowering, teeth bared. Throwing his head back, he let out an unearthly growl.

Tavian retreated towards his car, his pant leg torn and his ankle bleeding profusely. Slavering at the mouth, the three-legged dog hobbled after his wounded prey. Scooping up several large stones, Tavian whirled around and hurled them at the crazed animal. Despite a few direct hits, Cerberus kept on coming.

Frantically, Tavian ripped the satin cover off his car and threw it over his attacker. While the frenzied dog struggled to get free, he quickly punched his key remote. The gulls wings flew up and he darted inside just as Cerberus broke loose. Grabbing the door handle, Tavian slammed the wings shut in the nick of time. The enraged animal leapt up against the side of the car, raking his claws into the glossy orange enamel. Again and again. Scraping deep gouges into pristine skin of the six-hundred-and-fifty thousand-dollar sports car.

Tavian leaned on his tiger growl horn. Far from frightening his attacker, it just made Cerberus respond with more ferocious howls. Hearing the clamor, LeGrande ran out of the shed and grabbed hold of the enraged mongrel and dragged him back.

"You tie that bitch up or you're outta here!" Tavian yelled. He engaged the shift and floored the accelerator, showering man and dog in sharp gravel pellets as he fled the premises in reverse.

That afternoon, Tavian roared back to the Blast Furnace, popped open his gull wing doors, and took out a double-barreled shotgun. He found the three-legged dog chained to a stake in front of the shed and blasted a hole in his chest at point blank range. The Keeper and his crew came running out.

"Stand back!" Tavian ordered, waving them away with his shotgun.

As Cerberus twitched and groaned on the ground, Tavian calmly put his gun in his car and took out an axe. In one great swoop, he chopped the dog's head clean off, sending its blood gushing out of its body like a stream of water from an open fire hydrant.

"Whatthafuck!" LeGrande yelled.

"Bitch was dangerous," Tavian said. He pulled on a pair of latex gloves and put the severed head inside a clear plastic garbage bag. "Might have had rabies. Gotta have it tested."

Then he threw the head and gloves into a cardboard box on the floor of the passenger seat, jumped back behind the wheel, and blasted off.

Word of the incident traveled fast and brought Liz down from the office. She almost threw up at the gory scene. Cerberus had come to her rescue and had been cruelly slaughtered as a result.

"Who'd want to kill a crippled dog?" Tsonka asked.

"A madman," Liz said bitterly.

"Who happens to be our boss."

No one had anything to say about that.

"What we gonna do with the body?" J'Rod wondered. "He was Qwazi's dog. Followed him here last winter."

LeGrande kneeled down and picked up the headless body of the three-legged dog. "Only right to give him back to his master," he said.

Solemnly, he led the others into the Blast Furnace. Lifting the dead dog over his head, he paused for a moment as if he were a priest making an offering before an altar. Then with a heave, he threw the body into a cauldron of boiling pig iron. A moment later, Cerberus was vaporized into nothingness.

"Qwazi's got his dog back," LeGrande said. "Now he ain't gonna be so lonely anymore."

Later, when Liz returned to the Administration Building, she found the front door locked. After ringing the delivery bell, Bull came down with her coat and purse.

"You've been shit-canned," he said coldly without any trace of emotion. "No severance, no nothing. The boss said just get the fuck out and don't come back."

Liz was more relieved than surprised. She wouldn't have to pretend anymore. "My book bag," she said. "It's on the floor under my desk."

Bull pulled the door shut, locked it, and stomped back up the stairs. A few minutes later, the second floor window slid open and her book bag came flying out. On impact, it burst open, spilling its contents on the ground.

"You shoulda taken my advice!" the foreman hollered. "You coulda been his fuckin' wife! You coulda been rich! You stupid, fucking bitch!"

Silena

David was furious when he found out about Liz's firing. Unfortunately, he didn't have the liberty or leave to run down and punch Tavian in his hereditary harelip. Confined inside a small phone booth in the basement of Bancroft Hall, he felt utterly helpless, imprisoned in a glass cage. Outside the booth, Archie and half a dozen anxious plebes waited in line for their turn to call home.

"Hope you're gonna slap a sexual harassment suit on him," David told Liz when he finally calmed down.

She was in her apartment packing with one hand and holding her cell in the other. "I'm afraid that would be a waste of time. Only witnesses to the incidents were a dead dog, the Director of the CIA, and an unidentified bimbo. Good luck in getting any of them to testify."

"Comes down to a 'he said, she said' situation."

"These things usually do. Anyway, my time is better spent on your case. That will be my revenge."

A pugnacious, two-hundred-and-fifty pound linebacker butted in front of Archie and banged on the bifold door of the phone booth. "Come on hotshot! Get a move on!"

"Don't be so impatient, man," Archie scolded. "Cut Dave some slack."

"Fucker's had his five minutes!" the brute complained.

Inside the booth, David continued his conversation unfazed. "Working on my case won't pay your rent."

"No, it won't." Liz looked sadly at her small efficiency apartment. Located above a teashop on a cobblestoned street in Fells Point, it had a great water view of the Inner Harbor, assorted bridges, oil terminals, smoke stacks, cargo gantries, and the Domino Sugar Factory. The place had a lot of local color and character and she was really going to hate to leave.

"What are you gonna do?"

"Lou and Doc offered me a spare room in their home. I'd have to live on a steam grate if it weren't for them."

David sighed. "Wish I could come up and help you move."

"I can handle it. Don't want you to have to go AWOL for me. All my earthly belongings fit into two suitcases. I've learned to travel light."

The linebacker pounded on the door again. "Get the fuck off! I got shit to do!"

David reluctantly signed off and flung open the bifold door. "You got a problem, man?"

"Wish I could come up and help you move," the guy said in a sissified tone of voice.

David grabbed his collar and thrust him against the wall. Cocking his arm, he was about to break his knuckles in his face.

"Don't hit him, Dave," Archie intervened. "You'll just hurt your hand some more."

"You're right, Archie. Better save it for Tavian." David backed off and walked away.

The linebacker was beginning to think he was off the hook when Archie turned and slugged him in the stomach with a roundhouse right.

"My hand ain't broken, fucker. Don't you ever mess with my friend again."

Doubled in pain, the guy threw up on his spit-shined shoes.

"Thanks, man," David said. Despite his size, Archie was fearless. Not only that, he really packed a wallop.

"Hey, no problem. We're teammates, aren't we?"

"Yeah, teammates," David agreed. But not this year.

With her luggage rattling around in the bed of her green Tundra, Liz drove across town to the upscale Bolton Hill section of Baltimore. It was a small oasis of civility distinguished by 19th Century townhouses on shady, tree-lined boulevards. The community was only a short walk to theaters and art galleries and was a favorite residence of the city's cultural elite.

She found Louisa's cream-colored Mercedes convertible in front of a three-storied Victorian brownstone on a corner lot with a small ivy patch for a front yard. Raymond's Humvee was parked nearby in the dappled shadows of a large elm tree. Cloaked in its olive drab, black and brown camouflage, it was practically invisible.

Doc met her at the curb and despite her protests, picked up her two overstuffed bags himself. In his overalls and jaunty cap, it seemed somehow appropriate.

"Bet you didn't know I worked as a part-time valet in high-school, Miss Mancini," he said. "Welcome to Hotel Moses. Cocktails are at five and dinner at six. Casual dress will be fine. Follow me and we'll drop these off downstairs."

He led her around to the back of the house and down some steps to the basement entrance. Liz was delighted. The small room that Louisa had offered her turned out to be a suite that had been used by her mother when she was alive. Besides the bedroom, there was a kitchenette, bathroom, and small sitting room. Raymond had moved in a desk, telephone, computer, fax machine, and a set of law books.

"It's wonderful, Doc. You know, I don't have the money now, but I'm going to pay you a fair rent."

"The only payback I want is for you to use your time to work on the mummy suit. Beating the Blackburns in court is payback enough for me."

"Gotta deal."

"Come on, Lou's waiting for us upstairs. We'll give you a tour."

The place was impressive with its twelve-foot high ceilings, hardwood floors, and lace curtains on the windows. Elegant chandeliers hung from the ceilings and the walls were decorated in a variety of Victorian floral motifs designed by William Morris. The furniture, like Raymond, himself, was a study in contrast. Antiques, mostly from the Louis XIV era graced every room. Their upholstery, however, had long since disintegrated and had been replaced by a dazzling assortment of African textiles and animal skins that the couple had collected on their many trips to Africa. They had traveled there, not as tourists, but as a doctor and lawyer determined to donate their professional services to the people of their impoverished homelands. Sightseeing had been put off until sometime in the future.

In the heart of the house, hanging over the fireplace, was a framed genealogy that traced the couple's roots back four hundred years.

"My people immigrated from the Gold Coast after the American Civil War," Louisa told Liz. "They settled in Boston and found work as custodians in the colleges there. Eventually, they were able to get educated themselves and over time they managed to improve their condition and prosper."

"Far different story on my side," Doc said sadly. "My people were slaves. Most of the details came from my paternal grandma. Lady Laetitia was what everyone called her. Pop took me to meet her when I was a kid. Lived out on the neck of Tilghman Island in a lean-to with her daughter's family. She was ninety-four years old at the time and had nary a tooth in her head but her memory was prodigious. Pop made a tape recording of her recollections. Seems my ancestors were from the Congo, captured in battle by an African warlord and sold to white slavers. A great many of them died in chains and were thrown into the Atlantic, Those that survived the voyage were auctioned off at ports along the Chesapeake. Some family members were separated from each other and lost track of altogether. A few fell into Blackburn hands. Even at ninety-four, Laetitia wept for them when she told us of the cruel abuses they had suffered.

The master of Kings Oak at that time was Caecilius, III. The family knew him as Trey but his slaves called him Trinity because he was the size of three men and wielded the power of life and death over them like a three-personed god. He was fat at a time when most men were lean, struggling to scratch out a living from the land. Trey's appetite was prodigious, both for fine food and the flesh of young women. He kept his wife's belly full of babies and when she couldn't take him anymore he went after his slave women. One in particular. A beautiful girl named Silena who was a deaf-mute. She pleased him so much that he excused her from manual labor and gave her a cabin of her very own. The menfolk, black and white together, were forbidden from coming anywhere near it or her. Like I said, Trey was a big man and so he moved a sturdy four-poster inside her cabin, more for his comfort than hers. It had been shipped over from England and was complete with draw curtains and a canopy. Got a lot of use, it seems. Over the next five years, Silena gave birth to seven light-skinned babies. The first six times, Trinity came down to her cabin and snatched the baby away. He was afraid his wife would kill him if she found out what he had been up to. So he killed the baby instead. Not personally, of course. Gave it to his white overseer who smothered it and buried the little body in an unmarked grave. By the time the seventh one was born, Silena was determined her child would live. She bathed her little girl in Black Walnut dye which turned her skin as dark as coal. When Trey saw the black baby, he figured one of the bucks had gotten to his woman before him. None would confess and so all the men on the plantation were given twenty lashes and warned that one or all of them would die if his woman ever had another black baby. Fortunately, he let this one live. Even so, Silena was heart-broken and couldn't bear to have another child. And she didn't. She died of complications during her next pregnancy. Death was the only freedom she could find."

Raymond pointed to her place on the genealogical tree. "Silena's last child was named Hannah and she was Laetitia's grandmother."

"I don't see Trey's name next to Silena's on the chart," Liz observed.

"That's 'cause we're not a hundred percent sure he was Hannah's father. Trey visited Silena three times a week and his three sons secretly filled in for him on the other nights. They let her alone on Sundays when Trey's wife made all of them go to church with her. That's when the foreman came calling. Could have been any one of them."

Liz shook her head. "Makes me sick to think of it."

"Me, too. Laetitia was an octoroon and still had her grandmother's light skin. That makes me 1/32nd white."

For the first time since Liz had known him, Raymond removed his Ivy League cap. There on his right forehead just down from the hairline was a small white splotch.

"Makes me crazy to think I might have a little Blackburn blood in me," he said, running his hand over his unsightly birthmark. "A little Blackburn poison." His voice broke and his eyes moistened. "I'd slice open my veins and bleed it out if I could."

Louisa put her arm around him and gave him a hug.

Liz realized that the professor's interest in the bog mummy case was far deeper and more personal than she thought. Raymond Moses was going to get even with the Blackburns if it was the last thing he did. And she was, too.

Resolve

Rage against the Blackburns fueled David's determination to rebuild his body and regain his strength. With Dr. Zegusa's permission, he began to work out with the lacrosse team in the weight room, even though he wouldn't be allowed to play until next season. It would be an arduous task to be sure, but he was inspired by the indomitable spirit and courage of the ancestors who lived in his blood.

First and foremost, there was the example of Great Standing Bear. When he was just a boy, he won his name in a confrontation with a black bear that had wandered into the village in search of food while the men were away hunting. Raising his arms above his head, the boy puffed up his chest and made a fearsome face. Startled, the beast backed away, then turned tail and was chased out of the village by the boy's mighty roar. His bravery saved the women and children of the tribe and made him werowance when he came of age.

David thought, too, of the great werowance's oldest son who rose to glory in the dead of night when the fearsome Nanticokes were putting his father's hunting lodge to the torch. With fangs of fire biting into the backbone of his bow, he sent a flaming arrow into the eye of the enemy chieftain, slaying him on the spot and sending his warriors into a panicked retreat. Thus did Burning Bow earn his name and a place of honor in the history of the tribe.

In his company, too, was brave Hawk-in-the-Heart. Without weapons, he battled a pack of hungry wolves, hammering them with his hands, slinging them by their tails, and smashing their skulls against the ground. He sacrificed himself to save the lives of his people while the ravenous beasts ripped out his bowels.

His ancestors had won their names by selfless acts of courage against overwhelming odds. David was all too aware of his own shortcomings. He had yet to fulfill the promise of his secret Choptank name. The name that Grandfather Two Tongues had bestowed on him at birth. The name that was a prophecy of things to come.

NAGPRA

"Section 4 is my favorite part," Liz told Raymond. They were discussing the Native American Graves Protection and Repatriation Act in the professor's living room after dinner.

"Ah, yes," Raymond said. "Illegal trafficking of human remains." He had changed out of his overalls into a Harvard sweat suit and was resting comfortably in his zebra-skinned massage chair. "It's one of my favorite passages, too," he added, putting his feet up on a matching ottoman.

"If you two are going to be talking shop," Louisa interjected "I'm going up to watch TV."

"*General Hospital* must be on," Raymond whispered loudly to Liz. "Her favorite show."

"Better than the *Law and Order* episode going on down here," Lou shot back. She bounded off the cheetah-skinned sofa and made her exit up the stairs.

"Night, night," Raymond said. Fiddling with the chair's remote, he turned his attention back to his favorite student.

"Believe it or not, Miss Mancini, this contraption's got four different massages. Think I'll start with the kneading program." He punched a button and the mechanical fingers in back of the chair began to undulate. "Ooh, that feels sooo good. I can control the ottoman, too. It's great for the calves and dawgs. Now where were we?"

"Section 4, Doc. It says Septimus could be fined and imprisoned for up to twelve months—if we can prove he illegally profited from the mummies."

"A year in the slammer doesn't seem nearly enough, does it?"

"Maybe we can suggest a year per mummy," Liz said. "There were two hundred and ten as I remember."

"That's more like it."

"But first we have to find proof that he made an illegal profit."

"The scoundrel made a bundle, you can be sure of that," Raymond said. "I'm sure Mr. Roche would have advised him to make an 'in-kind' donation to the museum. That would have been the smart thing to do. The donor is allowed to set the value of the gift which can then be legally deducted from his income tax."

"And since the mummies are priceless, there's no telling what value he put on them," Liz added.

"Exactly. We need to find out just how much it was. I want the jury to hear that. It will make their eyes pop out of their sockets."

Raymond raised the remote and switched over to the rolling massage. "Ah, this one's Heaven itself. Helps me roll with the punches."

"I'll see about subpoenaing a copy of Septimus' tax return," Liz said, scribbling a reminder on her yellow note pad.

"Good, but don't waste time on his personal one. We need the return for Blackburn Steelworks. It's the holding company for all the family's financial interests. Found that out in my slave reparation lawsuit. The scoundrel transferred all his personal assets to it so that they would be protected under his corporate shield: brokerage accounts, art works, real estate, the works."

"Got it."

"If the corporate tax return becomes a problem, you can get an appraisal from the museum. The donor is required to file one. And that stuff's public information."

"I'll get it one way or the other, Doc. We really have the goods on Septimus this time. Don't see how he can get out of this one."

Raymond suddenly clicked off his massage. The zebra-skinned chair stopped shaking and he sat as still as if he had just died.

"Something the matter, Doc? You look a little worried."

"To tell you the truth, Miss Mancini, there is one small technicality that's been bothering me."

"Oh?"

"But don't worry, I'll think of a way around it." Raymond leaned back in his chair and selected all four massages at once. He closed his eyes and his body began to shake like he was a patient undergoing shock therapy.

Albino Buck

The twenty-four-point albino stopped in his tracks, his pink nostrils sniffing the breeze. Downwind, three bow hunters watched silently from camouflaged platforms that were strapped to the topmost branches of a nearby elm. Slowly, Septimus raised his crossbow and took aim. The buck was standing broadside about a hundred feet away but the 4x scope brought him a lot closer. With a loud twang, the carbon shaft rocketed across the clearing at 335 feet per second and struck the startled stag in the neck with such force that it passed clean through his body. Wounded, the buck cried out and bolted into a nearby thicket.

"Damn it!"

"Your sight must be out of adjustment, Mr. Chairman," Laurence Roche said diplomatically. He knew from experience that when things went wrong, it was never the boss's fault.

"Can't be going too far, Dad," Tavian said. "Snow White's pumping blood like you hit an artery."

"Let's go finish it off," his father said.

One by one, the three men unharnessed their safety belts and climbed down the ladder. Once on the ground, they had no trouble following the trail of blood that was splattered over tall grasses and thorny bushes. None of them seemed the least bit concerned about the Indian legend that claimed it was bad luck to kill an albino deer.

"As you were saying, Mr. Roche," Septimus said. "Before the buck paid us a call..."

"I was telling you not to worry, boss. Raymond Moses doesn't have a case. It's true that NAGPRA requires native remains to be turned over to their tribe for reburial, but..."

Septimus cut him off. "And lose 32 million in tax deductions? No way."

"Let me finish, boss. You may have read about the Kennewick Man case. It was in the news a year or two ago. The skeletal remains of a prehistoric man were found washed up near the Columbia River in the state of Washington. Five different tribes claimed him under NAGPRA. A group of scientists countersued under the Archeological Resources and Protection Act, arguing that they should be allowed to keep the body for further study. The Federal Court of Appeals ruled in their favor. It's a precedent that should help us in our case. We'll contend that you donated the mummies for scientific study and are thus entitled to claim a tax deduction."

Septimus was reassured by the news. "Make sure we use all our influence to get a judge who is familiar with that case and congenial to our cause."

"Already working on it, boss."

The trail of blood splatter ended at a small stream.

"I think we lost him," Tavian said.

"Look over there." Roche's beady, bloodshot eyes rarely missed a detail, whether it was in a legal brief or elsewhere. "Whitey went downstream and came out where those overturned rocks are. You can see what looks like wet footprints on the bank. Must have climbed up over that ridge of pines."

Once again the men picked up the blood trail like hounds on the hunt. But Septimus couldn't get his mind off the lawsuit.

"Raymond Moses is a crafty bastard. He probably knows all about the Kennewick Man case. There's more here than meets the eye, Mr. Roche. The suit is not just about the mummies. Moses wants to get us into court so that Indian punk can have a public stage to whine about his people's stolen lands."

"Your ancestor won Kings Oak by Right of Discovery," Roche said. "Can't be contested. No way, no how."

"Maybe they think the bad publicity will make us want to pay them off," Tavian said.

Roche shrugged. "Maybe that's it."

"They'd be wrong of course," Septimus said sternly. "I'd never submit to blackmail."

"Of course not."

"What about the parchment?"

"You said it had been burned, boss."

"I meant the Choptank copy, Mr. Roche. That's what worries me. There's no telling what they'll say it means."

"Carter Seymour assured us there's no way it can be translated. He's an expert and he ought to know."

Septimus stared at him. "Sometimes experts don't know everything, Mr. Roche. You should know that better than anyone."

The little gnome was duly chastised. His boss was undoubtedly referring to Roche's colossal failure to have his first wife, Sheila Ann, sign a prenuptial agreement. The divorce had left him almost destitute. Despite the experience, Roche hadn't had the nerve to suggest a prenup to his next three wives either for fear they'd leave him. Now about seventy-five percent of his salary went to alimony.

Over the rise, they found the buck lying still against the trunk of an oak tree. Streams of blood ran down his neck like a red hand with elongated fingers.

"I get to skin it," Tavian said. He took the coiled rope off his shoulder and unsheathed his serrated, skinning knife. "Gonna pretend it's an Injun."

"Take off the head first," his father ordered. "Make sure you get plenty of cape with it."

"It's gonna look great in your den, Mr. Chairman," Roche said.

"I've got just the place for it over the hearth," Septimus said. "Right above the Founder's musket."

As Tavian approached, the buck suddenly twitched.

"It's not dead, yet," Septimus said. Raising his crossbow once again, he glanced over at his son.

"I want that Indian parchment found and destroyed. Do you understand? As soon as possible."

"Yes, Dad."

And with that Septimus shot the albino through the heart.

Ancestors in the Blood

"Ouch!" David said. He averted his eyes as the needle punctured the vein in his arm.

Operating the syringe was a Pakistani lady in a white lab coat and yellow turban. Her eyes were exotically accentuated with thick black liner, and a vermillion bindi was painted in the center of her forehead.

After filling the barrel with blood, she drew out the needle and gave David a cotton swab to hold in the crook of his elbow.

"Please to tell me, Mr. Waterfield. That was not hurting you, no?"

"No, ma'am. Not much."

"How long will it be before we can get his DNA profile, Dr. Rasheed?" Liz asked.

"Six to eight weeks," the lady doctor said. Depressing the plunger, she squirted David's blood into a glass vial.

"And how about the DNA from the mummies? When can we expect those profiles?"

"They are telling me we just got the tissue samples from the museum yesterday. Two-hundred ten of them. The extraction process with them is more, how you say, complicated. The specimens they are so old. This is true also for the blood X on the parchment."

"We go to court in mid-August," Liz told her. "That's five months away. We need to see the profiles as soon as possible. We've got lots of work to do."

"We do our best," Dr. Rasheed promised. "Should be no problem."

David rolled down his sleeve and slipped into his dress blue jacket. After thanking Dr. Rasheed, he and Liz made their way back down the narrow corridor. On either side were clean white labs filled with busy technicians, racks of test tubes, and whirling centrifuges. As they entered the lobby, David stopped to look at the photo enlargements on the walls: microscopic images of blood platelets and colorful renderings of the double helix. What particularly fascinated him were the blown-up bands of DNA test strips.

"They look kinda like bar codes you'd find in a store," he said.

"Or tattooed on Raymond's butt," Liz added. She went on to tell him the story about the professor's mooning days at Harvard Law.

"Doc's a real character," David said. "But very generous. This has gotta be an expensive process."

"It is," Liz agreed. "But he insisted that we do it. It's the only way to scientifically establish that you are a lineal descendant of the mummies. And the law requires that before the museum is obliged to give them back to you for reburial."

"I don't know how I can ever repay him."

"You can't. Me either. For my room and board, I mean. But repayment is the last thing on Ray and Lou's minds. They've already got plenty of money. What they want is for justice to be done."

Like the ancestors who live in my blood, David thought.

Outside in the parking lot, they got into Liz's truck. She had been kind enough to pick David up in Annapolis and drive him all they way to Rockville to the DNA lab.

"I don't have to be back at the Academy until two," David told her. "Treat you to lunch?"

"Great idea, I'm starved."

They headed south on I-295 and turned into a strip mall that advertised a Health Food Deli on the premises. To their surprise it turned out to be a greasy, fast food dive instead. The owner, who was leaning on the cash register, had pork chop cheeks, a triple chin, and a belly that looked eight months pregnant. He was a walking advertisement that said "Eat Somewhere Else."

"Hey," David said, "I thought your sign said you were a deli."

"That was the last owner. Went of business. Haven't had time to change the sign."

"Do you have anything remotely healthy," Liz asked.

"Just what's on the menu, ma'am."

"I can't have the chicken because it causes pfiesteria in fish. And I don't want a fish sandwich because of the mercury that might be in it. And I bet the vegetables in your salads were grown with fertilizers."

A young black couple looked up from a table in the corner.

"Hey lady, not so loud," the owner said. "I have other customers here."

"And forget the burgers," David added. "Cows poop in the Bay and cause the nutrients that kill the grasses."

The disgusted young couple got up and left without finishing their fries.

"You're gonna cause me to go out of business if you stay here any longer," the owner complained. "So what it'll be?"

"An ice cube in a cup and a glass of bottled water," Liz said.

"Make that two," David added.

Back on the road, the conversation turned to the state of David's health.

"Dr. Zegusa said my knee needs another month to heal," he told Liz. "Got me on a lot of stretches and leg lifts but says it won't be strong enough to play this year. You know, with all the running and cutting I'd have to do."

"That's too bad. How's the coach taking it?"

"Not well at all. He talked me into sitting on the bench with the team this season. I think it's more for his sake than the other guys. Made me the chief statistician and head cheerleader."

"Quite an honor," Liz laughed.

"So far, we've done pretty well. Won our first two games without me."

"Must be a good cheerleader."

"Unfortunately, next weekend we play Princeton. That should keep me busy."

"They're tough, huh."

David nodded. "And experienced. Everyone's back from last year's championship team. Just hope we can give them a good game. Why don't you come down and we can get together for a bite afterwards?"

"Great idea! I've never seen a lacrosse game before."

"That reminds me, I promised LeGrande and his buddies that I'd get them into a game sometime. They've never seen one either."

"I remember. It was that night at the Pig Iron Pub. They've never been ten miles from the mill before and I volunteered to drive them down and be their bodyguard."

"Heaven help anyone who messes with you."

Liz laughed. "I'll call them and see if they can come. It'll be a real treat for them, and me, too."

Tiger Meat

Game day morning and Liz's truck had vanished from a side street near Raymond's house. She figured it had been taken sometime in the middle of the night.

"Damn!" Liz sank down to the curb and put her hands over her face.

There was no need to call the cops. She knew very well who the culprit was: Dundalk Bank and Trust. A wholly owned subsidiary of Blackburn Steelworks, it offered employees a small discount on car loans. Since her termination, she had been receiving increasingly hostile dunning letters that threatened immediate repossession unless she could catch up on her back payments. A series of cranky phone calls followed soon after. She was pretty sure it was Tavian on the other end of the line. His telltale lisp was pretty hard to disguise. Without a job, there was no way she could keep up. Despite her pleas for more time, the bank had finally made good on its threats. And it couldn't have come at a worse time.

Not wanting to disappoint David, she called LeGrande on her cell phone and arranged for them all to meet at the Greyhound station in Dundalk. It was not as convenient, but it would get them to Annapolis all the same.

It was the Blast Furnace boys first day off in two months and the men acted like truant school boys, tromping down the aisle of the bus in steel-toed boondockers that were as heavy as concrete blocks. All of them were dressed up in their very best clothes, which looked very much like their worst clothes except that they had newer patches on their knees and elbows.

LeGrande rode next to Liz as befitted the Keeper of the Blast Furnace while the other men filled in around them.

"Things ain't the same at the mill anymore, Miss Mancini," LeGrande complained as they headed across the Francis Scott Key Bridge. "Without you and Qwazi, I mean. No one laughs much anymore."

"I know, Lee. But things are gonna change. You'll see. We'll nail those bastards."

"Sure hope you do. A nail gun between the eyes would be good."

The bus stopped frequently, loading and unloading its passengers. But it didn't seem to bother the steelmen.

"Only other vehicle I ever rode in what was this long," Kenyatta said, "is my cream-colored, Cadillac stretch limo."

"Say what?" Mandala said.

"You heard me. Got a TV and bar in the back and a hot tub, too."

"Why didn't we take it today?"

"Hell, I gotta give the driver some time off. What you think—I'm a slave driver?"

"A liar be a better name," J'Rod said.

Passing through Arnold, they caught sight of the Academy complex across the Severn River. Surrounded by bright blue water and crisp white sails, it was a far different world than the charcoal-covered mill town they were used to.

Exiting on Main Street near State Circle, they walked several blocks down Maryland Avenue to Gate 3. Up ahead was a guardhouse manned by two marines in camouflage fatigues and armed with automatic weapons. As Liz and her friends walked towards them, a sports car zoomed up and startled them with a tiger growl horn. Jumping aside, they were dismayed to see Tavian at the wheel of his hot-orange Ferrari Enzo and a male passenger sitting beside him. Tavian seemed as surprised as they were.

"What the hell!" they heard him say.

Liz was beside herself. She had forgotten that Tavian was a Princeton grad. Just her rotten luck that he was here, too.

"Good news!" Tavian hollered as he pulled around them. "Insurance said my buggy was a total loss and bought me an identical replacement. Ain't it cool? Best of all, the lab tests came back negative for rabies. The cur was clean." He grinned at them sadistically from ear to ear. "Isn't it great! I'm gonna be okay!"

LeGrande flexed his muscles and started for the car. Liz grabbed his arm and stopped him.

"He's still your boss, Lee. Let it go."

Tavian gunned his motor.

But he's not mine anymore, Liz thought.

"Hey, Tavian!" she yelled at the top of her lungs. "Rape anybody lately!"

Tavian face flushed. He peeled out, then slammed his brakes at the guardhouse. Instead of arresting him for reckless driving, the two marines on duty snapped to attention and saluted, not the driver, but his passenger. Even in civvies, they recognized him as Captain Cyrus Van Aiken, winner of a Purple Heart and head of internal security at the Academy.

"You might want to check out those people in back of us," Tavian told the guards. "Look kinda Un-American to me."

"Do it!" Cy barked.

"Yes, sir." The marines saluted again as Tavian cruised through the gate, thrusting his middle finger up at the group behind him.

When Liz and her friends got to the guardhouse, the marines performed a "random" search. After frisking the men and patting them down, they took their names and addresses before letting them pass through. It was a humiliating way to start the day but the boys from the Blast Furnace weren't about to let it ruin their outing.

Once inside the Academy grounds, they were overawed. Its red brick sidewalks, stately limestone buildings, historic monuments, and impeccable landscaping looked spectacular in the springtime sun. They were stunned by the sleek-looking F-4 Phantom on display near the lacrosse field that overlooked Spa Creek. But most of all, it was the appearance of Rip Miller Field itself that impressed them the most.

"Looka that green," Tsonka said. "It be so bright it hurts your eyes."

"My eyes used to it," Kenyatta said. "Same kind of grass I got on my estate in Ireland."

"You got no estate and that ain't grass anyways," Mandala said. "That's astroturf, bro."

But Kenyatta wasn't listening, already transported to his imaginary world far away.

"Think I'll put some of that Astro-stuff in my front yard," J'Rod said. "Won't have to do no mo mowing."

"You don't mow now," Tsonka said. "You got nuthing but dirt and dog shit at your place."

"You gotta point there."

"You could dye it green, bro," LeGrande suggested.

"No, he can't," Kenyatta said, back from his momentary trip to the Emerald Isle. "Everyone know dog shit don't look good in green."

As they filed into the bleachers, they found only a smattering of loyal fans on hand to root for the starless Navy team. Chief among them was Admiral Shaw who had come without his wife, Mitzi. In contrast, the seats on the visitor's side of the field were packed with orange and black clad preppies from Princeton and their rich alumni, eager to see their top-ranked Tigers devour the lowly Midshipmen.

"We outnumbered," LeGrande complained.

"Yeah, but our side weighs more than they do," Mandala said in a voice as deep and heavy as his three-hundred and fifty pound body.

Helene was already there and had saved Liz six seats near mid-field. With her were Archie's parents, each wearing a T-shirt with a gold "Navy" on the front. Like their son, they both had auburn hair and a faceful of freckles. After all the introductions had been made, Liz sat down next to Helene. As always, she was attired in the Uniform of the Day in anticipation of a visit to her boyfriend's room after the game.

"Archibald's starting at goal today," she told Liz.

"Hank and I are so excited," Frieda Unger added.

"Haven't missed one of his games since grade school," her husband added proudly, a camcorder hanging from his shoulder.

"That's great," Liz said. "David has to wait another year to play. The guys and I just came down to watch him cheerlead."

"Hope he ain't wearing no dress," J'Rod said.

"But pompoms be okay," Kenyatta joked.

The hometown crowd let out a holler as the Midshipmen ran out on the field, resplendent in their shiny, blue helmets and shorts and white shirts with big gold numbers on them. Coach Sleazak came out next followed by his injured star suited up in gray sweats. Walking with a slight limp, David carried a bag of sticks over his shoulder and a box of balls under his arm.

"I hate that punk!" Tavian said, as he tracked him across the field in his binoculars.

"Hate him all you want," Cy said "but the punk's an awesome lacrosse player. Sleazak's secret weapon. Fast as hell. Can even dunk from the back of the goal like the Gait brothers used to do. And get this, he plays with an old-fashioned wooden stick!"

"Yeah, well it looks like he's not playing today."

"As I understand it," Cy said with a wry smile "he was injured playing baseball. Out for the season. But Sleazak expects him to be back next year. Thinks he can lead the team to the National Title."

"Maybe not," Tavian said with more than a trace of bitterness in his voice. "I have a feeling the punk's accident prone and won't be back at all."

Cy knew just what he meant.

A female mid from Tennessee stepped out on the field and sang the National Anthem with a countrified twang. The crowd joined in, as they did in every sporting event in Maryland, with a loud "O" on the "O say can you see" line. It was their way of calling attention to the state's beloved Orioles.

Afterwards, the mayhem began in earnest. Princeton's potent, All-American offense wasted no time in putting on a show, much to Archie's dismay. Their offense was choreographed like an intricate ballet danced in double time. Against them the Navy long sticks were completely outmanned. Archie was peppered with an unrelenting hail of shots that made him feel like he was on the receiving end of a Biblical stoning of epic proportions.

"They're trying to hurt him!" Archie's mom cried out in alarm.

"But they haven't scored on him yet," Helene said hopefully.

Just then, Archie made an acrobatic save that so startled the opposition that they stopped in their tracks. He saw his chance and sprinted out of the goal and headed down field.

The Navy crowd rose to their feet and roared. David had never seen his roommate move so fast. He was practically running out of his shoes.

"Go, Archie, go!" While Frieda cheered, Hank rolled his camcorder. Helene and Liz jumped up and down. So did the boys from the Blast Furnace. For a moment, Liz was afraid they might bring down the bleachers.

Archie blazed past the defenders and raced into the clear, with only the opposing goalie in the way of his glory.

Coach Sleazak was so excited he ran down the sidelines with him, screaming and pumping his fists.

Archie reared back to fire. Unfortunately, he stepped on a shoelace and tumbled face first into the Astroturf.

The crowd groaned. They groaned even louder when the Tigers picked up the loose ball, passed the length of the field, and spooned the ball easily in Navy's untended goal.

Things got worse from there. With Archie's confidence gone, the Tigers couldn't miss. To make matters worse, Navy's attack was sluggish in the extreme. Even the hotshot Armbruister was playing poorly, leading all players in dropped balls and missed passes, a statistic he steadily improved upon all afternoon until he had to leave the game with a broken nose. This one was particularly gruesome. His cartilage was smashed flat leaving a shapeless flap of flesh hanging down like a broken blood bag.

Admiral Shaw abandoned ship at halftime, utterly disgusted. The final score was thirteen to two. You couldn't tell the sweat from the tears on Coach Sleazak's agonized face. It was going to be a long, dismal season.

Liz hung her head. It was bad enough that the Middies had lost so badly, but worse than that, she knew Tavian was sitting across the field gloating in his team's victory. Still, she vowed to be upbeat and not tell David about his presence on the other side of the field. That would just make him angry and he really couldn't do anything about it anyway. As the spectators began to clear away, Helene and the Ungers went off to console Archie. Liz and the steelmen stepped down the bleachers to see David.

"Hey, all I can say is wait until next year," she told him. "Princeton won't have a chance."

"We'll see," David said. "Right now, I'm just happy you all came down."

"Man, this inspired us to start us a team at the mill," LeGrande said. "Figure we can use shovels for sticks and a piece of coal for a ball."

"What'll you use for a goal?" David asked.

"Way I figure it," Tsonka said "the bad boy's fancy-ass sports car will do just fine."

David laughed. An image of Tavian's Ferrari loaded up like a coal bin came to mind.

David emptied a bag of sticks on the artificial turf. "These might be better than shovels. Some of them are broken but most are just bent. We're just gonna throw them away. Maybe you guys can fix 'em."

"Hey, thanks," J'Rod said. "No problem, we handy."

They picked out a hard rubber ball and five crooked, titanium poles. Mandala straightened them out like they were nothing more than wire coat hangers.

"Let's play ball!" LeGrande shouted.

He led the other men onto the field in their steel-toed boondockers. In their wake was a trail of crushed plastic footprints that would take a week to regain their shape. Throwing and catching were skills that seemed to elude them. Most of their energy was spent chasing down loose balls. What they were very good at was checking each other with bone-jarring blocks that would have rendered most players unconscious.

As they watched from the sidelines, Liz filled David in on the lawsuit.

"Just heard they've assigned a judge to our case," she said.

"Good."

"Not really. It's going to be Jason Andrews."

"Don't tell me. A Blackburn crony, right?"

"You got it. Septimus took him on a big game hunt in Africa last year. Old prep school buddies."

"Might be a short trial."

"Doc will do everything he can. You know that."

"I know."

"Duck!" Tsonka screamed.

David reached out and caught the hard rubber ball an arm's length from Liz's head.

"Hey! The goal's over that way," he joked as he threw it back.

"I think they really enjoyed coming down," Liz said. "It's like a holiday for them. For me, too."

"Speaking of holidays, firsties graduate at the end of May. There's a lot of cool stuff going on down here. The Blue Angels are flying and us lowly plebes have to scale the Herndon Monument. There's a dance afterwards with a live band. Thought we could double date with Archie and Helene. How about it?"

"A real date? I thought you'd never ask." Liz leaned over and gave him a hug and a kiss on the cheek.

David blushed. He was well aware that Public Displays of Affection were not permitted on the grounds of the United States Naval Academy. Still in the aftermath of the game, no one seemed to notice. Or so it seemed.

Across the field, Tavian put down his binoculars in disgust and turned to his friend. "Bancroft Hall, third floor, Room 311."

"Know it well," Cy said. "Consider it done."

G.M.O. CALLAGHAN

Obelisk

The blast of a starting gun! A frenzied mob in gym shorts and T-shirts bolted out of the confines of Tecumseh Courtyard. Racing down the red brick path, they flew through a cheering gauntlet of parents, upperclassmen, and curious tourists. From the bandstand across the Yard came a brassy Sousa march.

The stampeding herd followed the path to a roped-off clearing in front of the chapel where the Herndon Monument arose twenty-one feet into the air. At the peak of the obelisk was a blue-bordered Dixie cup cover, the hated symbol of plebehood. The plebes' task was to climb up and replace it with a midshipman's hard-brimmed hat. Only then could they advance up the next rung of the ladder to become third-class midshipmen. The only problem was that the monolith was covered with two hundred pounds of lard.

Liz had arrived early, dressed in dungarees and driving Louisa's cream-colored, Mercedes SL Convertible.

"Wow, things must be looking up for you," Helene said. Today, she was outfitted in crisp, summer whites.

"Wish it were mine," Liz said "but it belongs to a friend."

Lou had insisted on loaning it to Liz after she heard about her truck being taken away. Liz had to admit it was a lot more convenient than the bus and more appropriate for an end-of-

318

year celebration. She and Helene had staked out their places right behind the spectator retaining rope and in front of on-lookers that had grown ten deep since their arrival. As always, Archie's dutiful parents were there to videotape the event for posterity.

Behind them, twelve-foot scaffolds had been set up for the convenience of professional photographers. The annual scaling of Herndon was a made-to-order media event, a tradition the TV stations and newspapers never tired of covering.

"There's Archibald!" Helene said excitedly. Despite his short stature, his flaming red hair made him stand out in any crowd.

"Where's David?" Liz scanned the mob. But her man was nowhere to be seen.

The whooping and hollering died out as the plebes confronted the magnitude of their challenge. Never had the Herndon Monument seemed taller than it was today. The thick layer of lard made it look as difficult and treacherous to scale as Mount Everest. Some took off their sneakers and began to throw them at the Dixie cup cap in a fruitless attempt to knock it off its perch, not knowing it had been securely wired down by upperclassmen.

Archie spotted Helene and Liz in the crowd.

"Hey! Look at this!" he shouted.

They watched as he took off his shoes, tied the laces together, and whirled them around his head like he was an Olympic hammer thrower. His shot wasn't even close, missing by a mile and landing in the branches of a tulip poplar tree.

"Shit!" he said.

"Archibald has never been able to throw straight," Helene told Liz. "That's why he became a goalie. He can catch almost anything you throw at him."

Anything but a Princeton shot, Liz thought. She looked around for David again. She knew there was no way he would voluntarily miss out on the Herndon climb and began to worry that maybe he had gotten sick.

The barrage of tennis shoes continued. Several soles stuck in the lard as futile reminders of the task ahead. It was clear there would be no easy way out today. There never was.

In previous years, the plebe class, after hours of frustration, usually came together and formed a human pyramid that would allow one of them to climb to the top. Scaling Herndon was an exercise that was designed to promote teamwork.

But not today.

"Move aside," a voice commanded.

Liz recognized it immediately.

The class fell silent as David Waterfield emerged from the throng and walked confidently up to the face of the unscalable monument. Gone was the limp of only last month. Pulling off his T-shirt, he stunned the crowd with his well-muscled physique.

"Dave's really gotten himself buffed up," Helene said to Liz, her voice laced with envy.

"Uh huh."

He surprised them further by ripping his shirt in two. Tying the ends together, he spun them around into a makeshift rope.

"What's he doing?" Helene asked.

"Not a clue."

Stepping out of his sneakers, David slapped the rope around the shaft of the monument. Then leaning back and pulling tight, he slowly began to climb up one step at a time, sliding the rope up as he went, like a lumberjack scaling a tree.

"Go David! Go!"

Liz focused in on his feet and ankles. The blisters he had received from his contact with the toxic waste in Miss Applebaum's schoolroom had flared up again. She knew the pain had never completely subsided and was amazed that his will power was so strong that he was able to ignore it.

"To the top! To the top!" his fellow plebes shouted. They moved in underneath him, supporting him as he ascended ever upwards. The Navy band joined in with a drum roll that swelled with each arduous step. Like circus acrobats, his classmates climbed up on each other's backs and shoulders to buttress him from a fall. But there was no need to be concerned. In five minutes, David was at the summit of Mount Herndon. Gripping the rope in one hand, he snatched away the hated Dixie cup cover and tossed it back into the crowd. Archie threw him the hard hat and David slapped it on top, then slid down into the arms of his classmates.

"Plebes no more!" they shouted. "Plebes no more!"

Even Liz and Helene joined in the cheer. So did Midshipman Sasser, the saucy black woman who was David's squad leader during Plebe Summer. She remembered how she teased him and the other men about climbing Herndon. How she boasted that a woman would be first to the top. Someday, maybe, but not today. This was David Waterfield's time to shine.

The band reprised their rousing Sousa march. Lifting David on their shoulders, the mob carried him over to the steps of the

Chapel where Admiral Oliver Shaw had watched the whole incident unfold. It was one of the shortest climbs on record. Not the teamwork that he was expecting, but a superlative physical effort by an individual. An individual who had worked extremely hard to regain his full strength. An individual who had made the Superintendent's List this past semester despite his debilitating accident. An individual who was, first and foremost, a leader of men.

"According to tradition," Admiral Shaw announced, "the first plebe up the pole is destined to become the first admiral in the class. Unfortunately, the Academy historian tells me that this hasn't happened yet, which means it's more of an unfulfilled prophecy than an active tradition. This year, I have a feeling that's going to change."

With that, he took off his shoulder boards, with their four gold stars, and handed them to David Waterfield.

"Congratulations, son," he said. "And good luck."

The plebes roared their approval and Liz and Helene hugged each other.

"Thank you, sir. I'll do my best," David said. But first, there was another prophecy that needed to be fulfilled—the one foretold so long ago by Grandfather Two Tongues. The prophecy of his secret Choptank name.

That evening, a formal ball was held inside spacious Dahlgren Hall with music provided by a twelve-piece orchestra. The atmosphere was magical. In the vaulted ceiling above the dance floor, thousands of tiny white lights were arranged into a series of arches that extended the length of the building. It was as if the stars had realigned themselves in honor of the occasion.

Black tie was the order of the night. David looked magnificent in a white dinner jacket with gold buttons running down the front. He wore dark, navy-blue trousers that were almost black and had a gold cummerbund wrapped around his waist. In his left hand, he carried a pair of white gloves, a bit uncertain whether to put them on or stash them under his cummerbund.

On his right arm, Liz looked absolutely gorgeous in a strapless, royal blue silk gown, borrowed at Louisa's insistence from her own closet. It was the perfect color, matching the glow in her bright indigo eyes. She wore her wavy, brown hair woven into tiny plaits that were coiled on top of her head to resemble a crown. Around her neck hung a single strand of creamy-white pearls augmented by a pair of matching earrings. They had once belonged to her mother and even though they were imitations, they made Liz's skin warm with the remembrance of maternal love. On her wrist was a corsage that David had given her, an exotic orchid with purple-pink petals and an indescribably seductive scent. For the first time in her life, Liz felt really special.

Dancing next to them were Archie and Helene. As they waltzed around the floor, they seemed to be mirror images of each other, except that like the other female mids, Helene was uniformed in the ladies' version of dinner dress whites with a gold cummerbund around her waist and a dark, navy blue skirt that touched her toes. It was the same one, with a few alterations, that her mother had worn at the U.S. Navy Birthday Ball ten years earlier.

"They're a perfect couple, don't you think," David said to Liz as they moved clumsily around the floor. She was making a concerted effort not to step on his spit shined shoes and badly damaged feet.

"Made for each other," Liz agreed.

Just like you and me, David thought.

"So what happens now?" Liz asked.

"What do you mean?"

"You know. Now that school's over?"

"Our summers are broken into thirds. In June, I'll be training at sea. In July, I'll be back at the Yard. And then in August, I'll have one month of liberty."

"Perfect timing. Won't be a problem for you to come to court then."

"Looking forward to it."

"What'll you be doing at sea?"

"I'll be on a submarine with Archie. We really lucked out. Usually upperclassmen get those assignments, but they had some unfilled billets and we got them."

"A sub?" A trace of concern crept into Liz's voice.

"It's just for three weeks. Only two of them underwater. It'll be okay."

"Where are you going?"

"Naples, Istanbul, and back."

"I've never been to Europe," Liz said. "My parents were from Italy. My aunt still lives in Sperlonga, just south of Rome. She's not too far from Naples. Give me the dates you'll be there and I'll e-mail Aunt Claudia you're coming. She loves to show relatives around."

"Relatives?" David smiled. They weren't that close yet.

"And acquaintances, too," Liz said.

He didn't think they were that far apart either. Their relationship was somewhere in-between, but moving closer and closer all the time.

The waltz faded away with a graceful flourish and the conductor took the mike and announced a ten-minute break. Archie gave Helene a big kiss and she whispered in his ear. His eyes lit up and he looked over at David.

"Babe and I are gonna take a little break, too," he winked. "Back in half an hour." With that he took her arm and headed straight for the exit.

"Sneaking up to the room again, eh?" Liz asked.

David nodded. "Helene's our third roommate."

"Isn't it risky?"

"Very. But they've got it down to a science. She goes in the west entrance and he goes in the south and they meet up inside. Security has never stopped them."

"He must really love her."

"He does. Says he can't do without her. They're going to get married right after graduation."

"That's three years away. Why wait?"

"There's a rule that midshipmen can't marry until they have a commission. Just this winter, a firstie got kicked out for having a secret wife."

"Jeez, couldn't he have made it to the end of the year?"

David shook his head. "His girl was pregnant. Didn't think it was the right thing to do for the baby."

"What a terrible dilemma," Liz said.

"Worst part is the guy even has to pay the Navy back for the cost of his education. A hundred-and-thirty-six grand! His life is ruined. Even so, he said he'd do it all over again. He really loves his girl."

The musicians returned from their break, fortified by nips from their vest pocket flasks. One by one, they sat down and took up their instruments. The conductor waved his baton and the magic of the evening began all over again.

True to their promise, Archie and Helene returned to the dance floor on schedule, none the worse for wear, although Helene's hair looked a little disheveled and her skirt wasn't quite straight.

"Any problems with security?" David asked.

"None." Archie said. "At the west entrance, the Mate of the Deck's got his nose buried in a paperback and on the south, the guy's half asleep. Went right by them."

Helene looked over at Liz. "We're about the same size," she said. "Wanna switch clothes?"

"Uh huh," Liz said unexpectedly, before her internal censor had a chance to assert itself. David's heart leapt at the implication.

There was an awkward silence before David spoke up.

"I'll show you my Grandfather's stick," he said, then reddened when he realized how suggestive it sounded.

"Archibald let me hold it," Helene said. "You'll like it, Liz. It's really cool. Zataka something."

"ZaStakaZappa," David said.

Liz nodded. But a lacrosse stick wasn't quite what she had in mind. Without further discussion, the four of them hurried to the other side of the dance floor. There, the girls found a ladies room with vacant stalls next to each other. It was a tight fit, but swap was managed without anyone being the wiser.

"You're about to be a lucky man, Dave," Archie said.

"Just my luck I'll be caught."

"Whatever, man. She's worth it."

And when Liz returned in Helene's white jacket and long black skirt, David knew that Archie was right. Liz was worth whatever happened.

"I feel weird," Liz said. "Like I'm in someone else's skin."

"Me, too," Helene said, running her hand over her new satin gown. "But you'll get used to it. Look around you. There are a thousand people here. No one's gonna notice."

"Most of them don't know us and those that do aren't paying any attention," David said. "Let's just dance a while until you get your sea legs."

It was a slow dance and Liz gradually became more secure. No MP's rushed over to arrest her. No one even looked askance at her.

"It's time now," she whispered.

"Let's go," David said, leading her off the dance floor and towards the exit.

Satisfied with themselves, Archie and Helene did a high-five.

Outside Bancroft, David gave Liz his room number and instructions on how to get up to the third floor. "Just walk right by the Mate of the Deck, make a left and go down to the fifth door. Room 311." He handed her his key. "Just wait for me inside. I'll be there in five minutes."

Pumped up with adrenalin, Liz walked inside as naturally as possible.

In the meantime, David hurried around to the south entrance and ran up the stairs to the third floor. The place was completely quiet; the passageways, empty. Everyone was off partying. David started to double time. Coming around the corner, he ran smack into a Marine officer.

"Sorry, sir! " David jumped back, snapped to attention, and saluted. "My fault, sir!"

"Jesus! Watch where you're going!" the Captain scolded. He continued past David without even stopping to return his salute. David couldn't help but notice that the man walked with a slight limp. He hoped he hadn't hurt him.

At the end of the hall, he saw Liz push his door open and shut the door behind her. His pace quickened and his heart raced. There was nothing like a little danger to heighten the excitement of the moment. Opening the door, he found Liz standing back against the wall with a horrified expression on her face. Then he saw why. His room had been thoroughly ransacked. Closets had been emptied, uniforms thrown on the floor, drawers overturned, and books scattered everywhere. Even his rack had been stripped of its covers and his mattress gutted.

"Must have just happened," Liz said. "Archie and Helene were just here."

David noticed his trash can sitting on top of his desk. When he looked inside, his heart broke. ZaStakaZappa! It had been cut into dozens of small pieces by an electric saw. The elaborately carved stick that had taken Grandfather Two Tongues three months to make had been utterly destroyed.

David was too grieved to speak. His pain was unbearable. It was as if his own backbone had suddenly collapsed and his vertebrae were laying on the ground in pieces. He felt utterly helpless. Sinking down on his chair, he cradled his head in his hands and gave in to despair. Without ZaStakaZappa how could he ever fulfill the prophecy of his secret Choptank name?

Liz put her arms around him. "Who would do such a horrible thing?" she wondered.

The answer was in the ceiling. Overhead, dozens of Styrofoam tiles had been punched out at random, some over David's rack.

"The parchment!" David gasped. "Someone was looking for the parchment!"

"The Blackburns!"

Climbing up on his bed, he reached inside a vacant square and groped around for the oblong box. David let out a sigh of relief. "It is still here. I must have pushed it back a little further than usual."

He took it out and opened it. The peace pipe, wampum belt, and parchment were still inside.

"We've got to get the parchment out of here," Liz warned. "Looks like they're willing to do anything to get it."

David nodded. "You're right, I can't keep it here any longer."

"Doc has a safe in his office. I can take it there."

"Good idea."

Liz turned around and lifted the back of her jacket. Carefully, David slid the parchment under her gold cummerbund. He could see the edge of her pink panties and the temptation to go further was overwhelming.

"You'd better go back to your car now. I've gotta find another hiding place for the box before I notify the Officer of the Deck."

So much for their romantic evening alone.

Liz adjusted her clothes and headed for the door. "One thing is bothering me," she said, turning around to face David. "Why would Septimus want to steal your parchment anyway? The guy at the museum said it couldn't be translated and the Blackburns have the English original."

"Maybe they're afraid somebody else can interpret it."

Liz's eyes brightened with a sudden revelation. "Of course! Why didn't I think of that before?"

"What before?"

"Blackburn's wife! She's bound to know something about it."

"His wife?"

"Ex-wife actually. Her name is Felicia. Lou told me about her. They had a nasty divorce."

"What makes you think she'd tell us anything?" David asked.

"Don't you watch any detective movies? There's no better source of family secrets than a jilted wife."

Nun's Tale

South of St. Michaels, Liz pulled over to a picnic area by the side of the road. Here, in a blackened barbeque pit, David placed the remains of his beloved ZaStakaZappa. Shutting his dotted eyelids, he looked inwards into the distant dreams of his past. And slowly, out of the darkness, emerged a vision. His mother was clapping her hands and singing to him on his seventh birthday. And he saw the hallowed figure of Grandfather Two Tongues presenting him with a gift wrapped in gray cloth woven from Shadow Woman's loom. Like a snake shedding its skin, the great stick emerged into David's hands. How thrilled he had been! For it was a stick, Grandfather said, that would save the world. It was no accident that he had given it to his grandson on the same day that he told him the meaning of his secret Choptank name.

When the scene had vanished from his inner eye, David doused the pile of wooden disks with lighter fluid and lit it with a match. A column of fire and smoke shot into the sky sending ZaStakaZappa back into the arms of the ancient ones who dwelt in the clouds. Someday, he believed, its essence would return to the earth in the tears of his ancestors. The Cycle of History would repeat itself again as it always had. In time, the burning wood would be reborn in the shape of a hickory tree. In time, a passerby would use a broken limb as a walking stick. In time, a craftsman would shape the cane into a baggataway stick. And in time, another man would wield it to save the world. But it would not be David Waterfield. His time had passed. And so had the prophecy of his secret Choptank name.

After scattering the ashes in the wildflowers at the edge of the woods, David returned to the car and they continued on down the highway in silence. After they passed over the drawbridge, the highway narrowed to a single lane blacktop and then merged onto a dirt road. Liz spotted the steeple in the trees and pulled over next to a historic marker.

"There it is. Convent of the Blessed Virgin. Established 1640."

"Looks like this is as close as we can get," David said. "I'd say it's about a mile to a mile-and-a-half away."

"What are we waiting for? Don't think they'll be sending a tourist tram for us."

Leaving Lou's Mercedes on the shoulder, they headed off through knee-high grass that left their blue jeans and socks dotted with cockleburs. A dark halo of gnats swarmed around their heads and when they waved them off, mosquitoes attacked their hands and the back of their necks.

Eventually, they came to a path that led them to a glade of sassafras trees that overlooked the Choptank. A light breeze was blowing from the south, stirring the reeds along the bank into a gentle rustle. On the shoreline, a solitary Great Blue Heron waded quietly. Stopping suddenly, it thrust its spear-like bill into the water and brought forth a squirming salamander. Straightening its S-shaped neck, the heron swallowed it whole. The meal complete, the great bird paused for a moment to study the human intruders.

"Kraaaakk," it said, *"kraaaak."* Then with a frantic flapping of wings, it took flight, tucking its long legs under its belly and gliding over the inlet toward the great oak on the point, its leaves green and golden in the morning sun.

Further on, the path disappeared into a thick pine forest. A "No Trespassing" sign was nailed into one of the trees. Streams of dark sap ran down the trunk like sacred blood on a crucifix. Venturing ahead, they came to a high brick wall, so overgrown with ivy that its presence in the woods was camouflaged. Around the side, they found an iron gate that was better suited to a prison than a monastery. Bolted next to it was a hand bell which Liz promptly rang.

A few moments later, the Mother Superior arrived on a walking stick, bent over at a ninety-degree angle. Despite the summer heat, she wore a brown woolen tunic, white wimple, and black head cloth.

"I'm afraid we're not open to the public," she said, lifting her head to reveal a deep, vertical crease bisecting her forehead. "Only to members of the order."

"We've come to see Sister Felicia," Liz said.

The nun looked surprised. "No one has come to see Sister Felicia for twenty-five years."

"I'm a friend of her family," Liz explained. "Lately, I've been thinking that I have the calling, too. I really need to get her advice." She was surprised at how easy it was for her to lie. She was definitely going to Hell if there was one.

The old woman's stern demeanor lightened a bit, pleased by the prospect of a new recruit and a very pretty one at that.

"We haven't had a new nun in a decade," she said. "Our order is very strict. It's not for everyone. You have to give up all your worldly goods and human contacts."

The Mother Superior cast a cold, suspicious eye on David, dressed in his dead father's tattered blue jeans and long-sleeved red-flannel shirt. All that saved him from looking like cheap white trash was that his skin was brown.

"This is my step-brother," Liz explained. "I have no other family." She was beginning to burn already

"Very well. You may speak with Sister Felicia," the old nun said, unlatching the gate. "I believe I saw her in the back garden."

Inside the brick enclosure was a small church and adjoining dormitory. Like the outer walls, they were swallowed in ivy and gave the appearance of being an organic structure that had grown up in the woods independent of the hand of man. Liz and David followed a trail of stepping-stones that led them around back to an old graveyard. Jutting out of the moss-covered ground were ancient tombstones that resembled the tablets of the Ten Commandments. A few lay shattered on the ground as if thrown down by Moses himself.

They were suddenly aware of a nun sitting on a bench under the shade of a chestnut tree. Her head was bowed and her lashless eyes were sealed in prayer. In her lap, a pair of child-like hands fidgeted with a string of olive-wood, rosary beads. They waited until she was finished before gently intruding on her quietude.

"Sister Felicia," Liz said gently.

She looked up at them with a sixty-four year-old face as flawless and smooth as if Michelangelo had carved it in marble. Her appearance hadn't changed much from the newspaper clipping Petra had showed her or the portrait she had seen on the cafeteria wall. Like her son, she had the pale blonde hair and hooded green eyes of her Habsburg forebears. Like him too, she had a subtle scar that bisected her upper lip.

"I'm Liz Mancini and this is David Waterfield. We really need your help."

Surprised at the intrusion of outsiders, Sister Felicia retrieved her glasses from a leash around her neck and put them on. Rising from her bench she came forward cautiously, slowing to a standstill in front of David. She studied him for a moment before speaking.

"So you've come at last," she said in an Eastern European accent delivered with a slight hiss. "I was wondering if you would ever find me."

David was speechless.

"I've seen you before, young man. You're the Choptank boy. The one that caused such a commotion at the museum."

"You saw me on the news?"

She nodded. "I'm not supposed to have a TV, of course. It's against the rules. But it's just a two-and-a-half inch battery-powered Casio. Small enough to keep in my pocket and the reception is good enough to keep me in touch with the outside world. I like the operas they show on public TV from time to time. Don't get to go to them anymore. You won't tell Mother Superior on me will you? We're all sinners after all, aren't we?"

"Our lips are sealed," David promised.

"I heard you speak about your ancestor's parchment. The one written in the Choptank tongue."

"Yes. That's what we came to ask you about."

Sister Felicia waved her hand in a dismissive way. "I know nothing about its contents. My former husband kept many secrets from me. I can't help you, I'm afraid."

She smiled enigmatically, turned away, and went back to her bench under the chestnut tree.

David and Liz looked deflated. Another dead end.

"We're sorry to have disturbed you, sister," David apologized. He took Liz's arm and turned to walk away.

"Not so fast young man," Sister Felicia said quickly. "I said I couldn't help you. But there's someone here in the garden who might be able to."

David's heart stopped. He looked around. There was no one present but the three of them.

"You're standing on him."

He looked down at his feet. What he thought was a stepping-stone was, in fact, a grave marker. Moving aside quickly, he dropped to his knees for a closer examination. Chiseled on the granite face was a name that had been badly eroded by the elements and the passage of time. It took him a moment to piece the letters together.

"Francisco de Genoa!" he gasped. Beneath him was the Jesuit missionary mentioned in the Founder's diary, the man who wrote the Choptank parchment. Black Robe!

"His body was buried here after he was killed by the natives," Sister Felicia said. "Not by the Choptanks, you understand. They were long gone by then. Susquahanocks. A raiding party. Frightful barbarians really. Children of the devil. Father de Genoa tried his best to baptize them but they baptized him instead—in boiling water."

"How awful," Liz said.

"Only his body is here. His heart and his brains were sent to the Vatican in accordance with his last testament. It was his desire to have the rest of his remains planted under the Kings Oak, but the Founder wouldn't permit it. They put him way out here instead."

"Not surprising, I guess," David said.

"No. Not surprising at all. After that, they used this place as a pauper's graveyard. We've got a great many slaves and indentured servants underfoot. A few assorted mistresses, too. And their aborted babies, I'm afraid. Most of them are unmarked. Over the years, our nunnery grew up around the cemetery. Unwanted women who found their rightful place in the service of God."

"I'm sorry," Liz said.

"Don't be. Some of us are quite happy here." Her remark seemed to be self-exclusive. Then, she turned her green eyes on David. "This Francisco de Genoa, he labored for years to learn your people's language."

"Forgive me for saying so, but it didn't help us much."

"All he could do was try. They say it took him two years to translate the holy catechism into your tongue."

"The catechism?"

"Yes, it was a beautiful work. I saw it myself once. And his vocabulary, too. A work of love."

David was stunned. He could scarcely believe his ears. "A vocabulary? You mean, like a dictionary?"

"Yes, of course. He spent his youth learning the Choptank language and writing the words down in his vocabulary the way they sounded to him. Only then could he have translated the catechism into their tongue. It was his life's work. The man should be canonized." Her eyes met David's and her lips bent into a subtle smile. "Perhaps this vocabulary of his might be of some use to you."

"Is it here?" he asked. "Can I see it?"

"They would never keep so priceless a relic here. His work was sent to the Vatican when he died. It was in the same box with the urns that contained his heart and brains. Like I said, I saw it there on display once in the Pope's Secret Archives. My husband took me there to see it twenty-three years ago."

"So Septimus knew about it, too," Liz said.

"Indeed. He said he was interested in it for historical reasons and had been negotiating to buy it from the church. That wasn't unusual. The Blackburn family had been doing business with the Vatican for a long time, beginning back when the Founder purchased his first indulgence from Pope Innocent, the tenth."

"To gain forgiveness for slaughtering my people," David guessed.

"No doubt and other mortal sins as well," Sister Felicia said. "The fourth Caecilius was a frequent visitor there, too. On three occasions, in fact. Each time seeking the Pontiff's permission to divorce his latest wife. None of them had been able to deliver him a son and namesake and he felt he had been unjustly cursed. After some pretty hefty donations to the church, he got his annulments and the right of his eldest daughter to carry the Blackburn name into her marriage. Even so, three generations passed before the family finally bore another son and the name carried on naturally without anymore help from the Holy See."

"What happened with the vocabulary?" David asked anxiously.

338

"Septimus arranged an audience with the Pope, himself. It was right after his election by the College of Cardinals. I went along, too. He expected to have no trouble with the final negotiations since price was no object to him. But to his amazement, the new pontiff flatly refused to consider the transaction. My husband was very, very upset. When the Holy Father turned his back, Septimus lost his temper and made a rude gesture to him."

"He flipped him the bird?" David asked in utter disbelief.

Sister Felicia nodded. "Indeed he did. I was aghast! The Carmelengo saw it, too, and my husband was immediately excommunicated. Such a horrible feeling. I felt as if we had been damned for eternity."

Shamed by the remembrance, Sister Felicia looked down and her eyes welled with tears. Her punishment had been to bear the baby of the devil, the hairy creature with a harelip and four-inch tail.

Liz patted her on the back. "I'm so sorry, Sister. So sorry."

"It was God's will," Felicia said at last. "He works in mysterious ways."

"He certainly does," Liz added.

"You've been such a help to us, Sister," David said. "I don't know how to thank you."

"The vocabulary is still there, young man. Find it and use it. That will be thanks enough for me."

She seemed nervous now, wringing her rosary in her hands. "Forgive me. Revenge is a sin, too. Much worse than the others. I've been very wicked today. You must excuse me now for I have a lot of praying to do."

She turned away from them and began to walk back towards the convent, worrying her beads in her hands and reciting a stream of Hail Marys under her breath.

Liz could scarcely contain her excitement. "The Vatican! You realize that's in Rome..."

"...and Rome isn't too far from Naples!" David said, finishing the thought.

"I'll ask Aunt Claudia to take you there. You can use the vocabulary to translate the parchment. What a stroke of luck!"

Or Fate.

They hurried back out the gates of the monastery. Joyfully they retraced their way through the woods, like children who had just been told a wonderful secret they could only share with each other. When they got back to the river, they ran in with their clothes on, splashing handfuls of water up into the air. And when they came down, it was like a shower of diamonds falling into the river. David had never been so happy in all his life. He pulled Liz to him and kissed her. She wouldn't let him go, kissing him back slow and tender. They wanted to share this moment and each other more than they ever thought possible.

In the waters of the Choptank, they shed the last remainder of their reticence and flung their clothes back to the shore. At last, they were free of all restraints, floating in a timeless sea, primordial and pristine. A light breeze stirred the waters and the gentle undulation of the waves brought their bodies close together. In the waters of the Choptank, they embraced in their full nakedness. Their blood rose like the surging tide, heating their flesh from within. She felt him harden against her and her legs went limp.

He picked her up in his arms and carried her out of the river and into the glade of sassafras trees, laying her down gently on a bed of wild flowers. Her body was like the earth itself. A pair of sacred mountains sloped down to a smooth and fertile plain that led, in turn, to a sweet-scented forest. Hidden within was a forbidden cave that marked the entrance to a secret underground river. He arose and covered her like the heavens covered the earth before the rains came, rumbling over the mountains and plains. She parted in awe of him and his power penetrated deep inside, illuminating her with great shafts of lighting, until, at length, his mighty fire was quenched in the waters of her secret river.

Afterwards, they lay spent on the bed of wild flowers, the rising tide of the Choptank washing over its banks. In the silence of his satisfaction, David heard the water lapping at the shore. *"Chop tank,"* it seemed to say as it rose and fell. *"Chop tank."* The sound of itself mimicked in the name that his ancestors had given it. And all around him, he heard the wind singing through the sassafras trees, celebrating his renewal in a long, lost language that Nature had not forgotten.

Leviathan

It was a killer whale made of steel, a twenty-first century sea monster with x-ray eyes and a nuclear heart. At a moment's notice it could belch fire out of its blowholes and hurl thirty-two, nuclear-tipped Trident missiles halfway across the globe from five fathoms under the sea. Nearly six hundred feet long and with a beam of thirty-six feet, it could attain speeds of up to forty knots while remaining utterly silent. State of the art, next generation stealth technology made it the biggest, fastest, quietest, and most lethal boomer in the history of the American Navy. And the most expensive, too. It was largely responsible for an ever-rising tide of red ink that was all but ignored in the bottomless, black pit of the super-secret, Defense budget.

And now, docked in the berth where she had been born, encircled by gargantuan cranes and gantries, she awaited her formal christening. A large American banner was mounted on her conning tower and her nose was wrapped in red, white, and blue bunting with a five-pointed white star at the tip.

On the land, facing the bow, was a flag-festooned platform filled with assorted dignitaries. Liz and Helene settled into uncomfortable, metal folding chairs on the ground in front of the platform. Already in attendance were a large group of locals, mostly laborers and their families, who were pretending to enjoy being back at their workplace on an unpaid Saturday morning. As usual, Helene was wearing her mother's uniform. To show her support for David, Liz had put on a navy blue dress accented with a gold scarf. It made her indigo eyes stand out all the more.

The Commissioning Ceremony began with a multi-denominational invocation by a Navy Chaplin. Thereafter, the crew of one-hundred-and-twenty men, outfitted in crisp dress whites marched smartly up the gangplank to the cheers of the crowd. Each was a highly trained submariner who had won a coveted dolphin insignia at Groton and had served with distinction on other ships in the nuclear fleet. Bringing up the rear were ten lowly Naval Academy trainees. Nonetheless, Liz and Helene were filled with pride as their men passed before them.

"Don't they look great," Helene said. "Men in uniform really turn me on."

Liz nodded, doing her best to mask her sadness. She and David had finally become whole and now they were being ripped apart again. Half of her was about to be dragged away into the deep and silent sea. Their month long separation seemed like an eternity. Her one consolation was that Aunt Claudia would be waiting for David on the other side of the ocean.

"Wish I could go with Archibald," Helene sighed.

"You should have stowed away, girl. You'd fit right in."

"Don't think I didn't think about it. Unfortunately, subs have all male crews. Plus, I have to stay and look after my dad."

Liz remembered her sad situation. Helene's mother had been tragically killed and her father incapacitated by alcoholism. She was forced to drop out of school and work two jobs to make ends meet. That was the reason she wasn't attending the Academy with Archie in the first place.

Formed up on deck, the crew snapped to attention as the pint-sized Secretary of Defense strode across the stage and climbed up on a step stool behind the podium. After ordering the men to parade rest, the honorable Karl Darren embarked on a long-winded speech designed to justify the importance of the new sub to the United States Navy. Laden with top-heavy platitudes and bombastic ballast, his speech, had it been a ship, would have immediately capsized and sunk to the bottom of the sea.

"In conclusion," he said finally, "I would be remiss on this special occasion, if I did not recognize a gentleman whose dedication, determination, and drive were most responsible for completing this important project on time—the Chairman of Blackburn Steelworks, the Honorable Caecilius Blackburn, himself."

An ovation arose from the dignitaries on the platform, complemented by a small smattering of polite applause from the conscripted crowd below. Septimus stood up and acknowledged the acclaim with a nod to his cronies on the platform, an insincere wave to the groundlings, and a mock salute to the crewmen on deck. As he surveyed their faces, he was suddenly rocked by the recognition of an enemy in their midst.

Bolts of anger shot out of David's eyes like poison-tipped arrows.

Alarmed by his enemy's presence on his billion-dollar boat, the Chairman's heart raced wildly. His hand went to his chest and he sat down quickly to regain his composure, a response that many took to be the result of being overwhelmed by adulation.

The ceremony culminated with the announcement that the new sub would henceforth be named the *U.S.S. Chesapeake*. The captain officially assumed his command and the ship's pennant was hoisted from a mast atop the conning tower. The Navy Band struck up *Anchors Aweigh* and the newly commissioned sub backed out of its berth. Liz and Helene jumped up and down and waved frantically, excited and sad at the same time. They wondered, as all women did whose men went away to the sea, if they would ever see their loved ones again.

From his seat on the platform, Septimus turned away and spat on the ground. "Damn him straight to Hell," he cursed under his breath.

With its crew still at parade rest, *Chessie* made its way down the James River and through historic Hampton Roads, crossing waters where once the Civil War ironclads, Monitor and Merrimac, waged battle over the wooden bones of sunken Union ships. Their descendants, great steel destroyers and aircraft carriers, were visible on the shore berthed at the Norfolk Naval Base, the largest military complex in the world.

At last, she entered the baptismal waters of the great bay whose name she now proudly bore and sailed through the bridge and tunnel system that leapt in and out of the water like a seventeen-mile long sea serpent. Encountering the roaring wind and rollicking whitecaps of the Atlantic, the captain ordered his dolphins below to change into their work clothes.

The first order of business was a maneuver known as "Angles and Dangles," a series of steep dives designed to determine if all the equipment on board was properly secured. A loose lock, or even an unsecured ballpoint pen or shoe, could spell disaster, alerting enemy sonar to the sub's presence. As they cleared the continental shelf, the skipper ordered the tanks flooded and soon afterwards *Chessie* nosed down at a thirty-degree angle. David and Archie held tightly to the rails along the bulkheads, struggling to keep their feet from slipping out from under them. The dolphin boys, on the other hand, made a sport of the exercise. They held a contest to see who could slide down the central passageway without spilling coffee out of their Styrofoam cups. It was all done in complete silence, of course. Submariners on the *Chessie* were not allowed to speak above a quiet whisper.

The winner of the contest was the ship's medic, a pop-eyed petty officer with long arms, big ears, and an exceptional sense of balance. Tattooed on his forearm was a cartoon caduceus with a winged staff and vicious intertwined vipers. It was not surprising that the crew's nickname for him was Doctor Snakes. His specialty was nuclear medicine and he was the one man on board that no one wanted to see professionally.

The maneuver successfully completed, the *Chessie* leveled out on a course that would take her across the Atlantic. In the eerie silence, a feeling of intense claustrophobia and imminent danger pervaded the place. Three-dozen nuclear-tipped Trident missiles were poised vertically underneath the hatches amidships, ready for launching. Elsewhere, an assortment of tomahawks, torpedoes, mines, and depth charges were stockpiled in every available space, some even stowed in the living quarters and heads. Potentially, the most dangerous device on board was the S6G nuclear reactor, which occupied all four decks in the middle of the sub. Fueled by highly enriched Uranium-235, the reactor operated by transforming the power of a nuclear bomb into a slow, controlled explosion that provided enough energy to run the engines almost indefinitely.

Running through the middle of the reactor chamber was a single passageway that led from the bridge to the engine room in the stern. The dolphin boys called it the "birth canal" for it was almost as tight and difficult to squeeze through. Lined in four inches of lead, the entrance was marked with a large radiation trefoil and a warning in red block letters:

SAFE EGRESS LIMITED TO 10 SECONDS

During the cruise, the nine Academy trainees were scheduled to rotate through the major departments of the sub. David and Archie were assigned to the first engine room rotation. Joining them were two third-class basketball string beans, Crane and Olijah. All of them had to pass through the birth canal on their way to the engine room. At 6'9", the two forwards practically had to crawl through the tunnel on all fours. Archie and David waited patiently for them to clear the passage before starting in themselves.

"Remember to keep your hands over your balls when you go through, Dave," Archie whispered. "Everything else is expendable."

"Yes, mother," David said.

At the other end of the tunnel were the turbines, generators, and gears that operated the propeller. It didn't take the two of them long to realize that it was the very worst place to be. The equipment generated quite a bit of heat that had a lot to do with making the crew of Machinist's Mates and Boilermakers even more irascible than normal. Most of them could hardly mask their envy and utter disdain for the squeaky-clean midshipmen in their midst.

After eight hours in the sweatshop, the trainees scurried back through the lead-lined tunnel to the crew quarters. After a long hot shower, David and Archie eagerly headed up to the mess buffet. Submarine food had a reputation of being outstanding, a perk for serving in the toughest and most lonely assignment in the Navy. *Chessie's* mess was no exception. Her menu included prime rib, lobster tails, sautéed mushrooms, baked potatoes, beef rice soup, oven-baked bread, and chocolate cake for dessert.

David and Archie went back for seconds and thirds on the lobster tails.

"If we continue to stuff ourselves like this, we'll never make it through the hatch," David whispered. "We'll have to spend the rest of our lives trapped in this tin can."

"Then I'm definitely not going back for fourths," Archie said softly. "I can't wait to get off this fucking ship. I gotta tell you, Dave, this place gives me the creeps. All we gotta do is spring a little leak and the ship will sink like a ton of bricks. They say drowning is the worst way to go."

"You're not going to drown, Archie. You'd be crushed flat before that could happen."

"That's reassuring. Thanks."

"Take my advice and don't even think about it. Keep focused on life back home. Your parents. Helene. You'll be okay."

"Yeah, you're right, Dave. When I think about Babe, I don't care where I am. Good idea."

On the way out of the mess, David pocketed an orange. "Hey Archie, maybe we can paint this black and use it as a ball."

"You mean like Armbruister used to do in high school?"

"Right. We can play catch in the corridors after the lights are out. Should be good for our eyes."

"Yeah, as long as we don't miss it. Any sound and the dolphin boys will be all over us."

"That'll just help us keep our concentration," David said.

Along with the rest of their shift, they headed into the crew lounge to put on earphones and watch a video. David found a roll of black masking tape and when the lights went out, he went to work on the orange.

Unfortunately, the movie was *The Perfect Storm* and did nothing to allay Archie's fear of the sea. When it was over, his face was a pale shade of blue. It was as if he had been holding his breath for the last third of the movie.

"Forget about it, Archie. It's just a story," David said quietly, neglecting to mention that it was based on a true story. "There's nothing to worry about." But it had left its mark on David, too. Even he was beginning to feel the weight of impending doom.

At ten p.m., it was time for them to head for their racks. On *Chessie,* like other nuclear boomers, the number of bunks was a third less than the actual crew size. It was a structural feature designed to allow the sub to carry a maximum amount of firepower. Because of this, the dolphins had to sleep in shifts, sharing their racks with each other, a practice known as "hot berthing." The previous occupants were just leaving for their assignments when David and Archie arrived.

"Hey! You fart in my rack, I'll kill you," one of them said in a hard whisper. He was a Third Class Gunner's Mate with a greasy face and a bulbous nose pocked with enlarged pores.

"And don't even think about looking at my fuckin' pinups," his buck-toothed buddy cautioned. "They're private property."

"Don't worry," Archie said. "We're not into boys."

The two turned on him. "You little shit!"

David stepped in to separate them. "You better hurry on, men. You'll be late for your detail."

One look at his big hands and thick arms and the two thugs backed off and went on their way.

"Thanks, Dave." Archie said, climbing into the top bunk. "I'll let you have the bottom one."

"Great," David said. "You've got pinups on the wall, I get to sleep over a dozen torpedoes."

"Sweet dreams. Wake me up when you want to play catch."

Drawing back the privacy curtains, David turned over the grease-stained pillow and lay down on the still warm mattress with his hands crossed over his chest like a corpse inside a coffin. Outside the sub's three-inch-thick bulkhead, he imagined monsters of the deep swimming in tandem with the great steel Leviathan. First came a school of hammerhead sharks, then a pair of giant squids followed by a pod of Killer Whales. Together they glided over the Abyssal Plains and through deep canyons in the earth's crust formed by mountain ranges that dwarfed the peaks of Everest.

Slowly, David drifted into a superficial slumber, sleeping as his ancestors had with his eyes wide open. His sight turned inward, away from the suffocating claustrophobia of his confinement. Before him was the great oak of his ancestors and the mighty river that ran through the blood of his people. On the far bank, Liz was waiting for him on a bed of wildflowers under the shade of a sassafras tree. Her soft indigo eyes opened wide and took him inside herself. He replayed their act of union over and over again. It was the happiest moment of his life.

He saw Shadow Woman working at her loom and his little sisters playing with the nanny goat. The sight of them brought back the pain of separation. He missed his mother terribly. She had sacrificed herself daily so that her only son could leave home in search of his legacy. His little sisters, too, had left a hole in his heart. He remembered how they liked to crawl up on his lap and beg him to read them stories out of his schoolbooks. He felt as close to them as if they had been his natural sisters. When they were just babies, their real parents had worked themselves to death in the toxic waste dump at the edge of the village, dying from accidental pricks of an infectious syringe. Shadow Woman had taken the little ones into the family and raised them as her own, renaming them Winking Star and Jumping Bug. Ironically, the added hardship was a balm to his mother's melancholia. She took delight in combing their waist-long hair and making them new dresses from discarded feedbags. Grandfather Two Tongues doted on the little girls, fasting through two meals a day to make sure they got the food they needed. The thought of Tequetamo brought a troubled vision of tarantulas and scorpions crawling over his burial mound. David peered inside the grave and saw the old wisoe rotting away in the hostile red earth. Earth that was not the ashes of his ancestors. Earth that was nobody's ashes. And as he thought about him, he felt the old man's gnarled hand on top of his head and heard his quavering voice sing out the seven sacred syllables of his secret Choptank name. The name that could never be revealed to a white man. The name that was a prophecy of things to come.

Suddenly, the heat inside David's berth became unbearable. His open eyeballs sizzled like fried eggs. On his left, the bulkhead was glowing red hot, liquefying into molten steel. From out of it, a half-melted, human face emerged, gasping for breath, its skin bubbling and bursting like magma in the cone of an erupting volcano.

David bolted upright, banging his head on the top of his bunk.

"Save yourself!" the fiery face shrieked. "Get out! Get out! This ship is cursed!" It submerged again and the liquid steel closed over it, turning cold and grey and hard.

Archie's head poked down from the bunk above. "Hey, Dave," he whispered. "Be quiet! You're having a freakin' nightmare!"

David wasn't so sure. It was more like a warning. The melting face had a diamond stud in its ear lobe. He and the rest of the crew were trapped inside the steel tomb of Qwazi Lightfoot.

"Hey, wanna play catch?" Archie asked.

"Not tonight, man. Not tonight."

The next day, disaster struck. After a particularly grueling day in the engine room, David, Archie, and the two basketball string beans headed for the shower stalls. A few minutes of soap, shampoo, and hot water, made them feel almost human again.

Archie was the first to sound the alarm.

"What the fuck!" The hair he had been shampooing was now in his hand.

Crane was next, followed by Olijah, then David. Their eyebrows and eyelashes were wiped away, chest and pubic hair, too. The bottoms of the shower stalls looked like the unswept floor of a barbershop.

With towels wrapped around their waists, the scared young men hurried to sickbay. Shocked by their bald bodies, Doctor Snakes put down his cup of coffee and grabbed his Geiger counter. As it passed over them, it chattered like a wild monkey.

"Eight hundred Roentgens!" Doctor Snakes whispered is a raspy voice that sounded like he was suffering from throat cancer. The muscles of his cheeks twitched in alarm. He was on his fifth cup of coffee and his nerves were already on edge.

"Eight hundred? Is that bad?" Archie asked as calmly as he could.

"Sweet Jesus!" The chief's face turned as red as the bulb on the end of a thermometer. "You boys got Radiation Sickness! Where the fuck you been?"

"Mostly the engine room," Olijah said.

"How long did it take you guys to go through the tunnel?"

"Sign said we had ten seconds," David said softly.

"Twenty seconds!" His popped-eyes look like they were ready to shoot out of his head. "Fuck! It shoulda said five! Someone in the print shop made a big fuckin' mistake!"

"Shit!"

"Hey! Keep your voices down."

"Sorry. What can we do?"

"I feel sick."

"Are we gonna die, doc?" Archie whined and wrapped his arms around himself for protection.

The tattooed man hedged. "I can't lie to you boys. All of you are man enough to hear it."

"Hear what?" Crane asked.

"Fact is, there's not a reliable cure at present."

"Shit!"

"Fuck!"

"Oh God!"

"Hey, keep your fuckin' voices down. Just hold on. Keep cool. There are medical breakthroughs all the time. In fact, there's a new serum they're experimenting with that's made from the blood of Central Asian tortoises. They found out they can take forty-thousand Roentgens compared to eight-hundred for humans."

"How can we get it, doc?" Olijah asked.

Snakes shook his head. "Like I said, boys, it's only experimental at this point. Right now all I can do is give you anti-radiation pills. They help prevent nausea. If you make it to Naples, we'll take you to the hospital right away. Maybe they can do something for you."

A sense of despair fell over the men. Olijah went into shock. Crane cried shamelessly. Archie curled up in the fetal position on the floor of sickbay and had to be carried back to his bunk.

David sank down to the deck and buried his face in his hands. He thought of Liz and his mother and two sisters. Miss Applebaum, too. He was never going to see any of them again.

"What's the hell is that shit?" Snakes asked.

He looked up to see the medic hovering directly over him. "What's what?"

"On top of your head. First I thought you had ring worm. But no—you got a tattoo of some kind."

"I do?" It was news to David.

Snakes brought over two hand mirrors and held them up so David could see.

Sure enough, there in the middle of his bare pate was a zigzagged line that ended in many small jagged forks. David was stunned. All he could think of was that Two Tongues must have tattooed the emblem on his head when he was a baby. It was just like the absentminded old man to forget to tell him about it.

"What's it mean, Waterfield?" Snakes asked. "You belong to some kind of gang? Or a cult, maybe? Some kind of devil worship, I bet."

The medic's insults brought David back to his feet. "That is not for you to know. That is not for any white man to know." And with that he turned away and left the infirmary.

"Up yours!" Snakes leaned back and flipped a double bird at David's back.

With such a dire prognosis, David and the other doomed men were advised to draw up their wills and get their lives in order. David poured his heart out in a farewell letter to Liz.

> *My darling Liz,*
> *I love you more than I can say. I will always cherish the memory of the wonderful times we had together. I wish that time had given me the opportunity to ask you to marry me. We could*

have had such a wonderful life together. But that was not to be. Fate is cruel and my time is just about over. I want you to know that I will always be thinking of you. Wherever you go, whatever you do, I will be there with you. Love, David.

Another one was addressed to Miss Applebaum. He thanked his teacher for all she had done for him over the years. It was she who taught him the power of learning and the power of love. He could never repay her for all her kindnesses.

But his most poignant words were reserved for his mother.

I am not afraid to die, for I know I will go into the Great Sea of Ancestors and that someday, I will arise in another form. Grandfather Two Tongues taught me so. But I am ashamed, mother. I have failed my people. I am fated to die without fulfilling the mission of my secret name. Forgive me, for I cannot forgive myself.

Unable to sleep, his waking dreams were filled with the sacred mourning rituals of his ancestors. He saw them smear their bodies in the blood of a slaughtered elk and fill their mouths with the ashes of a bitterroot tree. He saw them dip the ends of their hair in oil and light them with a flaming torch. He saw great halos of fire ringing the heads of Great Standing Bear, Three-Legged Coyote, Black Moon Rising, Two Tongues, and the other werowances and wisoes who lived in his blood. Dancing together in a circle, they wailed louder and louder as the flames burned closer and closer to their skulls, until at last the women smothered them with blankets. David thought mostly of his beloved Tequetamo: Two Tongues, Grandfather, and mentor. How could he face him now in the Great Sea of Ancestors? He had let everyone down. His people's loss would never be avenged. David was inconsolable.

For the next several days, the dolphins steered clear of the trainees like they were a radioactive shipwreck. Confined to a corner table in the mess deck next to the trash bin, four scared, hairless men awaited their fate like a group of condemned prisoners on death row.

A week after they were stricken, Snakes approached the doomed men at breakfast, a cup of coffee in one hand and a half-eaten donut in the other. Several of his cronies followed close behind, edging toward the trainees like they were approaching a leper colony.

"Found something that will make you guys feel a little better," Snakes whispered, licking the sugar off his fingertips.

The despondent trainees looked up from their trays of untouched chow. One of the medic's cronies, a pinheaded First Class Torpedoman, produced a paper bag from behind his back. With a theatrical flourish, he upended its contents. A dozen empty pink plastic bottles bounced around on the tabletop.

David picked one up and read the label out loud. "Nair Hair Remover!"

"For Totally Touchable Skin!" Archie finished. "Shit!"

Olijah and Crane looked at each other in amazement. "What the fuck!"

"Not so loud, men," Snakes cautioned.

"It was all a joke!" David said. "A fucking joke!"

"Don't get pissed," the tattooed medic said softly. "Nair in the soap and shampoo dispensers is like a rite of initiation on boomers."

"Yeah, we do it to all the new guys," a Damage Controlman confided.

"From now on, you trainees will take the radiation warnings even more seriously than before."

"Jesus!" Olijah said.

"Don't worry," Snakes promised, "your hair will all grow back by the time we get back home."

"Except for the pubes," the Torpedoman added. "They never grow back."

The pranksters couldn't help it. They howled so loud their laughter was overheard five miles away in the submarines of three nations. Foreign sonar men were astounded in three different languages. To some, it was the sound of the Americans mocking their incompetence. To others, it was the unearthly wail of a dying dog.

Secret Archives

The sixth fleet was headquartered just north of Naples on the Gulf of Gaeta. During the Middle Ages, it was an important harbor guarded by two castles that stood sentry on a rocky promontory that jutted out into the sea. In recent times, the town had become something of a tourist resort, famous for its walled city, ruined Roman villas, and white, sandy beach. The base headquarters was located atop Monte Orlando in the center of town, overlooking the gulf and the Formia Mountains on the far shore. At the foot of the mount, a long-armed pier reached out into the harbor and offered assistance to incoming vessels.

On the last morning in port, David and Archie were finally granted an eight-hour liberty. As they followed Snakes and his cronies down the gangplank, they marveled at the way the dolphin boys had mastered the art of saluting the ensign with one hand while balancing a cup of coffee, cigarette, and donut in the other.

"Assholes," David said, still whispering.

At the end of the pier, the liberty detail was met by a welcoming committee composed of ladies from the local whorehouses. Shrieking and flapping their arms, they descended on their prey like a flock of harpies.

"Hey back off, bitches," Snakes yelled. "You'll make us spill our coffee."

But the whores didn't seem to understand English. Coffee splattered on spit-shined shoes and summer whites were bombarded with big, brown spots.

Competition for the men was keen, even for the two strange, prickly-headed creatures. With faint outlines for eyebrows, they resembled visiting aliens more than human beings. The women did anything and everything to get their attention. Some displayed themselves in suggestive poses. Others were more direct, raising their skirts and lowering their blouses. The old ones who had no other assets took out their false teeth and wiggled their tongues.

David shooed them away and walked out into the parking lot, looking in vain for the yellow Isetta Liz said would meet him. Archie followed close behind, doing his best to ignore the ladies' shameless show of lewdness by focusing his attention on Helene.

"While you're gone, Dave, I'm just gonna roam around the town. Maybe I can find an Internet Cafe and e-mail Babe."

"Good plan, Archibald. Keep you out of trouble."

"Who you calling bald? Better look at yourself in a mirror."

David didn't have to consult a mirror to know how weird he looked. All he could hope for was that his hair would grow out by the time the *Chessie* returned to Annapolis.

After a vigorous round of haggling, the Snakes and his cronies chose their partners. Squashing their butts on the pier, they tossed their coffee cups in an already overflowing trash can and headed into town to find a cheap motel.

"Those assholes sure like their coffee," Archie said.

"Yeah, they drink way too much. They're too dumb to know it's not good for them."

Like a good boy scout, Archie went back and picked up the litter they had left behind and crushed it down in the trash can.

David's eyes suddenly brightened. "Maybe we could do them a favor."

"Like what?"

"Like warn them about the dangers of caffeine."

"How would we do that?"

"Easy. We could slip a laxative into their coffee pot when they aren't looking."

Archie caught on right away. "You mean like in some kind of rite of initiation?"

"Exactly. We'd be doing them a great service."

"I'll see if I can find a pharmacy."

"Better yet, a veterinarian," David said. "Horse laxative would be best."

"No question."

"Get some clothespins while you're at it. We'll clip 'em on our noses. Gonna get kinda stinky in there."

"Skipper's gonna have to sail home with the hatches open."

"Difficult in a submarine."

"I'll see what I can find," Archie said. "Gonna be a blast going back."

They exchanged a high five and Archie hurried away on his mission. No sooner had he dropped out of sight, than a tooting horn announced the arrival of a tiny, three-wheeled Isetta that was the shape and color of a lopsided lemon. Popping out of the front hood, which also served as the vehicle's only door, was a jolly middle-aged woman in a loose-fitting, green-frilled mumu designed to conceal her Rubenesque figure. She had a set of triple chins that made her laugh in triplicate and chocolate-colored hair that was piled up in an elaborate beehive. It was so high off her forehead that she was forced to drive with her sunroof open. There was no doubt in David's mind who she was.

She had no problem spotting David either but was too polite to pay much attention to his odd appearance. "You musta be Davie," she threw open her arms without waiting for confirmation. "I'm a Elizabeth's Aunt Claudia."

David found himself instantly engulfed in huge maternal breasts. "Glad to meet you Mrs. Panzoni," he said after he had regained his breath.

"No, no, no," she waved her hands. "You call me Aunt Claudia. I'm a everybody's Aunt Claudia. You call me that, okay, Davie?"

"Okay," he threw up his hands in mock surrender. "You win. Aunt Claudia it is."

Crammed inside the two-seater, they slowly puttered up the steep hillside to the main street of the town. Dodging a fleet of careening motor scooters, Aunt Claudia wove her way through narrow, cobblestoned lanes lined with old cathedrals, open-air market houses, and picturesque piazzas.

"Hold on, Davie. I know a shortcut."

Turning the wheel sharply, she drove into an alley only slightly larger than the width of her three-wheeled vehicle. Skillfully navigating an obstacle course of garbage cans and laundry lines, she exited on the other side of town unscathed. A few turns later they were on the Autostrada del Sole, headed north towards Rome and Vatican City.

Aunt Claudia did most of the talking. She loved to hold forth, both with her mouth and her hands. She seemed to leave the wheel unattended for minutes at a time while she embellished her favorite stories with dramatic gestures. But her little car just kept chugging ever onwards like a well-trained horse that knew the way back home.

"Anybody tell you, Davie? You looka like an Italian."

"I'm Choptank," he couldn't resist telling her.

"Choptank," she looked puzzled. "I never heard of that country. You sure you not Italian?"

David was sure.

The drive to Rome took about two hours. Picturesque landscapes rushed past their windows like a parade of canvases created by Renaissance masters. There were sheep-filled pastures, rolling vineyards, and on distant hilltops, the ruins of Roman villas guarded by groves of stately, cypress trees.

Claudia took the opportunity to fill David in on her family history since the year One. Just in case he got to be a relative sometime. She told him how her sister, Maria, and her boyfriend, Alfonso, eloped and worked their way to Baltimore on a tramp steamer. Elizabeth was born a couple of years later. She was the first real American in the family and they were all so proud. But things in America were not as good as they thought. The family had a hard time making ends meet. Alfonso had to take a job in a steel mill. It only paid minimum wage, but he managed to keep food on the table. When Elizabeth was only twelve, Alfonso got sick and died, leaving Maria to raise Elizabeth alone. Claudia said the family sent money, and that helped some. Maria scraped by and somehow saved enough to send Elizabeth to community college. But then, the great tragedy of tragedies befell them. The year after her daughter graduated, Maria became ill and died.

"I'm sorry," David said.

"It was all so sad," Claudia sniffled back a tear. "But Elizabeth, she work her way through it. With the help of friends from the old country, you understand."

David did.

"Sometimes, even now, I can't help but think of the poor little thing, all alone over there, so far from home."

"She does just fine, Aunt Claudia" David assured her. "She's a hard worker, has a whole lot of friends, and is going to be a lawyer someday."

"And she has you, too, huh, Davie?" She wasn't afraid to pry.

"Yeah," David smiled, remembering his last liberty with her. "She's sure got me."

At last they approached the outskirts of the Eternal City. For the sake of time, Claudia exited onto the Grande Raccordo Anulare that encircled Rome and avoided the traffic congestion that clogged the historic areas. Since she didn't have time to give David a proper tour, she described the highlights in vivid words and expansive gestures. The Pantheon, Colosseum, Trevi Fountain, Spanish Steps, and Forum, all came alive inside her tiny three-wheeled car. Miraculously, she avoided crashing into oncoming traffic despite the fact that her hands and attention were otherwise occupied. As if it had a mind of its own, her Isetta turned off the ring road, crossed the Tiber River, and headed down the Via della Conciliazione. At the end of the street, the magnificent dome of St. Peter's Basilica rose up to meet them. David could hardly contain his excitement. His long journey was almost over.

Parking was always a problem around the Vatican, but Claudia managed to pull off a minor miracle. Finding a narrow sliver of space between a Fiat and a Lancia, she backed in between them and parked perpendicular to the curb. It was a fortuitous arrangement that gave them plenty of room to extricate themselves from the front door.

Nearby at the Arch of the Bells, a contingent of Swiss Guards stood sentinel, resplendent in shiny metal helmets with rooster-red plumes, white-ruffed collars, breastplates, and blue-and-yellow striped breeches. They were armed to the teeth with medieval halberds, pikes, and swords.

"We got an appointment," Aunt Claudia said in Italian, pulling a letter out of her purse and handing it to the captain.

After its authenticity was verified by a phone call, the guard waved them through the gate toward the great dome of St. Peter's Basilica. Hurrying across the Piazza San Pietro, they sent waves of pigeons undulating into the air, over and around the ancient Egyptian obelisk that stood in the center of the ellipse and through semicircular colonnades that were adorned on top with statues of angels and saints.

"After we through," Aunt Claudia promised, "I'm a gonna take you on a tour and show you the Basilica and Sistina. You gotta see it all."

"Great," said David. "After we're through."

He followed her down a narrow alley that led behind the Basilica. There, lurking in its shadow, was the Vatican Museum, the repository of the Pope's Secret Archives. In this place, six thousand miles from home, was the secret key that would unlock the riddle of the past. In this place was the end of a trail of blood and tears that began more than three-and-a-half centuries ago.

They made their way up a magnificent spiral stairway and down a series of long vaulted corridors lined with Renaissance statuary. Magnificent frescoes adorned their ceilings and their walls were hung with ornate tapestries and great paintings in gilded frames. Awe-inspiring works by Michelangelo, Leonardo da Vinci, Titian, and Raphael were everywhere. In the distance, the faint incantations of a Gregorian chant filled the air like incense made of frankincense and myrrh.

At the end of the corridor, was a set of double doors that led into the Archives. Inside was a dark chamber festooned with heavy curtains that eliminated the possibility of daylight damaging the rare collections within. Priceless medieval incunabula were everywhere, stored on shelves that rose up to the ceiling and were reachable only on wooden ladders. Many volumes dated back more than a thousand years. Among them, the handwritten proceedings of the trial of Galileo, tried and convicted of heresy for maintaining that the earth revolved around the sun. Here, too, was Henry VIII's petition to annul his marriage to Catherine of Aragon, an action that lead to the Church of England's separation from Rome. There were other historical documents as well. Among them, an important treaty with Napoleon Bonaparte, letters from the Great Khan of Mongolia, and crude hand-drawn maps of the ancient world.

Aunt Claudia disappeared into a corner alcove and returned with a slender bookmark of a man dressed in a long, black cassock. His eyes were of an unearthly shade of blue and the few remaining strands of his golden hair were curled into a wreath that encircled his crown like a garland of oak leaves.

"Davie, this is Monsignor Alighieri. He is Assistant Librarian and has agreed to help us."

"Thank you, sir," David said as he shook the man's pale, skeleton-like hand.

The Monsignor said something in Italian.

"He no speak English," Aunt Claudia explained. "But no you worry, I'm a good at transportation."

David knew what she meant.

She spoke to him again, and he could make out the words "Francisco de Genoa."

The librarian nodded pleasantly and beckoned for them to follow him down a thickly carpeted aisle lined on either side with marble busts of past popes and princes of the church. Leaving the reading room, they entered a dimly lit corridor filled with ancient volumes that had once provided the very foundations of western civilization.

"Luigi, my husband, he knows the Monsignor's cousin," Aunt Claudia whispered to David. "That is how we got in so easily. He says to Luigi that Monsignor Alighieri is a direct descendant of Dante."

David remembered the poet from Miss Applebaum's class. Dante's masterwork was *The Divine Comedy*, an allegorical journey through the circles of Hell, with a pit stop in Purgatory before finally passing on to Paradise. It was a voyage that reminded David of his own personal passage.

"There is no better person in all of Italy to guide us on our quest," Aunt Claudia said. She wanted to make sure David understood the significance of what she had told him.

"You did well, Aunt Claudia. Very well, indeed."

The corridor led into a labyrinth of narrow passageways, some barely wide enough for Aunt Claudia to squeeze through. In others, she had to walk sideways, which she accomplished with characteristic good humor. Periodically, they encountered piles of priceless leather-bound books stacked in the aisles. With David's assistance, Aunt Claudia managed to climb over them without knocking any over.

At last, they came to an alcove that contained shelves of wooden boxes of all sizes and shapes, all covered in a thick layer of cobwebs. The librarian retrieved a small ladder from an adjoining alcove and climbed up to the top shelf. Clearing away the curtain of cobwebs, he selected a small wooden box, blew off a layer of dust, and checked the label. Then he smiled and carried it back down the ladder.

"It looks like a small coffin," Aunt Claudia said. She crossed herself in anticipation of finding a mummified baby inside.

David's heart was pumping so hard, he could hardly hear.

With great care, Monsignor Alighieri brought the ancient box out into the light. Donning a pair of white cotton gloves, he slowly cracked open the lid and the three of them craned their necks to look inside. At the bottom of the box, a thin leather-bound volume lay in a pile of debris. Its back was broken and its face cracked and discolored like the skin of a decaying corpse.

Reaching inside, the librarian carefully brought forth the mortal remains of the mind of Francisco de Genoa. As he lifted open the cover, David's high expectations plunged into utter disappointment. The document was written in black ink on decaying black leaves that had been riddled with wormholes. It was completely and utterly unreadable.

"Oh, no!" David said sadly. "Oh, no."

Partially covered by the debris at the bottom of the box was a white card with printing on it. Monsignor Alighieri picked it up and read it carefully. Then turned and spoke to Aunt Claudia.

"He say, hey, not to worry about it," she translated. "Just follow him."

After replacing the book and chest on the top shelf, the librarian led his visitors back through the maze of stacks and down a narrow stairway. At the bottom was an ancient underground crypt that had been renovated into an information technology lab. Here, technicians wearing white coats over their black cassocks were busily working at a network of scanners, monitors, and computers. Everywhere, there were piles of deteriorating books and unbound manuscripts waiting their turn to be transformed, a leaf at a time, into high-resolution color images that would last as long as the world itself.

The Monsignor turned and explained it all to Aunt Claudia. To David's untrained ear there was a certain rhyme and meter to the way he spoke. The man was Dante's descendant in speech as well as blood. When the librarian finished, Aunt Claudia turned to David and translated as best she could.

"Monsignor, he tell me that they make here finger copies that are stored on C somethings."

"You mean digital copies stored on CD-ROMs, don't you?"

"Yes. That is what I mean."

The librarian spoke again.

"He says that you are fortunate," Aunt Claudia said. "The de Genoa book, it was in a section of the archives that was one of the first to be restored. Says it was made a year ago."

While Aunt Claudia was talking, the Monsignor handed the white card to one of the technicians and instructed him to call up the de Genoa file. A few clicks later, the image of the leather cover came up on the monitor, followed by a page that was completely black.

"This is 'before', the Monsignor say," Aunt Claudia told David. "Now watch. You gonna see a miracle."

The technician fiddled with the controls, adjusting color filters and fine-tuning the contrast and brightness. Miraculously, writing began to appear. *Ad Gloria Dei* it announced with a flourish. Underneath was the signature *Francisco de Genoa, S.J.* and the date *Dies X Junius MDCXXXV*. The tenth of June, 1635.

Monsignor Alighieri smiled and spoke again.

"He smiling," Aunt Claudia told David, "because he says all these files, they are made available to everyone in the world on the Vatican Internet website. You no need to have come here, you could have clicked on it."

David was utterly amazed. He had no idea that the Vatican even had a website. The light of the Information Age had dawned on its dark, medieval face in the form of high tech computer monitors.

In the leaves that followed, written across wormholes and watermarks, were the Choptank words of the Catholic catechism, Lord's Prayer, Ten Commandments, Hail Mary, and the Book of Genesis. They were the long, laborious, multi-syllabic words that Francisco de Genoa had transcribed so long ago in a doomed effort to convert the savages to Catholicism and save their souls from perdition. As in Grandfather's parchment, some letters were written in block form while others were joined together in cursive. The vowels were overwritten with accent marks, bars, double dots, and half moons to aid in pronunciation. A great many words had no vowels at all.

At the back of the volume was an extended vocabulary, a labor of love that had taken the Jesuit priest more than a decade to compile.

"Nuts!" David said.

"What's the matter, Davie?" Aunt Claudia asked. "Something wrong?"

"The meanings, Aunt Claudia. They're in some other language."

She relayed David's concern to the Monsignor.

"*Latina lingua*," he answered with a smile.

"Latin," Aunt Claudia said.

David took a photocopy of Grandfather's parchment out of his pocket and showed it to Monsignor Aligheri. "Aunt Claudia, would you ask him if he would help us translate?"

She nodded and rephrased his request in Italian.

The librarian nodded his head.

"Of course he would," Aunt Claudia told David. "Is this not the Vatican? Is Latin not the language of God?"

In a few moments, a laser printer zapped out the full seventy-five pages of de Genoa's vocabulary. With that in hand, the Monsignor motioned for the visitors to follow him. Retracing their path up the steps and around the labyrinth, they returned to the main reading room of the Secret Archives.

Monsignor Alighieri led them into the corner alcove that served as the Assistant Librarian's office. It was a small space furnished with ornate mahogany furniture and a pedestal that held the marble bust of Dante. Sitting down at his desk, he took the pages of de Genoa's vocabulary and put them down next to David's parchment.

David and Aunt Claudia sat down and watched patiently as the librarian transcribed each word from the parchment onto a lined yellow tablet. Then he carefully leafed through the vocabulary pages in search of its meaning. When he found it, he wrote it down first in Latin and then, under it, his Italian translation. It was like watching a human Rosetta stone at work.

The translation went slowly and time, itself, seemed to stand still. Several times Monsignor Aligheri turned over the pages of his yellow tablet and continued scribbling. Occasionally, to David's consternation, he would stop for a moment, smile quizzically, shake his head, and then continue on with his work.

"What the heck is he smiling about?" David whispered to Aunt Claudia. He stopped her when she started to relay his question to Monsignor Aligheri. "Just thinking out loud," David told her. "No need to translate."

Nevertheless, the librarian's reaction unnerved him, and the suspense became unbearable.

At last, Monsignor Aligheri completed his work and began to read the Italian translation a line at a time, pausing for Aunt Claudia to turn it into English.

"Great Standing Bear, Emperor of the Choptank people who live at the Center of the World speaks. My knees bend and my head bows to the wishes of the mighty King from across the great water. I accept the Lord of the Great Canoe as my brother. His people shall be as my children. We will never smite them with axes, shoot them with arrows, boil them in water, poison their food, or cut off their heads. My hunting ground shall be as their hunting ground. As token of peace, I give to the Lord of the Great Canoe all the deer in my wilderness, and also all foxes, wolves, possums, otters, raccoons, beavers, bears, rabbits, squirrels, elks, snakes, frogs, lizards, and all other living things save my own people. From my water, I give all fish, turtles, crabs, oysters, clams, snails, shrimp, eels, jellyfish, stingrays, starfish, sea horses and all other swimming things. From my sky, I give the sun, moon, clouds, lightning, thunder, rain, and all mockingbirds, eagles, hawks, owls, vultures, ducks, pigeons, geese, blackbirds, cardinals, hummingbirds, swans, turkeys, crows, ospreys, moths, mosquitoes, firebugs, and butterflies. From my earth, I give all trees, bushes, vines, wildflowers, weeds, tobacco, corn, squash, gourds, pumpkins, beans, herbs, rocks, dirt, sand, seashells, bones, caves, cliffs, creeks, rivers, and marshland that lie in

> *the peninsula of the great oak, the place known to one and all as the Center of the World."*

Claudia looked up with tears in her eyes. David could hardly mask his disappointment. His worst fears had been realized. Grandfather's parchment was not what he had hoped for. It was only a catalogue that formalized the theft of his people's land. A theft that was, in any case, already legal by Right of Discovery according to Dr. Moses. There was nothing here that would allow him to challenge that claim. Lord Blackburn had stolen it fair and square. Grandfather's parchment was nothing but a bill of sale. David hung his head in sorrow for the treachery that had befallen his ancestors.

Claudia embraced him. "I'm sorry, Davie. I'm so sorry."

David regained his composure. "Tell Monsignor Alighieri that I thank him for his trouble."

While she was doing so, he walked outside to be by himself. Down the hall, he found a marble bench under a painting of the Crucifixion and sat down, burying his face in his hands. It had all been for naught. His coming to the Chesapeake was a terrible mistake, a cosmic joke. It would have been better for him to have never known about his lost heritage.

He heard the clicking of frantic footsteps on the marble floor and looked up to see Aunt Claudia careening down the corridor. When she reached him, she was puffing and panting.

"Monsignor Alighieri...," she said trying to regain her breath, "...he wants to know...," she was still huffing and puffing.

David looked up. "What? What does he want to know?"

Aunt Claudia took a deep breath. "He wants to know if you want to hear the rest of the document?"

"There's more?"

"Yes, yes, he says there's more." Claudia took his hand and pulled him back down the hall and into library.

"I'm sorry, Monsignor," David apologized. "I thought you had finished.

Aunt Claudia translated and the librarian nodded and smiled cryptically.

When they were seated again, he turned the page in his yellow tablet and picked up where he had left off. Aunt Claudia resumed her translation.

"The Lord of the Great Canoe speaks. I accept the gift of Great Standing Bear, Emperor of the Choptanks. He shall be as my brother. His men shall be as my men. His children shall be as my children. His wives shall be as my wives. In my arms I will protect them from their enemies. As a token of friendship and to pay the Emperor for the loss of his hunting ground at the Center of the World, I give to him five crossbows and ten thundersticks with fire powder and lighting twigs. To his wives, I give a great treasure chest of jewels, cloth, mirrors, and precious metals. To his men, I give twenty hoes and ten rakes. To ease their withdrawal from the Center of the World, the Lord of the Great Canoe gives to the Emperor of the Choptank people, now and forevermore, a new homeland across the Chesapeake, a piece of land known to one and all as..."

Monsignor Alighieri paused as he turned to the next page in his yellow pad.

"Punto," he said at last. "Punto d'Airone!"

"...the Point of the Herons!"

Echoes of the words flew around the room. Free at last, like birds that had been caged for centuries.

David Waterfield was stunned. Like the shyster he was, Lord Blackburn had traded damaged goods for something of value. His men had already burned Herons Poynte to the ground in their misguided hunt for game. Living woods and wildlife would not return for decades and would never be of any use to him.

"Oh, Davie, is this good?" Aunt Claudia asked.

David took her in his arms and hugged her. Tears were streaming down his cheeks. "Yes, Aunt Claudia. Very, very good." He had no doubt what he would do now.

Aunt Claudia hugged the Monsignor on impulse. His eyes were ringed in red. He seemed to sense without knowing why or how, that a miracle had just occurred. That in this holy place an ancient injustice had been undone.

David was in a daze. Aunt Claudia thanked the Monsignor profusely. Stuffing de Genoa's vocabulary, the copy of the parchment, and the librarian's translation into her purse, she quickly led David out of the Secret Archives. She was only too well aware that he had a ship to catch. As they hurried through a series of galleries into an ornate vaulted corridor, they heard singing coming from the Sistine Chapel. Aunt

Claudia steered David to the side of the corridor next to a group of gawking tourists with binoculars around their necks.

"It's High Mass, the tourist guide told Aunt Claudia, checking his watch. "It's putting us way behind schedule, but it's almost over."

A few minutes later, a pair of Swiss guards opened the great doors and the glorious intertwined voices of a choir filled the corridor.

" Alleluia!" they sang. "Alleluia!!"

A thurifer emerged from the gate in the portcullis swinging a brass censer that filled the air with sweet-smelling incense. Next came a crucifer carrying a long staff with a cross on top. Aunt Claudia and several other tourists bowed their heads and crossed themselves. Several acolytes followed with long candles in brass holders. After them, came a bishop in full regalia. His robes were woven of purple silk accented by a golden stole and a pectoral cross. Crowning his head was a white miter, elaborately ornamented in gilded brocade. On his right hand was a ring with a large amethyst set in a circle of diamonds that signified his marriage to the church.

David couldn't help but notice that the bishop's left hand held the symbol of a lowly shepherd, a golden crosier.

La crosse, he thought. The name the black robes had given baggataway. Perhaps it was some kind of omen, or maybe just a strange coincidence. Perhaps it was ZaStakaZappa in another guise, born again in gold.

As the celebrants filed out into the corridor, the choir continued to sing. Looking into the Sistine Chapel, David marveled at the elaborate frescoes that adorned the altar and ceiling: the Last Judgment, Adam and Eve, The Garden of

Eden, and the Great Flood. The history of the world as seen through Christian eyes. The glorious song of the choir reverberated around the vaulted ceiling as if it were the angels of Michelangelo who mouthed the words. It was a song of great joy and celebration, a song about redemption and resurrection. To David Waterfield, it was a song about the Chesapeake.

Sea Change

The kitchen phone jangled.

"Let the machine take it," Raymond said impatiently.

They had just sat down for breakfast and he and Louisa were already running late. Independent as ever, his wife ignored him and checked the Caller ID window.

"What do you know! It's an overseas line!" She tossed the handset across the table to Liz.

It was David, his voice trembling with excitement. "Hey, I can't believe I finally got through. You won't believe it! I'm calling from a pay phone at the Vatican and the calling instructions are in Latin."

Liz cut to the chase. "What about the vocabulary?" she asked.

When David told her the news, she couldn't believe her ears.

"Hey, Doc!" she yelled. "You gotta hear this!"

Raymond ran into the living room and picked up the other line.

"Are you sure, son?" he asked incredulously after David repeated the story. "Are you really sure?"

"That's the way it translates, Doc. Monsignor Aligheri said he checked it twice."

"Hot damn!" the professor shouted at the top of his lungs. "Holy hot damn!"

"Raymond!" Louisa was aghast at his complete lapse in manners. "You know I don't permit swearing in this house. Especially not in front of our guest!"

"I can't help it, Lou! We just got the Blackburns by the balls!"

Liz nodded vigorously and Louisa's mouth dropped open. "God damn!" she screamed. "God damn!"

It was just the loophole they needed in court. The Blackburns could argue ownership of their land by virtue of the King's Right of Discovery until they were blue in the face. It simply didn't matter. Part of what Lord Baltimore had given to Caecilius Blackburn, he had given back freely to the Choptanks. Now and forevermore! Of course, at the time, Herons Poynte had been burnt to ashes and the Founder thought he was getting away with highway robbery. He had no idea that, in time, it would become the financial cornerstone of his family's empire. The implications were enormous.

"Listen, David," Liz said. "You've got to make copies of the vocabulary and the bishop's translation. And get his name, too. Everything."

"Already have. I just now faxed them to the number you gave me."

"You faxed them already! They're coming here!" Raymond was as excited as a young boy on Christmas morning. Portable phones in hand, the three of them galloped downstairs to Liz's study. The printer was chatting busily away.

"They're coming in now!" Liz gasped. "We can't wait to read them! When will you be back?"

"Three weeks."

Even as he spoke, David suddenly remembered the time. It was almost two and he was due back at the base at five. The sub was scheduled to go on maneuvers in the Adriatic before heading to Istanbul and then back to Newport News.

"I'll call you as soon as I get back to the Academy," he said hurriedly. "Gotta run or I'll be late for the ship. Oh, before I forget, Aunt Claudia sends her love."

"Tell her I love her, too," Liz said before she let David go.

He cradled the receiver and looked at his watch again. It was going to be close. The crazy Roman rush hour was just starting to gear up but Aunt Claudia wasn't daunted.

"Don't worry, Davie, we gotta just enough time," she tried to assure him. But her voice was strained with anxiety.

The traffic was stop and go. Front bumpers banged into back bumpers, tempers flared, and streams of impatient pedestrians risked their lives to dart across the street. Everyone was anxious to get home.

Home, David thought. He envisioned his ancestors paddling across the Chesapeake to what they thought was their new hunting ground at Herons Point. He could imagine them arriving in their dugout canoes, their arms aching from the long trip. He could feel their dismay at discovering their new land burnt to the ground, its once plentiful game gone. Filled with anger at the white man's trickery, Great Standing Bear and his warriors had returned to set things right. What they didn't know was that their new muskets didn't have any ammunition. Many were massacred and their bodies dumped in the peat bog. Those who escaped began their endless migration to the south. Eventually, they joined the Cherokee on the Trail of Tears, the long sad march across the country to desolate reservations in the Indian Territory of Oklahoma.

"No, no, no, no, no," Aunt Claudia was suddenly hysterical. Her little yellow car was starting to cough and wheeze like a sick child. Fumes were leaking out the rear. Traffic came to a standstill behind her. She put her hands over her ears to block out the cacophony of horns.

David pulled himself out the front door and opened up the engine compartment which was forwards of the left rear tire. Engulfed in a cloud of black smoke, his anxiety turned to outright panic. How on earth was he going to make it back on time? The *Chessie* sailed in three hours. Even under the best circumstances it would be tight.

Claudia sensed his dismay. "Don't worry, Davie, someone come along and give us a helping hand soon."

Several passing motorists gave them the finger instead. The traffic swept around them like a rampaging river that was too big for its banks. All they could do was sit and wait for it to subside and for help to come along.

An hour later, Claudia's face lit up. "Here it is! Here it is!" She pointed to a taxicab that was headed their way, weaving in and out of traffic like a violinist in a work by Vivaldi. Help was on the way. Taking her life in her hands, Claudia stepped out into the busy street and commandeered the cab.

"You go on, Davie, " she said pulling open the door. "Hurry or you miss a your plane."

"Sub," Aunt Claudia, "I'm gonna miss my sub. But it's okay. I can't leave you here alone." He slammed the door shut and waved the cabby on.

"Oh, no. Oh, no."

"Don't worry, Aunt Claudia. Everything is going to be fine."

David's stomach knotted up in a monkey's fist of conflicting emotions. He was ecstatic over the translation and distressed that he was definitely going to miss the boat. And that was a cardinal sin in the Navy. He wondered what the punishment would be. Dismissal from the Academy? A few months in the brig? Court martial? He didn't have a clue. All he knew was that it was wrong to abandon an old lady in her time of need, an old lady who had done her best to help him.

"You a good boy," she said gratefully. "You crazy in the head, but you a good boy. I see now why Elizabeth she loves you. Before, I not so sure. You thinka I don't notice? You gotta no hair, no eyebrows, and no eyelashes!"

"My shipmates played a practical joke on me," David explained, thankful that she hadn't seen the tattoo on the top of his head. "But everything will grow out, Aunt Claudia. I promise. By the next time you see me."

She immediately thought he was talking about a wedding. And the very idea calmed her down considerably. A happy and contented woman, she seemed oblivious to the curses and middle fingers coming from the cars careening around her.

It was another hour before help arrived in the form of a paddy wagon with a cargo of student radicals caged in the back. The polizia radioed for a tow truck that took still another hour to arrive. When they finally got to the garage, David telephoned the base to tell them what had happened. He wasn't surprised to hear that the *Chessie* had left on schedule and that he was technically AWOL. They ordered him to report back to the base on the double.

The mechanic operated on the car like he was a skilled craftsman called in to repair a damaged Stradivarius. Finally, after endless tinkering and fine-tuning, he had the problem all patched up.

At last, Claudia was able to give David a ride back to the base at Gaeta, apologizing all the way. "It's a my fault. I don't know whata to do. Elizabeth she killa me."

It was two in the morning when she let him out at the front gate. "Don't you worry, Davie, everything is gonna be okay."

He admired her faith. He didn't have the same kind of confidence. A marine with an automatic rifle hanging from his shoulder came over to the car and formally took David into custody. It was all over now. He was officially in hot shit.

He was confined to the barracks until space was available on a cargo plane headed back to the states. Alone in his Spartan quarters, David took the time to think about the future that had been made possible by the translation of the parchment. If the courts decided to give Herons Point back to his tribe, he would immediately shut down Blackburn Steelworks, freeing the environment from a habitual polluter of the air and water. He envisioned liquidating all the mill's assets to provide generous life-long pensions to employees who would lose their jobs. Every one would be happy, except, of course, the Blackburns.

David shut his dotted eyelids and imagined the future unfolding before him like a time-lapse movie. Silver and gold clouds streaked across the sky, the stars spun wildly, and the sun and moon raced each other around the world. As the seasons cycled before him, he saw thousands of tiny green shoots squiggle up through concrete cracks and grow so large and hard that they caused it to crumble. From every direction, vines slithered across the ground like green snakes and spiraled up around brick buildings, eating away the mortar that held them together. He heard the mighty rush of the wind and saw the tumbling of towers and the collapse of gigantic work sheds. Over time, the relentless hand of the weather corroded exposed furnaces and heavy machinery. Great trees burst through brick floors and thrust their mighty limbs through rusted metal, turning it to dust. His eyes flickered and he saw a green mantle of wild grasses spread over the ruins and a river running so clear that it mirrored the sky. He smelled the comings and goings of wildflowers that freshened the air with their sweet scents and brought the return of butterflies and birds. And he heard the crank of the Great Blue Heron and saw a flock nesting in the rookeries along the waters' edge. Yes, in the fullness of time, Nature herself would reclaim what had been taken from her. Herons Point would become itself again.

After two weeks of confinement, David was notified that he would be put on a Lockheed C-5A Galaxy cargo plane bound for the Patuxent Naval Air Station. Located in southern Maryland, the base was only a few hours drive from the Naval Academy. The timing was perfect. His hair, eyebrows, and lashes had grown back enough to make him look human again. Still, David was apprehensive about what lay ahead.

Strapped to the side of the cargo bay, his only companions were several bullet-riddled Black Hawks that were going home for repair. As his plane headed out over the Atlantic, he looked down and wondered about Archie. Had he been able to buy the horse laxative? If so, had he carried out their planned revenge? Had the *Chessie's* heads been turned into horse stalls? David wasn't sure Archie would have the nerve to execute the plan by himself. But even if that were the case, his mind would be so occupied with the plot that he would probably forget about his fear of the deep. And that was good enough for David.

Eight hours later, the plane swooped down over the Chesapeake Bay and landed on a runway next to the Patuxent River. As David disembarked, he was intercepted by a pair of poker-faced men from the Shore Patrol. After escorting him into the back of their van, they drove north towards Annapolis and the Naval Academy without uttering a single word. Since it was a Saturday, they had been instructed to take David to Buchanan House, the residence of the Superintendent. Located next to the Chapel, it was an imposing Beaux Arts mansion with a great mansard roof. Rank, as always, had its privileges.

Mitzi Shaw answered the doorbell and was somewhat taken aback by the armed Shore Patrolmen. A delicate blonde fitness fanatic, she was attired in white tennis togs and had a Wilson U.S. Open racket bag slung over her shoulder.

"Oh my," she said. "I don't allow guns in the house. You gentlemen stay outside." She turned to David. "I assume you're Mr. Waterfield."

"Yes, ma'am," David said politely.

"I'm running late. Oliver is waiting for you out back."

She directed him down the hallway to a pair of French doors that opened onto the veranda. Once he was on his way, she bid the Shore Patrolmen good day, shut the door behind her, and cut across the front lawn towards the tennis courts around the corner.

Inside, Buchanan House was a living museum. Allusions to the sea were everywhere. Portraits of naval heroes and seascapes of famous battles hung from the walls along with several antique barometers and an elaborate knot collection. Down the hall, a fleet of model sailing ships were displayed on a long table next to a reproduction of John Harrison's longitude chronometer, the remarkable 18th century innovation that changed navigation forever.

On the other side of the double doors was a wraparound porch with a white railing and a green-and-white striped awning overhead. The view was magnificent, looking out over a formal garden with Black-Eyed Susans in full bloom. At the bottom of the steps, a gardener in a straw hat was on his knees weeding a flower bed. Only, it wasn't a gardener, David suddenly realized. It was Admiral Shaw, himself, dressed in cut-off blue jeans and a dirty T-shirt. Seeing David on the porch, he stabbed his spade in the ground, climbed back to his feet, and stomped up the steps. Taking off his gardening gloves, he stuffed them into his back pocket.

David snapped to attention and saluted.

"At ease," Oliver Shaw said, looking David square in the eye. "Good to see you, son."

"Good to see you, too, sir."

"Take a load off." The Admiral gestured to a rattan sofa next to the wall. David sat down and the Superintendent leaned back against the railing.

"You look fit, Mr. Waterfield. Climbing Herndon must have agreed with you. No one would ever know you had a serious accident seven months ago."

"Thank you, sir."

"Before we get started, I want to tell you how much I'm looking forward to seeing you play next season. You're a helluva athlete."

It was the first indication that David was going to be coming back. Evidently, being expelled was not in the cards today.

"Thank you, sir," David repeated. He couldn't figure out what was going on here.

"Do you think we'll have it all together this spring? I understand we've landed a couple of blue chip prospects this year."

"Yes, sir," David said. "Coach Sleazak's really psyched. Not only that but Archie's come a long way at goal. With a little luck, he could be All-Conference."

Oliver Shaw stared at him for what seemed like an eternity. Unable to put it off any longer, he took a deep breath and his words took on an ominous tone.

"I'm sorry to tell you this, son, but there's been a terrible tragedy."

The unexpected turn in the conversation stunned David.

"I was informed this morning that the *Chessie* is missing at sea. All our indications are that she suffered an accident in the deep and broke up. All aboard are presumed dead."

David felt like he had been hit over the head again with a baseball bat. The horror was so abstract at first, a broad concept that rapidly filled out in flesh and blood.

"Archie!" he gasped. Archie was dead! And so were nine other midshipmen and a crew of one-hundred-and-twenty officers and men.

"I'm afraid so."

"No!" David refused to believe it. "There must be some mistake, sir."

"There's no mistake, son. We've got satellites tracking all our ships at sea and we've found an oil slick just north of the Canary Islands that was in her projected route home. There's no doubt about it. The *Chesapeake* has gone down."

David fought back the tears. He thought of Archie and how much he hated to be cooped up in the stale close quarters. He couldn't imagine how horrible it was for him. It wasn't manly to cry in front of an officer. But Admiral Shaw had already started, heartsick over the fine young men who had met such a dreadful death in the depths of the sea. With great effort, the Superintendent regained his self-control.

"You were lucky," he said at last.

"I should be dead, too, sir," David lamented. "My God! I should be dead!"

"The report was that you stayed to protect a helpless old woman. You weren't thinking of yourself. Usually that doesn't matter much in AWOL situations. But in this case, evidently, your priorities were right. I don't know what all this means, but I do know that you've been punished enough already."

David lowered his head between his knees and wept until he had no more tears to cry.

"You can go now," Admiral Shaw said when he was sure David was back in control of his emotions. "My people tracked down your girl. She's waiting for you in T-Court."

David nodded and the Superintendent escorted him back through the house and out the front door, dismissing the MP's.

Numb with grief, David forgot his salute and walked slowly into the park across the street. Admiral Shaw hated to see him go. Now, he had to face the awful task of calling the parents of the other nine men.

Across the way, Liz waited patiently on a bench near the statue of Tecumseh. When she saw David approaching, she ran to embrace him. Tears were shed for both the joy of their reunion and the sadness over the loss of so many young lives.

Nearby, a platoon of new plebes ran by, high-porting their sea bags over their heads as a squad leader screamed at them. Life was going on as usual at the United States Naval Academy, even without the crew of the *U.S.S. Chesapeake*.

Memorial

Eternal Father, strong to save,
Whose arm hath bound the restless wave,
Who bidst the mighty ocean deep
Its own appointed limits keep;
Oh, hear us when we cry to thee
For those in peril on the sea!
Amen.

July began on a dark and somber note. Nine gallant midshipmen were eulogized in the Cathedral of the Navy and remembered in marble on the cemetery wall at Hospital Point. Nine names were chiseled in stone, while nine lifeless bodies floundered in a tin can at the bottom of a cruel and unforgiving sea. Forever.

When the ceremony was over, David and Liz went over and embraced Helene. During the service, she had been resolute and stoic. For all appearances, she was a first-class midshipman in complete control of her emotions. But in David's arms, her feeling of loss rushed to the surface and she trembled in grief. She was Archie's girl and he was gone and so were all her dreams of a lifetime together. They would never be newlyweds. They would never rush down the steps of the chapel arm-in-arm, ducking through a tunnel of swords. Never.

Archie's parents were inconsolable, their eyes swollen and bloodshot, their faces white with grief. Outliving a child was the worst misfortune that a parent could suffer. After the service, Admiral Shaw had presented them with an American flag. In accordance with military tradition, it was folded thirteen times into a triangle that symbolized both the thirteen original colonies and the tri-cornered hats of the soldiers who had sacrificed so much during the War of Independence. Like countless mothers before her, Frieda Unger clutched it tightly to her chest in memory of her fallen son.

David expressed his condolences to Archie's parents and told them what a fine son they had.

"He spoke well of you, too," Mrs. Unger said. "I'm glad he had such a nice friend."

"He was looking forward to playing lacrosse with you next year," Archie's father added. "Told me you were going to lead the team to a National Championship."

"The only way we could have won would have been with Archie guarding the goal," David said graciously. "Coach Sleazak told me we're going to dedicate the season to him."

The bereaved parents nodded and tried to smile. Even small consolations were helpful at a time like this. Slowly and silently, the five of them made their way towards the Unger's minivan. It was the kind of car a proud parent would drive. Its bumpers were plastered with Annapolis Panthers lacrosse stickers and a couple of Navy decals were visible in the rear window. The back was loaded up with Archie's uniforms and computer.

"It was really thoughtful of you to get his things together for us," Archie's mom told David.

She planned on preserving her son's uniforms in his bedroom closet. His goalie stick would be hung over his bed, lacrosse posters would be tacked all over the bedroom walls, and his high school trophies would be displayed in his bookcase. The room would become a memorial to her lost son, a lost son who would never come home again.

"But there's one thing we want you to have," Hank Unger added. He opened the door and took out his son's titanium attackman stick and handed it to David.

"Archie would have wanted you to have this. He told us what happened to your Grandfather's stick."

David was overcome by the gesture. "I'll play with it always," he said, "for both of us. Archie's spirit will always be with me on the field."

They all hugged again, and then the Ungers got in their van and drove away from the Academy, away from their hopes for the future and into a lifetime of memories and tears.

"What will you do now?" David asked Helene.

"Archibald was really looking after me," she said. "I didn't know it, but he put me down as the beneficiary on his life insurance policy."

"How thoughtful," Liz said.

"It's not a lot, but it's enough for me to quit my job, provide for my father, and finish high school. Then I want to go to the Naval Academy Prep School and eventually get admitted here."

"Archie would be so proud of you," David said. The illusion she had been living had ended. Now it was time to start a new reality.

Revelations

Far from the smokestacks of Herons Point, the seventh incarnation of the Founder's name stood aloof on the rooftop garden atop his corporate headquarters. From his vantage point high above Charles Street, the proud panorama of the City of Baltimore spread out before him. To his left was the magnificent Inner Harbor, dominated by I. M. Pei's soaring Trade Tower and the glass pyramids of the National Aquarium. Across the harbor, he could see historic Federal Hill and to his right, the twin stadiums at Camden Yards. Many of these and, in fact, much of the remainder of the city and its environs had been built on skeletons of Blackburn Steel, a fact which made the Chairman feel enlarged and omnipotent, as if he were the Greek god Zeus surveying his world from the heights of Mount Olympus.

He took a deep breath and his lungs tingled with satisfaction. It was Monday and the air was always especially clean and clear on Mondays. Most of the heavy industry on the Patapsco had closed over the weekend, giving the prevailing winds a chance to sweep the smoke out of the sky and redistribute it to the surrounding suburbs. Blackburn Steelworks was an exception. It operated seven days a week, a full eight hours during the daytime and another surreptitious shift at night.

With its black budget defense projects, it was too lucrative to be allowed to sit idle. Upon its success rested the well being of two dozen other companies, both foreign and domestic, that were headquartered in the fifty-two floors beneath his Gucci-clad feet. The integrated iron and steel mill that his great-grandfather founded was nothing less than the very foundation of the Blackburn Empire.

"Excuse, master," Mikada whispered quietly as she minced out of the penthouse in dainty little steps. "They waiting for you now. Come now, master, you see."

Septimus turned and followed his geisha inside the white-on-white world of his ultra modern penthouse. Surrounded by soft, subtle shades of cream and enveloped in the pervasive smell of vanilla, the Chairman felt purified. There was not a spot or speck of dirt anywhere to be seen. It was as if all of it had been banished from his presence and confined to the grimy worksheds of Blackburn Steel. Even the inside of his private elevator was rendered in shades of white. A delicate, crystal chandelier hung from the ceiling and the sides were paneled in mother of pearl. Mikada punched a button and took her master down to the boardroom.

The Chairman's attorney, Laurence Roche, three aides, and a secretary jumped to their feet to greet him. As usual, the bleary-eyed Roche was dressed in a seersucker suit, wrinkled shirt, and large clip-on bow tie that served to mask his hyperactive Adam's apple.

"Please be seated," Septimus said. "All of you,"

The Chairman assumed his place at the head of the table with Mikada standing behind him ready to massage his neck and shoulders at the first hint of approaching stress. To his great annoyance, one seat was empty. Septimus fumed for a few minutes before Tavian stumbled into the room and took his place at the far end of the table. Exercising the prerogative of a prince, he was casually attired in a maroon golf shirt and pleated slacks patterned in the family's black and tan tartan.

"Nice of you to join us," the elder Blackburn chided. He considered Tavian's attendance to be mandatory on-the-job training for the day, far distant, when his only begotten son would assume command of the family's multi-national enterprise.

"Sorry, I'm late, Dad," Tavian apologized. "Couldn't find my putter."

After the meeting, Tavian and his hollow-legged buddy, Cy Van Aiken, were scheduled to play eighteen holes at the exclusive Baltimore Country Club, then hook up with a couple of hot babes for a night on the town. Neither of them was very good at golf, but they were pretty much assured of a hole-in-one later in the bedroom.

Reaching inside his vest pocket, the Chairman took out the Founder's tobacco pouch and filled his pipe bowl with Windsor Blend. As he lit up, he instructed his attorney to bring him up to date on current business matters. Switching on her tape-recorder, the secretary started taking notes in shorthand.

"Mr. Chairman, I assume you've heard about the *Chessie*," Roche began.

"Indeed I did. Saw it on the news a few nights ago. A great pity."

Deep down inside, Septimus knew it must have been the sub-standard steel. Break-up under stress had always been a possibility. Although he would never acknowledge it, Bull Wolinski had warned him about that.

"The Pentagon has informed us it will be conducting a thorough investigation," Roche said.

The Chairman wasn't worried. Instead, he felt smugly satisfied that his judgment had proved correct once again. It was true that an accident had occurred, but with evidence scattered in one of the deepest and most inaccessible parts of the Atlantic, the results were a foregone conclusion. No fault would be found, no blame assessed. The reputation of Blackburn Steelworks would remain unsullied.

"We can expect the Navy to order a replacement sub shortly," Roche said.

Septimus smiled subtly. "I'm sure we can find a way to accommodate them."

It was another chance to gouge the living eyes out of the federal government, an unexpected bonus for Blackburn Steel.

Roche hesitated for a moment. "The latest word on the accident is that there was one survivor."

The Chairman's eyes sharpened.

"Waterfield," Roche explained. "Apparently he was AWOL in Rome when it happened."

"Oh really?" Septimus frowned and his face became a fist. Mikada began to massage his neck and shoulders.

Roche mustered forth all his courage to continue. "Mr. Chairman, there's something important I need to tell you. There's been...er...a new development in the mummy case."

"New development? What are you talking about?"

Roche took a deep breath. "Mr. Chairman, I've been notified that the plaintiffs have expanded the scope of their suit."

"Go on."

Sweating profusely, Roche took the cardboard-backed handkerchief out of his breast pocket and blotted his brow.

"Mr. Chairman," he continued, "Waterfield has found the de Genoa vocabulary in the Vatican. The plaintiffs have been able to translate the parchment."

Tavian was incredulous. "What the fuck is he talking about, Dad?"

But his father said nothing.

"They are challenging your ownership of Herons Point, Mr. Chairman. They say the Founder gave it to the Choptanks to induce them to vacate Kings Oak peacefully."

"That's ridiculous!" Tavian blurted out.

His father, however, was stone-faced silent.

"Furthermore," Roche added, "the plaintiffs are asserting that the steel mill was built at Herons Point without the tribe's permission. That, in fact, tribal land was used illegally by your great-grandfather as collateral to finance the construction of the mill. Thus, they claim that under Maryland law, Blackburn Steel belongs to the descendants of the Choptank tribe. And so do all of the companies that are held in its name. Moses remembered that you transferred all your assets to Blackburn Steelworks during the slave reparations lawsuit so that they could be protected by the corporate shield. Thus they are claiming all your brokerage accounts, art work, jewelry, and personal effects. Real estate assets, too, including Black Steeple and Kings Oak. Even the bodies of the mummies that you donated to the museum. In short, everything you own."

"Shiiiit!" Tavian leaned back in his chair and let out a howl. "That's absurd! Isn't it, Dad? They've gone crazy. The dumb fucks!"

The Chairman didn't move a muscle. Suddenly and unexpectedly, his worst fear had been realized. A specter from the past had returned to confront him and demand restitution for the wrongs that had been committed against an entire people. His own father had warned him of this possibility when he had solemnly instructed him in the duties of the Chairmanship. He had spoken to him of the great responsibilities he would bear to future, unborn generations. He had let him read for himself the old parchment deed that was the very basis of the family power and the potential for their downfall. It had shaken him to the core. Septimus had always wondered why his great-grandfather hadn't repurchased Herons Point from the Choptanks when he decided to build a steel plant there. His father had told him that there was no one to buy it from. The tribe was long gone by then, persecuted westward by the steady advance of the white man. The family figured it was unlikely that any of them would ever return. They were wrong. Their luck had finally run out.

"Mr. Chairman," Laurence Roche said calmly, "in view of this new development, I've asked for and received a six month's continuance from the court. There will be much work for us to do to prepare our defense."

But Septimus wasn't listening now. He had lived in fear of this moment of reckoning ever since his father had first shown him the parchment, fear that threatened to turn into panic when the Choptank punk first appeared at Kings Oak. But not until today did he realize that David Waterfield had, by some miracle, managed to find the vocabulary and have the Choptank parchment translated into English. For the first time in his life, he didn't know what to do. Waves of panic shot through his whole being. His mind ran screaming in circles. He felt the cornerstone of his empire being pulled out from under him. Fifty-two stories of interlocking companies began to tumble down on him like a house of cards. His heart raced out of control and a riot of blood gushed to his head. An electric shock sent him reeling back, overturning his chair. And before his eyes the world went black.

"My God!" Roche said. "He fainted!"

But it was obvious to the others that it was more serious than that. The Chairman's face was turning blue. Mikada knelt down at his side, felt his pulse, and listened to his heart.

"Master's heart stop!" she screamed. "Somebody call 911!"

While Roche punched his cell phone, Mikada regained her composure. In her line of work, she had already had several older gentlemen go out on her, but Septimus was the first to do so without any participation on her part. She had watched medics try to revive her customers with CPR and now her untrained hands tried to emulate them. Her fists pounded her boss's chest like they did when she was angry with him, trying desperately to beat the life back into him.

Tavian looked down at the undignified tangle of arms and legs sprawled out on the white carpet. It was the first time he had ever seen his father out of control, the first time he had ever seen him as a victim. He looked weak and helpless now, lying amid a pool of coffee, scattered papers, and the spilled contents of his pipe and tobacco pouch. To make matters worse, a foul odor rose up from him as his bowels evacuated down the legs of his Armani trousers and spilled out over the immaculate, snow-white carpet. Roche threw his seersucker jacket over his boss, saying it would help prevent him from going into shock. But it looked like the Chairman was well on his way there now.

Mikada stopped pounding for a moment and put her ear to her master's chest. "Heart beating now!" she said excitedly, full of wonder at the miracle her tiny hands had performed.

A State Police helicopter was visible through the glass wall. Although it was a tight squeeze, it managed to set down on the rooftop heliport next to the corporate copter. While its rotors kept turning, two medics rushed down to the boardroom and took away the Chairman's limp body strapped to a gurney. With the patient secured inside, the chopper lifted off and banked towards the helipad at the University of Maryland Hospital. The whole incident had taken only ten minutes.

Six hours passed before Septimus had regained enough strength to summon his son to his side. The stroke had affected the left lobe of his brain and his right side was paralyzed. With great difficulty, he was able to speak out of the left corner of his mouth.

As best he could, the father told the son about the validity of the parchment deed. He described his futile attempt to buy de Genoa's vocabulary from the Vatican twenty-four years earlier, an action that had resulted in his excommunication from the church and the sacrifice of his very soul. Most of all, he voiced his deep concern over the pending lawsuit. David was a local sports hero, a Naval Academy Midshipman with an untarnished reputation. He fretted that a jury, which would undoubtedly be made up of a preponderance of minorities, would have a natural bias towards the Choptank punk. If they decided to confirm the tribe's title to Herons Point or even if they managed to shut down Blackburn Steel, it was all over. Everything would fall down around them. Both of them knew without saying so, that the standard method of solving problems—a large cash payment—wouldn't work in this instance. David Waterfield was after something money couldn't buy. His lost birthright.

Tavian understood the seriousness of it. He had never seen his father cry. But now tears were streaming down the left side of the old man's face while his right side remained frozen in passivity. It was a sight pitiful and grotesque at the same time.

A purple-haired nurse with heavily tattooed forearms came rushing into the room and quickly administered a sedative.

"That gonna make you feel better, Mr. Blackburn," she said. "You be in dreamland soon."

She wiped his tears away with a tissue, wadded it up, and hooked it into a waste can in the corner of the room.

Three points, she thought.

Had Septimus known that Shakela had tended David Waterfield in this very same room and bed, he would have immediately died.

Tavian leaned over and held his father's hand. "Don't worry, Dad. I'll fix everything. I know just what to do."

The stricken old man looked up at him. Everything—the entire future of the Blackburn family—rested in his son's untested hands. Now, he was more afraid than ever.

"My tobacco pouch," the old man struggled to say. "Would you...get it for me?"

"There's no smoking in here, Dad."

"Not gonna smoke...my good luck charm. You know the legend about it."

"Yes, Dad. You told me many times."

"Been asking for that darn pouch since he came in," Shakela said. "Checked his clothes, but it not there."

"Don't worry, Dad, it will show up. You'll see."

The Chairman closed his eyes, resigned to whatever Fate had in store for him.

Dutifully, Tavian kissed his father's forehead and left the room. On his way down the hall, he slipped his hand in his pocket and felt the Founder's pouch bulging inside. The mighty balls of Great Standing Bear were his now and his alone. The power had passed.

The Shaft

Bancroft Hall was completely dark and utterly silent, like a submarine hiding at the bottom of the ocean, waiting for an enemy to pass overhead. Inside, a thousand midshipmen were stretched out in their racks awaiting the dreaded six-thirty reveille that would set them off and running on the last month of their summer training routine. Alone among their number was one who slumbered lightly under open eyes, a Choptank warrior alert for the sudden move of an enemy.

The overhead lights inexplicably began to flicker on and off like a ship signaling in Morse code. David hit the floor, certain that something was amiss.

An amplified voice boomed over the PA in the passageway.

"All hands on deck! Everybody up! On the double!"

"The fuck's going on?" David's roommate sat bolt upright in his bunk. "It's only 0200," Mazurski said. Reveille had come four hours too soon. But this wasn't reveille.

"A surprise inspection," David guessed. "They must be looking for something."

Up and down the corridor, weary bodies staggered out of their rooms in sleepy confusion, all of them bundled up in navy-blue bathrobes and matching flip-flops.

"Attention on deck!" came the command at the end of the hall.

A ragged chain reaction rolled down the line just as David and Masurski stumbled into place. Around the corner came the Officer of the Day followed by a bowlegged man in a blue blazer with a gold badge pinned to his pocket. Under the brim of his white Stetson hat were a pair of bullet-hole eyes and a hook nose that ended in a cowcatcher mustache. He wore a western string tie around his neck and a wide, rawhide belt around his waist. On the front was a big metal buckle with the initials WBG hooked together like they could have come off the end of a branding iron.

"Shit! It's Wild Bill Granger!" Mazurski whispered. "Someone's in hot shit."

Close behind him were three special agents of the Naval Criminal Investigative Service decked out in identical blue blazers. Two of them were nondescript undercover men with their jackets pulled back just enough to reveal shoulder holsters. The third was a petite female with a butch haircut who was sliding down the slickly buffed deck on the leash of a powerful, jet-black German shepherd.

"He's got the Gestapo with him," David whispered.

As they made their way down the corridor, Wild Bill and his storm troopers stopped by each room in turn, staying only for the dog to take a few sniffs.

"Drugs," Mazurski said. "They're looking for drugs."

The agents headed down toward David's room. At first, they went right by, but then the shepherd got a whiff of something and turned back. Stopping in front of David's feet, she sniffed and snorted through enlarged black nostrils.

"Seems like Velma likes you, son," Granger said in his Texas twang. "Maybe she's just crazy 'bout them blisters on your feet or maybe she smells somethun' else."

Velma nosed through David's legs towards his open door, forcing him to step over her tightened leash.

"Like to ask you boys for permission to search the premises," Wild Bill said.

His politeness was just a formality. If they denied him permission, it would be tantamount to admitting there were drugs inside. It would only bring him back with a proper search warrant and a really bad attitude.

"No problem, sir," David agreed.

"No problem at all, sir," Mazurski seconded.

"After you boys then," Granger said in mock politeness, giving them a nudge inside.

Immediately Velma got extremely excited, causing her to run in circles around the room, urinating all over the floor.

"Hey, man! I spent two hours buffing that deck!" Mazurski was really ticked off.

"We've got an inspection tomorrow," David explained.

Wild Bill apologized with a shrug of the shoulders. "When you gotta go, you gotta go. Know what I mean?"

Barking and yelping like crazy, the shepherd zeroed in on one of the closets.

"Whose clothes are those?" Granger asked.

"Mine, sir," David said.

"Stand back, son."

Carefully, Granger slid the closet door. There was nothing inside but an array of dry-cleaned uniforms ready for inspection. Some were on hangers while others were folded neatly on shelves. One by one, Wild Bill flung them out on the floor for the shepherd to smell. But Velma ignored them. The bitch wouldn't shut up. Straining at her leash, she growled at the empty closet.

"What's she doing, Wild Bill?" the little lady with the butch haircut said. "Everything's out'n there."

"Maybe not everthang, Lucy," Granger said.

He pulled over David's chair and stepped up on it. Slowly, he ran his hand over the top of the closet, searching for the object of Velma's frenzy.

"You boys did a good job of cleaning," Granger said. "Can't find a speck of dirt up here. Uh oh. What's this?"

He brought down a lacrosse stick and held it out over the dog's head. Velma barked her head off, slavering at the mouth.

"This your stick, son?"

David nodded. It was the one Archie's parents had given him.

Granger inspected it carefully. It had an innocent-looking titanium shaft. But he knew better. The rubber plug at the bottom made him very suspicious. Prying out the stopper, he shook the stick hard. Five small plastic bags of chalky, white tablets fell on the floor.

"Well looky here," Wild Bill said. "Funny place to hide your aspirins, ain't it."

David was dumbfounded. "That's not my stuff, sir." He couldn't believe it was Archie's either. Someone had set him up.

"Right," Granger said. He had heard every denial in the book. It wasn't his job to separate bullshit from believability.

Lucy opened one of the bags, stuck in a finger, and took a taste. Her eyes crossed for a moment. Then she turned and nodded to Wild Bill.

"I'm taking you into custody, son," Granger announced solemnly, taking a flash card out of his wallet. As many times as he had advised midshipmen of their Article 31-B Rights, he could never remember them. He found a cheat sheet was safer than trusting his memory and giving some left-wing lawyer a way to get them off the hook. He ticked them off, one at a time, but David didn't hear a word. A profound state of shock had left him speechless.

Lucy produced a camera and proceeded to take flash pictures of the crime scene. Wild Bill was only too happy to pose for her, holding up the lacrosse stick and pill bags as if they were trophies of some kind.

"You better get dressed, kid, you're gonna go with us for a while."

"But I'm innocent, sir."

"I'm not asking. I'm telling."

David sorted through the pile of clothes that had been thrown on the floor. The uniform of the day smelled of dog pee but he had no choice but to put it on. When he had finished dressing, one of the male agents grabbed his arms and pulled them behind his back while the other produced a set of stainless steel handcuffs that just barely managed to fit over David's thick wrists.

"Sorry kid, one size fits all," the agent apologized.

David winced when he finally managed to clamp them shut.

"I'll call Liz for you, Dave," Mazurski promised.

"Thanks, man."

Then they pushed David out the door and proudly paraded him down the hall in front of the whole wing like he was an escaped fugitive that had been tracked down and captured. Public Enemy Number One. David hung his head down. It was too painful to look up at his friends. He felt, as innocent men must have felt many times in the past, as if he were on his way to a lynching or a crucifixion.

Article 32

The investigation of David Waterfield was concluded in record time. A week after the bust, an Article 32 Hearing under the Uniform Code of Military Justice was held in Rickover Hall. The purpose was to determine if there was enough evidence for a trial by court martial.

Raymond and Liz drove down from Baltimore to be at David's side. Both as lawyers and friends, they were especially concerned that David had not been forthcoming with the investigating officers. He had refused to tell them that the lacrosse stick had been given to him just weeks earlier by Archie's parents.

"That's like saying Archie did drugs," David said. "I know he didn't. He was a stand-up guy. I can't destroy his reputation. His parents would never get over it. The truth is someone got into my room and planted the drugs."

"The same someone who broke into your room and sawed up ZaStakaZappa," Liz added.

"I think we all know who's behind this," Raymond said. "We just don't know how to prove it yet."

The presiding officer, Captain Marshall Solomon, entered the chamber and called the proceeding to order. He was a thin, wiry man who wore a black patch over his left eye as a result of a fencing accident his last year in law school. His opponent's foil had lost its protective tip and slipped between the wire mesh in his face mask, skewing his eye like a toothpick in a stuffed olive. He was, of course, compensated by a huge cash settlement and was fitted with a Cryolite glass eye at the military's expense. Even though it wasn't necessary, Captain Solomon still liked to wear his eye patch whenever he was in court or presiding at a hearing. It made him feel a bit like a swashbuckler ready to cross swords again in the verbal arena, a man to be feared and respected for his ability to thrust and parry. If Justice were supposed to be blind, at least he was halfway there.

Wild Bill Granger was the first to testify. He revealed that it was an anonymous telephone call that had drawn him and his investigators to Bancroft Hall in search of drug violations. He told how Velma had sniffed out David's room and led him to find the lacrosse stick over his closet. The suspect, he said, identified it as his own. Inside the shaft were five small bags of white pills.

"And what did you determine they were," Captain Solomon asked.

"Ecstasy. Nasty stuff. Street value of over five-thousand dollars."

Raymond bit his lip. Even if Archie weren't an addict or a dealer, the fact that the drugs were found in his stick would have cast a reasonable doubt on David's guilt. The charges against his client would be summarily dismissed. But the professor had promised, with great reluctance, to respect David's decision not to tarnish Archie's memory.

Next, Captain Solomon summoned forth the Academy's security officer. A snappy marine came forward with a slight limp and sat down at the table in front of him. David had seen the man before but hadn't known his name. Now he did. Captain Cyrus Van Aiken, III.

"That's the guy I almost ran into in Bancroft," he whispered to Liz. "The night of the formal ball."

Liz remembered. "I got bad news. I saw the creep at the tent party at Kings Oak last fall. He's Tavian's best friend. I bet he's the one who ransacked your room and cut up ZaStakaZappa."

David started to come out of his chair but Raymond and Liz restrained him before he did himself any more harm.

At Solomon's prodding, Van Aiken told of having received David's computer from the NCIS agents.

"And what did you discover?"

"There was nothing incriminating on the hard drive. No lists of clients, or anything relating to drugs," Van Aiken testified.

David and Liz were pleasantly surprised. At least no evidence had been planted there.

"However," Van Aiken continued, "when I was lifting up the tower, I heard a strange rattle inside. We took off the metal casing and discovered something wedged inside next to the chips and hard drive."

He reached in his brief case and took out a large plastic bag. Inside was Grandfather Two Tongue's oblong wooden box.

Liz looked at David. She had always wondered where David had hidden it after she had taken the parchment to Raymond's safe.

Van Aiken brought forth another plastic bag. "Inside, the box, I found this pipe and a small bag of powder."

"Are these yours?" Captain Solomon asked David.

"I object," Raymond intervened.

David answered anyway. "Yes, sir. They're mine." The truth was the truth. He wouldn't deny it no matter what. Raymond sighed and Liz reached over and squeezed David's hand.

"They belonged to my grandfather," David continued. "I couldn't bear to part with them. Since plebes are forbidden to have personal things in their rooms, I hid them in the tower."

Captain Van Aiken went on to explain how laboratory analysis had identified the powder and residue in the pipe's bowl as peyote.

"Have you ever smoked this pipe, Mr. Waterfield?" Solomon asked.

"Object," Raymond said. "Use of peyote in Native American religious rites is protected by the first and fourteenth amendments to the Constitution. My client doesn't have to answer that question."

"Of course, Dr. Moses. I asked only because the usage of one drug can sometimes lead to experimentation with another."

The damage done, Raymond set about trying to rehabilitate his client. He called forth Midshipman Oscar Taylor to testify. He had been on duty as the Officer of the Deck the night of the formal ball. Under the professor's questioning, Taylor told of having been summoned to David's room to find that it had been broken into and thoroughly ransacked. He mentioned how holes had been punched into the ceiling tiles and how David's wooden stick had been cut into pieces.

Raymond turned to Captain Solomon. "We believe someone is out to destroy Mr. Waterfield's reputation. Someone planted the Ecstasy in his lacrosse stick. Perhaps the same someone who broke into his room in this instance." He paused and glanced over at Captain Van Aiken. "We contend that Mr. Waterfield is being framed. He is considered by all who know him to be a man of high morality who would never engage in any activity involving drugs."

As proof, he summoned a series of witnesses to testify to David's good character: his roommate, Mazurski; Coach Sleazak; and most importantly, the Superintendent of the Naval Academy himself.

"I have never known such a fine young man," Oliver Shaw said. "Mr. Waterfield has consistently demonstrated great personal character and outstanding leadership potential. Last semester, he made the Superintendent's List. All of this, despite having sustained serious injuries at the start of the school year."

Far from ending the matter, Admiral Shaw's remark caused the one-eyed judge to question David on his use of painkillers.

"I've taken nothing except what Dr. Zegusa prescribed for me when I was in the hospital," David testified. "Ecstasy wasn't one of them. The Academy has had four random drug tests this year and I have never had any illegal substance show up in my urine."

But despite David's denial and the testimony of Admiral Shaw and the others, Captain Solomon ruled that there was ample evidence to proceed with a trial by court martial. A date certain was set one month away, but it might have just as well been held right then and there. The verdict was a foregone conclusion. There was no defense for the evidence presented. No way to prove that David had been set up. Nothing that

Raymond's eloquence could completely smooth over or explain away.

Thirty days later, the presiding officer weighed the evidence and ruled that David Waterfield was guilty as charged. The sentence was lighter than usual since the prosecution had failed to prove that David had ever taken the pills himself or sold them to others. And, of course, Superintendent Shaw's testimony regarding the character of the defendant was a moderating influence. Nevertheless, the sentence was almost too heavy for David to bear. He was suspended from the Academy for a year during which time he would be confined to the Marine Corps Brig at Quantico, Virginia.

Liz felt sick to her stomach, a nauseating revulsion for Justice gone terribly awry. For the first time, she was ashamed to be studying law. In the wrong hands, it was so easily manipulated to convict the innocent and let the powerful go free.

After the proceeding was adjourned, the court granted David a few minutes to be alone with his friends.

"Oh, David. They won't get away with this," Liz promised, her eyes red from weeping. "I won't let them."

David was too dejected to speak.

"Don't worry, son, this thing isn't over yet," Dr. Moses assured him. "Not by a long shot. And we've still got the parchment suit ahead. Justice will prevail, I promise."

David nodded but deep down inside he didn't really believe it. Justice in America had always been for the white man, not for Native Americans or people of color. David leaned over and kissed Liz goodbye and thanked Raymond for his help. Then he was handcuffed and escorted out of Rickover Hall by the military police.

Despite Raymond's request that the transfer be handled discreetly, the press had been notified by an anonymous phone call. The networks, cable news, and Washington bureaus of all the major newspapers had assembled outside on the lawn. David's story had all the elements needed to capture public attention. Another star athlete had been caught doing drugs. This time the prestigious United States Naval Academy was the background. The Native American element added another fresh new angle. It was the kind of thing that sold newspapers and increased TV ratings.

David Waterfield scuffled slowly down the sidewalk through a frenzied gauntlet. Reporters stoned him with pointed questions that sounded like insults and accusations. TV cameras ripped off his image into their electronic eyes. Mobile vans uplinked them to satellites and spread his disgrace all over the country and, indeed, the world. What would his mother and sisters think? And Miss Applebaum? It made him cry to think of the hurt that his loved ones would suffer.

A Shore Patrolman with big hands pressed his head down and guided him inside the rear compartment of a white van. Before the doors shut, David took one last look at freedom. Liz. Raymond. Admiral Shaw. Mazurski. Coach Sleazak. His teammates. All of them soured by the unfairness of the verdict against him. Lurking behind them was the smirking marine officer who had no doubt set him up. David's eyes flashed in anger. Someday, he would have his revenge, for himself and all his people.

The Brig

The Quantico Military Reservation was located twenty miles south of Mount Vernon on the western bank of the Potomac River. All told, it covered about a hundred square miles of prime Virginia countryside that had been stolen from Manohoacs Indians centuries ago. Besides the brig, it housed training facilities for the FBI and DEA, a war college, helicopter school, and an airfield. In addition there were a variety of support facilities including an eighteen-hole golf course, several swimming pools, tennis courts, and an officer's club. Somewhat symbolically, the brig was located at the far edge of the base across the railroad tracks and next to the garbage dump. It was a low-rise complex that could have been mistaken for a barracks except for the iron bars on the windows and the coiled razor wire atop the chain link fence that surrounded it.

Inside the walls were inmates from all branches of the armed services. Only one of them was innocent. Like so many of his ancestors, David Waterfield had been falsely accused, convicted, and incarcerated. It had happened so often to his people that they came to expect imprisonment as their natural state. Grandfather Two Tongues had told him that the early years of the nineteenth century were the worst. White settlers in the southeast had gone mad with gold fever. Ignoring the rulings of their own Supreme Court, they uprooted the Cherokee from their ancient homeland in the Appalachian Mountains. Innocent farmers were rounded up at bayonet point. Children were kidnapped at schools. Families were taken from their beds in the dead of night. All of them were herded like animals into overcrowded stockades. Their abandoned homes were ransacked. Bodies of the dead were dug up from their graves. All in a search for Cherokee gold that did not exist.

Those who resisted the bluecoats were treated harshly, the old wisoe said. He told David the sad story of his ancestor, Kicking Calf, who had won his name by his ability to fight with his feet as well as his fists. During the battle of Buzzards' Tree, he was surrounded by bluecoats, knocked unconscious by the butt of a rifle, and captured. As an example to the other prisoners, his arms were tied behind his back and a noose slipped over his head. Then he was strung up in front of them, kicking until his windpipe severed and his neck snapped. Afterwards, the bluecoats cut him down and hacked off his right foot above the ankle. Coated in iron, it was used as a doorstop at the entrance to the general's office in the stockade.

David was determined not to be another victim of the system. Someday, he would reclaim his innocence and fulfill the prophecy of his secret Choptank name. But first he had to work his way back to freedom. The rigorous regimen inside the brig was designed to rehabilitate inmates so they could be reintroduced into society. Mornings were broken into a two-hour Drug Rehabilitation class followed by an Anger Management Seminar. In it, the instructor demonstrated the techniques of Verbal Judo as a way to control and redirect hostility through semantics. Manual labor was the order of the afternoon. For twelve cents an hour, David was required to work in a sweatshop making mahogany furniture for the brass in the Pentagon.

At night he was confined to a cell that was only a little larger than his bunk on the *Chessie*. Instead of steel and water, he was surrounded by a foot of concrete. But the feeling of impending doom was the same. He imagined the walls of his cell slowly closing in on him like a tightening vice. He felt his lungs shrink and his breathing grow shallow. Inevitably, he thought of poor Archie sinking to the bottom of the sea, waiting for the sides of the sub to collapse on him like a crumpled tin can. Only the thought of Liz gave him hope and the courage to endure.

It was a month before she was allowed to visit. The anticipation of seeing her was almost more than David could bear. He thought he would pass out when he walked into the interview room and saw her sitting behind the thick Plexiglas partition. She was Joan of Arc with indigo eyes and skin that gave off a soft, tender glow even under the harsh, fluorescent lighting. She was clearly startled by David's appearance. The man in the orange prison fatigues and handcuffs was a stark contrast to the neatly pressed midshipman she was used to seeing. His hair was beginning to grow out now and was at a particularly unkempt stage, somewhere between being too short to matter and not quite long enough to comb or shave. His eyes were downcast and the pain of humiliation was clearly visible in his face. The guard nudged him into his seat in front of the Plexiglas window, removed his handcuffs, and went outside so they could have some privacy.

Liz picked up the phone and so did he. The ultimate long distance call.

"David," was all she could say.

"Hey. Thanks for coming. I've missed you so much. How have you been?"

Liz did her best to be upbeat and positive. "Coping as best I can."

"Yeah, me too."

"You won't believe it, but I finally landed a new job."

"Hey, that's great. Where?

"The Maryland Law Library down on Pratt Street," Liz said. "I'm a research assistant. The pay's not great but I'll be able to keep up my tuition and get a room of my own. Not only that, but Raymond forced the bank to give me back my Tundra."

"Looks like things are looking up."

"Not everything," Liz said. "I heard LeGrande and the others guys were laid off at the mill."

"Tavian," David guessed.

"Yep. He just wanted to punish them for defending you at the Pig Iron Pub. Let them go on the spur of the moment without any severance."

"Sounds familiar."

"Yeah, well...so what have they got you doing?" It was time for her to change the subject.

"They're trying their best to straighten me out, hardened criminal that I am," David said. "Every morning I have to sit through four hours of training classes. Pretty boring stuff."

"I don't know how you stand it."

"Actually it's not too bad. I've discovered there's an advantage to being able to sleep with your eyes open."

Liz smiled. "And just what is it that you think about when you're sleeping?"

"You," he said gently. "Just you."

"Oh David."

"Been thinking about what happens after I get out of this place."

Their eyes touched through three inches of scratched Plexiglas.

"I want us to get married."

Liz hadn't allowed herself think about such a possibility. The wells of her eyes overflowed.

"Yes, yes, of course. That's what I want, too."

David was relieved. It wasn't the most conventional of proposals, but it was successful.

Liz dabbed her cheeks with a tissue. "When were you thinking?"

"I have some things to do first. After I get out of here, I need to clear my name. Then I want to finish up at the Academy."

Liz felt a sharp pang in her stomach. He was talking about four years. How could she ever wait that long?

"We'll do it at the Navy Chapel during Commissioning Week," David said. "You know, one of those weddings that take place every fifteen minutes."

She tried to smile. "Like Archie and Helene were planning."

"Right."

"Why do we have to wait so long?" Liz couldn't help but ask, even though she already knew the answer.

"It's against Academy rules to be married," David said. "They would never let me back in."

Her eyes dropped to the floor and she took a deep breath. "What about a family? Do you think you'd ever want to have any children?"

"Someday," he said quietly. "After things have gotten back to normal."

His vision turned inwards and he peered off into the future. His eyes submerged themselves into the crystalline depths of the Great Sea of Ancestors, into the liquid essence of ancient ones and the primordial elements of the unborn. He saw his ghost swimming with a child of his own blood, a son with his father's broad shoulders and flowing brown hair. A son drawn ever upwards toward the shimmering light which danced across the surface. A son who would break through the barrier to breathe and be born again.

Liz began to cry again.

"Is something the matter? Did I say something to upset you?"

"I'm sorry," she said. "It's just that I'm so happy." But that wasn't it at all.

"Now, now. It's okay," David said. "Everything is going to work out fine. Someday all of this will be behind us and we'll just forget it ever happened."

"I don't think so, Dave. I'll never forget this. And I'm never going to rest until those Blackburns pay for everything they've done to us."

"Hate doesn't solve anything, Liz. It just takes you down with it. Forget about them. Just think about us."

The guard came back in the room and signaled the end of their meeting. David asked Liz not to come back and see him. It was such a long drive for her and it would just upset them both. It was only another eleven months until he would be released. They had often gone months at a time without seeing each other at the Academy. Telephone calls and letters would do until then.

He hung up the phone but maintained eye contact with Liz. The guard snapped on his handcuffs and led him shuffling out of the room, his eyes connected to hers until the metal door slid shut and severed their souls in two.

Liz managed to contain her feelings until she had left the building and climbed back inside her truck. Putting on her sunglasses, she stared into the rear-view mirror and wished that she were dead.

Deliverance

"Push, push, push," Dr. Lumamba urged.

An agonizing wail cut through the soothing strains of a Mozart piano sonata that had been piped into the delivery room.

"Keep on! You've almost there!"

Another shriek was followed by the cry of a newborn.

"It's a girl!" Louisa announced. "You have a beautiful little girl!"

The mother's pain turned into an overwhelming sense of joy. "Oh my God! Oh my God!"

Louisa clamped off the umbilical cord and handed the stupefied father a pair of scissors. It was a moment filled with magical symbolism. Cleaned of its waxy residue, the miracle child was dressed in a cotton shirt, pampers, and a knit cap. Swaddled in a pink blanket, she was handed back into her mother's arms.

"She's so beautiful," she cried. "So beautiful."

"Thank you Dr. Lumamba," the father said. "Thank you so much."

The baby's name was Seychelle. She was the third one Louisa had delivered in an eighteen hour period and Baby Number 2,762 since she had begun her practice eighteen years ago. Most of those were normal, healthy births. A small percentage of them were breech deliveries and caesarians. Tragically, some were premature, some died on arrival, and some were so defective they were aborted before birth. When that happened, Louisa was as devastated as the parents and couldn't sleep for many nights afterwards. But tonight was a victory. Louisa breathed easy. She was three for three today and on top of the world. But lurking beneath her sense of satisfaction was a trace of sadness, too. She was keenly aware that giving birth was an experience she would never be sharing. After the first five years of marriage to Raymond, she had found out that she could never have children. The problem was hers, not Rays. To his credit, he supported her emotionally and stayed with her even though she knew there was nothing more in the world he wanted than a son or daughter to carry on the family lineage. They had talked about adoption from time to time but had decided that it was not for them. The children she delivered would be her surrogates. And indeed, they were. Louisa kept up with them as much as she could, sending birthday cards until her boys and girls grew up, left home, and started their own families.

"Do you mind?" The happy father handed Dr. Lumamba his camcorder, "Would you take a video of us?"

"I'd be delighted," Lou said, fumbling with the camcorder. "But you'll have to show me how this thing works."

After a short lesson, the beaming father snuggled up next to his exhausted wife with the crying newborn between them. Miraculously, just as the camera's red light blinked on, baby Seychelle stopped crying, gurgled, and put her fist in her mouth.

"Hey, great shot!" Louisa said. "Maybe I can have a career as a photographer when I retire."

"And Seychelle can be a model," her proud father said.

When Louisa was finished, she took a snapshot of the baby girl for herself on her digital camera. After congratulating the new parents, she excused herself from the delivery room, leaving her nurses to finish the job. Back in the locker room, she scrubbed up and changed into her street clothes.

It was nine p.m. when Louisa finally returned to her office down the hall from the nursery. The walls were covered in corkboard from floor to ceiling. Two were filled with snapshots of her previous deliveries. Downloading her camera into her computer, she printed out the three new ones. As she thumbtacked them in place, she realized she would have to start on the third wall soon. By the time she retired, she figured she would have all four walls and the ceiling full of newborn babies. Her kids, all of them. Sitting back down at her computer, she looked over her schedule for the next day. A caesarian was scheduled in the early morning and a vaginal would no doubt be coming later that night. At times like this, she was thankful for the sleep sofa in her office.

Her solitude was interrupted by a call from the receptionist at the front desk. "Excuse me, Dr. Lumamba, a lady is here to see you."

An emergency! Louisa thought. "Send her in right away."

It was Liz. Her eyes were red and full of tears.

Louisa hurried over to her. "Honey, honey, what's the matter? Are you okay?"

"Oh, Lou, you've got to help me."

"Of course, honey. You know you can count on me."

She put her arms around her, sat her down on her sofa, and waited for Liz to finish crying. Dabbing her eyes, she finally regained her composure.

"Want to tell me about it now?" Louisa asked.

"Oh Lou, I'm pregnant."

Louisa's eyes lit up. "Oh honey, that's wonderful. Oh I'm so happy for you. It's nothing to cry about."

Liz shook her head. "No, no, its horrible. I can't have it. I need to get an abortion."

Louisa was shocked.

"I'm two months gone," Liz explained. "David is the father." She started crying again. "I thought I was safe, but I wasn't."

Lou rubbed her back. "It's okay, it's okay. It doesn't matter if you're not married. You love each other."

"He doesn't know. I went to see him today at Quantico. I wanted to tell him. But I couldn't. He's determined to clear his name and go back to the Academy next year. They won't let him in if he has a wife or child. Then he'd have to repay the entire cost of his education. He'll be ruined. I can't be a part of that."

"Now, now, calm down," Louisa said.

Liz's voice broke and she started sobbing. "You've got to help me, Lou. I've got no one else to turn to."

Louisa's eyes reddened and her heart shattered once again. "Of course, I'll help you, honey. Of course, I will."

G.M.O. CALLAGHAN

Temple of Themis

The Blackburns used every trick in the book to postpone the parchment trial. A secretary had inadvertently misfiled some of the key documents, they claimed the first time. Next, Laurence Roche had come down unexpectedly with the swine flu. After that, it was a computer glitch that caused them to lose some essential data. But, in the final analysis, the trial could only be delayed, not canceled. After endless months of continuances, a date of May 4th was finally set in stone.

By that time, Liz had recovered her health and gotten her life back in order. Throughout her ordeal, she had kept in touch with David through letters and phone calls, as he wished. She was always cheerful and upbeat, never bothering him with her problems. At his suggestion, she wrote his mother and Miss Applebaum and kept them informed of the progress of the case.

At last, the morning of the trial arrived. The legal foot dragging of the defense hadn't bothered Raymond Moses one bit. In his opinion, all it did was give him even more time to prepare. He had never worked so hard on anything before in his life, especially a *pro bono* case. This one was as well laid out as any he had ever been involved in and he had never been more confident of the outcome. He was certain the trial was going to be sensational. It was bound to create a lot of publicity and maybe even set a few precedents. And, of course, it would bring long overdue justice to those who had suffered so long.

As soon as Raymond drove his Humvee into the District Court parking lot, the local paparazzi swarmed all over him with live mikes and uplinked Betacams in one of the spontaneous ambushes they liked to call an interview.

"Dr. Moses! Dr. Moses!" they chanted, each trying to yell louder than the other.

"No comment," he announced, as he climbed out of his vehicle.

Today he was outfitted in a desert camouflage jacket, a TV-friendly blue dress shirt, red plaid bow tie, denim coveralls, and, of course, the omnipresent Ivy League cap. In honor of the occasion, he had replaced his oxford cordovans with the kind of rubber muck boots one would wear to clean out a horse's stall. He felt the symbolism was appropriate, even if it went unnoticed by the reporters.

"Dr. Moses! Over here! One question!"

Rather enjoying the attention, Raymond plunged into the pack of journalism jackals, cradling his brief case with both hands for fear one of them might actually snatch it from him to get a scoop on the day's agenda. Barking questions at him, they hounded him across the parking lot, nipping at his heels. Some raced around to get a front view. Others walked backwards up steep steps that led to a columned temple of Justice that seemed out of place in downtown Baltimore. Perpetually encircled by the shadows of skyscrapers, its white marble facade was always rendered in a compromising shade of gray.

The stream of questions continued flowing uphill, punctuated by the flash and whir of motorized Nikons. The trial hadn't even started and already it was becoming a three-ring media circus. Raymond was more than ready to be the ringmaster.

"I'll have something for you later," he promised, drawing the frenzied pack after him into the blades of a rotating glass door.

In the lobby, the professor and the media horde encountered Laurence Roche huddling with his legal team. Sensing fresh meat, the pack abandoned their quarry and circled around their new victim.

Unlike Raymond, Roche was willing to talk. In fact, he couldn't wait to be on camera.

"What's Mr. Blackburn think of this?" yelled a newsman from Court TV.

"He couldn't care less," Roche asserted coldly. "The Chairman thinks the whole thing is nothing more than a cheap publicity stunt."

"Will he be attending the trial?" someone else shouted.

Roche shook his head and smiled curtly. "No, Mr. Blackburn is on a skiing holiday in Gstaad."

Watching from his den at Kings Oak Manor, the Chairman's stroke-stricken face bent into half a smile. He had always been impressed by how well his attorney lied. The vacation story seemed to be a pleasing cover for his absence. Unfortunately, it made him aware, once more, that not only would he never be skiing again, but he probably wouldn't even be able to walk, eat, or go to the bathroom by himself. Since his stroke, he had been confined to a motorized wheel chair that moved between floors on an electronic lift installed on the railings of the staircase. When he was angry, Septimus rode it around the house with reckless abandon like a petulant child in a bumper car. And now he was very, very angry. Slipping into gear, he throttled forward and zoomed out of the den.

The sound of shattering antiques brought Nero and Cissy running in from the east wing. They found their master in the foyer, next to a toppled pedestal and shattered pieces of a priceless Ming Dynasty vase. Saliva drooled from the corner of his mouth.

"Look what you done broke, Mr. B." Nero chided. "Been in the fambly a hundert years."

Septimus spit on it and lurched forward, careening down the long portrait gallery, knocking off several paintings in the process. A small colonial boy, who had been crushed to death by a horse, had his frame smashed once again. Twin matrons who had never married were ripped completely in two. A Victorian gentleman in a top hat was run over by a pair of hard rubber wheels.

"Be careful, Mr. B, you gonna cut yourself, you don't watch out," Cissy called.

Nero hurried after him. "As long as you be breaking this shit, might as well break this one, too," he said under his breath. He reached over and yanked another portrait off the wall. It was the big man known as Trinity, the cruel slave owner who forced his white seed into the body of Silena. Like venom from an albino rattlesnake, it had infected the blood of all who flowed from her child, Hannah. Raising the image of Trinity over his head, Nero smashed it to the floor, shattering glass and frame.

"That's wrong, Nero. Shouldna gone and done that."

"Wrong what Trinity did, woman. This here what his ass deserve."

He stamped his foot on Trinity's face and ground in the broken glass.

When they caught up with their crippled master, he had circled back into the den and was watching the television again as if nothing had happened.

"You just sit there nice and easy, Mr. B. Time for your medication. I be right back."

On the screen, Tavian was shown coming into the courtroom. Stylishly dressed in a silver sharkskin suit and red power tie, he caused a commotion usually reserved for celebrities at a movie premiere. The place was packed, society people from Ruxton were forced to rub elbows with street people right off the steam grates of West Baltimore Street. LeGrande and the Blast Furnace boys were there, too, taking time out from the unemployment line to get seats in the second row.

"All we gotta do is stare at them jury folks" LeGrande said, his white-tinged hair sticking out of his head like the quills of a porcupine.

"Yeah, bro, make us some faces, let 'em know who we be rooting for." J'Rod demonstrated the point with a menacing glare.

"That be good," Mandala said, his three-hundred-and-fifty pound bulk spilling over his seat on two sides.

"Show some happy teeth for David. A little tongue for the other dude." This time it was Kenyatta who demonstrated the looks.

"Right on, bros. Right on," Tsonka agreed.

Sitting behind them were an assortment of people of color. A few of them claimed descent from the Choptanks of Great

Standing Bear. Instead of fleeing across the Bay after his murder, their ancestors had followed Red-Eyed Owl and taken refuge in the dark woods of the southern shore. Later, they mixed their blood with black slaves, poor whites, and half-breeds. Unaware of their own heritage, they had come to court out of curiosity, eager to find out who they were and what they might become.

Raymond had just taken his place at the plaintiff's table when Liz entered the chamber with four visitors. The tinkling of small bells drew everyone's attention, that and the flash of color in the drab courtroom. The chamber buzzed with excitement. Necks craned to the cause of the commotion like a flock of startled flamingos. Holding their chins high, a middle-aged woman and two young girls followed Liz down the central aisle. Their skin was the color of terra cotta and they wore their hair in waist-long braids, plaited and decorated with colorful wooden beads. Their garments were even more spectacular, made out of seed-bag burlap that had been dyed in bright primary colors. Woven into them were primitive designs of horned animals, long-legged birds, flying fish, and monsters with claws. Around their wrists and ankles were bracelets and bells cut from tin cans. On their feet were sandals made from the soles of discarded tennis shoes. Following behind them was a hunched-over, old woman outfitted in her Sunday-Go-To-Meeting best: a dark blue dress with small, white polka-dots; cream-colored gloves; and a matching hat with a narrow veil at the top like Mamie Eisenhower used to wear.

Raymond arose and greeted David's mother warmly.

"How was your flight from Oklahoma, Mrs. Waterfield," he asked.

"My name not 'Mrs. Waterfield'. But I am my son's mother. You can call me Shadow Woman, but you can never know my real name."

"Oh, sorry."

"Didn't fly either," Lydia Applebaum added. "Drove 'em up here myself. Took us seven days." Behind her wire-rimmed bifocals, her blue eyes were big and bloodshot.

"Had to go real slow," Winking Star interjected. "Rocinante has another hole in the floor."

"But no one fell through," Jumping Bug added, sounding a bit disappointed.

"So glad you got here safely," Raymond said patting the girls on top of their heads. Then he returned his attention to Miss Applebaum. "So you're David's teacher. I've heard a lot about you. I'm really pleased to meet you."

"Was his teacher. Retired now." Despite her love of teaching, Lydia Applebaum never regretted the sacrifices she had made to get David back home.

"Where is my son?" Shadow Woman said. "Where is my David?"

"Yeah, where is David?" the two little girls repeated.

Raymond cleared his throat. "You'll see him soon. I promise you it won't be long. Everything is going to turn out all right. Just bear with me."

A major part of his strategy was to downplay David's role in the whole affair. Yet he knew Roche wouldn't miss the opportunity to drag Shadow Woman's son to the stand and question his character in front of the entire courtroom. He dreaded the spectacle for her sake.

Liz showed the four visitors to their seats in the row behind the plaintiff's table. Lou was there, too, determined to show her support for Raymond and Liz. She greeted David's family and assured them they were in good hands. Then she leaned forward and rubbed her husband's neck.

"Win this one, Ray, I'll give you back your Fatboy."

"You gotta deal, babe. My leather jacket and pants, too."

"You drive a hard bargain, but okay." Then she reached over and took Liz's hand. "It's gonna be okay, girl. Everything going to work out just fine. You'll see."

"Thanks for being here today, Lou," Liz said. "And thanks for everything else you've done for me." They both knew just what she meant.

Soon afterwards, a dozen jurors filed into the courtroom. Four black males, three white men, three white women, and two Hispanic females took their seats in the jury box. It had taken weeks to select them. Anyone whom Raymond wanted, Roche had found fault with and vice versa. The prosecution and defense finally settled on a bland group that didn't read newspapers or watch TV or even talk to their neighbors. They had no opinions about anything. They were pure and untarnished and altogether uninformed about whatever was happening in the world around them. Raymond liked to think of them as twelve blank tablets on which to work his will, but deep down inside he feared their minds were nothing but mush.

The bailiff, a stocky policewoman in a curly blonde wig, entered the chamber and turned to the spectators.

"Oyez, oyez, oyez," she called out. "The United States District Court for the District of Maryland is now in session. The Right Honorable Judge Jason Andrews presiding. All Rise."

Everyone stood on her command. Court etiquette demanded Raymond remove his cap during the proceedings. Now the unsightly white splotch on his forehead, the insidious mark of a rapacious slave master, was on display for everyone to see. He immediately felt diminished and inferior.

Judge Jason Andrews strode in confidently from his chambers, his black robes rustling behind him. He was an aristocratic-looking gentleman with a thick head of hair dyed a lustrous shade of reddish-brown in emulation of his hero, Ronald Reagan. Like the Gipper, he combed his mane into a Gibraltar-like promontory on the right side of his head, which made him appear to be somewhat lopsided. Gathering up his robes, His Honor assumed his seat behind a massive mahogany bench. Elevated two feet off the floor, it was decorated with a classical carving of the Greek goddess, Themis. As usual, she was blindfolded and held a set of scales in one hand and a sword in the other.

But if Justice was blind, the judge was not. Raymond watched carefully as His Honor nodded subtly in the direction of Tavian who was standing just behind Roche and his team of three-piece suits. Raymond knew full well that Judge Andrews was a crony of the Blackburns. An ambitious man who had cast his sights on the State House, the Judge was undoubtedly getting some heavy donations from Septimus and his friends. However, the publicity he would be receiving in the trial was also important. His ear would likely be tuned to how public opinion was moving. In the final analysis, his primary loyalty would be to the ballot box.

The opening statements were brief and to the point. Regaining his poise, Raymond declared that he would prove that the Blackburn family had stolen the land at Herons Point from the Choptank tribe. On the other side, Roche promised to prove that it was the plaintiffs who were attempting to steal property that Lord Baltimore had granted to the first Caecilius Blackburn.

The plaintiffs presented their case first. Raymond called Dr. Herbert Crawford, the Director of the Maryland State Archives, to the stand. He was a tall, thin man with a hearing aid implanted in his left ear. A pair of half moon glasses were balanced on the tip of his nose and secured by a leash that hung down from the temples. It was an arrangement that suggested an occasionally forgetful nature. Although he couldn't recollect what he had for breakfast that morning, Dr. Crawford had a long memory for historical details.

"For reasons unknown," he lectured the court "Lord Baltimore granted Caecilius Blackburn the title of Court-Baron and with it as much land in the New World as he could cover on a map with the print of his hand."

Raymond passed a photo-enlargement of Lord Blackburn's charter to the jury foreman.

"This is clearly stated in the first paragraph of the document you see before you. Please notice the great seal of Lord Baltimore at the bottom of the page."

When each member of the jury had looked at it, Dr. Crawford continued with his presentation. "Unfortunately, when the time came for Caecilius to claim his prize, he had had a bit too much to drink and missed his mark completely."

Dr. Moses held up another photo-enlargement that showed the black handprint in the middle of the Bay. The jury cackled in amusement.

"Sorta like a game of pin the tail on the donkey," Raymond interjected.

"Indeed," Crawford agreed. "The gentleman was fortunate to have gotten anything. You can see the tip of the little finger of his left hand barely reached Herons Point and the heel of his thumb just barely touched the peninsula of the great oak."

At Raymond's direction, Dr. Crawford went on to outline the history of the Blackburn's settlement in Maryland as related in the Founder's *Generall Historie*. Starting from the beginning of the journey in England, he described events all the way up to the Founder's first encounter with Great Standing Bear and the Choptank people. And, of course, he mentioned the role of the Jesuit priest, Francisco de Genoa, in writing down a treaty between the two parties, first in English and then translating it phonetically into the Indians' native tongue.

"Have you seen these documents?" Raymond asked.

"They are not a matter of public record, Dr. Moses. To my knowledge no one but the principals has ever seen them."

"Thank you, Dr. Crawford, that's all I have for you. Your witness, Mr. Roche."

The bleary-eyed man in the seersucker suit rose halfway from his seat. "No questions here, your honor."

The historical record stood as stated.

Next, Raymond called Shadow Woman to the stand.

Under his gentle guidance, the old woman recited the painful history of her tribe that had been passed down by word of mouth from one generation to the other. She repeated the story that Grandfather Two Tongues had told the night of the tornado. Tears flooded her eyes when she spoke of the arrival of the English cavaliers and their deadly fire sticks. Her voice broke into sobs as she recounted the raping and killing that took place at the Center of the World. Especially poignant was her grief at how the survivors had been forced to leave their homeland and wander in exile for more than three-and-a-half centuries.

"The white man forced us to live in the Indian Territory with the Cherokee," she said sadly "and then they came and took that away from us, too."

The jury was clearly moved by her story.

At this point, Raymond took the oblong, wooden box off the evidence table and held it in front of her.

"Would you please identify this box for the jury?" he asked.

"It belong to Two Tongues," Shadow Woman said. "Sacred things from the ancestors."

Raymond opened the lid and took out a plastic evidence bag. "And this?"

"That is the lightning pipe that held the breath of our ancestors since our time began."

Raymond put it back inside and took out a second bag. "What can you tell me about this?"

"That a wampum belt," Shadow Woman said. "Woven into it is a picture of our homeland. The Center of the World where the great tree of our ancestors stands."

"What about this," Raymond asked. He took out the third bag containing the Chopank parchment.

Shadow Woman shrugged her shoulders and shook her head. "No can read."

"Thank, you. Your witness, Mr. Roche."

This time, Roche was primed for cross-examination.

"I'm curious about one of these items in Mr. Two Tongues' box." He reached in and took out one of the evidence bags.

"Peace pipe," she said.

"Yes ma'am, so you indicated. We took the liberty of having the substance inside the bowl analyzed. It was peyote. Are you are familiar with the drug peyote?"

"Sacred cactus," she answered with a nod.

"Have you ever smoked the sacred cactus, ma'am?"

Before Raymond could object, Shadow Woman stuck out her tongue and made a face. "Never! Taste bad. Only men smoke."

"Then have you ever breathed in the fumes accidentally? Like when Mr. Two Tongues was smoking?"

She looked at Dr. Moses for guidance. Reluctantly, he nodded.

"Only one time," she said softly.

"Perhaps on the occasion when Mr. Two Tongues told you this outlandish tale you've repeated here today?"

"No tale. Truth."

"Peyote is a hallucinogenic, ma'am," Roche said. "Perhaps the story you heard was nothing but a delusion."

"No delusion."

"Thank you. You're excused. That's all, your honor."

Frowning in displeasure, Shadow Woman left the stand and took her seat between her adopted daughters in the row behind Liz. Unnoticed by the officers of the court, a young white juror pantomimed smoking a reefer to the delight of the lady next to him. J'Rod and Mandala chastised them with their menacing faces but it was too late. It was clear that Roche's questioning had made an impact on all the members of the jury.

"If it please the court," Raymond resumed. "I would like to display an enlargement of the parchment that was found in the bottom of the box, your honor. The original is far too fragile to pass around."

"Go ahead, Dr. Moses."

On cue, two of the professor's grad students carried in a five-by-seven-foot, color photograph and placed it on an easel in view of the entire courtroom. A murmur arose from the spectators. The long, unfathomable words mystified and intrigued everyone, even those in the jury who couldn't read very well anyway. Especially puzzling were the strange pronunciation marks, the mixture of cursive and block letters, and the words that had no vowels at all. At the bottom of the page, a crude red X and the ornate signature of Caecilius Blackburn were clearly visible.

Dr. Moses turned and addressed the jurors. "What you have before you, ladies and gentlemen of the jury, is the Choptank copy of the peace treaty mentioned in the *Generall Historie* which Dr. Crawford spoke about earlier. Since the tribe had no written language, these words were rendered on the page as they sounded to the ear of the Jesuit scribe, Francisco de Genoa. For centuries, no one understood what these words meant. Even members of the tribe had forgotten their meaning. Until now."

LeGrande and his boys turned their heads and grinned at the jury causing several to shift uncomfortably in their seats. Lydia Applebaum put her arm around Shadow Woman and gave her a reassuring hug. The Blackburns were about to get their comeuppance.

Raymond stopped for a moment to take a sip of water while the court studied the parchment blow-up. "My next witness," he continued, "will be Monsignor Antonio Alighieri of the Vatican Library."

Accompanied by a female translator from the Vatican Embassy in Washington, the slim, bookmark of a man slipped into the stand. Through his interpreter, he told how de Genoa had compiled a Choptank vocabulary so that he could translate the word of God to the heathens. After his murder at the hands of a hostile tribe, the priest's effects, including his vocabulary, were shipped to the Vatican for safekeeping.

At Raymond's prodding, Monsignor Alighieri spoke, too, of how David Waterfield had come to the Vatican in search of the Jesuit's vocabulary. He was pleased to say that he had shown him the work and had translated the Choptank parchment for him. Glossed over in his account was what the translation actually said. The courtroom spectators and TV audience were on the edges of their seats.

"Thank you, Monsignor," Raymond said. "Your witness, Mr. Roche."

"Nothing here, your honor." Roche knew it was not wise to question the integrity of a church official. Especially since he knew that many of the jurors were religious people.

Next, Raymond called Dr. Florence Vetterer to the stand. A heavy, wild-eyed woman with Medusa-like hair emerged from the audience and made her way to the box with the help of a cane. She told the court that her specialty was the field of comparative linguistics, which she taught to a select group of graduate students at Harvard. Left unmentioned was her avocation as a well-regarded poet with several books of verse to her credit.

At Raymond's prodding, Dr. Vetterer testified that she and her team of Ivy League experts had used de Genoa's vocabulary to independently check the accuracy of the Vatican's translation.

"And what were your conclusions," Raymond asked.

"We found our translation matched the one done for Mr. Waterfield by Monsignor Alighieri of the Vatican."

"Would you be so kind as to read your translation to the court?"

"It would be my pleasure," Dr. Vetterer answered.

She began by first reading a passage of the parchment in the Choptank tongue. This she did as if she were chanting the words of a great epic poem.

"*GrrrraaTamenTatinke PotaPowHatant shupTunke ShumMaTecu tanKamatu mazaKanna Becu.*"

Then, referring to a single typewritten page, she would translate the passage into English.

"Great Standing Bear, Emperor of the Choptank people who live at the Center of the World speaks."

Gradually the people in the courtroom began to sense the correlation between the two languages. Clearly enunciating every syllable, Dr. Vetterer drew out the drama of every word, and thrilled them with the sounds of a long-lost world.

Everyone in the room was astonished at the way the Founder itemized every rock, insect, animal, bird, fish, and blade of grass that Lord Baltimore had granted him.

"Greedy little bastard," LeGrande whispered to his crew in the front row.

"You ask me," Tsonka said, "there was a piece of deer shit he forgot to mention."

At last, Dr. Vetterer reached the final passage. After reciting the Choptank words, she paused for dramatic effect, then delivered the *coup de grace.*

"To ease their withdrawal from the Center of the World, the Lord of the Great Canoe gives to the Emperor and the Choptank people, now and forevermore, a new homeland across the Chesapeake—a piece of land known to one and all as the Point of the Herons."

A collective gasp arose from the spectators in the courtroom. The jury was astounded. Reporters ran outside to their cameras and cell phones.

"I rest my case," Raymond shouted over the noisy din.

Judge Andrews banged his gavel and adjourned for the day.

Outside the courtroom, TV newsmen who were doing stand-ups in front of the building, flocked to Raymond as he descended the stairs. Ignoring their questions, he waved them off. There would be plenty of time to talk to them after the jury had rendered a verdict in favor of his client. Even minds of mush could not help being persuaded by the evidence he had presented.

Smoke and Mirrors

The next day Laurence Roche began the Blackburn defense with a bang, strutting out in front of the jury like a bantam rooster about to do battle.

"Get ready to start making faces," Tsonka told the Blast Furnace boys.

"May have to do mo than that," Mandala said, crossing his enormous arms in front of him.

Roche adjusted his tie and cleared his throat. "The defense calls Mr. Simon Guilford to the stand."

A distinguished gentleman in a three-piece suit came forward. He had wavy, gray hair and a nervous tic in the left eye.

"Who the heck is he?" Liz asked Raymond. "This guy's not on our list."

Dr. Moses bounded to his feet. "We object your honor. This is the first we have heard of this witness."

The Judge looked at the counsel for the defense. "What's going on here, Mr. Roche?"

"Your honor, I was about to explain. Some vital information was discovered yesterday evening while our investigators were combing through the personal effects of Mr. Blackburn's late father. It led our investigators to this gentlemen who can explain its significance further."

"Objection overruled, Dr. Moses. You may continue, Mr. Roche."

Raymond sat down. "The scoundrels are up to something," he whispered to Liz.

"Yeah, but what?" They were about to find out.

Under Roche's questioning, the winking witness revealed that he was the President of the Tred Avon Bank and Trust Company of Talbot County, Maryland.

"Was the late Caecilius Blackburn, the sixth, a customer of your bank, Mr. Guilford?"

"Yes, he was. Until his death in 1972."

"What happened to his accounts then?"

"They were transferred to a competitor, a savings and loan owned by his son, the seventh Mr. Blackburn."

"Was everything taken from your bank?"

"Not everything. One item was inadvertently left behind."

Roche bent his finger to the back of the room and Sheriff Turner trotted forward carrying a large safety deposit box wrapped in crime scene tape.

Again, Raymond leapt to his feet. "Objection! We know nothing about this!"

"Overruled," Judge Andrews said sternly. "The defense may continue."

"Is this it, Mr. Guilford?" Roche asked.

"Yes, sir, it is."

"Has any one opened this box besides the late Mr. Blackburn?"

"No. I brought our log as you requested." He handed Roche a spiral notebook that he, in turn, gave to the clerk of the court to enter into evidence.

"Did you open the box for our investigators last night?" Roche asked.

"No, sir. It takes two keys to open it. The bank has a key, but your people did not."

"Is that when Sheriff Turner was summoned to take the box into custody?"

"Yes, sir." The tick in his left eye got worse.

Roche turned to address the judge. "It might interest the court to know that in the wee hours of this morning our staff was able to locate the late Mr. Blackburn's key." He reached inside his breast pocket and drew out an iron key with an oval head and an elaborately notched flag. He held it aloft for all to see.

"How fortuitous," Judge Andrews said.

"With your help, Mr. Guilford," Roche said, "we can now open the box. You brought along the bank's key, didn't you?"

"Yes, sir, I did." He produced a second key, the mirror image of the first.

"I must object again, your honor," Raymond declared loudly. "This is an outrageous charade." He was jumping up and down so much that he was starting to get winded.

"Aren't you curious, Dr. Moses?" the judge asked. "I must say, I am. Please continue, Mr. Roche."

Sheriff Turner was instructed to remove the crime scene tape. Thereafter, the two keys were inserted in the lock and rotated in opposing directions until they caused a click in the tumbler.

Roche paused for effect, then slowly creaked open the lid and looked inside. "My, my. What have we here?" He smiled broadly.

The judge, the jury, and the courtroom were all eager to know. But Roche took his good time about it. Taking out a pair of cotton gloves, he carefully put them on, a finger at a time. It was a calculated moment, almost as dramatic as when O.J Simpson tried on his own murder gloves. They didn't fit, but these did.

With everyone's eyes on the safety deposit box, Roche slowly reached inside, then gingerly removed a document mounted in a glass picture frame. He perused it for a moment, arching his eyebrows as if he were seeing it for the first time. Then he turned to the jury and dropped his bombshell.

"What we have here, ladies and gentlemen of the jury, is the original English version of Lord Blackburn's parchment!"

Again Raymond bounded to his feet. "Your Honor, this is an ambush! The plaintiffs subpoenaed the defense for this document and were told that it no longer existed."

"Mr. Roche?"

"Indeed, that is what we thought, your honor, until last night's fortuitous discovery."

"Sit down, Dr. Moses. You may continue, Mr. Roche."

"As you can see, the parchment has suffered some damage from a fire that occurred at the Blackburn estate some forty years ago."

He waved the frame in front of his adversary, then turned around and paraded it in front of the judge and jury. Scorch marks were evident on its face and its edges were burned black. Unlike the Choptank parchment, a red seal was impressed at the bottom. The handwriting, however, seemed identical, complete with a flowery signature and crude X.

With all eyes riveted on the document, Roche continued.

"Everyone, including the seventh Mr. Blackburn, was under the impression that this parchment had been destroyed by a terrible fire at Kings Oak Manor. What he didn't know was that a servant, now deceased, risked his life to save it. My client's father sent it away for restoration and conservation. Like I said, it was discovered only yesterday in a fire proof, safety deposit box belonging to the late Mr. Blackburn."

"Outrageous!" Raymond said under his breath. Unconsciously, his hand went up to his forehead to cover the white birthmark that was his fatal flaw. Surely it had grown larger today, like a fast-growing cancer that was threatening to consume him.

"We didn't have time to produce a nice big blow-up for you to read as Dr. Moses did with his 'version.' Therefore, I would like to have Mr. Guilford, as a disinterested party, read the document to us so that we may all learn what it says at the same time."

His white-gloved hands held the glass frame up in front of the nervous banker. Mr. Guilford wiped his brow with his handkerchief and slipped on his reading glasses.

"The penmanship is a bit hard to read," he said, "and some of the spellings are kinda funny, but I think I can make it out all right."

"Do your best, Mr. Guilford."

With twitching eyes and a quavering voice, the banker began to read.

"Caecilius Blackburn, humble servant of His Most Sovereign Majesty, Charles, King of England, Scotland, France, and Ireland, and Great Standing Bear, mighty..." He paused, unable to make out the next word.

Roche took a look. "Werowance. That's what the chief was called."

Guilford continued, "...mighty werowance of the Choptank people and ruler of the land of the Great Oak do this treaty make. Great Standing Bear humbly acknowledges the superiority and higher sovereignty of the King of England who hath won his territory in the New World by Right of Discovery. As proof of his allegiance to the crown, the werowance agrees to honor Lord Baltimore's charter and surrender his lands at the Center of the World to Caecilius Blackburn. Furthermore, he pledges to take the Choptank people away in peace, never to return. To compensate the tribe for their loss and to protect them from the attacks of hostile..." Guilford paused again and directed Roche's attention to the next word. "It says 'salvages'," he said.

"That's seventeenth century English for 'savages'," Roche told him. "Please continue."

"Very well. To compensate the tribe for their loss and to protect them from the attacks of hostile savages, Caecilius Blackburn conveys to Great Standing Bear and the Chopank people, a gift of five crossbows and ten muskets, along with a parcel of arrows, ramrods, wads, flints, two barrels of black powder, and match. To bind this agreement, Caecilius Blackburn hath set his seal and hand and Great Standing Bear has made his mark in his own blood."

The blinking banker removed his glasses and folded them back in their case.

"Is that all?" Roche asked.

"No, sir. At the bottom of the page, there's a large red X and the signature of Caecilius Blackburn. Underneath them is the word 'witness' and the name Francisco de Genoa, S.J."

"Is that the document in its entirety, Mr. Guilford?"

"No, there's a date. The tenth of June, in the year of our Lord, 1635. That's all it says."

"Hogwash," Raymond said.

"Dr. Moses, please constrain your comments," Judge Andrews scolded.

Ignoring the comment, Roche turned to the jury and summarized the significance of the document. "Please note, ladies and gentlemen, that in this original document there is no mention whatsoever of Lord Blackburn giving 'the point of the herons' to the Choptanks as the plaintiffs would have you believe."

The excited jury appeared to buy into the story completely. Tavian grinned so hard his harelip almost split open. Behind the plaintiff's table, Liz and Raymond could only shake their heads in dismay. The audacity of the lie left them speechless.

Roche pressed forward, taking his white cotton gloves off a finger at a time as he spoke. "Now you are probably wondering who could have hated the Blackburn family so much that he would create a counterfeit document in a blatant attempt to steal their land? Who could have committed such a despicable act?"

The jurors thought about it for a moment. Some of them shrugged their shoulders. Others didn't even understand the question.

Roche answered his own question. "The defense calls David Waterfield to the stand."

The side door next to the jury box opened and two burly Shore Patrolmen escorted in their prisoner. David's hands were cuffed and he was dressed in an orange prison jumpsuit with a black number stenciled on his chest. His hair had grown long and was pulled back in a ponytail the way it was when he was a boy.

Shadow Woman stood up and shrieked out from across the room. "Oh David! David! What have they done to you?"

Tears burst from her eyes like broken blood vessels. Jumping Bug and Winking Star tore away from her and ran towards their brother. Intercepted by officers of the court, they were carried kicking and screaming back to their seats. The courtroom was in an uproar.

"Order! Order!" Judge Andrews pounded his gavel and brought the courtroom back in control.

David hung his head. He had never been so humiliated in all his life. To be put on public display before his own mother! He slumped down in the stand and fixed his eyes on the floor, not wanting to see the pain in her eyes. Not wanting to see his little sisters or Liz. Or Miss Applebaum either. Not wanting any of them to see him so disgraced. He wished he were dead.

Despite his unkempt appearance, Liz took heart. Only two months remained of David's sentence. After that they could begin their life together again, regardless of the outcome of the trial.

The lady bailiff in the curly blonde wig came forward with a Bible and one of the MPs unlocked David's handcuffs. Placing his right palm down on the cover, David swore to tell "the truth, the whole truth, and nothing but the truth." But he didn't need the white man's gospel to prevent him from perjury. The honor of his people lived in his blood and his conscience was clear. He couldn't help but think that it would be far more appropriate for Laurence Roche to swear on the

Bible. David had already seen how unscrupulous lawyers could twist the simple truth into a grotesque and outrageous lie.

The defense wasted no time in going on the attack. "You are, I believe, what is now commonly referred to as a Native American," Roche said. "Is that correct?"

"I am."

"And, uh, what tribe do you belong to?"

"Choptank."

"Are you now or have you ever been a midshipman at the United States Naval Academy?"

"I still am."

"Are you now incarcerated at the Quantico Marine Brig?"

"Yes."

"And on what charge?"

"Possession of drugs. I was framed."

The remark caused another outburst in the courtroom. Anger seethed from LeGrande Collins and the Blast Furnace Boys in the second row. Judge Andrews hammered his gavel like he was driving nails into his desk. The defense asked that the second part of the answer be stricken from the record and the judge agreed.

"The witness will confine his answers to the questions asked or risk contempt of court," he said sharply. "Is that understood?"

"Yes, sir."

Roche held up a small book. "Have you ever seen this journal before, Mr. Waterfield? *A Generall Historie of Caecilius Blackburn His Colonye in Maria-Land.*"

"I have."

"Did you, in fact, ever check it out of Nimitz Library?"

"I did."

"And just when would that have been?"

David thought for a moment. "Sometime in early October of my plebe year."

Roche looked down at his notes. "October 3rd to be exact."

"If you say so."

"Did you read Caecilius Blackburn's account of the founding of his colony?"

"Yes, sir, I did."

"So on October 3rd of your plebe year, you read about the existence of a phonetic parchment written in the Choptank language."

"I already knew..."

Roche cut him off. "Yes or no, Mr. Waterfield. On October 3rd, you read about the existence of a phonetic parchment."

"Yes."

"That will be all for the moment, Mr. Waterfield. But don't go away," Roche added with a barely suppressed chuckle.

The Shore Patrolmen came forward and escorted the prisoner off the stand and to a seat in the front of the courtroom.

Next up was Captain Cyrus Van Aiken, resplendent in his Marine dress uniform. His chestful of ribbons was a testimony to his bravery and honor, a stark contrast to black numbers stenciled on David's orange prison jumpsuit.

"As Chief of Security at the United States Naval Academy," Roche began "was it your responsibility to examine evidence against the accused?"

"Yes, sir, it was."

Under Roche's questioning, Van Aiken told the court about the raid on David's room and the discovery of drugs in the shaft of his lacrosse stick.

"I object, your honor," Raymond said forcefully. "That case was adjudicated last summer and has nothing to do with this one."

"What about it, Mr. Roche?" the judge asked.

"Bear with me, your honor. The connection will soon become apparent."

Judge Andrews nodded and waved him on.

"Thank you, your honor," Roche said. He turned to Van Aiken and continued his line of questioning. "Besides the drugs, Captain, did you discover anything else of a suspicious nature?"

"Yes, sir, we did. Rolled up inside the hollow shaft, we found several blank sheets of parchment paper. Looked pretty old."

Raymond jumped to his feet. "Move to strike your Honor. We were not told of this."

Roche smiled. "Sorry, your Honor. Again, we became aware of this important fact only last night."

"Overruled, Dr. Moses. Let's see where this is going."

Roche picked an evidence bag off the table and showed the parchment sheets to the jury. To their untrained eyes they looked identical to the paper used in the Choptank document. Turning back to the marine captain on the stand, Roche continued his line of questioning.

"Captain Van Aiken, did you have the occasion to have the age of the parchment sheets established?"

"Yes, sir. Experts have reported that they are approximately four-hundred years-old."

"Were you able to trace where these sheets came from?

"Not specifically, sir. But we have been told that blank sheets are sometimes available in antique stores."

"Did you find anything else of interest in Mr. Waterfield's room, Captain?"

Van Aiken nodded. "My office was asked to examine Mr. Waterfield's hard drive for any suspicious drug-related data. We made a printout of everything that was on it. E-mails, term papers, Internet activity. Things like that. And we recovered all items that had been deleted."

Roche handed him a stack of paper. "Would these be the printouts you made from the hard drive?"

Van Aiken flipped through them. "Yes, sir. It appears so."

"Please examine the three circled lines on page seventy-four and tell the court what these entries refer to."

The Captain quickly found them. "The first one is the Internet address for the Vatican web site."

"And the line after that?"

"It shows the web address of the Vatican Library."

"And the third?"

"It's the address for Francisco de Genoa's Choptank catechism and vocabulary."

Raymond cradled his head in his hands.

Tavian couldn't help but gloat. Everyone thought the raid on David's room was about drugs. But drugs were never the main thing. They were only a pretext to allow a search of David's room and plant evidence. It was the parchment paper and hard drive all along.

"Thank you, Captain," Roche said. "Please tell the court when these addresses were first accessed."

"First date was December 30th of Mr. Waterfield's plebe year." Van Aiken said. "It was called up many times after that."

"December 30th!" Roche declared dramatically. "In other words, it was approximately three months after Mr. Waterfield had learned of the existence of a Choptank parchment from *A Generall Historie* and six months before his trip to the Vatican! Plenty of time for him to have forged a new document, wouldn't you say?"

Raymond was about to object again when the old lady behind him leapt out of her seat. She stomped her foot on the floor and smacked her hands together.

"That's a god-damned lie!" Lydia Applebaum shouted. "David Waterfield would never do that!"

The court went crazy. David looked across the room and for the first time recognized his old mentor in the crowd, her enormous blue eyes ablaze, her fist clenched and her jaw set, determined to defend him to the end.

Judge Andrews banged his gavel again. "Quiet in the courtroom!"

"David Waterfield would never do that!" Miss Applebaum yelled. "I know him better than anyone! I was his teacher!"

"Sit down, please!" the Judge said sharply.

With Lou's help, Liz eased the combative, old woman back down in her seat. She clamped her mouth shut and crossed her arms defiantly.

When the commotion finally settled down, Roche continued.

"Captain Van Aiken, may I ask why these things were not brought up at Mr. Waterfield's court martial?"

"We didn't know what they meant. They didn't seem to have anything to do with the drug charge."

Miss Applebaum bolted up again. "David Waterfield would never do drugs either! Somebody set him up!"

"That's right!" LeGrande shouted. "He was fuckin' framed."

The Blast Furnace Boys were outraged. They had seen it happen before and now it was happening again. Lies. White man lies. Anything to keep the Truth from coming to light.

The Judge pounded the gavel so hard the right side of his Reagan hair-do collapsed. "I'm telling you people, refrain from these outbursts! Next time you'll be removed from the courtroom. That goes for everyone."

"Don't you tell me when to shut up, sonny!" Miss Applebaum shot back, as if His Honor were some punk kid in her class that had sassed her. "I know just what to do with your kind!"

The court was astounded by the old lady's audacity.

"Get that woman out of here!" Judge Andrews shouted.

The blonde female bailiff rushed over and seized her by the arm.

"Get your goddamn hands off me!" Lydia Applebaum shouted. In the ensuing scuffle, she knocked off the bailiff's blonde wig.

"Bitch!" the bailiff said under her breath.

"You're hurting her!" Liz complained.

Grabbing the old lady around the waist, the bailiff picked her up and carried her kicking and screaming out the door. The Blast Furnace Boys rose up in a body, steel-making muscles bulging in their biceps, insults steaming from their mouths. They had just fucking had it. And so had many other outraged spectators.

Judge Andrews couldn't put up with it anymore. The rule of law was disintegrating into outright rebellion. He hammered his gavel so hard the head flung off. You could just barely hear him over the din.

"Clear the court," he shouted. "The party's over. Reconvene tomorrow at the same time." His Honor arose and quickly retreated to the solitude of his private chambers.

Raymond Moses was aghast. Months of work had just been dismantled in under an hour. He was filled with despair. He could read the jury's mind. The case was down the toilet. There would be no justice for David Waterfield. No justice for anyone.

The MP's ordered David to stand up while they put his cuffs back on him. Across the room, he caught sight of Tavian smirking at him, flipping him the bird with both hands. Turning away, Tavian laughed all the way out of the courtroom.

David looked around and saw Liz with her arms around his mother and his little sisters clinging to her skirt. For the first time since they were in the courtroom together, their eyes met for what would later seem like an eternity. In fact, it was a quick parting glance that would have to last them each a lifetime.

"Come on, punk," one of the Shore Patrolmen said to David. "Time to go."

They pushed him toward the side door. And David's pulse began beating to the sound of distant drums. They pushed him again. And his blood turned to fire. They pushed him once more and it was one time too many. From deep inside his soul, the voice of Grandfather Two Tongues arose and called out his secret Choptank name. And a thousand werowances and warriors screamed out for revenge. It was time. After 365 years of treachery, it was time. Gathering up all his strength, David

Waterfield whirled around with a double-fisted roundhouse swing. It caught one of the Shore Patrolmen across the jaw, sending him careening back into the jury box. His partner got it in the side of the head, the edge of the cuffs splitting his cheek wide open. Several state troopers came running from the back of the room, but the Blast Furnace boys stepped out into the aisle, positioning themselves between David and the troopers.

"David!" Liz screamed.

Before he could answer, LeGrande grabbed David by the arm and pushed him through the door next to the jury room. Drawing their billy clubs, the troopers tried to beat their way through the human barricade. But the Blast Furnace boys wouldn't budge, fending off their blows with their forearms.

"Hey, these little clubs ain't nuthin'," J'Rod said.

"Toothpicks," Mandala added, grabbing a billy club and breaking it in two.

"Y'all got any baseball bats?" Tsonka asked the astounded troopers. "We used to that."

At the end of the hall, LeGrande raised a window and helped David down the fire escape. Leaping down to a pavement littered with broken bottles, they followed a narrow, graffiti-lined alleyway until it emptied into Calvert Street. Parked right across from the courthouse was a dirty red beetle with Oklahoma plates. Rocinante!

Miss Applebaum had just unlocked the doors when she saw them coming.

"Quick! Get in the backseat!" she yelled. "Watch out for the hole in the floor."

They ducked inside and she slammed the door shut just in time. The police came pouring down the steps of the courthouse, weapons at the ready.

"They couldn't have gotten far," one of the troopers said as he and his partner jumped into a squad car and peeled away down the street, light bars flashing and sirens blaring. They must have seen too many cop shows on TV. This time the chase was beginning before the flight.

After the cars and motorcycles had cleared out, the old lady looked back over the seat at her star pupil lying handcuffed on the floor in a prison jumpsuit.

"It's good to see you again, Mr. Waterfield."

"And you, Miss Applebaum."

"Can I give you a lift?"

"You already did, Miss Applebaum. You already did."

Just then a hot-orange Ferrari Enzo crept out of the underground parking lot across the street, growling like a savage beast on the prowl.

David peered over the top of the back seat. "Tavian!"

"Who's Tavian?"

"Dude who set him up!" LeGrande said.

The Ferrari took off like a rocket ship.

"Let's get him, Rosie!" The old lady smashed her foot down on the accelerator of her twenty-three year-old VW. The turtle was in pursuit of the hare all over again.

Retribution

Reports of the escape were already breaking on drive-time radio. But Tavian wasn't tuned in to the hard news. He was too busy lip-syncing the lyrics of a punk rock rhapsody on his CD, curling his lower lip and snarling the way they did on MTV, wrinkling up his nose as if something stunk. Stopping for the light at Fayette and Green, he was too interested in checking himself out in the rear view mirror to notice who was following him.

Lydia Applebaum, her eyes just clearing the top of her steering wheel, snuck into the lane on his left, hiding behind a blue Toyota Corona with a collection of stuffed animals suction-cupped to the back window. It gave her just enough of a vantage point to see Tavian take off his tie, then reach into his glove compartment and retrieve a leather pouch. Opening it up, he took a pinch of a white substance and stuck it up his nose.

"I don't believe it," Miss Applebaum said indignantly. "The jerk's snorting cocaine in broad daylight."

Her passengers peeked up over the back seat. "If I can catch him with it," David said, "then maybe they'll start to believe that I was set up."

The light turned and the orange tiger gunned across the intersection. Rocinante crawled after it, using the Corona as a shield.

"There's a tool box under the passenger seat," Miss Applebaum said back over her shoulder. "Maybe you can get the cuffs off."

LeGrande found a hammer and screwdriver and got to work trying to pry open one of the chain links. It was a lot harder than it looked in the movies, cramped in the backseat with the car lurching down the road and a gaping hole in the floorboard.

At the next intersection, the Corona went through a yellow light and they found themselves coming right up alongside Tavian. Rocinante coughed and wheezed like she was trying to catch her breath while the Ferrari Enzo shook to the beat of heavy metal. Miss Applebaum turned her head away, trying to look disinterested. LeGrande kept down while David peered up over the edge of the side window. Tavian wasn't paying any attention to them, muting his music while he made a call on his cell phone.

"Hey, good job today, Cy. Those retards on the jury bought it hook, line, and sinker. Time to party, man. Yeah! Meet me at the Yacht Club at four. We'll take the new bimbos out for the weekend. And bring some more candy."

With the verdict practically assured, it was time for Tavian to kick back and enjoy the sweet smell of victory. He put another pinch up his nose as the light turned green, trapping a bag lady with a shopping cart full of trash in the middle of the crosswalk. Highly annoyed, Tavian leaned on his tiger growl horn, then peeled out around the startled woman with one hand on the wheel. Rosie chugged out after him, winding through the unwitting roadblocks of rush hour traffic. Tavian was really flying now, eager to make his rendezvous.

"We're gonna lose him, man," LeGrande lamented. "No way we can keep up."

"That's okay," David said calmly. "I know where he's going." He had traveled the roads between Baltimore and Annapolis several times with Liz. The Yacht Club was just down from the Academy next to the Eastport Bridge. He remembered the strange feeling of *deja vu* that had come over him when he had first seen it. Like he had somehow seen it before, not in the past, but in the future. And so he would.

He directed Miss Applebaum into a southbound lane of the Baltimore Beltway while LeGrande continued working on the cuffs. Unfortunately, he fumbled the hammer and dropped it out of the hole in the floor.

"We gotta stop!"

"No way," David said. "He'll get too far ahead."

"Shit!"

"Watch your language, sonny," Miss Applebaum scolded. "No swearing allowed in this car."

"Sorry, ma'am." LeGrande was duly chastised.

For the next twenty minutes, the little old lady pushed her beloved Rocinante to its outer limits. Its body shuddered like it was going through the sound barrier. But the speedometer only read forty-five.

By the time they merged onto Route 97 South towards Annapolis, LeGrande finally managed to pry open a link in the middle of the chain with the screwdriver, leaving David with a stainless steel bracelet on each wrist.

"Now you best be getting out of that orange jumpsuit," LeGrande said. "Put on my clothes."

"You gonna wear my prison suit?"

"Naw. I got on jockey shorts. Black. Looks like a Speedo. People think I be going swimming."

Two grown men frantically undressing in the back of a Volkswagen beetle brought the attention of passing cars. Some of the gawkers were horrified, some shook their heads, and a few just honked their horns. Miss Applebaum just smiled pleasantly at them and waved.

Once he was in LeGrande's jeans and chambray shirt, David stuffed the orange jumpsuit out the hole in the floor.

"Now you look normal," LeGrande said. "Except for your ponytail."

The words hadn't been out of his mouth a minute before a siren sounded from behind them.

Miss Applebaum caught the cop in her side view mirror. "Uh oh. Here comes the law."

Cruising alongside, a motorcycle cop waved Rosie off the road and onto a gravel shoulder next to a drainage ditch. Pulling up in front of them, a bowlegged man with a butt as big as his potbelly hopped off his bike and ambled back to the VW.

"Afternoon, officer," Miss Applebaum said pleasantly. "What seems to be the trouble?"

"Expired plates, ma'am," he said curtly. "Need your registration and driver's license."

"Excuse me, young man," she said, "but shouldn't you be chasing that green SUV up ahead? They tossed that orange trash out the window."

"Your registration and driver's license, please."

Since she had retired Lydia Applebaum hadn't bothered to renew her license. In fact, she wasn't sure she knew where it was. As she nervously fumbled through her purse, the officer turned his attention to the men in the back seat. Something looked suspicious. A brown-skinned man in a ponytail was sitting on his hands in the back seat. Next to him was an African-American with long black hair bleached white at the tips and dressed in a sleeveless T-shirt and black jockey shorts. Up front a nervous old white biddy was rummaging through her glove compartment like a raccoon going through a garbage can. The thought occurred to him that maybe they were kidnapping her.

"Lady, you okay?" he asked her.

"Fine, officer, just fine. Give me another second."

He looked back at David and caught a glimmer of the metal cuffs on his wrist. "Mind getting out, sir."

That did it. Miss Applebaum floored the accelerator and peeled out before David even had a chance to reply. Cutting into traffic, she clipped the front of the policeman's motorcycle and sent it tumbling down the embankment.

"Dammit!" she said, belatedly clamping her hand over her mouth. "Pardon me," she added contritely, more concerned over her lapse of decorum than the damaged motorcycle. Once again she had broken her own rule against swearing, not to mention the laws of the great state of Maryland. But this time she had no choice. Time was of the essence and she had to get David to the Yacht Club as fast as possible.

At David's direction, she took Route 50 to the Rowe Boulevard exit and headed towards the State House dome, hiding Rocinante in the heavy flow of rush hour traffic as much as she could. They had just entered Church Circle when a couple of squad cars with flashing light bars lit up their rear-view mirror.

"Gonna catch us sure!" LeGrande shouted, careful not to swear.

"Just so they don't catch us until I get Tavian," David said calmly.

"Go, Rosie, go!" Miss Applebaum shouted.

Meanwhile, Tavian zoomed into the parking lot beside the Annapolis Yacht Club. Overlooking Spa Creek at the Eastport Bridge, the three-leveled contemporary facility was surrounded by a maze of million dollar boats and a parking lot full of Mercedes, BMWs, Jaguars, and one newly arrived hot-orange Enzo Ferrari.

The gull wings flew up and Tavian eagerly jumped out carrying two large brown paper bags. He had taken a detour to load up on provisions. A half-dozen six-packs, assorted snacks, and a carton of Trojan rubbers filled the bill. After an intense week in court, the prospect of a wild weekend on the water was just what the doctor ordered. Ready for some serious recreation, he hurried down the long dock that led to his orange-and-black cigarette boat. Dancing on its lines, *Tiger Shark* was bow out and ready to boogie.

He found his buddy, Cy, and two buxom babes in thong bikinis waiting for him in the V-berth. One was a gorgeous blonde with beach ball boobs; the other, a brunette with thick lips and killer buns.

"I'm Shannon," the blonde said.

"And I'm Rita."

He greeted each with an open mouth kiss and a rub on the rear end. "I'll take Shannon first," he said. "We can switch off later."

"Awesome," Rita said.

"Okay by me," Cy agreed. He had already gotten out of his uniform and into a T-shirt and shorts. Removing the artificial limb from his puckered stump, he plopped it down on the galley table. Inside was a virtual cornucopia of club drugs: E-bombs, Banana Splits, Bromos, Cloud Nines, Tachas, and Toonies. All neatly packaged in individual plastic baggies.

"This enough candy for you?" Cy asked.

"Fuckin' A."

Tavian slipped out of his silver sharkskin jacket and was preparing to change into his sailing clothes when he heard the sound of gunfire. Scrambling back up to the cockpit, he was astounded to see David Waterfield at the far end of the dock, racing towards him with two state troopers in hot pursuit. The sight threw him into a panic. His blood enemy, the law, and a boatload of illegal drugs were a disastrous combination. Immediately, he fired up his engines and threw off the bowlines.

"Get rid of that shit!" he yelled to Cy.

In a panic, the one-legged marine and the two bimbos started scooping the contraband back into the hollow compartment of his prosthetic limb

Falling to one knee, the lead trooper took aim. Several shots followed, riddling the cabin of the million-dollar Gulfstar cruiser in the next berth. With no time to throw off the stern lines, Tavian revved up his twin 500 horsepower engines and rammed the throttle forward. *Tiger Shark* reared back on its haunches and blasted away from the dock, pulling out the pilings in the process.

David leapt out over the water just as the planks in the dock collapsed like a cascading line of dominoes, sending the pursuing troopers into the drink. Miraculously, he managed to catch hold of one of the stern lines.

Tiger Shark burst through the tranquil waters of Spa Creek, pulling David behind it like a fish on a line. Tidal waves of wake rippled back on cruisers tethered to public moorings. One man was tossed out of his hammock and another couple lost their barbequed steak overboard. Near the Academy seawall, a group of plebes in sunfish sailboats were amazed to see the speeding cigarette boat cut across their midst. Swamped with water, a half dozen tipped over.

Inside *Tiger Shark,* Shannon and Rita were trying to get Cy's prosthesis back on when Tavian veered suddenly, sending them sprawling in a heap. Separated from the stump, the hollow leg bounced around the bulkheads spewing its contents across the cabin.

"Get them the fuck out!" Tavian cried over the roar of his engines. He looked back and saw David hanging on his stern line. More troopers were arriving at the dock. Taking the Founder's pouch out of his pocket, Tavian hurled it into the Chesapeake, into the Great Sea of Ancestors, where the water spirit of Great Standing Bear was waiting to become whole.

The Maryland Marine police received a call for help from the squad car at the Yacht Club. A traffic copter was immediately diverted from its duties over Route 50 and deployed out in a wide arc over the Bay. Its task was akin to finding a needle in a haystack. The Chesapeake was filling up with pleasure boats that had gotten the jump on what forecasters promised would be a great weekend. And there was the usual heavy traffic in the middle of the Bay, a foreign tanker and an empty container ship coming down from Baltimore and a coal-bearing barge on its way up.

Tavian glanced back quickly and saw that David had climbed onto the swim platform. One of his legs was already inside the boat! Tavian knew just what to do. He started weaving back and forth in an effort to throw David off. Inside the cabin, Cy and the two bimbos banged around the bulkheads, but David hung on for his life.

Since that maneuver hadn't worked, Tavian began to do some tight, high-powered turns, first to the port and then to the starboard. But somehow David managed to get the rest of his body into the cockpit.

Overhead, the traffic copter spotted the crazy wake patterns in an area south of Annapolis near Thomas Point Light. A man in a white dress shirt and slacks was at the helm and a ratty-looking bum with a ponytail was crawling towards him from the stern.

Tavian straightened the wheel and blasted off towards the dead zone in the middle of the Bay. The copter stayed with him, radioing the cigarette boat's position to a Marine Police hovercraft that was already cruising south of the Bay Bridge. Taking up the challenge, the hovercraft raised itself in the water and blasted off on a cushion of air, swooping over the surface of the Chesapeake like a low-altitude fighter.

David worked his way up toward the wheel, fighting the steep incline and G-forces that kept pushing him back. His heart beat like the war drums of his ancestors. His blood raced like their war canoes. Inside his head, Great Standing Bear roared out for revenge.

Tiger Shark was on full throttle now and still David was inching his way ever closer. Tavian looked back and David lurched forward to wrest control of the wheel from his enemy. The hovercraft spotted the zigzagging boat weaving in and out of a heavily congested area. Through his binoculars, the captain could see two figures fighting at the helm. From overhead, the copter radioed that the boat had just turned into a collision course with a coal barge.

David was beginning to get the upper hand when Cy emerged from the cabin and rammed the end of a crab net into his groin, knocking the breath out of him. A sharp elbow from Tavian sent David sprawling back on the starboard locker.

Tavian looked back over his shoulder at his fallen foe and exulted. "You've fucking had it, asshole!" A couple more quick turns and he might be able to throw him out altogether.

"Watch out!" Cy screamed and dove back inside.

Tavian whirled around and saw it coming at him. A tug was bearing down on him like a locomotive. Spinning the wheel away from the on-coming bow, he steered into the deadly space between the tug and the barge that followed it. An invisible cable suddenly sprang into sight. Tavian's eyes popped open. He yanked the throttle into reverse. But it was too late. The cold silver edge, pulled taut by two hundred tons of coal, swept down on him with a vengeance. Raking over the boat's bow, it sliced through his windshield and finally, to his unspeakable horror, his own neck.

Tiger Shark spun around to a standstill. Tavian fell to his knees and his head toppled off his body and bounced into the bay. A fountain of blood spurted out of his neck like a geyser, turning the cockpit into a sea of red.

David jumped to his feet and grabbed the shaft of the crab net. In his tight grip it became ZaStakaZappa in another guise. Leaning over the side, he ensnared the floating head in the net and brought it back on board, as if somehow it could be reattached to its body long enough to confess its treachery. Tavian's eyes were wide open, his mouth agape, as if he could still sense the fatal dismemberment he had just suffered. David's blood screamed out in triumph. His enemy's head was in his net. An entire dynasty had been severed at the top, never to live again. He held the bloody ball high over his head, an exalted trophy of war. And in that very moment, he became his secret Choptank name.

"I am ShaKraaKaPowHaZakka!" he shouted to the sky. "The Sword of Lightning! Redeemer of the Sacred Tree!"

And from the cloudless sky came the thunder of a thousand great werowances and warriors. After more than three-and-a-half centuries, the Choptank people had been avenged, now and forevermore.

The hovercraft pulled alongside and an officer yelled at him through a bullhorn.

"Drop the stick, son, and put your hands up. You're under arrest."

The officer started to read his Miranda Rights, but David ignored him. The law didn't understand before, and it wouldn't understand now, not with the head of his enemy in his net.

One of the other officers reached down for his side arm. On reflex, David cocked back the net and hurled the bloody head into his chest, knocking the horrified man off his feet. The others drew their guns and took aim as David dove off the side of the boat. A hail of bullets followed him into the smooth, still waters of the Chesapeake, waters that mirrored the sky overhead and masked the target underneath. The officers emptied their guns, reloaded, and waited for him to resurface. Fifteen minutes went by, then an hour. But there was no sign of David Waterfield. The sun sank into the Chesapeake, turning the water into a sacrificial shade of red.

No one could say if David Waterfield had been hit. No one saw if he had come up for air. No one knew if he was dead or if he was still alive. He had just disappeared somewhere between the surface of the water and the sky which it reflected.

David Waterfield had become a legend.

Judgment Day

Vindication came a week too late. Before a packed courtroom, Captain Cyrus Van Aiken confessed to everything that Tavian had ordered him to do. He told about the destruction of David's wooden stick, the drug set-up, the planted parchment paper, and the bogus computer files. Most importantly, he told the court about the Blackburns' fear of the Choptank parchment and Septimus' destruction of the English original. It had been Tavian's idea to create a clever English forgery in its place and portray David's copy as a fake.

In the front row, five women in mourning black huddled together for support. Nothing could bring David Waterfield back to them, but it was some consolation that his lost honor and dignity had been restored.

Roche did his best to paint Van Aiken as a crazed drug addict who had agreed to testify in return for leniency. But it didn't make any difference. It only took fifteen minutes for the jury to render a unanimous verdict in favor of the plaintiffs.

The spectators in the courtroom whooped and hollered and jumped for joy. Reporters raced outside to file their stories, and the five women in black hugged each other and wept.

Listening on the radio from their jail cell, LeGrande and the Blast Furnace boys nodded in satisfaction. They had done their part to help David fulfill his destiny, but they had lost a good friend in the process.

Sensing a popular cause that might possibly fuel his rise to the State House, Judge Andrews forgot all about his loyalties to the Blackburn family and ordered maximum penalties under the law.

"The court hereby orders that title to the land at Herons Point be returned to the remaining members of the Choptank tribe," he said sternly. "Further, the defendants are ordered to pay back rent on the property for the last three-hundred-and-sixty-five years. For this purpose, the assets of Blackburn Steelworks, including Kings Oak, Black Steeple, Blackburn Shipbuilding, and other subsidiaries including the poultry farms and cattle herds will be turned over to a court-appointed fiduciary to administer on behalf of the Choptank people."

Including interest, the fines amounted to more than five billion dollars. The net worth of the most powerful family in the state had suddenly become less than zero. As a further show of good faith, Judge Andrews ordered the incarcerated steelmen released from jail and Lydia Applebaum cleared of the charges of aiding a criminal and reckless driving. Because of his illness, the court spared Septimus the further humiliation of a prison term. It was enough that he had been totally ruined.

Outside the temple of law, Dr. Raymond Moses descended in full glory. Following behind him, their hands linked together, were the five women in black. At the bottom of the steps, Raymond stopped to address the assembled press.

"It was David's wish that the ashes of his ancestors, including his grandfather, be scattered under the great white oak which his people regarded as the Center of the World. As for Herons Point, it was his desire that Blackburn Steelworks be immediately shut down. Income from the Blackburn estate is to be used to provide life-long pensions for all employees who will lose their jobs, including those whose livelihoods were terminated unfairly by the mill's management. Medical settlements are to be given to those whose health has been compromised or ended altogether. Reparations will also be paid to the descendants of the African slaves who suffered at the hands of the Blackburns. The remaining funds will underwrite efforts to clean-up the dead zone in the Bay.

It was David's wish that title to Herons Point be conveyed to the State of Maryland with the proviso that the steel mill be torn down and the land turned into a park for all the people to enjoy. What David wanted most of all was for the air and water pollution to stop. Today is just a beginning. There is much to do. "

All who heard his words understood their import. David Waterfield's dream was to become a reality. The pollution from the foundry would cease. The victims would get a new lease on life. The Chesapeake would have another chance.

Firestorm

The great fieldstone hearth blazed like a funeral pyre and the shadow of Death danced triumphantly through the den, mocking memories of eternal youth foolishly preserved in golden picture frames.

Alone in a wheel chair by the window sat the seventh incarnation of the Founder's name, an invalid in black silk pajamas wrapped in a heavy woolen shawl. As he stared into the void, a look of alarm animated the left side of his face while the right remained frozen in peaceful placidity. Raging outside was a storm as vicious and cruel as the one that swirled inside his head. A golden afternoon had been snuffed out in its prime. Power lines had been severed. His estate plunged into utter darkness. Worse than that was the infernal clamor of the wind. A monster with many mouths, it howled and shrieked at him like a thousand wild savages exulting in their final triumph.

He didn't much care. There was little life left in him now. His mighty empire was no more and his blood had been spilled with the blood of his son. With him had died the future of an unbroken lineage that branched back to the beginnings of time. Bitter tears bled down the left side of his face and into the corner of his mouth. How cruel it was for Fate to seize the son before the father, to deny a dying man his one last chance at immortality in the shape of future generations to come. From within himself, he heard the shrill voices of the unborn damning him for his failure to insure the continuation of the line.

The wind became more violent, beating its fists against the walls and pounding on the windowpanes. The very foundations of the house shuddered from the onslaught. On a sideboard next to the window, a finger of flame trembled inside an antique hurricane lantern, as if it, too, were afraid.

"Come away from there, Mr. B," Cissy said. Her pale white hands grabbed the handles of her master's wheel chair and rolled him closer to the fireplace. "You be more comfy over t'here."

Septimus grumbled at her disagreeably. Despite her faithful service to him, he still found it disturbing to be confronted with her ghastly albino skin and piggish, pink eyes.

"Looks like we a li'l short of firewood, Mr. B. I be back in a jiffy. You gonna miss all this help we've been giving ya when you gots to go to the state home for the indigent."

As she hurried away, Nero entered the den carrying a silver tray. "Time for your medicine, Mr. B," he said, lowering a saucer of pills and a glass of water in front of his master.

Disgusted by the sight of the white splotches on Nero's face, Septimus head-butted the tray out of his hands and spit at him.

"That's fine you do dat, Mr. B. You de boss if that how you want it to be."

Across the room, a latch failed and a pair of casement windows flew open, one of them narrowly missing the hurricane lantern on the sideboard. Nero hurried over to stop the blast of cold air. For a moment, he stood at the open window listening to the savage howls of the wind as if it was somehow speaking to him. Then he turned to the man in the wheel chair.

"Oh looky here, Mr. B, the window done knocked over the lantern."

Nero waited until his master wheeled around to face him, then reached over and deliberately swept the lantern off the sideboard. The glass chimney shattered on the hardwood floor and the exposed wick ignited a pool of kerosene that had spilled out of the reservoir in the base. A river of fire surged onto the fine oriental carpet.

Septimus's mouth dropped open and he struggled to speak. But the words of alarm stuck inside his throat.

Cissy came back in the room and dropped her logs on the floor. "Don't you just stand around, Nero, we gotta snuff that fire out 'fore it take hold." Snatching the shawl from her master's shoulder, she ran over to beat-out the flames.

Nero caught her arm. "It too late, woman. There ain't nuthin we can do now. This is God's will. Ain't nothing we can do but get us out of this house fast. Go fetch the boy and get the other brothers and sisters out of their cabins."

Cissy looked back at the wretch in the wheel chair, the cruel and ruthless master who seemed to delight in abusing his servants as much as his ancestors had the slaves they had treated like so much livestock. His face looked like the masks of comedy and tragedy fused together; the right side, frozen in contentment; the left, frantic with fear.

"Forgive us, Lord," Cissy whispered. Then she turned and ran out of the room crying for her six-fingered son. "Zaccariah! Zaccariah!"

The flames on the rug leapt into the curtains. Nero walked up to his trembling master. "Anything I can get you 'fore I go, Mr. B.? Some warm milk or a sugar cookie?"

Septimus had turned as mute as the slave girl, Silena.

"Not hungry, tonight, huh, Mr. B. Guess I can't blame you none. Sleep tight, Mr. B., sleep your ass tight." He turned his back on the only master he had ever known. Rushing out of the den, he ran through the portrait gallery and threw open the front door. Darting outside, he disappeared into the blackness of the night.

Inside the den, the wind whipped the fire into a whirling frenzy. Out of its body came a ravenous beast with seven flaming heads and blazing wings and a spiny serpentine tail. Rampaging through the room, it let out a mighty roar and shot out twenty tongues that torched everything in sight. Over the hearth, the white buck's head burst into flames. Walls wilted. Furniture exploded. The Founder's musket melted like butter. Presidents, popes, and pop stars were incinerated into ashes. Trapped inside its shrinking coils, the seventh incarnation of the Founder's name shrieked out for help.

"Nero! Nero!" he screamed. But Nero was in the stables sending the frightened thoroughbreds skittering into the night.

When Septimus opened his mouth again, the breath of the beast blasted into him like a blowtorch, exploding his lungs like cheap rubber balloons. Fangs of flame bit into the leg of his black silk pajamas and rushed up over him in a fury, melting his flesh, licking the meat off his bones, cremating him alive.

By morning there was nothing left. The wind had fanned the blaze from one building to another, consuming the guesthouses, horse stalls, car barn, gazebo, and boathouse. Even the long pier and the boats that had been docked next to it were gone. All physical evidence of the Blackburns had disappeared from the face of the earth.

Return of the Blood

Five years had passed since David Waterfield had been lost beneath the surface of the Chesapeake, but Liz still missed him as if it were only yesterday. Each year, on the anniversary of his death, she returned to the quiet, secret place where their love had been consummated.

Across the inlet, the great white oak still dominated the peninsula, its strong boughs glowing green and golden in the afternoon sun. Nature had reclaimed the land around it now and it looked much like it had four hundred years ago—a sacred place where the earth came together with the water and sky at the Center of the World.

As David wished, the water spirits of his ancestors had been returned to the clouds on funeral pyres and their ashes scattered on the rich, loamy soil underneath the great oak. Already their essence had been drawn through its roots and up into its mighty shaft, to live again in the outermost ring of the annular circles that contained the history of the place and the living tissue of all who had become part of the earth around them.

Overhead, in the deep cerulean sky, ice crystal clouds swirled around the crown of the great oak and made it appear to be spinning counterclockwise on its axis, as if it were turning back time itself.

For a moment, the breeze fell away, the clouds stopped, and the earth, itself, seemed to stand still. The surface of the Choptank became as smooth and shiny as a mirror. And in the woods, the warblers and thrushes ceased their singing and the cicadas fell utterly silent.

Then suddenly, from the mighty boughs of the ancient tree, a thousand green tongues began to chatter in excitement. And the world began to turn again. With an air of expectation, Liz arose from her bed of wildflowers and made her way down to the water's edge and waited for a miracle to occur.

In the river beyond, the water parted and a solitary figure burst through the surface, gasping for air and shaking beads of silver and gold from his broad shoulders and long brown hair. The very image of David Waterfield, himself! The child he had dreamed about. The son he had never known. The secret Liz had never found the right time to tell. The boy ran into his mother's arms and she felt his heart beating with the immortal blood of a thousand werowances and warriors.

A great song of nature filled her soul, in the rustling of the leaves, the gentle rhythm of the waves, the chirping of cicadas, and the call of the Great Blue Heron. It was a hymn of faith and renewal. David Waterfield was not dead. He lived on in the body and mind of his child, in the blood that ran through his veins like the great ancestral river that flowed out from the hearts of the ancient ones into a future filled with hope and promise.

Acknowledgments

The author wishes to thank Burt Kummerow, former director of Historic St. Mary's City, for his insights into early Maryland History and especially the Piscataway catechism of Father Andrew White, which inspired this story. I would also like to express my gratitude to A. Robert Cole who first introduced me to the subject of Maryland history and to Duncan and Diane Hood for sharing the story of the De Courcy family's land grant by fingerprint. Special thanks to my wife, Carolyn, for all the editing she did on my manuscript and to Lee Boynton for his wonderful visualization of the cover image.

Thanks also to Bob Rau, Professor Emeritus of the United States Naval Academy, for his valuable advice and to his wife, Grace Ann, who was kind enough to critique my story. I am also indebted to Barbara Levin for her eagle-eyed proof-reading of the manuscript. Todd Brunner, Christopher Brianas, and Maureen and Dennis Sullivan also helped me by offering valuable tips on the life at the Academy.

I also want to express by appreciation to Fred Miller for his information on log canoe racing and Pat Truby for his very helpful ideas on graphic design. In addition, Gerald Sweeney, Katherine Burke, Mac Nelson, and Gary and Pat Quinn gave me some valuable insights into marketing techniques. Ronald S. Wade, the Director of the Maryland State Anatomy Board, was very helpful in sharing his thoughts on bog mummies with me. Thanks also to Debbie Siddon of Apple Computer for her technical assistance.

Many of my ideas were influenced and inspired by accounts in other non-fiction books. The atrocities committed against American Indians were based on accounts found in Dee Brown's *Bury My Heart at Wounded Knee*. Tom Horton's *Bay Country* gave me many insights into the wondrous ecology of the Chesapeake. I am also indebted to Mark Reutter for the excellent account of the Maryland steel industry contained in his non-fiction book, *Making Steel*.

Thanks also to Maryland Writers Association and the Santa Fe Writers Project for their timely encouragement in this project.

Any errors of fact or fiction that I may have made in this work are entirely mine.

About the Author

A long-time resident of Annapolis, Maryland, the author is an avid sailor and environmentalist. His work as a documentary and commercial filmmaker has won him many national awards. His feature film script, *The Last Foxhunt*, was honored by a Gold Medal at the Houston International Film Festival. Mr. Callaghan graduated from Kenyon College with a BA in English Literature and received a MA in the same subject from Northwestern University. He can be reached through his website at www.HeronsPoynte.com or by e-mail at HeronsPoynte@mac.com.

About the Cover Art

The *Herons Poynte* cover was painted in watercolor by Lee Boynton of Annapolis, Maryland. A painter of light, Mr. Boynton employs warm sensuous colors to infuse his compositions. He feels that the translucent quality of the watercolor medium is especially suited to expressing the delicate beauty of light. Mr. Boynton studied under Impressionist master Henry Hensche at the Cape Cod School of Art in Provincetown, MA. His complex, life-long fascination with the sea is reflected in his fluid and powerful renderings of the changing moods of nature along the coast of Maine and on the Chesapeake Bay. His work has been selected for leading national and international exhibitions, most notably the national Arts for the Parks Top 100 Exhibition in Jackson, Wyoming, and the Mystic International Exhibition at Mystic Seaport in Mystic, Connecticut. Visit his online gallery at www.leeboynton.com.